THE
GOLD SEEKERS

VOLUME VII OF THE AUSTRALIANS

William Stuart Long

A DELL BOOK

Created by the producers of
**The Kent Family Chronicles,
Wagons West,** and **A Woman's
Estate** by Roberta Gellis.

Chairman of the Board: Lyle Kenyon Engel

Published by
Dell Publishing Co., Inc.
1 Dag Hammarskjold Plaza
New York, New York 10017

Produced by Book Creations, Inc.
Chairman of the Board: Lyle Kenyon Engel

Dell ® TM 681510, Dell Publishing Co., Inc.

ISBN: 0-440-13169-3

Printed in the United States of America
First printing—July 1985

WAS IT VISION OR MADNESS THAT DROVE THEM TO PIT THEIR WILES AGAINST A HARSH LAND, AN ELUSIVE TREASURE—AND EACH OTHER?

Luke Murphy—Driven halfway round the world by a passion for vengeance, in Australia he found friendship, love, and a destiny of blood and honor.

Mercy Bancroft—Lovely and defenseless, she lived in thrall to one man—until she found protection with the enemy who'd sworn to destroy him.

Elizabeth Tempest—The daughter of Rick and Katie, she grew up innocent amid hardship and unearthly beauty. Luke Murphy taught her what it was to be a woman.

Captain Red Broome—A born commander, he was the best and the brightest of the sons of the founders. But would his duty to ship and crown make him betray his highest ideals?

Captain Jasper Morgan—He was a blackguard with a hundred names and a thousand deceptions—and one chilling obsession: the insatiable lust for gold.

DRIVEN BY PASSION, GREED AND GLITTERING DREAMS OF THE FUTURE, THEY WERE . . .

THE GOLD SEEKERS

*Other books in THE AUSTRALIANS series
by William Stuart Long*

This book is dedicated to my brother-in-law, Squadron Leader John Chisholm Ward, a seventh-generation descendant of one of Australia's pioneer families.

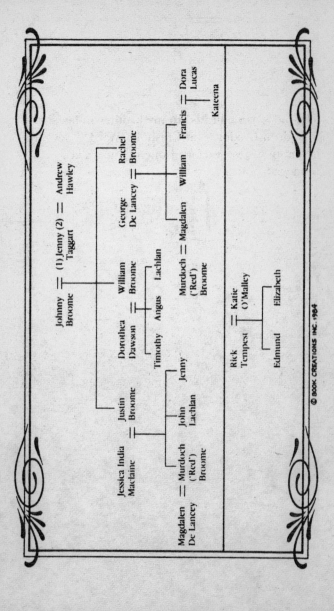

Jessica India
Maclaine

Magdalen = Murdoch
De Lancey   ('Red')
            Broome

John
Lachlan

Jenny

Justin
Broome

Johnny = (1) Jenny (2) = Andrew
Broome   Taggart   Hawley

Timothy   Angus   Lachlan

Dorothea =
Dawson

William
Broome

George   Rachel
De Lancey Broome

Murdoch = Magdalen
('Red')
Broome

William

Francis = Dora
          Lucas

Kateena

Rick = Katie
Tempest O'Malley

Edmund   Elizabeth

© BOOK CREATIONS INC. 1984

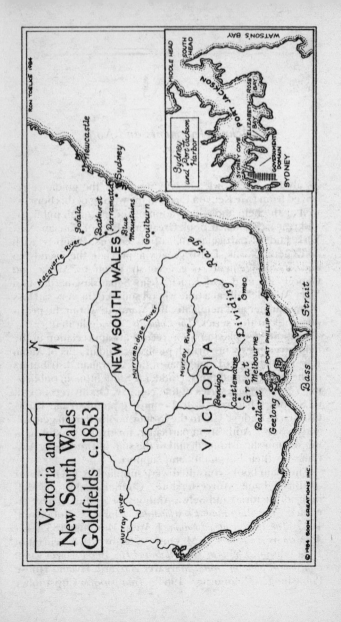

Victoria and
New South Wales
Goldfields c.1853

Acknowledgments and Notes

As always, I acknowledge very gratefully the guidance received from Lyle Kenyon Engel in the writing of this book, as well as the help and cooperation of the editorial, publicity, and research staffs at Book Creations, Inc., of Canaan, New York, and, in particular, that of my editors, Philip D. Rich and Glenn Novak. I also greatly appreciate the friendship and encouragement so generously given by Marla and George Engel, Carol Krach, Jean Sepanski-Guarda, and Mary Ann McNally at a time when I suffered the very sad loss of my partner and helpmate, Bill Mann, to whom the previous book in this series, *The Colonists*, was dedicated.

I should also like to put on record my appreciation of the help given me by my British publisher, Aidan Ellis of Aidan Ellis Publishing Ltd., and that of the Australian distributors of the paperback editions, Hodder & Stoughton, in publicizing *The Australians* series in that country. On my recent visit to Sydney I had reason to be most grateful to Ian Parry-Okeden of Radio 2 UE, to the Sydney booksellers in general, and to Selwa Anthony in particular, for the successful signing session she arranged, and to the staff of Doubleday Australia for their hospitality and support.

The main books consulted were supplied by E. G. Glover of Birlingham, Worcestershire, Conrad Bailey of Melbourne, Victoria, and Selwa Anthony of Sydney. These included: *The Australian Encyclopaedia:* Angus & Robertson, 1927; *The History of Tasmania:* J. West, Dowling, 1852; *The Macarthurs of Camden:* S. M. Onslow, Rigby, 1973, reprint of 1914 edition; *Elizabeth Macarthur and Her World:* Hazel King; *Punishment Short of Death:* Margaret Hazzard, Hyland House Publishing, Melbourne, 1984; *Transported:* Christopher

Sweeney, Macmillan of Australia, 1981; *Australian Explorers:* Kathleen Fitzpatrick, Oxford University Press, 1958; *History of Australia:* Marjorie Barnard, Angus & Robertson, 1962 (copy supplied by Bay Books); *The Gold Seekers:* Norman Bartlett, Readers Book Club, London, 1965; *Unwilling Emigrants:* Alexandra Hasluck, Oxford University Press, 1959; *New Zealand:* Reginald Horsley, T. C. & E. C. Jack, Edinburgh, 1912; *Australian Historical Monographs:* various titles, edited by George Mackaness, Ford, Sydney, 1956; *The Beginning:* Appleyard & Manford, University of Western Australia Press, 1979; *Australia:* W. H. Lang, Caxton Publishing Co., London, reprint; *Practical Experiences at the Diggings:* W. Hall, 1852, reprint; *Notes of a Gold Digger:* J. Bonwick, 1852, reprint; *The Baltimore Clipper:* Irving Chapelle, Bonanza Books, New York, 1930. I have also taken the liberty of adapting, from one of my earlier works, material pertaining to the Crimea battles, which are part of the historical record.

Research on my behalf was undertaken in Sydney by Vera Koenigswarter and in London by Judith Farrington, and by Book Creations' researcher Kathleen Halverson, for the gold rush in California. I am indebted to all three, and to Ian Cottam of York for the loan of his books, and to Ada Broadley for her unfailing help and support in the domestic field.

This book, like the others in the series, is written as a novel, with fictional characters superimposed on the narrative. Their adventures and misadventures are based on fact and, at times, may seem more credible than those of the real-life characters with whom their stories are interwoven. Nevertheless, I have not embroidered or exaggerated the actions of any of them, save where it was expedient to dramatize these a little in order to avoid writing "dull" history. Leaders of the Eureka stockade episode are, in all save one case, called by their real names and their actions accurately described, and—lest I give offense unwittingly to any descendants—the one I have fictionalized has had his name changed slightly since I cannot prove that all his actions were as heinous as they are here portrayed.

Part One

THE LURE OF RICHES

CHAPTER I

"Keep her going, young Luke!" Daniel Murphy urged cheerfully. He grinned as, with powerful arms, he shoveled the contents of his barrow into the slanting, oblong box of the gold-mining rocker they were working. "This one may yield more than dust. Others have made big strikes—why shouldn't we? Morgan says the gold's here, and he knows what he's doing, don't he?"

His brother Luke, standing thigh-deep in the cold, murky waters of the creek, responded with an indifferent shrug.

"Does he, Dan?" he questioned. "Does he?" But not waiting for an answer, and with now-practiced skill, he bailed water into the cradle and began shaking it on its rockers in order to separate the mass of sand and gravel. Larger fragments of rock and useless pebbles were retained by a perforated metal sheet secured across the upper part of the box, the rest falling through into the sloping bottom, for the water to wash it past a series of slats or riffles. At the end of each day, someone would carefully scoop from behind the riffles the particles of gold that had settled there, mixed, inevitably, with sand.

Luke straightened up, smothering a sigh. Unlike his older brother, Daniel, who was a well-muscled six feet, he was small and slight and, just past his eighteenth birthday, the younger by three years. Until four months ago, when Captain Jasper Morgan had entered their lives on his way to the goldfields, both he and Dan had been content enough to work on their father's small, isolated farm in California's Sacramento Valley, raising hogs and horses and supplying the gold rush travelers and the mining camps with food and timber in addition to replacements for their worn-out teams.

Their father was a Mormon. Although he had been one of

the early converts, he had found existence under Brigham
Young in Great Salt Lake City too restrictive and had deserted the New Zion in order to return to the life and work
he knew and loved best. But he had retained the principles
of his faith, and the all-prevailing gold fever now gripping
the state of California in the year 1850 had left him un-
moved, for he had heeded the Mormon leader's stern injunction that gold was for paving city streets and not for
personal enrichment.

Luke, bareheaded under the relentless sun, mopped his
brow as he watched his brother walk away, pushing the
heavy barrow in the direction of the bank, where their two
companions were toiling with picks and spades.

The coming of Captain Jasper Morgan had changed everything. Handsome, elegant, and worldly-wise, Morgan
had an eloquent tongue and an answer for any argument. He
had charmed them all initially and had even contrived to
refute Brigham Young's dictum by listing the advantages
certain to accrue to those who had the wit and knowledge to
prospect successfully for the gold that, he had claimed, was
there for the taking. He had that knowledge; in a matter of a
few weeks, his musical Welsh voice had asserted—or at most
a couple of months—he would find a suitable site, and the
skill he had acquired in the coal and tin mines of his native
land would ensure success beyond the dreams of avarice.

But he needed help, Morgan had conceded—strong arms
and young men accustomed to hard labor, since he himself
—Luke smiled wryly at the memory—he himself, having followed a military profession and lived as a gentleman, was
deficient on that score.

Dan had been eager to take him up on the offer of a
partnership. Dan, for all their strict upbringing and their
Mormon principles, had always hankered after the chance to
join the thousands of gold seekers who had come flooding
into the bleak, inhospitable land since James Marshall's discovery at Sutter's Mill. And Luke's smile widened into one of
deep affection. Where Dan went, he went, too. When their
father had given his consent and their mother her cautious
approval, they had signed the deeds of partnership, and
leaving in their places the two old Mexicans Morgan had

brought with him from San Francisco, they had undertaken
the chore of driving their new partner's wagon, with its tents
and mining gear, to the site he had chosen.

It had been a weary journey, through abandoned diggings
and deserted mining camps, for the gold-hungry invaders
were constantly moving on as news of fresh strikes reached
them and new arrivals added daily to their number, now
rumored to be more than one hundred thousand. California
had been ceded to the United States by Mexico and was now
a state of the Union; millions of empty acres, uncultivated
and uninhabited, were—as Morgan had said of the gold they
were yielding—there for the taking. The miners formed
their own committees, elected leaders, and made what laws
they deemed necessary, and any man might stake a claim and
hold it for as long as he continued to work it and left his tools
or his tent on the site.

But Morgan did not share these democratic notions. He
had a theory which, Luke reflected sullenly, he had not seen
fit to divulge either to Dan or himself or to the two other
men—both Australians and brothers, by the name of Gardener, Frank and Tom—whom he had also picked up on the
way and taken into partnership.

They had passed through the largely canvas city of Sacramento, on through the sealike valley, and through the oak-
clad foothills to the broad plateau of the Sierra, then down
once again to the Feather River region, where finally Morgan
had ordered a halt. They had set up camp in a dim gorge,
known locally as Windy Gully, through the steep, rocky
center of which ran a shallow stream. Morgan had displayed
a secretive expertise while he made a survey of his chosen
site but had finally pronounced the rocks gold-bearing and
assured his anxious partners that the stream, conscientiously worked, would yield as much alluvial gold as they
could wish for.

He had supervised the setting up of their rocker, had
doled out spades and buckets from the wagon, and, having
instructed them as to the procedure they must follow, had
taken two of the horses and absented himself for almost
three weeks. He— Dan came back, trundling another bar-

rowload of sand and pebbles, and Luke dealt with it in
brooding silence.

"Cheer up, lad," his brother said. "It'll be grub time soon,
and Frankie trapped us a couple o' plump buck rabbits, so
we'll eat well at least. Even if we don't have much to show for
a hard day's work."

"We never do have much," Luke retorted, refusing to be
placated. "A few bags of dust, that's all, and sweat enough to
find that." He shook the rocker box with angry violence.
"And there's Captain Morgan, always giving orders and
never lending us a hand himself! Some partnership this is,
with the four of us doing all the work."

"He's learnt us what to do, Luke," Dan reminded him.
"And paid for the wagon and the horses and the supplies."
He jerked his head skyward. " 'Twill be sundown in half an
hour. You'll feel differently when you've a decent meal inside you."

Maybe he would, Luke agreed, but without conviction, his
resentment of Jasper Morgan growing. The captain had returned after his three-week-long absence, bringing, it was
true, more supplies and a second wagon. He had also
brought a girl with him—his daughter, according to Tom
Gardener, the only one to have seen her—and instead of
living with the rest of them in the tents, he had moved into
the storekeeper's house at Flycatcher's Bend, three miles
away, and spent less time than before on their claim.

Luke scowled up at the setting sun, shivering now that the
upper part of his body was deprived of its earlier warmth,
and found himself wondering about the girl, Morgan's
daughter. Morgan kept her well out of sight, which, in view
of the proximity of the area's main mining camp, was perhaps understandable. The men there were, on the whole,
sober and well behaved; but there were more than two hundred of them, and inevitably there were a few that stepped
over the traces, given the opportunity. They were men from
all corners of the earth—Americans, of course, and British,
Australians, Negroes from the southern states, Mexicans,
Germans, Frenchmen, a few Irish, and a small bunch from
Chile.

The elected camp committee had drawn up the bylaws,

which were strictly and sometimes brutally enforced. But
some of the miners struck it rich and then went to celebrate
their good fortune by getting drunk, despite the extortion-
ate price the storekeepers in the locality charged for liquor,
most of which was rotgut stuff, illicitly distilled. The camps
themselves were primitive; in some there were a few rough
timber huts, but most of the miners slept under canvas. A
handful of the men—those who had exhausted their grubstakes in their quest for a strike—existed without even a tent;
and a pretty young female—and Morgan's girl *was* pretty,
Tom had asserted—would clearly be a sore temptation to
such men, the more so since they had, for the most part,
been deprived of feminine company for a long time.

Even so, Luke told himself sourly, Jasper Morgan had no
call to spend half his time with her, leaving his partners to do
all the work on the claim. They were not paid a wage, and
because he had supplied their food and equipment, Morgan
had demanded and arbitrarily taken a fifty percent share of
their so-far meager returns.

"The captain's a gentleman," Dan always reminded him
when he voiced his doubts. "And like he says, his word is his
bond. He'll not cheat us, Luke."

But was he really a gentleman? Certainly Morgan talked
with all the arrogant assurance that went with social superi-
ority. His commission, he had told them, had been granted
by the Queen of England, and he had fought in the Carlist
War in Spain, as a soldier of fortune, with a splendid, jewel-
encrusted gold medal, bearing Queen Isabella's head, to
prove his claim and his courage. But for all that, and in spite
of the man's glib talk of past glories and wide travel, Luke's
doubts had not been set at rest. Rather, they had increased
and worried him more, particularly since the girl's arrival.
Her name was Mercy, Tom had said, which might or might
not be Welsh. Or it was, perhaps, a shortened form of Mercedes. . . .

"Hi, there, Luke old son!" Tom himself hailed him from
the creek bank, a big, genial fellow who, whatever the temperature, worked with his torso bared and in pants cut off
above the knee. He and his brother shared most of the heavy
digging with Dan, and in addition, Frankie Gardener had

volunteered to act as camp cook. "Frankie's roastin' them rabbits he snared, an' he says they won't be long. You c'n knock off now, lad, an' git into some dry clothes. I'll 'tend to the riffles."

"Thanks, Tom," Luke acknowledged gratefully. He straightened up, flexing his cramped muscles and conscious of the pangs of hunger. It had been a long day, and he hoped, as he did most days, that they would have more than sand and a sprinkling of gold dust to show for it, although such hopes were seldom fulfilled. Morgan would not hear of their moving on, however small their return; he had chosen the Windy Gully site, bringing all his expert knowledge to the task, and to abandon it would be to call that knowledge into question.

As Luke made his way along the water's edge, an appetizing smell of roasting meat greeted him, and he gave Frankie Gardener a friendly wave. At least he and Dan had struck it rich where the other members of their partnership were concerned, he reflected. The Gardeners were as fine a pair of men as any he had ever met—honest, hardworking, utterly dependable, and the best of company, even in the face of disappointment. He enjoyed listening to the yarns they told about Australia as they hunkered down beside their campfire in the evening. Both had been seamen until, like so many others, they had jumped ship in San Francisco and come to try their luck in the goldfields.

Neither of them planned to stay in America.

"Soon as we make a worthwhile strike, we'll be off back to Sydney Town," Tom had said many times, and smiled as he went on to talk of his wife and children and his longing to end what had become a three-year separation from them. He had talked also of a fellow Australian named Hargraves, Luke recalled, a merchant seaman serving in the same ship, with whom Jasper Morgan had had some dealings.

Frankie had said of Hargraves, "He has his head screwed on the right way, has Ned. Reckons the country in our Bathurst an' Goulburn areas is as like this here as to make no difference. So if there's gold here in California, then there's every chance there'll be gold in New South Wales, an' I, for one, can't wait to go back an' find out. All Tom an' me are waiting for is just one good strike an' we'll be hightailin' it home!"

But there had been no good strike; just a few small bags of dust, won after days and weeks of backbreaking toil and sweat. And it was backbreaking. Luke thought sourly. Each spadeful of earth took effort; each laden barrow must be wheeled over the rough ground to the cradle, tipped into it, rocked, and washed. Placer mining, it was called. Panning was easier but less rewarding, and in any case, after a day spent swilling river sand in a heavy metal pan, a man's muscles ached and his head reeled. And they were working their claim with the knowledge that other miners, more skilled and experienced than they themselves, had worked Windy Gully and moved on. Besides—

"Hey, Luke boy!" Frankie, hands cupped about his mouth, hailed him from the tent site. Luke obediently halted and looked up to the top of the rocky bank, some thirty feet above.

"Yeah, Frankie? You want something?"

"A bucket o' fresh water, lad. Make sure your bucket's clean—it's for makin' the coffee. Don't want to swaller no dust with our coffee, do we? Nor any nuggets, neither."

It was a jest that had long since worn thin, and Luke did not laugh. He glanced back to where Tom and Dan were busy scraping out the riffles and saw Dan shake his head in answer to his unspoken question. Just dust, then, he thought with bitterness—dust, a pinch of which would buy a drink or two, and a handful sell for twenty dollars; barely enough to keep them in flour and coffee, with prices what they were at the diggings. It took nearly an ounce of dust a day just to keep one miner fed and working. . . .

"Right," he called back, swallowing his disappointment. "I'll get your water, Frankie."

He returned to the stream, the water squelching out of his worn cowhide boots. Conscientiously he rinsed the bucket, then filled it with fresh creek water. The bank at this point was steep; there was an easier ascent a few yards back, but in his present mood of black depression, Luke did not bother to walk back.

That this was a mistake he quickly realized as his wet boots

slipped on the lichen-covered rock and he had to put out his
free hand swiftly to grasp the exposed roots of a scrubby
manzanita growing in a crevice, in order to avoid spilling the
contents of his bucket. He managed to steady himself, losing
only a few drops of the water, but then, without warning, the
manzanita roots lost their frail hold, and Luke found himself
having to cling to the edge of the crevice with both hands,
letting the bucket fall.

Cursing, he watched the bucket roll out of reach and was
about to go down to retrieve it when something in the interior of the crevice caught his eye. Where the roots of the
mountain shrub had been there were pebbles lying as they
might have done in a bird's nest; only the pebbles were
larger than any bird's eggs he had ever seen, and in the last,
faint rays of the setting sun they possessed a dull, reflected
gleam.

Scarcely daring to believe the evidence of his eyes, Luke
reached into the crevice and picked up one of the pebbles,
an impulsive shout strangled in his throat. Best to make
sure, he told himself, his heart pounding like a living thing
against his ribs. There had been so many failures, so many
dashed hopes; it wouldn't do to yell out to Dan and the
others that at long last he had made the strike they had
dreamed of. Not until he was sure.

It did not take him long to make sure. He had seen and
handled other nuggets before, and there was no mistake
about these: Weight and feel were right. They were gold!
And there were—God in heaven, there were eight of them,
varying in size and shape, the largest, as nearly as he could
guess, weighing around five pounds.

An even larger one was embedded in the rock. His hands
trembling, Luke took out his jackknife and, with infinite care
and some difficulty, pried it out. Again resisting the impulse
to call to the others, he filled his pockets with the smaller
nuggets and clambered down to fetch his bucket, into which
he placed his last find.

The light had almost gone, and he strode back to the
gentle ascent they usually took, mounting it as if he were
walking on air. Dan and Tom were spreading out the day's
small mixture of sand and dust to dry in front of the fire, and

Frankie, busy with his rabbits on their spits, observed, without turning around, his tone mildly reproachful, "That you, Luke? Took your time, didn't you? Let's have the water; these rabbits are just about done."

"I brought something better than water," Luke said. His voice was so hoarse with excitement that it sounded unnatural, even to himself, and Dan, quick to sense the emotional strain under which his brother was laboring, jumped up and grasped him by the shoulders.

"What is it, young Luke? What is it, boy?"

"This," Luke stammered, his throat tight. "We—we m-made it, Dan; we made our strike! Praise be to God!"

He dropped to his knees by the fire, and as the other three watched in stunned amazement, he turned out first his pockets and then upended the heavy bucket, placing his haul on the strip of canvas on which the few handfuls of dust and sand were drying.

They stared with mouths agape, momentarily bereft of words. Then Tom picked up the largest of the nuggets and leaped to his feet, emitting a wild, triumphant yell.

"Jesus, boys, we're rich! This must be worth—God Almighty, a bloody fortune! We can go home, Frankie! The kid's made it for us, and made it big! Luke, you're a marvel!"

One of the precious jackrabbits fell from its spit into the fire, but Frankie did not trouble to retrieve it. He wrung Luke's hand, his tanned face aglow and his blue, seaman's eyes full of tears as he sought vainly for words.

"Where?" he managed at last. "Where did you find all these, Luke?"

Luke told him, feeling suddenly as if it were all a dream and fearful that he might waken from it. "Pinch me," he pleaded. "I—I can't believe it, even now."

It was Dan who brought them down to earth. He rescued the charred remnants of their supper and said soberly, "Ain't you forgetting—half o' this belongs to Captain Morgan?"

"He didn't find them nuggets," Tom protested. "Young Luke did, on his own."

"We got a partnership agreement, Tom," Dan reminded him. "Morgan staked us, and he brought us here. He's enti-

tled to fifty percent; we four divide the rest between us." He
grinned at the young Australian's chagrin. "Why, for crying
out loud, lad, there's enough for all of us! That lump o' gold
you're holding must weigh ten or twelve pounds by itself,
and the storekeepers are paying sixteen dollars an *ounce*.
They pay more at the Branch Mint in 'Frisco by all accounts
—twenty dollars maybe."

Tom attempted to work out figures in his head and finally,
his smile returning, resorted to counting on his fingers.

"God!" he exclaimed, awed. "Oh, my God!"

"And there could be more," Dan pointed out, "buried in
the bank o' the creek where Luke found this little lot." He
gestured to the congealing rabbit meat. "Let's have our
meal, boys, an' put some coffee on. You fetch up the water,
Tom."

"I fancy going to the camp," Tom countered obstinately,
"and buyin' me a skinful o' whiskey to celebrate. We've
waited long enough for something we *can* celebrate, haven't
we?"

Dan sighed. "Not till we tell Morgan. He has a right to
know. Go fetch the water, lad. There'll be time enough to
celebrate. And Luke, get you into some dry gear. You don't
want to die of pneumonia, do you, now that we've made it at
last?"

They both obeyed him, and Frankie asked, taking out his
knife to slice the rabbits, "You aiming to tell Morgan tonight, Dan?"

"No." Dan's headshake was firm. "At first light we'll take a
good look at where Luke made his find. Then, when Morgan
does show up, we'll tell him and see what he has to say."

Next day, when Jasper Morgan arrived on horseback for
his accustomed daily visit to the scene of his partners' activities, he had plenty to say—little of it to their liking, Luke
thought rebelliously as he listened.

Tall and well dressed, with his Colt revolver slung as
always from his belt, Morgan dismounted and, throwing his
horse's rein to Frankie, inspected the nuggets with little
visible sign of emotion, apart from a gleam in his dark eyes
that swiftly faded. He said peremptorily, "There'll be no
going to the mining camp—understand that, all of you. If

there's even a whisper of our having made a find of this magnitude, the gully will be overrun. We want to keep it to ourselves, and we cannot hope to do so if any of you shoots his mouth off. If you want a drink to celebrate, I'll supply it."

He silenced Tom's objections with an icy glance and turned to Luke.

"I confess I'm astonished that you were the one to stumble on this find, boy. But for once your clumsiness has been turned to good account, has it not? Now wipe that inane grin off your face and show me where you found the nuggets. There's probably more gold there, and I must decide the best way to get it out. It may be just a random deposit, but if it's in or near bedrock, we'll have to sink a shaft and dig right into the hillside."

Luke seethed with resentment at Morgan's disparaging words, but a warning glance from Dan was sufficient to cause him to curb his tongue. He led the way in silence, and the others followed. Their early-morning search had revealed only two small nuggets that Luke had missed in his excitement, and Jasper Morgan, despite a minute inspection of the crevice where the manzanita had sunk its tenuous roots, found no more.

Nevertheless, he was optimistic, lecturing them on the geology of the gold-bearing region and reeling off technical terms as, with a small hammer he had sent Frankie to fetch from his saddlebag, he tapped at the rock and talked knowledgeably of lodes and seams and the upheaval of the Sierra millions of years before, when the earth's interior had opened, spewing out its riches.

He was a great talker, Luke reflected, and the fact that most of his lecture was beyond his partners' understanding did not appear to deter him. And he was unexpectedly deft and nimble, taking off his well-tailored jacket in order to climb up and down the bank in shirtsleeves and breeches, displaying more energy than he had since they had first come to Windy Gully.

He was not an old man, of course; Jasper Morgan could not be much more than forty—or forty-five, perhaps, at most. His hair was black, with only a powdering of gray at the temples, which added to his air of gentlemanly distinction, and he was still what women would consider good-looking, Luke decided, studying him with more than usual care. His face was strong and unlined, the mouth straight beneath its heavy mustache, the skin darkly and healthily tanned. Yet there was something about him that . . . Luke shrugged, unable to put a name to it or even to find a plausible reason for his mistrust. Yet it was there, constantly nagging at him and—

Dan's voice broke into his thoughts. "We're to give up placer work in the creek bed, Luke, and drive a shaft into the bank, right below where you found those nuggets. The captain says there's every chance of a rich seam in there—you heard him, didn't you? We'll need timber for props, which we're to cut, and more tools, as well as blasting powder, which he's going to bring in for us. He's setting off now, soon as he's had some coffee."

He went into detail, but Luke scarcely heard him. Jasper Morgan had donned his jacket, he saw, and was heading back to the tent site, deep in conversation with Frankie and Tom.

"He's not taking the nuggets, is he, Dan?" Luke asked, frowning. "Did he say he was?"

Dan shook his head. "No, he didn't. I reckon he'll leave 'em with us. But he did say that it'll be best if he takes the lot —nuggets and dust—to 'Frisco in a week or two. The U.S. Mint's paying twenty-two dollars an ounce, so we'd lose out if we take what they're paying here or in Sacramento."

"We'll lose a lot more if he doesn't come back," Luke objected.

"He'll come back," his brother asserted. "He always has, hasn't he? And there's the girl, his daughter. It's a rough trip to 'Frisco, Luke; he won't take her with him, so he'll have to come back. Besides, we've gotten a partnership agreement, ain't we? And Captain Morgan's a gentleman. You want to learn to trust folk more, Luke boy, and that's a fact. Come on." He put an arm around Luke's shoulders. "I'm dry, I don't know about you. Let's get us a cup o' coffee."

"All right," Luke conceded reluctantly. "But seeing what I found, I'd like to take a bag of dust to the old folk. Pa could do with it, and Ma will be wondering how we're getting

along. I could be there and back before Morgan brings us
the tools."

"Ask Morgan, boy. Sounds reasonable enough to me."
Dan smiled down at him. "Aye, and not such a bad idea at
that. You ask him."

Luke did so, making his request with restrained polite-
ness, but Jasper Morgan's refusal was terse. "There's much
to be done whilst I'm gone, and I'll not be gone more than
three or four days. Besides, boy, I don't want you blabbing
your head off about our strike; we've got to keep quiet about
it, understand?"

"I made the find," Luke reminded him.

"And now you want to trade on it, eh?"

"No, sir, not that. And I know how to keep a still tongue in
my head. I won't blab."

But Morgan was adamant. The find was a good one, but
compared with what he expected the site to yield, it was a
drop in the ocean.

"In any event," he finished loftily, "your esteemed father
has religious objections, has he not? Wants to pave streets
and tile houses with gold, not put it to sound commercial
use. You stay here and put your back into some tree felling,
boy. This claim has cost me plenty, and I want to see a return
for what I've spent. I shall not be gone long, as I told you."

He was as good as his word. By noon on the third day he
was there with the wagon, and once again he stripped to his
shirtsleeves and went energetically about the task at hand.
He left the hard work to his young partners, it was true, but
he would not permit any of them to handle the gunpowder.
That he was expert in its use Luke was forced to admit, and
as Dan frequently remarked, the carefully controlled explosions he arranged saved them hours of backbreaking toil.

The shaft was through the rock in less than a week, and
twenty feet into the hillside, with timber props installed at
regular intervals, three days later. Morgan spent hours underground, with an oil lantern and his small geologist's hammer. His reports were encouraging, although only a few
lumps of gold-bearing ore and two more nuggets, weighing
less than ten ounces, were unearthed. All the while he was
unusually garrulous, although when the *alcalde*—the elected

chairman of the miners' standing committee—appeared with two of his committee members from the camp at Thayer's Bend to inquire as to the reason for the explosions, Morgan gave them short shrift.

The *alcalde* was a white-haired veteran named Ephraim Crocker, who had come to the diggings in the spring of 1848. He listened to Jasper Morgan's curt explanation with unconcealed skepticism and then observed flatly, "You're plumb crazy, Cap'n."

"How I work my claim is my affair, Mr. Crocker," Morgan returned coldly, cutting short the old man's attempt to point out to him the disadvantages of tunneling into the hillside. "In any event, we are outside your jurisdiction here, I'll thank you to remember."

Crocker exchanged glances with his committeemen and shrugged his bowed shoulders.

"Have it your own way, mister. I was just tryin' to offer a piece o' friendly advice, that's all. Up to you whether or not you take it. I been around the diggings over two years, an' I learnt the hard way what works an' what don't. Alluvial gold's easy dealt with, but gold-bearing quartz is another matter—has to be crushed, don't it? And you ain't got the tools nor the men to git it out, even supposin' you find it."

He nodded to his companions, and they fell into step with him and moved away before Jasper Morgan could find words with which to reply. But Crocker's warning worried Luke, and that evening he took his brother aside with the intention of voicing his doubts, only to find that Dan now shared them.

"Maybe Morgan knows what he's doing—I've always given him credit for that. But"—Dan's expression was wary —"so does old Eph Crocker, that's for sure."

"I'd like to talk with Pa about it," Luke said.

To his relief, his brother nodded. "Yeah, Luke boy, I reckon the time's come when you should."

"Morgan wouldn't give me leave. He said there was too much work to be done."

"And we've done it," Dan returned, an edge to his voice. "We've done everything he's asked of us. I've been thinking, Luke, these last few days, wondering what good we're doing with this darned mine. We've nothing much to show for our work, have we? Not even as much dust as we were getting from the rocker or Frankie got panning."

He hesitated and then took a small buckskin bag of gold dust from the pocket of his coat. He passed it to Luke. "Set off home tonight, boy, and take this to Pa. It's only a fraction of the value of them nuggets you found, so I reckon you've earned it. And you can talk to Pa, ask his counsel."

"What'll Morgan say," Luke questioned anxiously, "when he finds out I've gone?"

"We'll cover for you. He won't find out. Anyway—" Again Dan hesitated, reddening a little. "Tom thinks he's preparing to go to 'Frisco. He had the new wagon out yesterday, when Tom went to the cabin for stores, and seemed like he was overhauling it, ready for a trip."

"Did he say he was going?"

Dan shook his head. "Not for definite, no. But he mentioned the price the Mint's paying for dust, and old Eph Crocker said the same when I asked him. Twenty-two dollars an ounce."

"Yeah, but—"

"Luke boy, we've got to trust him," Dan insisted, anticipating the question. "And like I told you, he won't take his little girl with him. He said he wouldn't. She's his daughter; he must come back for her. And twenty-two dollars an ounce is a lot more than sixteen, ain't it?"

It was, Luke had to concede, but he asked uneasily, "Dan, does Morgan have our gold—does he have all of it out at the cabin?"

Dan's color deepened. "Yes, he does."

"And you let him take it?"

"He said he wanted to weigh it, so's he could account for it to us. In writing, Luke—he promised me he would put it in writing before he left here. I just kept that one bag back, for you to take to Pa." Dan got to his feet. "If you're going, you'd best start out pretty soon, boy. I'll saddle your horse for you while you're getting your gear together."

"All right," Luke agreed. He looked up into his brother's honest, open face and said diffidently, "Dan, you've worked out what our strike is worth, haven't you?"

"Only roughly, in my head."

"Well, how much do you reckon?"

"You'd best not tell Pa," Dan warned. "But roughly, if it brings twenty-two dollars an ounce, around ten thousand dollars. Half o' that is Morgan's, and the four of us divide the rest." He grinned. "If we stick together and pool our shares, Luke boy, we could buy us a tidy spread."

"Yeah, Dan, we could!" Luke's heart lifted. It was a small fortune—a sum beyond his wildest dreams. A farm in the foothills, stocked with cattle and hogs—aye, and horses, too —he and Dan together. He could ask no more, and they would see Pa and Ma right, of course. Take land near them and build Pa the barn he had always hankered after and have a harmonium for Ma, shipped from the East. He flung his arms around his brother's neck and hugged him. "I'd no idea it would be so much."

"I'm only guessing," Dan reminded him. "We don't have scales. It could be less, or it could be a bit more. We'll know for sure when Morgan puts it in writing." He returned Luke's hug and then pushed him away with a playful slap across the boy's thin buttocks. "Off with you, boy, and get ready. Frankie'll give you what grub you'll need; I told him you'd probably be going in the next day or so. And you can take my mare; she's a better ride than that pinto of yours, and Pa'll be pleased to see she's come to no harm."

Luke's preparations were soon completed, and the moon had risen by the time he had made his brief farewells. He swung himself onto the back of Dan's bay mare, and with his blanket roll and small sack of provisions strapped to his saddle, he set off for home. The mining camp at Thayer's Bend was in darkness as he rode down its rutted track, his passing setting a few dogs barking but arousing no one else, and he did not pause there.

He had a long way to go, he reminded himself, but he was glad to be going, and spirits lightened with every mile. It would be great to see Ma and Pa again, great to tell Pa that he and Dan would soon be rich men and that they would be coming home for good the minute Jasper Morgan paid them their share and released them.

The mare trotted briskly along the shadowed track, picking her way carefully over the scars that countless wagon wheels had left in their wake, and Luke pursed his lips and whistled a cheerful little tune as he let her have her head.

CHAPTER II

Barely fourteen days since he had left the diggings, Luke found himself once more in sight of the huddle of tents and log cabins that constituted the Thayer's Bend mining camp.

The visit home, by which he had set so much store, had lasted exactly a day, and he was returning from it chastened and more than a little rebellious. Religious scruples had again affected his father; the old man had refused the bag of gold dust, and during the waking hours of his brief stay Luke had been compelled to listen to a seemingly endless tirade of condemnation and reproach concerning his evil ways and the ungodliness of the search for riches in which he was engaged.

Two missionaries from Great Salt Lake City had called at the farm during his absence, his mother had confided wryly.

"Fine young fellers they were—mannerly and decent. But since they was here, your pa's been having a real battle with his conscience. He feels now he shouldn't never have let you and Dan go to the goldfields. You've gone against the will of God, both of you, he says, and he only wants you back here if you pay over the gold you've found to the church. D'you reckon you can do that, Luke?"

He had hated having to reject her suggestion, Luke recalled, feeling unmanly tears pricking at his eyes. Throughout the long ride back, his mother's stricken face had haunted him, but he and Dan had worked too hard for their strike, he told himself, for either of them willingly to hand over the proceeds of their toil to a church to which they owed no real allegiance. True, they had been reared in the Mormon faith, but during the years their father had lapsed from its teachings, they, too, had lapsed by default, and their mother . . . He sighed. Ma had tried hard, for the old man's sake, but her heart had never really been in it, for she was of Irish descent and had been brought up as a Catholic. And she certainly did not hold with polygamy. . . .

His tired horse stumbled, and Luke forced himself to give his attention to his riding. He was stiff and saddlesore, but another half hour should see him in the camp, and from there it was only five miles up the valley to their own claim. He would take a bottle of whiskey with him, he decided—buy it in camp with a few ounces of the dust his pa had scorned—and let Dan have a drink or two before listening to his account of his trip home. Dan would be upset, he knew, but would surely agree that they should not be expected to hand over their share of the strike to the Mormon church.

It wanted an hour to sunset when he reached Thayer's Bend. The store was in a wood-built shanty in the center, kept by a man named Logan, assisted by his two young sons. Luke hitched his mare's rein to the post outside and, taking the small buckskin bag of dust from his saddlebag, walked stiffly into the store. Logan's elder son, Ted, was behind the counter, and to Luke's astonishment the boy eyed him as if he had seen a ghost. Not waiting to ask him what he wanted, Ted backed away and went scuttling to the rear of the store, shouting for his father.

"Pa, come an' see! It's one o' them Windy Gully fellers! Leastways it's him or his spittin' image!"

Logan himself appeared, a napkin tucked into his shirt, irritably cursing at what was evidently the interruption of his meal. But at the sight of Luke his eyes widened behind their rimless spectacles and the angry words died on his lips.

"Gawd Almighty!" he exclaimed, visibly startled. "You are one o' Captain Morgan's boys, ain't you, from the Windy Gully claim?"

"That's right, Mr. Logan," Luke assured him. "I'm Luke Murphy. I'm on my way back from visiting my folks in—" He broke off, conscious of the storekeeper's tension. "Is there something wrong?" He thought of the mine shaft and the confined space in which he and the others had been compelled to work, and drew in his breath sharply. "There's not been an—an accident, has there?"

Logan hesitated. He was known as a hard man, but there

was pity in his eyes as they met Luke's. Finally, he inclined his head.

"That's right, boy, there has—a real bad one. Truth to tell, we thought—that is, we didn't know you was visitin' your folks. You must've gone afore it happened. But maybe it'd be best if Eph Crocker told you—I'm just a storekeeper; I don't know nothin' about minin'. Ted—" He gestured to the door. "Cut across an' ask Mr. Crocker to step in here. Tell him—tell him as one o' the Windy Gully boys has shown up here, an' they ain't all—" He bit back the word he had been about to say, but Luke, a sick sensation in the pit of his stomach, guessed what it was.

"Dead?" he whispered brokenly. "You don't mean they—they're all dead? Dear God, Mr. Logan, you can't mean that?"

Logan said nothing. Turning away, he splashed a measure of whiskey into a pewter pot and thrust it into Luke's hands.

"Swallow that down, son," he urged. "Eph'll be here soon, an' he'll tell you."

The raw spirit choked him, and Luke put the pot down, his hand shaking. He had planned to buy a bottle of whiskey, he remembered, to celebrate his return and to console Dan for what he had to say concerning their father. But Dan would not—*could* not hear that now because he was dead—he and Frankie and Tom. Jasper Morgan, too, he supposed. All of them except himself.

Heralded by a breathless Ted, old Ephraim Crocker came hurrying into the store. He, too, had evidently been disturbed by the boy's summons while eating his evening meal and was still buttoning his jacket when he halted by Luke's side, his lined face grimly set. In a few gruff words he confirmed the storekeeper's story.

"I'm right sorry, lad, an' that's the truth. But they was usin' blastin' powder, see, an' the whole shaft caved in on top of them." He explained the circumstances. "I reckon it must've blown when they was inside. 'Twas a mighty loud explosion—a lot o' the stuff must've gone up at one an' the same time, see. I heard it from here an' guessed there was somethin' amiss. Half a dozen of us threw down our tools an' made for the gully as fast as we knowed how, but we was too

late. They was buried, an' there was no way we could get to
them.''

"You tried?" Luke managed, his throat tight. "Mr.
Crocker, you did try to get to them?"

The old man inclined his balding white head. He said
regretfully, "Oh, we tried all right, son, but it was hopeless.
Tons o' rock was brought down, you see, an' even if we'd
been able to shift it, there was no chance of any of them bein'
alive. No chance at all." He patted Luke's slumped shoulders in an awkward gesture of sympathy. "You best stop here
in camp tonight, an' I'll go out with you in the mornin', so's
you can see for yourself. You won't have eaten, I don't suppose?"

"No," Luke admitted dully. "But I don't want nothin'."
He was appalled by what Crocker had told him, and bewildered also, for had not Jasper Morgan always claimed to be
an expert at handling blasting powder? An expert would not
have permitted men to be inside the mine when a charge was
about to be set off, and in the past Morgan had been careful
—meticulously so. And the gunpowder had always been
kept at a safe distance, with only the amount required for
each charge taken to the rock face.

He started to say this, but Crocker exchanged glances with
the storekeeper and then said reluctantly, "Cap'n Morgan
wasn't there, son. He come through here in his wagon the
day before it happened. Stopped at the store for supplies an'
told Mr. Logan he was on his way to 'Frisco—that's right,
ain't it, Mike?" Logan nodded, and the miners' elected
leader went on, avoiding Luke's gaze, "So we all figure that
'twas an accident. Maybe your brother and those two Australian boys he worked with weren't—well, maybe they didn't
know how to handle the blasting powder. An' with the cap'n
not there . . ."

He left his sentence unfinished, hanging in the air between them, with all its implications as plain to Luke as if he
had voiced them. He bit back an indignant denial; Crocker
was not trying to hurt him, he knew, but Dan was—had been
—no fool. They all had learned to handle the powder
charges under Morgan's tuition, and Dan wasn't one to take
risks with other men's lives, any more than with his own. It

simply did not make sense. Luke's brows met in an unhappy
pucker as he tried to puzzle it out.

Jasper Morgan had gone to San Francisco, as he had said
he would, taking their gold—the partnership's gold—with
him, to sell to the United States Mint.

"Did the captain have the girl with him, Mr. Logan?" he
forced himself to ask. "His daughter, I mean?"

Once again the two older men exchanged glances, and
then Logan shook his head. "Nope, he was alone, Luke."

That, at least, was a relief, and Luke's expression lightened. If Morgan had left his daughter behind, he would have
to come back—Dan had been certain on that score. And
then, when he had paid them their share of the money,
they— Luke stiffened, and for all his effort to prevent it, a
sob escaped him, as he remembered.

Dan and the other two could not claim their shares. They
were dead, all three of them, which meant that as the only
other surviving partner he would have to claim their shares
as well as his own—fifty percent, the same as Morgan's. He
would find a way to send Tom's and Frankie's shares to their
folks in Australia; that was the least he could do, of course.
And maybe he could talk Pa into accepting Dan's—to give to
the church, if that was what he wanted to do. He . . .

Young Ted brought him a mug of scalding black coffee,
and Luke sipped it gratefully, preferring it to the whiskey.
Ephraim Crocker sat down and waited until he had drunk it,
then asked thoughtfully, "Why did Cap'n Morgan go to
'Frisco, son, d'you know? What reason had he?"

"He went to sell our gold to the Mint, Mr. Crocker," Luke
answered, and broke off, belatedly recalling Jasper Morgan's
insistence that he was not to talk of their strike to the men of
Thayer's Bend.

Crocker eyed him with narrowed lids. "You made a strike,
then?"

There was no point now in attempting to hide the truth.
Luke nodded. "Yes, a good one, sir." He described his find
and the manner in which he had made it and, when the old
man pressed him, gave him Dan's estimate of its worth.

Crocker's lips pursed in a silent whistle, and Logan said,
with more than a hint of resentment, "Captain Morgan

never said nothin' about that to me, boy. Never even hinted at it."

"No. He—that is, he told us to keep still tongues in our heads. He said if it was known, there'd be a rush to the gully, and he didn't want that."

Crocker grunted. "That's understandable," he conceded. "But you did no good with that mine o' yours, did you?"

"No, we didn't. But Captain Morgan said," Luke began, "that—"

"I know what he said," Crocker reminded him. "An' I know what *I* said. You was there; you heard me. I told him he was plumb crazy 'cause he hadn't the right tools nor enough men. He should've stuck to puddlin' like the rest o' us." He rose heavily to his feet, as if suddenly unwilling to continue the conversation. "Try an' get some sleep, boy. Mr. Logan here will fix you up, eh, Mike? An' I'll be along first thing in the mornin' so's we can go out to Windy Gully together." He laid a gnarled hand on Luke's shoulder in wordless sympathy and left the store.

Luke slept fitfully, sharing bed and blanket with young Ted Logan, and he still felt weary and dispirited when, soon after sunrise, he set off for Windy Gully with Ephraim Crocker and another elderly member of the miners' standing committee, named Roberts. The mine shaft, when they reached it, was a shapeless mass of rocks and earth. The entrance had collapsed on itself and was blocked completely; looking at it through tear-misted eyes, Luke understood, without Crocker's repeated explanation, why the would-be rescuers had abandoned their attempt to hack a way through to the entombed men. It would have taken hours, and the chances of finding anyone alive beneath the mass of debris would have been virtually nonexistent, even had they managed to get through to them.

Nevertheless, the thought of his brother's body's being left to lie there was more than he could bear to contemplate. Dan deserved better than that, he told himself. He deserved a proper burial, with words from the Bible read over him and a headstone to mark his last resting place. Dan and the two Australians—all three of them deserved that, and however long it took, he would see that they got what they deserved.

Ephraim Crocker shook his head when Luke told him what he intended to do, but there was a gleam of approval in his faded blue eyes for all that.

"I can't promise you no help, son," he said apologetically. "We've all of us gotten our claims to work. But if you've made up your mind, then I'm not about to try an' stop you. And happen there'll be some who'll lend a hand. You made a good strike here; when word about that spreads around, why, there'll likely be one or two that'll take it into their heads to come up here. Offer 'em half o' what they find, and that should lessen your work. An' when you're able to bring the bodies out, why, we'll give them Christian burial up at the camp. Mr. Roberts here is a lay preacher; he'll read over them, won't you, John?"

"Most willingly," Roberts agreed. "And I'll be glad to help you, boy."

Luke thanked them both. The small camp was as the three dead men had left it; the tents still in place, their bedding neatly rolled, the campfire cold, but the spits and the old iron kettle untouched. There were some tools, too—two picks and a shovel with a broken shaft, a rusting ax, and Jasper Morgan's small geologist's hammer. But the keg of blasting powder was empty.

One of Frankie's snares held the rotting remains of a rabbit; Luke threw the carcass away and, his throat aching, reset the snare. Crocker and Roberts took their leave, and when they had ridden off, he hobbled his tired mare and began his arduous task.

He worked for two days like a man possessed, throughout the daylight hours and then far into the night. The pinto he had left with Dan came in, but there was no sign of the Gardeners' two animals. Morgan, he decided, must have taken them, for they had never wandered far before, and one of the saddles was gone.

On the morning of the third day the lay preacher, John Roberts, came up with two others, bringing a gift of flour and a small bag of coffee. All three toiled with him for several hours, and Luke felt that at long last he had made progress. Evidently they must have shared his opinion, for at noon on the following day they returned, this time accompa-

nied by Ephraim Crocker, with a lantern and a supply of
tools.

"Mr. Roberts reckons we should get to the bodies before
nightfall if we work at it, son," he told Luke with gruff gentleness. "An' we didn't think as it was—well, fittin' for you to
be on your own." He hesitated and then said, looking down
at his dirt-encrusted boots, "Remember, they'll have been
buried in that shaft for nigh on three weeks. They won't
be—" He broke off, at a loss for words.

Luke nodded, tight-lipped. "I know, Mr. Crocker. I know
what to expect."

"All the same, son, you'd best let us go in first. We'll take
blankets with us, an'— Mr. Logan's bringin' up a wagon. It'll
all be done respectful-like an' proper, don't you worry."

"I'll go with you, sir," Luke asserted. There was a sick
sensation in the pit of his stomach, and he longed to take
advantage of the kindly old man's offer, but . . . Dan was
his brother, and he had a duty he could not shirk.

They broke through two hours later, finding themselves,
to Luke's bewilderment, in a small underground chamber,
untouched by the explosion, its roof still quite firmly held by
the props of timber that had collapsed elsewhere. And the
bodies were there; he saw them in the light of Crocker's
lantern, all three of them, lying huddled together as if they
were sleeping. He had expected them to be crushed under
the weight of earth and rock, had nerved himself for the
sight of blood and hideously shattered limbs, the dead faces
indistinguishable one from the other, but . . . they were
not. He recognized Dan's face instantly and had to bite back
a sob, his stomach churning.

"Leave this to us, Luke," John Roberts besought him.
"We'll bring them out." He tested one of the roof props with
both hands and nodded to Ephraim Crocker. "It's safe
enough. You got the blankets, Eph?"

Frankie's body was the nearest. Crocker spread out a blanket, and motioning Roberts to help him, he started to lift the
Australian's still form onto it, only to let it go, an exclamation of shocked horror escaping him.

"God Almighty, John, he's been shot! Shot in the back,

look for Christ's sake! It wasn't no explosion that killed him.
He was *shot!*"

One of the other men crawled through the narrow opening they had made, and he, too, swore in shocked tones.

"This poor fellow, too, Eph . . . and in the back just the
same."

"Get the boy out," Crocker ordered hoarsely.

"Come on, Luke, my son," John Roberts urged. "Do like
Eph says—out with you."

Luke tried to protest, but Roberts grasped him by the
shoulders and propelled him back to the open air. Then, an
arm about him, he led him to a pile of the rocks they had
shifted and bade him sit down.

"We'll say a prayer together, boy," he suggested consol-
ingly. "Don't try to kneel; the good Lord will understand
that you're weak from shock. Just close your eyes and listen,
eh?"

His prayer was delivered with deep sincerity and compassion, but Luke scarcely heard it, although he managed to
whisper a dutiful "amen" when the well-meaning preacher
paused for breath. And for all he was numb with shock from
the scene he had witnessed, his mind was racing, drawing
conclusions so appalling that he shrank from putting them
into words, even to John Roberts.

For who would believe him, he asked himself bitterly; who
would take his word against Jasper Morgan's—*Captain* Morgan's? And yet it had to be Morgan who had perpetrated the
horror they had found beneath the ruins of the mine shaft. It
had to be Morgan who had shot and killed—who had *murdered*—Dan and Tom and Frankie, since only he stood to gain
by their deaths. Morgan had taken their shares in the strike,
as well as his own fifty percent, and gone off to San Francisco
with all of it, intending to sell the dust and the nuggets to the
Mint at twenty-two dollars an ounce.

True, he had left the diggings the day before the explosion, but— Luke's hands clenched in futile anger at his sides.
Logan, the storekeeper, would bear witness to his departure,
but was that not just what the treacherous swine had intended? He could have come back, leaving his wagon well
hidden, without a soul's being any the wiser. . . . Had he

not taken the two extra horses and Tom's saddle, for which there had been no obvious need?

There was a stir by the entrance to the mine shaft, and hearing Ephraim Crocker's voice enjoining care, Luke felt wave after wave of nausea sweep over him. Bile rose in his throat, and he gagged.

Preacher Roberts brought his lengthy prayer abruptly to an end and rose from his knees.

"Stay where you are, Luke," he advised. "Eph's bringing them up now, I reckon. Best you don't look till they're decently covered."

But he had to look, Luke knew; he had to be sure. He stumbled to his feet, disregarding Roberts's proffered hand, and holding himself stiffly erect, he walked across the few yards that separated him from the bodies.

In the strong sunlight, the cause of all three deaths was plainly to be seen. Tom and Frankie had been shot from behind, but Dan's wound was in the chest, as if— Luke shuddered involuntarily. As if his brother had realized suddenly what was being done and, turning to face his killer, had sought vainly to grapple with him. Dan's mouth was open, frozen in death, and his eyes were wide with—what?

Not fear. Rather accusation, mingled with disbelief, when it must have dawned on him that the murdering devil holding the gun to his chest was the man—*the gentleman*—he had trusted: Captain Morgan, who had duped them into sinking a mine shaft which he must have known would yield no recoverable gold but which, instead, he had planned to transform into a tomb as soon as it was deep enough for its intended purpose.

Poor Dan would probably have had no time to voice his accusation before the Colt was fired, silencing him forever, and Morgan went squirming out, pausing only to light the fuse he had prepared before galloping to safety in the concealing darkness.

It all fitted, Luke thought dully; it had all gone according to plan—save, perhaps, for his own absence. But Morgan would not have worried unduly on that score. Once he had set off the explosion, the evidence of his evil crime would have been buried. Certainly he would not have imagined that anybody, least of all Dan Murphy's despised kid brother, was likely to dig down through tons of earth and rock, in order to bring out the bodies of his victims and, in so doing, reveal the truth.

Controlling himself took an effort of will, but Luke made it. He drew the edge of the blanket over Dan's dead face and rose, looking at Ephraim Crocker in mute question. He had not expected the old miner to reach the same conclusion as he had, or even to reason along similar lines, yet evidently Crocker had done just that, for lowering his voice, he said, "We'll bring the man that did this to justice, son, never fear. An' there's only one man that could've done it, only one that stood to gain, ain't there? But it'll have to be brought up before the committee and the evidence stated clearly, so that it's legal, understand?"

He motioned the two miners who had come out of the shaft with him to stand aside, and the storekeeper, Logan, drove his wagon carefully over the littered ground and drew up within a few yards of the blanket-covered bodies. The others held a brief, low-voiced conversation, and then Crocker took Luke's arm and led him out of earshot.

"We'll give them a Christian burial tomorrow mornin', Luke boy," he promised. "An' when that's done, I'll convene a meetin' o' the full committee. You'll likely be called on to tell the meetin' everything you can about the partnership terms you agreed to an' about Captain Morgan—and, o' course, the strike you made, so best git your gear together an' come in with us for the night. We must act fast, son, if we're to see justice done."

Luke nodded his understanding.

The funeral service, conducted by John Roberts, was attended by virtually every man in the Thayer's Bend camp. For Luke it was an ordeal, but he met it with frozen calm and was heartened by the expressions of sympathy he received and by the men's spontaneous kindness. Many had taken the trouble to don their best suits, with ties or cravats and high-crowned derbies, and all had sacrificed a considerable portion of their day's work in order, as one old-timer put it, "To show our respects to them poor young fellers, cut off in the prime of life."

The meeting of the camp committee took place immediately after Luke's partners had been laid to rest. Under Ephraim Crocker's chairmanship it was brisk and businesslike, but in spite of this, it proved a greater ordeal than the funeral had been, for Luke found himself cast in the role of principal witness.

After Crocker and Roberts had given evidence concerning the finding of the bodies and the fact that all three men had died from gunshot wounds, he was called to take the stand, addressed formally as Mr. Murphy. The formality added to Luke's uneasiness, but he answered the questions as truthfully and clearly as he could, describing the partnership agreement with Jasper Morgan in detail and then, prompted by Crocker, giving a minute description of his strike.

Asked to estimate its value, he could only answer lamely that he did not know. "Dan—my brother Dan told me that he guessed it would fetch around ten thousand dollars from the Mint in 'Frisco."

"And this was why Captain Morgan had the gold in his possession? He was to take it to 'Frisco with your consent— yours and your partners'?"

"The others must've consented," Luke answered, frowning as he tried to remember what Dan had told him. "I wasn't asked, but—well, Dan said we had to trust Captain Morgan, and that was good enough for me. He had scales and was going to weigh the gold and give us a signed paper stating how much there was."

"Did you receive such a paper, Mr. Murphy?" John Roberts asked.

"No, sir. I'd left for home before it was ready."

"*Did* you trust Captain Morgan?" one of the other committeemen demanded unexpectedly. When Luke hesitated, not certain how to reply, he added, "What I'm getting at is this: When you set out to visit your folks, you knew Morgan intended to take the gold to San Francisco, didn't you?"

"Yes. From what Dan said, I knew he was preparing to go."

"What made you think he would come back with your and

your partners' share of the price he got for the gold? Had you any guarantee, or did your brother ask for one?"

Luke shuffled his feet uneasily. He had never trusted Jasper Morgan, he thought with bitterness, although he had certainly never supposed him to be capable of murder.

"There's the girl, sir," he said lamely. "Morgan's daughter. He wasn't taking her to 'Frisco with him, and Dan said he would come back on her account. So I figured—"

Ephraim Crocker cut him short. "I've sent for the girl, son. We'll hear what she has to say as soon as she gits here." He took out his pocket watch and looked inquiringly at the faces of the members of his committee. "That's liable to be awhile yet. So if there's no more questions you want to ask young Luke here, we can adjourn for half an hour. Talkin's thirsty work."

"I do have a question, Eph," one of the younger men said. "It won't take above a minute." He turned to face Luke and said crisply, "We've been told that the wounds the murdered men suffered were most likely caused by shots fired at close range from a Colt forty-four. Did Captain Morgan carry a Colt forty-four, d'you know?"

Luke met his gaze and nodded. "Yes, sir, he did."

"Then I'd say that wraps it up, Eph," the questioner suggested. "Whatever Morgan's daughter has to tell us. I move that we bring in a verdict on the evidence we've heard."

"What verdict have you in mind, Sam?" Crocker asked, his gavel poised.

"Well, I don't know just how it'd have to be worded to make it legal," the man addressed as Sam conceded. "But what I have in mind is that this feller Jasper Morgan's guilty of murder and—what's it called?—larceny, and we ought to find accordingly. Then, when he comes back for his daughter, we'll hang him."

There was a stunned silence; then several voices were raised in assent. Ephraim Crocker rapped with his gavel. "He'd have to be charged an' put on trial, Sam," he demurred. "We got no right to condemn him without lettin' him plead. We ain't no lynch mob." He shrugged his bowed shoulders. "Let me think about it, eh? An' I guess we ought

to hear from the girl before we bring in a verdict. All right?
Then the meetin's adjourned till she gits here."

The girl was brought in an hour later, and although Tom
had said that she was pretty, Luke was taken aback by the
sight of her. She was more than pretty, he thought. She was
beautiful—a slim, delicate-featured young woman, with fair
hair, neatly braided about a shapely head, and skin that had
tanned to an exquisite golden brown.

She was very frightened, and her blue eyes were red-
rimmed, the lids swollen, as if she had been weeping cease-
lessly all the way to the camp. But she had courage. Faced by
the circle of inquisitors, she squared her thin shoulders and
held her head high, replying to Ephraim Crocker's request
that she submit to his committee's questions in a spirit of
cooperation.

"I will tell you what I can, sir. It may not be much."

She bore little resemblance to her father, Luke thought,
and she was younger than he had supposed—his own age or
even less. Old Ephraim Crocker, clearly moved by her appearance and bearing, offered a guarded warning. "This
meetin' has been convened to inquire into the deaths of the
three poor young fellers we found yesterday in a mine shaft
in Windy Gully."

He started to go into details, but the girl said, "There was
an explosion, wasn't there? I heard that there had been an
accident and men killed."

She seemed to be unaware of the fact that the three men
had been her father's partners, Luke realized, and as her
innocent blue gaze stared intently at Ephraim Crocker, it
was plain that she could have no notion of the suspicion with
which her father was now regarded. And there was no way to
break it to her gently, although, to his credit, the old man
tried. He explained about the gunshot wounds, and the girl
continued to regard him gravely. Only when he named the
dead men and, pointing to Luke, told her that his brother
was one of the victims, did her expression change.

She said softly but with genuine feeling, "Oh, I am sorry,
indeed I am, Mr. Murphy."

"Come to the point, Eph," the man who had advocated a

hanging put in impatiently, "or we'll be here all day. Tell her that her pa is the prime suspect."

"Well, now, I guess that's the truth, little missy," Ephraim Crocker said awkwardly. "All the evidence we've heard points to it, you see. Your father—Captain Jasper Morgan, that is—why, he's gone off to 'Frisco, an' we reckon he's taken—"

"Please!" The girl's interruption was shrill, the color draining from her cheeks as understanding dawned. But she controlled herself and added, with the same dignity that she had displayed during Crocker's attempted explanation, "You are mistaken. Captain Morgan is not my father. I bear no relation to him, sir—none at all."

There was another prolonged silence as the members of the committee slowly took in the implications of her denial. Luke was the first to find his tongue.

Crossing to her side, he asked quietly, "What is your name? Tom—Tom Gardener told us it was Mercy, and we thought you were Morgan's daughter. We took it for granted, I guess, because—well, Morgan's old enough to be your father, and Tom said . . . You remember Tom, don't you?"

"Yes, I remember him," the girl responded. She faced him unflinchingly, although Luke, feeling acutely sorry for her, saw tears in her eyes, and her hands, clasped tightly in front of her, were visibly trembling. "My name is Mercedes Louisa Bancroft, but I'm called Mercy. My—my father was Henry Bancroft, but he—he is dead. My mother also. They both died of the cholera a year ago, when our wagon train reached Fort Kearny on the way to the diggings. I—I came on with the train to Sacramento. I was alone, I—some of the folk on the train were good to me, those who had started with us from Illinois and knew my parents. But I—I did not want to be a burden to them. So I . . ." She choked on a sob. "I wanted to fend for myself, but—"

Ephraim Crocker rapped with his gavel, but the warning was unnecessary, for the men were silent and still, avoiding each other's eyes. They had all heard of the terrible cholera epidemic of '49, which had ravaged the Mississippi Valley and been carried to the Platte and Green rivers, along the route taken by many of the wagon trains from the East.

Crocker said, thinking to spare the girl from having to make revelations she might not care to admit to in front of strangers, "So you took employment with Jasper Morgan, did you, missy? An' he brought you here?"

Mercy Bancroft looked up at him gratefully, blinking back her tears. "Yes, sir. The captain told me that he had a cabin here and that he would pay me to cook and clean for him and give me my keep. He seemed to be a gentleman, and I thought—" She broke off, a wave of embarrassed color creeping into her pale cheeks.

Once again Ephraim Crocker sought to spare her. "I reckon that's all we need to be told on that score. Agreed?" He glanced about him, defying any of the members of his committee to raise objections. None did, and he went on. "But maybe you can help us to conclude this inquiry by sayin' whether or not Captain Morgan is likely to come back here. We know he's gone to 'Frisco, an' I guess we know why, but did he tell you as it was his intention to come back?"

"No, sir." The girl shook her head. "He'll not be back. He left me this." She took a small buckskin bag from the pocket of her dress. "He said that it was in lieu of wages and that I best return where I came from. But I—I couldn't do that. My folks came from Lawson, Illinois, but that's just a small farming community, and I don't have anyone there. And in Sacramento—" She bit her lower lip and did not go on.

The man named Sam said impatiently, "It's plain enough, Eph—Morgan's a murderer an' a damned thieving rogue. We'll not see hide nor hair of him back here if he's got anythin' to do with it. Let's quit wastin' time. We got claims to work, don't we?"

There was a concerted murmur of assent. Ephraim Crocker gave vent to a resigned sigh. "We got to do things legal, Sam," he pointed out. "An' there's this poor young woman here, orphaned an' left on her own. She's as much a victim as them poor young fellers we just laid to rest, ain't she?"

Several voices were raised, offering suggestions.

"We c'n take up a collection for the little girl."

"That skunk Morgan won't come back of his own free will, Eph. But we could send someone to bring him back."

"Sure we could! An' then put him on trial fer murder."

"We got to bring in a verdict against him. Put it to the vote, Eph."

Luke rose to his feet, knowing suddenly what he had to do, and they fell silent again, waiting for him to speak. He did so boldly, sensing the girl's eyes on him. "I'll go search for him and bring him back, Mr. Crocker. I owe my brother that. And Tom and Frankie Gardener were my partners, so if anyone goes, it ought to be me."

"I guess it ought," Ephraim Crocker confirmed. He looked worried, but before he could voice any doubts, the men stamped their feet, demanding a vote. It was agreed unanimously that Jasper Morgan was charged with murder and required to stand trial, and in a second vote Luke was authorized, on behalf of the miners' committee, to bring him back to Thayer's Bend in order to answer the charges. A hat was passed, and the men contributed generously before hastening off, intent on making up for the time they had lost.

"Take the little girl back to Morgan's place, will you, Luke?" Crocker requested before following their example. "An' I'll see you before you set off for 'Frisco."

It was as they were riding back together, the girl on Luke's saddlebow, that she made havoc of his plans.

"I'm coming with you to 'Frisco," she said with quiet but unexpected firmness. Shocked, he started to argue, but she cut him short. "I've no place else to go. In Sacramento I . . . I was working in a saloon. That was where Jasper Morgan found me, and I won't go back there. I wouldn't even if I was starving. And I can't stay here by myself."

Luke's arms, which had been clasping her waist, loosened their grip instinctively. Then, ashamed of his reaction, he apologized.

"But you're—you're a female. We can't travel together. It wouldn't be right. It wouldn't be respectable."

"I shall not trouble you, Luke. And I was brought up to be respectable. My parents were God-fearing folk. But Captain Morgan . . ." Mercy, her head lowered, left the sentence uncompleted, with all its unhappy implications evoking

Luke's pity. She added, with a swift change of tone, "You'll need me as a witness in San Francisco. If you go by yourself, it would be your word against his. And he—oh, Luke, you know him! Jasper Morgan would talk his way out, whatever the miners' committee think."

She was right on that count, Luke was forced to concede. "I'd planned on killing him," he admitted a trifle sullenly, "if he refused to come back here with me to stand his trial."

That notion, he realized, had been in the back of his mind ever since he had seen Dan's body, but until now he had not put it into words, even in his thoughts. Vengeance, a life for a life—even the Scriptures held that to be no more than justice. And Jasper Morgan had robbed three men of their lives; he had planned to kill them from the moment he had set them working on the useless, unproductive mine that was to become their tomb. . . .

Mercy Bancroft drew in her breath sharply. She turned to look at him over her shoulder, and Luke was taken aback by the naked pain he read in her eyes.

"I could kill him also," she said in a low, bitter voice, "for what he did to me. I did not know that any man could be capable of—of such cruelty." Her tone changed again, became pleading. "Please, Luke, take me with you! We could travel as brother and sister, and I swear I'll not be a burden or a trouble to you. And we will find him, truly we will!"

Luke yielded. It went against the grain to do so, but she had a right. Morgan had robbed him of his brother and his two partners, as well as of the strike he had made, but perhaps he had robbed this slender, defenseless girl of even more.

"I'll find him," he vowed. "If it takes me the rest of my days. Wherever he's gone, I'll follow him, Mercy! He's had almost a month's start, but there'll be no place in San Francisco where he can hide. There are bound to be people who'll remember him. Jasper Morgan is not a man to pass unrecognized in a crowd."

And he would not anticipate pursuit, Luke thought wryly, for had he not brought half a hillside down to hide the evidence of the crime he had committed?

Mercy was silent for a long moment. Then she said reluctantly, "He may not be in San Francisco by the time we get there. Have you thought of that, Luke? He may not even be in California."

"No," Luke admitted. He frowned. "Where else would he go?"

"He talked of Australia to me more than once," Mercy told him. And it was true. . . . Luke's heart sank as he recalled remarks Morgan had made in his own hearing. He had talked of a man named Hargraves, and Tom and Frankie had talked of him, too. Hargraves was an Australian who had suggested that there might well be gold among the rivers and mountains of his native land. The country was similar to California, he had claimed, and there had been rumors of gold finds there, rumors that Tom said had been suppressed. . . . Luke's frown deepened. Morgan might not anticipate pursuit, but he would make sure there was no risk of it.

"Well . . ." He shook off his momentary despondence. "If Morgan has gone to Australia," he said recklessly, "then I'll follow him there. But I think he'll still be in 'Frisco."

Mercy turned again to look at him, and Luke saw that for the first time she was smiling.

"We'll leave in the morning," she said practically, "and pray that he's still there. And don't tell me that it will be a rough journey, little brother," she added, her smile suddenly mocking as she saw him open his mouth to speak. "It can be no worse than crossing the Sierra with a wagon train." She waved a small brown-skinned hand in the direction of the distant mountains, already capped with snow.

Luke, deprived of his last argument, held his peace, but his arms tightened around her. It would, he told himself, be good to have a companion on the journey. Or for the first part of it, at least.

CHAPTER III

For both Mercy and Luke, San Francisco swiftly became a place of nightmare terror. Its vast harbor was a forest of masts and spars, thronged with abandoned ships whose crews had deserted to join the rush to the goldfields. And still more ships arrived, from all corners of the globe, to suffer the same fate as those that had come before and to swell the crowds of sullen and angry men, many of them unable to find shelter and lacking sufficient funds to pay for transport to the distant diggings—or even to feed themselves.

Prices were high, necessities in short supply, accommodations in the hotels and lodging houses at a premium. Most of the buildings were hastily constructed wooden shanties, the best-appointed being the saloons and gambling houses—although even some of these were housed in canvas tents or marquees—and spreading out from the town center was a mushroom city of tents, inhabited by people of all nations.

To walk the streets in daylight was an ordeal; at night it was fraught with peril, with robberies so commonplace as to excite no comment, violence and drunkenness seemingly unrestrained and certainly unpunished. There were vigilantes, a passerby told Luke, led by a man named Brannan and controlled by his committee, and San Francisco had a governor and two elected senators, but . . . He had shrugged and gestured to a block of blackened and burned-out buildings a short distance away, asserting grimly that it was the work of arsonists.

"*Them* the vigilantes did catch. They hanged four of 'em, flogged a couple, an' deported the rest. But it still goes on."

Their informant, moved perhaps by their youth and seem-

ing helplessness, directed them to one of the hulks that had
been towed close to the shore and scuttled.

"Jemmy Kemp was her cook, an' the skipper left him in
charge, see, when he an' the rest went off to the diggings,"
he explained. "Now he's turned her into a rooming house.
He'll give you somewhere to sleep if you tell him that Gene
Drucker sent you. It'll cost you, but you'll be all right aboard
the *Nancy Bray*, and Jem's an honest man."

They had found him so, although Luke had been outraged
by the rent demanded for the tiny two-berth cabin Kemp had
offered them. But it was shelter, and their meals were provided; there was no need for Mercy to show herself in the
streets anymore, and, the girl thought, as she stood on deck
watching yet another vessel nose her way into the harbor, it
would not be for much longer. Despite the delay, Jasper
Morgan's trail was still warm; Luke's initial inquiry at the
office of the United States Mint had elicited the information
that their quarry had been there barely a month before
them.

Mercy recalled the visit. The Mint was where they had
begun their search, and a talkative clerk had been ready
enough to tell them what they wanted to know, for clearly it
was not every day that a man brought a fortune in gold to be
redeemed for cash by the Mint, even in San Francisco.

"A fine gentleman," the clerk had said without prompting.
"I remember him well. A military officer, British, he told me,
who came out here in the paddle-steamer *Panama*. At the
beginning of the year it was, when the *Panama* made her best
passage from the East—a hundred and forty-two days. But
of course the new clipper ships out of Boston have cut that
record. The *Sea Witch* made it in ninety-seven days around
the Horn from New York. No paddle-wheeler will match
that."

He had been disposed to enlarge on the clipper's achieve-
ment, but Luke had brought him back to the subject of their
inquiry, and they had learned, to their profound astonishment, that Dan's estimate of ten thousand dollars had been
too low. The mint had paid Jasper Morgan more than twelve
thousand, and one nugget alone had been weighed by the

mint's chief assayer and found to turn the scale at thirteen pounds, four ounces.

"Lord alive!" Luke had confided in a hoarse whisper as Mercy stood beside him in the small, dimly lit clapboard office. "That was the nugget I found in the hole where the manzanita bush was growing, halfway up the riverbank. I knew it was big, but I never dreamed it would weigh that much."

And Jasper Morgan had robbed him of it, Mercy reflected bitterly, watching as the clerk counted out the meager payment for their own small bags of dust, while continuing to sing the praises of the British military gentleman, whose strike had set everyone employed at the Mint enviously talking. None of them, however, had been able to say or even hazard a guess as to Morgan's present whereabouts or his future plans.

"I figure he'll have gone back to his claim," the clerk had suggested. "In the Sacramento Valley, wasn't it? Or . . . no, the captain mentioned the Feather. If you're so set on finding him, maybe you should make for the Feather. There are river paddlers plying from here now, up as far as Sacramento and Marysville, and I hear tell there are stagecoaches running up the valley, if you can afford the fares."

Jasper Morgan had been able to afford the river steamer; that was probably how he had gained so long a start over them, Mercy decided, knowing his ways. He would not go back to Windy Gully, of course—however carefully he had covered his tracks, he would not take that risk. The area covered by the diggings had expanded; each day the gold seekers moved farther and farther afield as word of some new strike reached the camps, but Morgan, she was convinced, would not choose to remain in California.

Australia—Sydney, in the state of New South Wales, was surely more likely to be his destination. He had talked often of Sydney and the prospects of finding gold in the colony, she remembered, although at the time she had paid little heed to what he had said to her.

Old Jemmy Kemp poked his grizzled head through the open hatchway and, seeing Mercy, gave her a friendly wave.

"That brother o' yours ain't back yet?" he asked.

She shook her head. "Not yet, Mr. Kemp."

Luke spent his days in the seemingly profitless search; no one in the town had been able to offer him a single clue, and lately, under her prompting, he had begun to make inquiries on the waterfront, frequenting the seamen's bars and boarding ships that had not been entirely deserted, in the hope that if their quarry had left San Francisco, he had sought to take passage in a Pacific-bound vessel.

Mercy glanced up at the darkening sky, only half hearing what Jemmy Kemp was saying to her concerning the evening meal. The old ship's cook fed his lodgers very well, and there were half a dozen others, apart from her and Luke. But few stayed on board the *Nancy Bray* for long; they obtained their grubstakes, purchased their supplies, and set off for the fields, succeeded by new arrivals, whose sojourns were equally brief. Like Luke, they spent their days in town, returning to the hulk only to sleep, and their presence had not troubled her, since, without exception, they had treated her with respect. . . . She shivered, remembering the attitude of the men in the Sacramento saloon when she had worked there. And . . . Jasper Morgan's.

It would be a long time before she was able to forget the manner in which Jasper Morgan had treated her.

"Beef stew an' taters," Jemmy Kemp concluded, with pardonable pride. "Some farmers drove in a herd o' steers—on the skinny side, they was, but still it's good red meat, ain't it? See the boy don't miss it." His head vanished.

"Luke'll be here soon," Mercy called after him. She crossed the deck, the worn, ill-fitting boards creaking even under her light weight, and halted at the head of the rickety gangplank that linked the *Nancy Bray* to the foreshore. Luke usually returned before nightfall, fearing to leave her alone, but already there were lights shining through the misty haze that shrouded the town, and she could see no sign of him.

He was a strange young man, she thought indulgently; shy where women were concerned, to the point of embarrassment in their presence. And although their careful husbanding of their resources required them to share their sleeping accommodation, Luke never so much as touched her when they were alone together. True, he would take her arm when they went walking in the town, but this was rather in order to protect her, she knew, than any sort of gesture of affection or intimacy.

He was eighteen—a year her senior—but in many respects, and certainly in experience, he was an innocent child, whereas she herself . . . Mercy was conscious of an ache in her throat. Thanks to the cholera that had deprived her of the love and support of her parents, she herself had undergone a swift and painful transition into womanhood. And there could be no going back. She was what a cruel fate had made of her—what Jasper Morgan had made of her, with his glib tongue and the promises he had given but had not kept.

"On my word as a gentleman," he had said, "you will be safe with me." And she, in her foolish innocence, had trusted him, until disillusion had come with the first of many brutal beatings and demands that— The sound of running feet distracted her from her thoughts, and she peered into the gathering darkness, relief flooding over her as she recognized Luke.

He came splashing through the mud toward her, waving excitedly as he reached the foot of the gangplank and saw her standing there.

"You're so late," she began anxiously. "And I was worried, Luke. You—"

He brushed her words aside and, to Mercy's surprise, hugged her. "You were right!" he exclaimed. "Morgan *has* gone to Australia. I've found proof of it at last."

"Oh, Luke!" She could only stare at him, a prey to conflicting emotions and suddenly afraid. "Are you sure?"

"He was here only for a few days," Luke asserted. "Mercy, he bought a ship—a small brig called the *Banshee*—and sailed for Sydney a month ago. I met the man he bought the ship from, so there's no mistake." He made a wry grimace. "He bought her cheap, because her master could not keep his crew and couldn't replace them."

"But Jasper Morgan could?" Mercy suggested, an edge to her voice.

"Yes. It seems that Mr. Brannan's committee of vigilance has put the fear of God into Australian ex-convicts—the ones they call the Sydney ducks—who've been blamed for much of the robbery and violence here. They lynched two of them before we left Thayer's Bend, and they're holding another for trial. Some of their fellows reckoned it was time to quit San Francisco before the vigilantes caught up with them. The *Banshee*'s old owner said that more'n a score of them signed on to crew for Morgan, just to get away from here." Luke shrugged. "Double-dyed rogues they were, according to him, and I believed him!"

He did not enlarge overmuch on the story the old sea captain had told him of the ghastly scenes attending the execution of one of the "ducks" by the name of Jenkins, who had eventually met his end dangling from a rope suspended from a beam of the old Customs House in the plaza. That example had apparently been sufficient to make the other Australians understand that for them the time had come to leave California.

Mercy was silent for a long moment, studying his face in the dim light and reading the determination in it. She asked flatly, "What will you do, Luke?" knowing what his answer would be before he gave it.

"I shall go after him. I have to, Mercy—I owe it to Dan and the others." Diffidently he laid a hand on her arm. "You knew that when we started."

"How will you find a ship?" Mercy's voice was still carefully controlled. "You can't buy one, like he did."

"Every other ship in this harbor is seeking hands," Luke told her. "And the masters don't care if the men they sign on are landsmen—or ignorant farm boys, as Morgan used to call Dan and me." He shrugged. "I heard of a vessel that is bound for the Pacific islands and Sydney as soon as her master can sign half a dozen more hands. She is partly crewed by Javanese or Malays, and they've stayed with her. She's a fine new schooner, built in a Boston yard—the *Dolphin*—registered in Sydney, and her master is the owner. His name is Van Buren, and—" He broke off, avoiding her gaze. "That's why I'm late, Mercy. I went out to her with a couple of others from the diggings—Australians who want to go home."

"And you signed on?" For all her efforts to control it, Mercy's voice was not steady. She had always known where the pursuit of Jasper Morgan might lead, she told herself, just as she had known that Luke would follow his brother's murderer wherever he might seek to hide. "Did you sign on with—with Captain Van Buren, Luke?" she persisted wretchedly.

Luke nodded. "I had to—there might not be another Australia-bound ship for months. The *Dolphin*'s not going direct to Sydney—she's a trader, and as I told you, she will be calling at ports in the Pacific islands on the way. But she's the only one, Mercy. If we wait any longer, Morgan will be too far ahead of us. . . . I'll never catch up with him."

Mercy's small hands clenched convulsively by her sides. She wanted to plead with him not to abandon her, but no words would come. They had never discussed what they would do if the pursuit of Jasper Morgan were to lead to a journey halfway across the world; it was a subject she had been afraid to broach, lest the fear that Luke would leave her behind were to become reality. But he was looking questioningly at her now, she realized, and she forced a tremulous smile. He had said *we* and *us.* . . .

"You—you'll take me with you, Luke?"

"Did you suppose I'd leave you here alone?" he countered reproachfully. "Of course I'll take you, if you are willing to come. But it will mean leaving America, Mercy. Perhaps forever."

To abandon the only existence, the only land she had ever known would not be easy, Mercy realized, but what had life here given her, save heartbreak and despair, the grinding poverty of her childhood, the loss of the mother and father she had loved—and the humiliation that had been her lot with Jasper Morgan?

"I'll have few regrets on that score," she managed, her throat tight. "And I'm not afraid. I'll go with you gladly if Captain Van Buren is willing to take me. But my passage will be costly, and—" She had been about to remind him that she was female and that the *Dolphin*'s master might not welcome a female passenger, but Luke, she saw, was smiling, and instead, she asked uncertainly, "Luke, did you tell him about me? Did you ask if he would take me?"

"I told Captain Van Buren that I had a young sister, and I

offered to work my passage in return for yours. The *Dolphin*
is carrying a few passengers—there is cabin accommodation
on board." Luke's smile widened. "The other passengers
are missionaries, with their wives and children—good folk,
who were stranded here when the crew of their ship deserted. Captain Van Buren is carrying them for the cost of
their food only, and he says he will take you on the same
terms."

Mercy stared at him, again bereft of words. Finally she said
in a small, choked voice, "He must be a very good man, this
Captain Van Buren."

"I reckon he is," Luke confirmed. "I can sell the horses
tomorrow—the man at the livery stables will give me a fair
price for them. That should cover the cost of your food, near
enough, and we shall not be penniless when we reach Sydney. There's just one more obstacle in our way." He hesitated, eyeing Mercy with a hint of uncertainty. "The captain
wants to see and talk with you before he agrees to give you
passage."

"To make sure that I shall be fit company for his missionaries?" Mercy suggested wryly.

"I guess that's the reason. He has his crew to think of, too.
He said he would send a boat for us later this evening. Don't
worry, little sister." Luke reached for her hand and clasped it
between his own two work-roughened palms. "You will pass
muster . . . *I'm* the one that may not. I've never been to sea
in my life, and I've signed on as a seaman. We're lucky to be
here, Mercy—no ship's master would take me in any other
port."

It was true, Mercy knew; the great concourse of abandoned ships in San Francisco Harbor was a stroke of good
fortune, at least to them, and she took courage from Luke's
words. If he was willing to work his passage, then— A loud,
metallic banging interrupted her thoughts. Jemmy Kemp
was beating on a frying pan below, to summon them to the
evening meal; and as if they, too, had heard the sound, three
of the *Nancy Bray*'s other boarders came thudding across the
gangplank, all of them laughing and evidently in high spirits.

"We're off to the fields in the mornin'," one of them said.
"Off to make our fortunes, God willing! Change your mind

an' come with us, young Luke—what do you say, eh? We can use you."

Luke glanced at Mercy and then shook his head. "Thanks," he said quietly, "but I've other plans." He offered Mercy his arm, and she took it, managing to smile.

The three young fortune hunters stood courteously aside to allow her to precede them.

In the spacious stern cabin of the *Dolphin*, her master, Claus Van Buren, finished his evening meal and raised his glass in an oddly formal salute, a gleam of satisfaction lighting his dark eyes. He was a slim, tall man, of fine physique and a certain arrogance, who held himself erect, as if even in repose he were defying anyone who might feel inclined to question his ancestry or his claim to the aristocratic name he bore.

"Here's to a swift and safe passage, Saleh!" he said, addressing the white-bearded Javanese who had served his meal. "Thank God we shall soon be taking this ship to sea again, for I swear she is breaking her heart, just as I am, seeing this harbor full of vessels going to rot. We shall have our full complement by tomorrow evening."

Old Saleh eyed him pensively but accepted the brimming glass he was offered. His position, on the ship's books, was that of master's steward, but it was a privileged one, for he had been friend and mentor to the *Dolphin*'s owner for more than twenty years. His face was unlined, having the color and texture of ivory, which gave it a serenity that somehow belied the neatly trimmed white beard and the balding head. Saleh, Claus thought, was ageless.

The old man drank the toast and observed, his tone faintly skeptical, "Full in number, perhaps—not in nautical skills. And you will make no profit from your passengers, master."

"I made a profit from my cargo," Van Buren reminded him. "A thousand percent on lumber; and the flour sold at forty-four dollars a barrel, the potatoes at sixteen dollars a bushel—San Francisco prices, Saleh. And you know what our eastern fortune hunters paid to be conveyed here. I have almost covered the cost of this ship in a single voyage! Mr. Donald McKay is a genius when it comes to designing fast

sailing ships, and I do not begrudge a cent of what he asked
of me. The *Dolphin* is the finest vessel I have ever owned or
commanded—truly the finest. She will pay for herself ten
times over when we're back in Sydney. She will cause a
sensation when we drop anchor in the cove. No one will have
seen her like, I promise you, and the tea traders will gnash
their teeth with envy!"

Saleh's white brows rose, but Claus Van Buren ignored
the implied doubts and smiled quietly to himself, his pride in
his new 850-ton Boston-built clipper schooner proof against
any criticism. True, she had been costly, but he had sold the
old schooner *Lydia*—in which he had made the passage from
Sydney to Boston—for considerably more than she would
have fetched in Australia. The demand for ships to carry
gold prospectors from the eastern states to California was
now almost insatiable, and that had dictated the *Lydia*'s
price, as well as that of the *Dolphin* herself; and those who
had taken passage around the Horn on board his vessel had
been willing to pay highly for the privilege of reaching their
destination in under a hundred days.

The *Dolphin* had not beaten the *Sea Witch*'s record, but she
had taken only one day more. . . .

"Come now, Saleh," he urged, his smile widening into a
boyish grin. "I can afford to be generous to the men of God
and their families. Poor souls, they did not deserve to be
stranded in this den of iniquity simply because their ship's
company deserted to the goldfields and left them to fend for
themselves. Would you have me leave them here? There is
no other cargo I can load from this place, and who, save our
good missionaries, desires to leave it?"

"The young man you signed on this evening," Saleh
pointed out gravely. "The one whose sister you also agreed
to take for the cost of her food. That young man is from the
goldfields, master—a farm boy, on his own admission, who
will be of scant use as a seaman."

"Luke Murphy," Claus supplied. "But the two he brought
with him have served at sea—they both are Australians. And
they assured me that they would send out three others,
prime seamen, tomorrow morning."

"The boy Murphy is American. No doubt he will learn—

he is willing enough, I am sure. But, master, he is too anxious to leave here. Did he tell you why?"

Claus shook his head. The boy, he was forced to concede, had given no reason for his anxiety to leave San Francisco, and Saleh was right in suggesting that he was overly anxious. He had said that he had worked a claim on the Sacramento River with his elder brother and two others—Australians— who had been killed in an accidental collapse of a mine shaft. But he had not enlarged on his story, had given no details, and had apportioned no blame—and there was the sister. Few gold miners brought their wives with them to the field, fewer still their sisters, and Murphy was young—eighteen, he had said, his sister a year younger.

"I told the boy that he must bring his sister out to the ship this evening, Saleh," he offered defensively, "before I could agree to give her passage. They are living on a hulk on the foreshore, it seems. I sent a boat for them—they will be here soon. You can question them if you wish."

Saleh spread his hands in a negative gesture. "It is not for me to question them, master. But if you will permit me, I will be present when you speak with them."

"What do you fear—that the boy is a criminal, a fugitive from justice?"

The old Javanese repeated his shrug. "It is possible. This is a lawless place. One hears tales of vigilantes, who dispense summary justice and are greatly feared. Those they call the Hounds are said to kill and rob. Their victims are said to be Mexicans and Spaniards, people with dark skins, such as ourselves, who have been shown no mercy. And daily there are drunken brawls in the streets and in the saloons. In the fields, if rumor is to be believed, the gold miners make their own laws. There are many bad people here, with no respect for religion or the church."

"Luke Murphy told me he was brought up in the Mormon faith," Claus argued. "Mormons are good, God-fearing folk, Saleh. Besides, I liked the boy, and I felt sorry for him."

Saleh's bearded lips twitched into an indulgent smile. "You have not changed since your boyhood. Always you permit your heart to rule your head! I would not have you otherwise, master, but sometimes it is wise to exercise cau-

tion. In your desire to befriend this American boy, you are
perhaps recalling your own youth and the cruelty you suffered at the hands of your father and *Mevrouw* Van Buren,
the wife of your father."

Perhaps he was, Claus reflected ruefully. Perhaps he had
seen himself in the thin, wiry boy who had pleaded so earnestly to be given the chance to work his passage to Australia, for all his admitted lack of nautical skills . . . and who
had then begged, even more earnestly, to be allowed to
bring his sister with him.

His own initiation into seafaring had been harsh enough,
the *Dolphin*'s master recalled. He had been barely eleven
when his father, who had for so long refused to acknowledge
their kinship, had taken him to the Dutch East Indies as a
member of the old *Dorcas*'s crew and had expected him to
work as a man. He had done so; he had always done whatever his father had asked or expected of him, anticipating
neither praise nor reward and receiving none. But the big,
arrogant Dutchman who had sired him had, in the end, made
reparation. Dying, he had acknowledged him at last as his
lawful son and heir and had bequeathed to him the Van
Buren name and the three trading ships on which his present
prosperity was built.

Claus met Saleh's quizzical gaze and echoed the old man's
smile. He was a rich man now, the three ships grown to a
sizable fleet, which did a profitable trade with the Indies and
China. In the early days, Sydney's elitist society had been
reluctant to accept him because of his color and background
and the fact that, during his father's lifetime, he, like Saleh,
had been a servant in the fine house that was now his own.

But with the education he had acquired at the church
school in Windsor—a township on the Hawkesbury River—
his increasing wealth and influence had wrought a change.
The passing years had seen the end of convict transportation
and, with it, an end to the sharp divisions in the colony's
society. Emancipated convicts and their Australian-born off-
spring owned land, often held commissions in the British
armed forces, or, like himself, successfully engaged in trade,
and the gulf that had once existed had been bridged. New
South Wales was a state, with its own elected Legislative

Council—largely thanks to the untiring efforts of William Charles Wentworth, who was now campaigning for a still greater measure of self-government. Its population had risen to more than 190,000, and its export trade, particularly in wool, had never been more prosperous.

Successive governors, with the curtailment of their auto-cratic powers, had been less rigid in their social attitudes, and indeed, Claus reflected, the divisions, where they ex-isted, were between the large landowners and the middle-class traders and townsfolk, with the women they married chiefly responsible for the barriers erected between them.

He himself had never married, because at the time when he might have taken a wife, the social climate had not been right. He was in his thirty-eighth year, an age at which most men would have had sons working for them and daughters ready for marriage or even already married, with grandchil-dren in imminent prospect. Looking back over the years, he sought for reasons for his solitary state and sighed. In his case, of course, the choice had been limited; but apart from that, he had never met a woman with whom he had wanted to share his life—save one.

His expression softened. He had been barely twelve, an unhappy, friendless boy, when Alice Fairweather had en-tered the Van Buren household—as lost and friendless as he —and he had solemnly declared his intention to wed her when he should become a man. But Alice had been a woman grown already, and she had married long before he had been old enough to make good his promise. All he had been able to do was endow the school of which her husband, the Rev-erend Nathan Cox, was principal, and— Claus repeated his sigh. And become one of their pupils, forever in their debt for all that they had taught him of letters and the arts and of their own Christian beliefs.

For the rest . . . His smile returned as he again met old Saleh's searching eyes. He cherished his freedom. With no ties to hold him, he could roam the oceans, and his ports of call held women in plenty, ready and willing to satisfy his need for their company and then to let him go, with no more regret than he felt himself.

If he loved, it was the sea and his ships that held his heart.

And now, in the *Dolphin*, he had a vessel to surpass all others —a magnificent topsail clipper schooner, built of the best oak, white pine, and hackmatack, and sheathed with Taunton copper. With her sharply raked bow, her great length, and her towering expanse of sail, she was truly a tribute to the genius of her builder, the man they called the blue nose, Donald McKay.

McKay was both an artist and a craftsman; he designed every vessel built in his yard and personally supervised every detail of her construction. When Claus had originally contracted for construction of the *Dolphin*, nearly three years ago, McKay had wanted to build a three-masted, square-rigged clipper ship instead of the schooner Claus had specified; but much as he had been tempted to concur with McKay's initial plan, practical considerations had compelled him to reject it. He wanted speed, certainly, but not at the expense of his new vessel's carrying capacity, and the *Dolphin*'s fore-and-aft rig ensured that she could be worked by a smaller crew than a square-rigger would require. Because of her hull design, she could not carry as much cargo as the old *Lydia*, but Donald McKay had used her length brilliantly and with much ingenuity, and his insistence on fitting her with three masts was, Claus now conceded, yet another example of the genius of the young man from Nova Scotia.

On the difficult and stormy passage around the Horn, she had occasioned him few qualms, and— He heard the splash of oars, wafted through the open stern window, and a faint shout from his first mate from the deck above.

"The boy you are so determined to befriend," Saleh observed, with a hint of censure. "With his sister. Is it your wish that they should be offered refreshment, master?"

Claus shrugged in well-simulated indifference. "They probably will not expect it. Murphy has signed on as a deckhand, to work his passage. But the girl will be one of our passengers. Tea perhaps, or, if you are anxious to loosen their tongues, a glass of the excellent brandy in which we drank our toast." He gestured to his empty glass, and Saleh, his dark face expressionless, set out a cut glass decanter and fresh glasses.

He had scarcely done so when there was a knock on the

door of the cabin and the mate ushered in Luke Murphy and his sister. The boy, it was evident, was nervous and ill at ease, but his eyes lit up as he looked about him, taking in the luxurious fittings of the cabin and the gleaming mahogany of its woodwork. Then, quickly recovering himself, he faced Claus, cap in hand, and said quietly, "You wanted to talk with my sister, sir. Her name is Mercy. Captain Van Buren, Mercy."

The girl had been standing in shadow, but in response to the boy's introduction, she stepped forward, the light of the lantern suspended above her head falling full on her small, anxious face, and Claus drew a startled breath as he looked at her. She was so like Alice Cox had been, when she had first entered the Van Buren house in Bridge Street, that he was momentarily bereft of words. Slight and overthin, her fair hair tightly braided and her blue eyes innocent of guile, she might have been Alice standing there, fresh from the confines of a convict ship and uncertain of her welcome . . . frightened yet undefeated, and heartbreakingly vulnerable.

She dropped him an awkward curtsy, coloring under his unexpectedly lengthy scrutiny, and Claus, overcoming his surprise, pulled up a chair for her, conscious that Saleh, too, had noticed the resemblance, for his lined brown face no longer registered disapproval.

Both visitors refused the offer of brandy, and unbidden, Saleh brought tea from his pantry, serving it in the eggshell-thin china cups that normally were reserved for guests of importance. As they drank it, Claus endeavored to carry out his initial intention and question Luke Murphy concerning his reasons for wishing to leave San Francisco, but the boy politely evaded him. The most he admitted was that he had heard much about Australia from the two partners who had been killed in the mine accident on the Sacramento River and that he and Mercy had made up their minds to make a new life there.

"Tom Gardener had a wife and family in Sydney, sir, and their parents live there. I reckon—well, that I owe it to the two of them to go and see their folks. They won't know what happened, and maybe they'll be living in hope that Tom and

Frankie will be coming back. And there ain't nothing to keep us here in 'Frisco, sir, not anymore."

"What about the diggings? Are you not throwing away your chances of making your fortune?"

Luke Murphy's headshake was emphatic. "From what I've heard, there's gold to be found in Australia, if you know where to look. That's why a good few of the lads that came out here to seek for gold are going back home now."

"Not the ones who struck it rich, surely?" Claus suggested. He saw Luke exchange a glance with his sister and then again shake his head.

"Even those, sir. They've no reason to stay. And if there *is* gold in Australia—as a man named Edward Hargraves claimed—they'll go back as miners with experience, and that'll give them an advantage. They'll not lack work, sir, and I shan't either. They say Mr. Hargraves has gone back to Sydney."

Claus frowned, feeling strangely uneasy at the prospect of a gold rush to Australia. Would Sydney's great Port Jackson Harbor become a graveyard for shipping, as that of San Francisco was? Would gold seekers from all over the world converge there, invading the rich sheep pastures, panning the rivers, bringing their gambling saloons and their lawlessness with them? He had never heard of Edward Hargraves or his theories, but there might well be truth in his claim, for there had been rumors in the past, tales of shepherds and explorers who had found alluvial gold in the country beyond the Blue Mountains. The rumors had been denied; no governor of a penal colony was willing to take the risks that were inseparable from the admission that gold existed in anything like substantial quantities. But for all that . . . He expelled his breath in a long-drawn sigh.

Australia was no longer a convict colony; the men and women who had been transported there in chains were now free, working their own land or paid for their labor, if they did not possess the means to buy a farm or a sheep run or a roof over their head in town.

Hearing his sigh, Mercy asked shyly, "You do not want to see Sydney used as this town has been, Captain Van Buren?"

"No, that I do not," Claus confessed, with feeling. There

was a difference, of course; Sydney, thanks to the farsighted-
ness of the late Governor Macquarie, thirty years before, was
already a city, well planned, permanent, and orderly. The
more recently founded colonies now had their own fast-
growing towns and harbors on the coastline, their pastoral
settlements spreading out inland, whereas San Francisco—
founded in 1776 as a mission station, Claus had heard—had
long been a poor, thinly populated seaport, held in thrall by
its Spanish-Mexican past until, two years ago, the discovery
of gold had brought a vast influx of fortune hunters to waken
it to startled life. The small seaport and the shantytown it
fronted had been given no time, no breathing space in which
to develop. Its original inhabitants had been overwhelmed
by the flood of immigrants, arriving in their thousands to
spread throughout the new and hitherto sparsely settled
state of California, with no desire to remain there for longer
than it took to make their strikes and recoup their costs.

Now, only a little over two years since the millwright at
Sutter's Mill had made his momentous discovery, the population had risen to close on two hundred thousand, Claus
had heard. But it was not the sort of influx he wanted to see
in Australia, and looking at the thoughtful face of the girl
who had sought his opinion, he repeated emphatically, "No,
indeed, I do not, Miss Murphy! It would be a disaster."

"Then it is to be hoped that Mr. Hargraves is wrong," she
said, and lapsed again into attentive silence, leaving Luke to
continue the conversation.

The boy was no more informative; it was clear that he had
said all he intended to say concerning his reasons for wishing to make a new life in Australia. Even when pressed as to
the wishes of his family, he answered evasively; but when
Claus rose to signify that the interview was over, he sensed a
sudden return of his would-be passengers' initial anxiety.

"Are you willing to take us, sir?" the boy blurted out.
"We'll be no trouble to you, I give you my word. And I'll
work, sir—I'm used to hard work."

Claus held out his hand, aware that Saleh, playing the role
of unobtrusive observer, had silently inclined his head.
"Yes," he answered briskly. "I'll take you on the terms we
agreed, Luke. I shall be sending a boat to pick up my other

passengers and the new hands tomorrow afternoon. You can come aboard then, both of you. Provided I have my full complement, I shall aim to leave this port within forty-eight hours."

He cut short Luke's thanks, his eyes on the girl's face, which glowed with sudden radiance, as if she were embarrassed by the intensity of his gaze. She turned away, her cheeks flooding with color.

Saleh escorted them to the deck. Returning, he said softly, "That is a good young woman, master—truly good. But I think she has endured much suffering and remains sorely wounded in her innermost spirit. The boy, however—" He paused, his white brows furrowed. "The boy has not told you the whole truth, and I do not believe he will—at all events, not until he leaves the ship in Sydney. For all that, I think you can trust him."

"Yes," Claus agreed. "That was the opinion of them I had formed. And," he added, with a swift change of tone, "you noticed the girl's resemblance, did you not?"

"To Alice . . . yes, of a surety, master. It was striking— the eyes, the manner, the bright-as-gold hair. But the boy is dark. They do not look like brother and sister." Saleh again paused, for much longer this time, and said finally, "You would do well to remember that she is *not* Alice."

"I'm not likely to forget," Claus assured him. "But I was twelve years old when I first set eyes on Alice. Now I am close to forty, Saleh my friend."

"And a very rich man," the old Javanese cautioned.

Claus laughed, brushing the warning aside.

"Let us hope that Luke Murphy is wrong in supposing that the man—what was his name? Hargraves, was it not? Well, that Hargraves will discover gold in New South Wales. I dread the thought of returning to Sydney only to find it filled with fortune hunters."

"I echo your fears, master," Saleh said somberly. "Please God we may not!"

CHAPTER IV

The bark *Emma* dropped anchor in Sydney's busy cove on January 7, 1851, after a voyage of ninety-two days from San Francisco. All her passengers were Australian—men who had worked in the Californian goldfields with varying success since '49.

Edward Hammond Hargraves was responsible for their return, for his talk of a larger and richer source of the gold they were seeking, to be found beyond New South Wales's Blue Mountains, had finally convinced them—that and the fact that the vigilantes of San Francisco had resorted to lynch law in order to hasten their departure.

Hargraves was thirty-five, a black-bearded giant of a man, standing six feet five in his stockinged feet and turning the scale at nearly three hundred pounds. English by birth, he had come to Sydney almost twenty years earlier, as a cabin boy on board the *Wave*, a trading vessel commanded by a man named John Lister. At the age of eighteen, tiring of the sea and having survived a severe attack of fever in Batavia, Hargraves had married and settled on the land, initially in the Illawarra district and then at Gosford, on Brisbane Water.

"My means were always limited," he was wont to tell his friends. "I could never pay a man's wages, or even feed a convict and clothe him—not with a wife and five young children to support. But by heaven, I know the western foothills, and *now* I know gold-bearing country when I see it. California taught me that."

California, he reflected as he stood on the *Emma*'s deck with the others, watching the crew lower the bower anchor, California had taught him all he had gone there to learn—and much that he could have done without. He had seen what greed did to a man's soul, but he had kept his own dream intact, for all the scorn with which some of the Yankee miners had greeted his oft-repeated claim.

"There's no goddamned gold in that country of yours, Ned," one of the old forty-niners had scoffed. "And even if there was, that Queen Victoria o' yours wouldn't let you dig it!"

But there was, there had to be, Ned Hargraves told himself. Up there at Guyong, twenty miles from Bathurst, where he had gone in search of some strays from his small cattle herd some years before, the country was so similar to that in the Sierra Nevada that they might have been one and the same. He had mined in the Wood's Creek field, in the Stanislaus Valley, with fair success, and the dream had been born when he had washed his first pan of dust and found a nugget gleaming dully in his palm.

He would go to Guyong, he decided—now, at once, not even waiting to acquaint his wife and family with the fact of his return. Essie would not welcome him if, after his long absence, he went back to her without the fortune he had confidently predicted would be his when he left for California. But if he were to make his dream turn into reality . . . ah, she would welcome him then, right enough! And so would the Governor; surely anyone who brought proof that New South Wales possessed potential riches to rival, if not to exceed, those of California could count on being substantially rewarded.

As if reading his thoughts, the man beside him, James Esmond—a onetime coach driver known as Happy Jim, who hailed from the newly created state of Victoria—observed with a grin, "You still reckon they'll appoint you gold commissioner o' New South Wales, Ned?"

Ned Hargraves ignored the gibe. He said, with dignity, "I intend to visit friends in Guyong—very old friends, who keep the inn there. And I shall set off as soon as we are put ashore."

It took, however, somewhat longer than he had anticipated. He had first to shake off those who wanted to accompany him, then to arrange for the hire of a horse and a temporary loan, for, as always, his funds were limited. Finally, ten days after stepping ashore from the *Emma*'s long-boat, he was on his way, riding a big gray horse and leading another loaded with camping gear and the pan he had brought back with him from the Stanislaus Valley. A coach plied from Sydney to Bathurst, taking two days on the 150-mile journey over the Blue Mountains, but Hargraves, anxious to avoid attracting undue attention, decided to make his own way.

It was a decision he came to regret, for the country through which he was traveling was experiencing a severe drought. The steep, winding road leading up into the mountains was choked with dust, and the vehicles he encountered —mainly heavily laden ox-drawn wagons, bearing bales of wool destined for Sydney's growing export trade—came in procession, their yoked lines of plodding bullocks raising a lingering cloud of dust in their wake that seemed never to disperse.

All the creeks were dried up, and his horse, deprived of the means to slake its thirst and wearied by its rider's weight, began to show signs of sluggishness by the end of the second day. For several weary miles Ned Hargraves was compelled to walk, leading both the packhorse and his mount. His destination, the small township of Guyong, came in sight at last, two miles from Springfield, where—on his first visit to the area, seventeen years earlier—he had stayed with William Tom, a Methodist lay preacher, and his young family.

The inn, now kept by Susan Lister, the widow of his old sea captain, was a small, single-story weatherboard building, ringed by stables and other outbuildings and shaded by a clump of thickly growing eucalyptus trees. Despite its unpretentious appearance, Hargraves was pleasantly surprised when, having left his horses in the care of a shirtsleeved aboriginal boy, he entered to find the place scrupulously clean and pervaded by an appetizing aroma of roasting meat.

The proprietress herself came to greet him and, at first, gave no sign of recognition. She had aged, of course, in the intervening years, but then, he thought wryly, so had he: the *Wave*'s onetime cabin boy had been a slim waif twenty years ago, and Susan Lister a beautiful young woman, in the prime

of life. Now she was white-haired, though trim and erect, as
he remembered her, and—good heavens! The tall, handsome young man who had come from the back premises to
stand at his mother's side must be John—John Hardman
Australia Lister—who had been barely three years old when
they had last seen each other.

Ned Hargraves introduced himself and held out his hand,
beaming from one to the other of them as he watched their
expressions change from astonishment to genuine pleasure.
Susan Lister embraced him, and young John wrung his hand
and shouted to his sister to join them.

"Hey, Susannah, who d'you suppose has turned up? Meet
Ned Hargraves, the fellow who used to bounce you on his
knee when you were knee-high to a grasshopper!"

The girl, pretty and dark-haired, appeared, evidently from
the inn kitchen, for she wore an apron over her neat gingham dress, and her hands and arms were powdered with
flour. She shook hands solemnly, not sharing her family's
enthusiasm.

"You're so big!" she exclaimed. "Surely you can't be the
cabin boy Ma used to tell us about?"

"I am, Susie," Ned assured her. "The very same. And it
does my heart good to see you grown into a fine young
woman, indeed it does."

"You'll be ready for a meal," Mrs. Lister said practically.
"And the meal will be ready for you in half an hour. Johnny
will take you to your room, and the pump's outside in the
yard, so you can rid yourself of the stains of travel. We've still
plenty of water here in spite of the drought—it comes down
from the mountains, praise be." She eyed the unexpected
visitor curiously. "Where have you come from, Ned? Sydney, is it—or Gosford? That's where I heard you'd gone. To
farm, was it not?"

"That's in the past, ma'am," Ned corrected. "I'm back
from America—from two years in the California goldfields."

Over the meal he spoke at length of his experiences in the
Sierra Nevada, and urged on by Johnny Lister's eager questions, he finally revealed the purpose of his visit.

"You reckon there's gold here, Mr. Hargraves—here in
New South Wales?"

"I'm sure of it, Johnny. The country closely resembles the gold country in California. There are the same mountains, the same rivers and gullies." Warming to his theme, Ned Hargraves gave the boy chapter and verse, ending with a lecture on the geological features and the scientific explanations that accounted for the presence of gold in the rocks and riverbeds.

"Was there not a shepherd, a few years ago, who found a nugget near Lewes Ponds?" he asked.

Johnny nodded excitedly. "Aye, that there was. Old Yorky Macgregor claimed to have found a nugget, just lying in the creek near his hut. He took it to Sydney, but no one believed him."

"Or maybe they didn't want to, and it was deliberately suppressed." Ned shrugged. "There were tales and rumors before I left for San Francisco. I heard that a reverend gentleman by the name of Clarke reported finding gold-bearing quartz in the Wollondilly Valley and in a tributary of Cox's River, near Winburndale."

"Talking of quartz, sir . . ." Johnny jumped to his feet and, after crossing to the mantelshelf, picked up some small rock specimens, which he offered for the visitor's inspection. "Two young fellows were up this way a year or so back—geologists, they said they were. They stayed here, and they gave me these when they left." He pointed to the veins in one of the specimens, gleaming brightly in the lamplight. "They said these were gold. But how can anyone hope to extract it?"

"There are easier ways of getting gold," Ned told him. "Ways I learnt in the Californian diggings. The Yankee miners pan for it and use sluices and cradle rockers—oh, don't worry, the equipment's simple and don't cost above a few shillings. And the place to search is in the beds of streams and rivers—that's where alluvial gold is found, in the form of dust and nuggets." He subjected Johnny Lister to an unblinking scrutiny. "I aim to find gold here, Johnny, and I've brought my equipment with me. But it's a good while since I was here. Do you know this area well enough to act as my guide?"

Johnny did not hesitate. "I've roamed around these parts

since I was a kid, Mr. Hargraves. I know every creek and gully for miles—Ma'll tell you. I can take you anywhere you've a mind to go."

"He can, Ned," the widow Lister confirmed, a trifle sourly. "Always out there, Johnny is. Usually when I need him, he's off with his pal Willie Tom. But he can go with you if you want him, for old times' sake. Only you'll probably have to take Willie, too."

"Can we, sir?" the boy pleaded. "Can we take Willie with us?"

Ned sighed. The last thing he wanted was word of his intentions to get out, but . . . "All right, lad," he agreed. "But you'll both have to keep still tongues in your heads if we find gold. We don't want all the men who've come back from California rushing up here, do we? I'm aiming to strike a bargain with the government, understand?"

"You can trust me, sir," Johnny said earnestly. "I'll cut along and warn Willie now. I take it you want to start first thing tomorrow?"

"That's right. It won't take me long to prove my case, one way or the other." Ned stifled a weary yawn. "I think, if you'll excuse me, Mrs. Lister, I'll turn in now. We—" He smiled, struck by an odd thought, all his confidence returning. "We could make history tomorrow, you know, ma'am. And I've the strangest feeling that we're going to do just that!"

The feeling persisted the following morning, when he and the two young men left to begin their search. Young William Tom—son of the lay preacher who had been Ned's host on his first visit to the area—struck the only discordant note. A thickset, swarthy youth, he seemed to derive considerable pleasure from expressing his disbelief in the prospect of finding anything of value in the creeks and gullies to which they were bound, least of all gold. Examining the flat metal pan attached to Ned Hargraves's saddle, he said scornfully, "Why, this is a bloomin' fryin' pan, ain't it? How d'you reckon you'll make our fortunes with that, Mr. Hargraves? Be best if you let me cook up damper in it when we stop to eat!"

"We're not stopping to eat," Ned told him with asperity. "And when we *do* stop, it'll be where and when I say. When I find the right place, I'll show you how to make a fortune with my frying pan! How much farther is it to Summer Hill Creek, Johnny?"

Johnny Lister pointed ahead of them. "Down this valley, Mr. Hargraves, about another mile. Summer Hill joins with Lewes Ponds down there and what they call Yorky's Corner, where Old Yorky Macgregor used to have his hut. Yorky was—"

"The shepherd who reported that he'd found a sizable nugget," Ned finished for him. "Well, that's probably as good a place as any to make a start."

When they reached the junction of the two creeks, Ned's spirits rose. The drought had reduced the water level, leaving sand and gravel exposed, and lower down and on the opposite side of the Summer Hill Creek there was a sandbar that reminded him vividly of those he had worked in California's Stanislaus Valley. There he had found small nuggets of alluvial gold a few inches below the surface—as, no doubt, the now-dead Yorky had done—but a swift search revealed none here, so he unstrapped his pan and, squatting by the edge of the creek, gave his two young companions a lesson in panning for gold.

With only his fourth panful he let out a cry of triumph. "See!" he invited the skeptical Willie Tom. "I've struck pay dirt! Before heaven, I was right! This *is* gold country. Boys, you're looking at gold dust, and I'll take my oath that there's plenty more where this came from."

Despite this initial success, however, five more hours of careful panning yielded only a few grains of the precious metal. Ned Hargraves dried out their minute haul, wrapping it in his handkerchief.

"Tomorrow we'll try lower down," he said, clambering wearily to his feet. "I'll take a pick to the creek bank, and we'll construct a cradle as soon as I can find some suitable planks of wood. You can wash more dirt with a rocking cradle."

For the ensuing three weeks, aided by the two young men, Ned took gravel samples from a wide area of the Macquarie River valley, finding sufficient dust to confirm all his hopes and dreams. They encountered only a few shepherds and

stockmen in their methodical search, but for all their efforts
to conceal the reason for their presence, Ned became increasingly anxious lest word of what they had found come to
the ears of men lately returned from California.

"I must be the first to approach the Governor," he confided to Susan Lister. "We've worked hard, the lads and me,
and it's only right that we should claim a reward for what
we've achieved. I'll go back to Sydney in a day or so and seek
an interview with the authorities. The cradle's finished. I'll
show Johnny and young Willie how to operate it, and they
can set it up at Summer Hill Creek or on Yorky's Corner. I
guarantee they'll find gold in considerable quantity once
they start rocking—because it's there, Mrs. Lister. I'd stake
my life on it!"

Two days later, after extracting a promise of silence from
the Listers and Willie Tom, Ned mounted his big gray horse
and set off to retrace his steps to Sydney.

The two boys watched him go, and then, both now as
confident as their mentor, they loaded packhorses with the
cradle and their camping gear and left on their mission. It
was well into the afternoon when they reached their destination, descending the steep slope from Lucas Gully to reach
the creek half a mile from where Old Yorky's hut still stood.

"Let's boil the billy," Willie Tom suggested, mopping his
heated face, "before we start unloading our gear. I'm
parched, I don't know about you."

"All right," Johnny agreed readily, untying the blackened
billycan suspended from the pommel of his saddle. "We're
on our own, ain't we? We can take our time, without Ned
Hargraves to drive us. Here—" He handed the can to Willie.
"You get the water. I'll unsaddle the horses and hobble
them."

Willie grinned and slithered down the bank to the exposed sandbar. He dipped the billycan into the water and
then drew it back, smothering a gasp. In a crevice of the rock
just below the surface of the water he caught a glimpse of
something that emitted a faint yellowy luster. Scarcely daring to believe his luck, he thrust his hand into the crevice and
drew out a nugget about the size of a hen's egg. And it was
gold! Pure, alluvial gold, just as Hargraves had described.

He turned, scarcely able to contain his excitement, and yelled to Johnny to join him.

"Look!" he exclaimed in a strangled voice. "Stone the crows, John—just look what I've found! Hargraves was right —there's gold here sure enough. And to think I used to wonder if he was off his rocker!"

"He was always sure he was right, Willie," Johnny asserted loyally. "And we've got to give him the credit. We'd never have found anything if he hadn't told us how and shown us where to look, would we?"

"Maybe so." Will shrugged and bent to dip the billycan into the creek. "But he'll have his work cut out to convince Governor Fitzroy with the few grains o' dust he took with him, I'll warrant. He should've waited and taken this beaut with him."

In fact, Ned experienced considerable skepticism when he was finally received by the colonial secretary, Edward Deas Thomson, after cooling his heels in the anteroom for the best part of a day. A man of fifty and the son-in-law of a previous governor, Thomson wielded considerable influence in the colony, having held office for fourteen years and served in the administration for more than twenty.

He listened to his visitor's story in repressive silence, and when Ned produced the grains of gold dust to substantiate his claim, the secretary pointedly donned his spectacles in order to examine them.

"Hardly an impressive find, Mr. Hargraves," he observed with a noticeable lack of enthusiasm. "Ah, you were at the Calfornian gold diggings, you say?"

"That is so, sir. I spent over a year there." Resenting the colonial secretary's manner, Ned launched into his carefully prepared lecture but was abruptly cut short.

"I am sure you know what you are talking about, sir . . . whereas I do not," Thomson assured him with a thin smile. "But to expect payment from the government on such flimsy evidence as you have produced is—well, somewhat optimistic, to say the least. If you are correct concerning the existence of a goldfield in this colony, it would undoubtedly halt the emigration to California. But, Mr. Hargraves, it would do much else besides—none of it good or likely to benefit our pastoral society. There have been claims made before, you know, which earlier administrations deemed it wiser to suppress, for reasons that must be obvious to you."

"California has been opened up as a direct result of the gold finds there, Mr. Thomson," Ned argued. "The population of San Francisco quadrupled in the space of two years. Gold has brought prosperity and—"

"And lawlessness, from all accounts, sir." The colonial secretary's tone was discouraging. "Not to put too fine a point on it, lawlessness, in what has been until recently a penal colony, is not to be desired. We have our prosperity here, Mr. Hargraves, and a well-ordered, securely based prosperity. Frankly, I do not think that His Excellency Sir Charles Fitzroy will welcome your discovery—if that is what it is—or feel disposed to reward you for making it."

"But, sir," Ned began, unable to hide his chagrin, "gold, in the quantities I confidently estimate, will bring the colony more profit than wool or coal. And I'm asking only for a fair reward for the work I've done and the expense I've been put to. If His Excellency were to—"

"Put your request in writing, Mr. Hargraves," Thomson invited. "My clerk will supply you with pen and paper, and you may leave your letter with him when it is done. I will see that His Excellency receives it without delay."

Conscious of Thomson's disapproval, Ned had no choice but to agree to his suggestion. Back in the anteroom once more, he spent more than an hour on the composition of his letter to Governor Fitzroy. He would, he assured the Governor, reveal the exact location of his discovery on payment of a reward that was in keeping with its value to the colony; and as an added inducement he offered his expert services in the capacity of . . . Dark brows knit, he sought for a title. *Commissioner for gold . . . gold-bearing land commissioner* . . . By heaven, Essie would be impressed if he returned to her with an official appointment! And the two boys who had assisted him—Johnny Lister and Willie Tom—they, too, were deserving of reward.

"It waxes late, sir," the colonial secretary's clerk reminded him reproachfully. "Have you not yet done?"

"I'll not keep you above five minutes," Ned answered with dignity. He wrote *"Commissioner for Crown Lands"* and signed his name with a flourish. Five hundred pounds, he decided, would not be too much to ask in the first instance, or perhaps . . . He picked up the pen again and wrote: "I leave it to the generosity of the government to make such additional reward as may be commensurate with the benefit likely to accrue to this colony as a result of my discovery."

Leaving his epistle in the clerk's hands, he went out into the street and, on impulse, asked a passerby to direct him to the office of Sydney's leading newspaper, the *Morning Herald.*

Better, Ned Hargraves told himself, to be sure than sorry. Thomson had been the reverse of grateful, and as had happened in the past, he and Sir Charles Fitzroy might attempt to suppress the news of this momentous discovery. But were he to reveal it to the press, their hands would be effectively tied. He would insist that the *Herald* hold back publication until the Governor had replied to his report, but if he did not, or if his reply should be unfavorable, then . . . With a jaunty step, Ned followed the directions he had been given, his mouth set in a firm, determined line.

CHAPTER V

Dusk was falling when Jenny Broome descended from the smart curricle that had brought her from the picnic she had shared with William De Lancey to her parents' house in Elizabeth Bay, on the outskirts of Sydney.

William, a tall, handsome figure in his undress cavalry uniform, assisted her to alight, holding her hand for a trifle longer than good manners decreed.

"Did you enjoy our drive, Jenny?" he asked solicitously.

"Very much, Will," she assured him, withdrawing her hand from his clasp and reddening a little as she saw his dark eyes light up. Their families were old friends; William's father was one of the colony's most respected judges, as well as her uncle through marriage, and she and Will, with only a year separating them, had known each other since childhood. But William had been commissioned into the British Army and had been on active service in India for the past five years, so that now, try as she might to revive their childhood relationship, Jenny found herself curiously shy of him. She had never been so before, and despite his long absence, she should not, she knew, regard him as a stranger now, or even . . . She lowered her gaze. Even as a suitor, because there was Edmund Tempest, with whom there had long been an understanding—on her parents' part, as well as her own.

But Edmund, though, seemed always to be too occupied with his family's farm on the Macquarie River, beyond Bathurst, to have much time to spend on what had always been a somewhat desultory courtship in Sydney. . . . Jenny bit back a sigh.

"You'll come out with me again, won't you, Jenny?" William urged. "I'll not have much longer here; my leave will be up all too soon, confound it! But I hear the Fortieth Regi-

ment intends to give a ball in their mess when their C.O.
arrives, and I . . . that is, I'd deem it an honor as well as a
pleasure if you would permit me to escort you to it. And of
course there's the race meeting next week. I was thinking of
riding in the garrison officers' race."

Jenny hesitated, eyeing him uncertainly, taking in the
strong, high-boned lines of his face and suddenly very conscious of his masculine attraction. He was much more ma-
ture than Edmund, she recognized, and she had heard that
he had displayed remarkable courage in the recent war in
India against the Sikhs—sufficient, at all events, to have
earned him a commendation in the commander in chief's
dispatches. She had enjoyed his company this afternoon, for
all her shyness, but . . . guiltily she recalled the reason for
her haste to return home. Her mother's illness was causing
them all much anxiety, not least her father. The poor, dear
soul had seemingly been ailing for some considerable time
but had told nobody until her sudden collapse had caused
her to take to her bed, almost a month ago, with frequent
visits from Dr. Munro—of late twice a day.

"I don't know, Will," she evaded, unhappily. "There's my
mother, you see. I must be with her."

"Is she very ill?"

"I'm afraid she is." Jenny started to move toward the door
of the house, her conscience pricking her. "Dr. Munro has
been most kind and attentive, and Mama never complains,
but she's suffering a great deal of pain. I should not really
have left her today, but she insisted that I needed a break
and that it would do me good."

"And has it?" William questioned. "Has it, Jenny?"

"Yes," Jenny admitted. "I think it has, thank you, Will."

"Call on me," William begged, "anytime when you need a
break and can be spared. I'm sorry about your mother, Jenny
—truly sorry."

He took his leave at last, with flattering reluctance, and
Jenny hurried into the house. It was a pleasant, white-
painted brick house, overlooking Elizabeth Bay and the blue
expanse of the great harbor—quite a contrast from the cottage on the west side of Sydney Cove where she had spent
her childhood. Her father had built the new house ten years

ago, when he had been promoted to post rank in the Royal
Navy, and her mother loved it, the view of incoming ships a
constant source of joy to her. So often it had been her
father's ships for which she and her mother had watched and
waited together—always anxiously. But now his seagoing
days were over, and he worked instead at building ships and
superintending the construction of a new naval dockyard at
Cockatoo Island, where—to her father's disgust, she knew—
it was planned to build and repair steam-propelled vessels,
which even here were beginning to supersede the sailing
ships he loved so passionately.

The young Irish maid, Biddy, came to relieve her of her
hat and cloak, and Jenny, shocked and worried when she saw
that the girl was in tears, quickly asked how her mother was.
The doctor had called, Biddy told her, between sobs, soon
after Jenny had left for her outing with William De Lancey.

"Sure he must have hurted the poor mistress something
cruel, for I heard her cry out. An' she has not eaten all day,
Miss Jenny. Just a few sips a' de broth Cook made for her an'
she was tellin' me to take it away. 'I can't fancy it,' she said,
but she t'anked me for taking it up to her, like she always
does."

Such courtesy, Jenny thought, was typical of her mother,
who as a young girl had been in service herself, as lady's
maid to the wife of the late Governor Macquarie. Doubtless
that was why she treated all her own servants with unfailing
consideration, with the result that, like the weeping Biddy,
they adored her.

"Perhaps if you prepare a tea tray, Biddy," she suggested,
"I'll take it to her, and maybe I'll be able to persuade her to
eat a little."

Biddy wiped her streaming eyes with a corner of her apron
and hurried off to prepare the tray. She returned with it a few
minutes later and, still tearful, indicated the extra cups she
had set out.

"De master's wid herself, Miss Jenny. I was t'inking he
might take a cup."

Perhaps he would, Jenny thought, conscious of a lump in
her throat as she picked up the tray. Her mother's illness was
taking a terrible toll on her father; he tried to hide it, but he

had taken to spending more time with her than he did at the shipyard, and for all his studied cheerfulness, Jenny could sense his anxiety as if it were a living thing, tearing him apart. She should not have left them, she reproached herself; she should have turned a deaf ear to William De Lancey's blandishments and her mother's urging. It was easier for both of them when she was there, but perhaps when her brother John returned from the assignment his paper had sent him on, they could devise some plan, between them, that would help improve matters.

Resting the laden tray on her hip, Jenny knocked on the door of her mother's bedroom and went in.

Jessica Broome's thin, pale face lit with a smile as, propped up on her pillows, she recognized her daughter.

"You're back early, child—but the better for your outing, I trust. Did you enjoy yourself?"

Jenny set down the tray and bent to kiss her.

"Yes, I did, Mam," she answered. It took an effort to simulate enthusiasm, but she made it, as she described the picnic and listed those who had been there, achingly aware of her father's strained silence. But he poured tea and, in response to her gesture, carried a cup over to her, which, without asking whether or not her mother wanted it, she induced her to drink.

"I was reading some of Red's old letters aloud," Justin Broome said when Jenny returned the empty cup to the tray. He met her gaze, his own mutely unhappy, and she guessed that something must have occurred during her absence to add to his distress on her mother's account. He had talked to Dr. Munro, perhaps, or . . . Her teeth closed fiercely over her lower lip as she felt it tremble. The small, brass-bound wooden box, in which her elder brother Red's letters were kept, stood open on the table beside him. Her mother, she thought, without even a twinge of jealousy or resentment, had always loved Red deeply—more, much more than either Johnny or her—and she had hoarded his letters over the years. Clearly, judging by the state of them, they had often been taken out and read and reread, for the pages were creased and the ink was faded, in places almost illegible.

She had been a baby, Jenny reflected, when Red had

joined the Royal Navy frigate *Success* as a midshipman under
the command of the founder and first Governor of Perth,
Western Australia, now Admiral Sir James Stirling and a
member of the Board of Admiralty.

Red—whose given name was Murdoch—had made an excellent career in the navy, better even than their father's. It
was all there in the letters, some of which had been read to
her, but Jenny gave vent to a regretful sigh. If she had
thought of Will De Lancey as a stranger, how much more of
a stranger had her elder brother become after an absence
from his homeland of more than twenty years?

True, he had returned to Australia with his old captain,
James Stirling, when the British government had finally approved the establishment of a settlement on the Swan River
in 1829. But the new capital, Perth, was twenty-five hundred
miles from Sydney, and Red had then been only a very junior
member of Lieutenant Governor Stirling's staff—too junior
to be able to make the long journey to visit his family in any
official capacity, and without the means to pay for a passage
in a merchant ship.

In any event, Jenny recalled, he had found the initial mis-
management of the new settlement little to his liking and the
problems of its first, ill-chosen free settlers even less so, and
he had sought active service at sea in preference. Appointed
to H.M.S. *Dido*, an eighteen-gun corvette under the command of Captain the Honorable Henry Keppel—brother of
his fellow midshipman Tom Keppel of the *Success*—Red had
been almost continuously in action. First he had been in
China, where his ship had been engaged in the Opium War
of 1842, and then the corvette had been ordered to Borneo,
on an expedition for the suppression of piracy there and in
the rivers of Sarawak, whose white rajah, James Brooke, had
requested British government help. He—

"I'll go on reading, Jenny." Her father's voice broke into
her thoughts. "It gives your mother great pleasure to hear
Red's letters," he added almost apologetically, "for all they
are years out of date. But don't stay if you would rather not."

"I'll stay, Dad," Jenny answered.

She settled back in a chair by the window, watching her
mother's face. Jessica Broome's dark eyes were aglow, she

saw, her expression one of eager anticipation as she said softly, "He was telling us about the Dayaks, Justin, and about Mr. Brooke."

"Yes," Justin Broome acknowledged. He picked up one of the crumpled letters and searched for the place where he had left off. Clearing his throat, he commenced reading.

"The Dayaks are river pirates and headhunters, and they go about their evil business with great daring. Their war *prahus* are very swift, armed with brass guns and with forty or fifty oarsmen to propel them. But they are greatly in awe of Captain Keppel, whom they call the Rajah Laut, which means "Sea King," and of our *Dido*, for she has the speed to give chase when we encounter their *prahus* at sea. When they flee upriver to their strongholds, we chase them in our boats. . . ."

Justin Broome went on, reading automatically for quite some time, but he was barely aware of what he was saying. His mind and his thoughts were on Dr. Munro's visit earlier that day, and he heard again, in memory, the doctor's words. Munro had spoken quietly and compassionately, yet his voice boomed out now in Justin's ears, shutting out the sound of his own.

"It is a malignant growth, Captain Broome, stemming from the lump on your wife's breast. Regrettably, I was unable to remove it. . . ."

Such a small lump it had been, Justin recalled with sick bitterness, and Jessica had borne with heroic courage the appalling pain of the doctor's attempts to remove it. First the applications of acid had been tried and had failed, and then a surgeon's knife had cut into the scarred and wasted flesh, but all to no avail: the ghastly growth had seemingly spread to other parts of her body that no knife could reach.

His wife, his beloved wife, was dying, Munro had said, and all he could do now was administer laudanum to ease the agony she was enduring. He could not say how long Jessica would have. . . .

Justin lost his place in the letter, and his voice sounded harsh to his own ears as he found the right line again and went on reading, conscious that his daughter was looking at him in mute alarm.

Jenny would have to be told, he knew, and he would have to break the sad news to her as gently as he could, though perhaps she had sensed the truth, poor child. She was devoted to her mother, and since Jessica had been forced to abandon her brave pretense, Jenny had scarcely left the sickroom.

He came to the end of the letter he had been reading and, after folding it carefully, replaced it in its box.

"Have you had enough, dearest?" he asked. "Or shall I go on?"

"Only if it does not weary you too much," Jessica said. "Reading his letters seems to bring Red nearer. And when you read them aloud, it's as if he's here in the room with us, telling us in person of what he has done and where he has been." She smiled, her expression oddly wistful, so that Justin's heart went out to her in helpless pity. "I wonder if we should recognize him if he *were* in the room now. It's been so long, has it not? But perhaps he resembles you, Justin, now that he's grown to manhood—he did as a boy."

Damn Red to hell, Justin thought savagely, for his long absence! It would have meant so much to Jessica had she been able to see him now, but . . . He controlled himself and answered with a forced smile, "I never had red hair, my love. And now, damme, it's gray! But I don't imagine Red will have changed out of recognition." He picked up another letter from the bundle, but intercepting a warning glance from Jenny, he hesitated a moment. Jessica, her face drawn from the pain she must be enduring, raised her hand in a dismissive gesture.

"Perhaps that is enough for today, Justin dear," she said weakly. "Thank you for sparing me so much of your time." Justin muttered a disclaimer, and she mused, as if he had not spoken, "Will De Lancey told us that his sister, Magdalen, met Red when she was in England last year, didn't he, Jenny? He seemed to think that they saw a good deal of each other."

Jenny, thus appealed to, gave her confirmation, again with a warning glance at her father. "Yes, he did. But like all Australian families with sons in the services, Will and Mag-

dalen have been separated for years. And Magdalen wasn't
in London for long—she was in Scotland, with Judge De
Lancey's relatives, Will said. He met them, too, when he was
a cadet at Addiscombe. He said they were titled and very
grand."

Her mother eyed her reproachfully but said nothing, and
a knock on the door heralded Johnny to provide a welcome
distraction. Tall and deeply tanned, he crossed the room in
swift, impatient strides, and bending to kiss Jessica's cheek,
he smiled broadly and put a letter into her hand.

"From Red, Mam," he told her, well aware of the joy his
announcement would bring. "I called at the post office for
mail, and this was waiting. I knew you would want to have it
at once."

Justin, anxiously watching his wife's face, rose and took
the letter from her, for she had paled alarmingly, and her
hands were shaking as she sought vainly to break the seal.

"I'll read it to you, my love," he offered, and she thanked
him with eyes that, he saw, had filled with tears. He offered
up a silent prayer as he took the letter to the window in order
to take advantage of the daylight. Dear God, for my poor
Jessie's sake, he prayed, let this be the news for which she
has waited all these years! Let it be to tell her that our son is
coming home. . . .

His own hands shook as he opened the letter. It began
affectionately, as Red's letters always did, with inquiries as to
the health and well-being of his family and messages for all
of them. Justin read these slowly, his gaze straying to the
foot of the page, and for all his efforts to control it, his voice
rose as he read.

> "I have been appointed to the command of Her Majes-
> ty's ship *Galah*, a Symondite corvette of eighteen guns,
> and have today read my commission to the ship's com-
> pany at Sheerness, and—praise be to heaven—my or-
> ders are to proceed to Port Jackson, to relieve the *Otter*
> on the Australian station. The posting will be for two
> years at least, the actual duration depending on circum-
> stances, and I cannot find words to tell you, dearest

Mama, how happy I am to be coming home at last. . . ."

Justin broke off, his throat suddenly tight, as he heard Jessica cry out.

"Oh, thank God! Justin, it is the answer to prayer—truly what I have begged the good Lord to grant me. The sight of my son before I—" She bit back the words she had been about to utter, and Justin put down the letter and went to kneel beside the bed, reaching for her hands with both his own.

She knew, he thought dully. For all Dr. Munro's well-intentioned insistence that she should not be told how serious her condition was, Jessica had seen through the doctor's platitudes and promises, as she had seen through his own unconvincing expressions of hope for her recovery. But being the courageous woman she was, she had put on a show of believing them. He glanced across at Johnny and then at his daughter and saw that both had understood, reading the same meaning as he had into the words their mother had left unsaid.

Jenny made to rise, but her brother's hand held her back. "When was that letter written?" Johnny questioned practically. "It arrived here by the *Lady Frere*, and she made the passage in just over five months, I believe—she was held up at the Cape. So that Red's ship—what's she called?—the *Galah*, should be well on her way, Mam."

"If she sailed at once, Johnny." Justin retrieved the letter, in control of himself again. "This was written on February nineteenth." He cleared his throat. "I'll read the rest of it, shall I, my love?"

"Yes, if you please," Jessica whispered. "I expect Red will tell us when—when we may expect him."

But Red was unable to give a precise date, they learned as Justin read on.

"We have to complete our fitting out and muster a crew, and Their Lordships have instructed me to make a shakedown cruise to Lisbon with dispatches, so probably it will be six or eight weeks before we set course for

Australian waters. Rest assured that any delay will not be of my making, but we are to give passage to the future commandant of your new naval dockyard, Dad— one of the new breed of steam engineers now making their presence felt in the Royal Navy. Our passenger is an officer by the name of Lucas—a post captain, no less —and he is bringing his wife with him. . . ."

Justin smiled wryly. "Poor Red—his first command, and he's to have an engineer captain thrust upon him! A married engineer captain, too—the lad will have to give up his quarters to them, I fear." He did not wait for any comment from his listeners but continued his reading.

"However, Their Lordships have permitted me to choose my officers, and Cousin Timothy has already joined, as first lieutenant, and we are expecting young Francis De Lancey as our second, as soon as he can make the journey from Dunglass, in Scotland."

"Timothy—William and Dodie's eldest son," Jessica put in, with obvious pleasure. "They will be as delighted by this news as I am, Justin."

But with less reason, Justin thought. Young Timothy Broome had been one of Captain Keppel's mids in the *Maeander*, which had called at Sydney the previous February, so his family had seen him comparatively recently. Justin's brother, William, now owned some twenty thousand acres of land in the new state of Victoria—land he had acquired by running his sheep on it in the exercise of what were known as squatters' rights, for which the government required only nominal payment.

"And George De Lancey," Justin observed. "He hasn't seen Francis for several years." He finished his reading of the letter, which concluded with an enthusiastic description of the *Galah*, and observing with concern the weariness in his wife's small face, he carried the letter over to her and offered gently, "We'll leave you now, shall we, my dearest? Try to sleep for a little while. And then perhaps Jenny might persuade you to eat."

"Don't worry," Jenny said. "I'll see that she does, Dad. But I don't believe she will need too much persuading after Red's news, will you, Mam?"

The letter in her hand, Jessica managed an answering smile, and leaving the two women together, Justin took his son's arm and led the way downstairs to the small room he used as an office.

"Let's take a drink together, Johnny," he invited, "so that I may hear your news. When did you get back from Goulburn?"

"Oh, I was back in Sydney before noon," Johnny told him. "My trip proved a complete waste of time. But . . ." He accepted the glass of brandy his father had poured for him and raised it in salute. "Your very good health, sir. However," he went on, "something of momentous interest *did* occur, and I've been anxious to tell you about it. When I returned to the office, there was a fellow by the name of Hargraves—Edward Hammond Hargraves—waiting to see me. He's an interesting fellow—very tall and stout, with a luxuriant black beard. He used to farm at Gosford, he told me, but hied him off to California to join the American gold rush. He failed to strike it rich, but he claims to know all there is to know about gold-seeking."

"And do you think he does?" Justin questioned.

"Yes, Dad, I do—he struck me as pretty truthful. And his story is that he realized there was a strong similarity between the country beyond Bathurst and in the Macquarie River valley and the goldfields of California." Johnny shrugged his broad shoulders and grinned. "He came back here to prove the point, and he claims to have done so. . . . Anyway, he produced a few specks of gold dust, which he told me he'd shown to Secretary Deas Thomson."

Justin's interest was suddenly kindled. "Did he tell where he found the dust?"

"Beyond saying it was in the Macquarie River area, he didn't. He's hoping for financial reward from the government. That was why he went to see Thomson, from whom—"

"From whom," Justin put in, "he received no encouragement?"

Johnny eyed him thoughtfully. 'Exactly so. How did you guess, sir?"

"Because," Justin answered, "more years ago than I care to remember, Rick Tempest and I found alluvial gold at Pengallon when we were in partnership there. . . ." Memory stirred, and he recalled vividly the events that had followed their discovery.

Rick had found the nuggets in the riverbank, but within hours of his having done so, the two of them had been subjected to a murderous attack by a gang of convict escapers. Rick had been shot and severely wounded before help had arrived.

"We reported our find to Governor Macquarie," Justin added. "And as I had anticipated—and repeatedly warned Rick—His Excellency very wisely insisted that it was not to be made public. He had the terms of our lease altered, so as to exclude mineral rights in it for twenty years." He frowned, hearing again in memory Lachlan Macquarie's voice and seeing, too, the dismay that had been mirrored in the Governor's face when he had been informed of Rick's discovery.

"God in heaven!" he had exclaimed. *"If word of this should be allowed to spread, the consequences could be disastrous! The convicts could not be controlled. There would be mass escapes, and every escaper would be up in the mountains, in the new grazing lands, searching for gold. And not only the convicts—free men, too, the settlers, men of the garrison. The colony would swiftly become ungovernable. . . . The people would starve if they were permitted to squander the bounties of nature in a wild quest for gold. I cannot run the risk of it."*

Those who had followed Governor Macquarie at the helm of the colony's destiny had shared this view, Justin reminded himself—and rightly so. He started to enlarge on the subject but then broke off, realizing that Johnny—a well-informed journalist—needed no convincing.

"They all kept quiet concerning the possibility of a gold find here, Dad. Brisbane, Darling, Gipps—Strzelecki found gold-bearing quartz near Hartley, and Sir George Gipps swore him to silence, and he did the same when the parson William Clarke went prospecting along Cox's River and the

Wollondilly. And then there was that shepherd, the fellow they called Old Yorky—Hargraves knew about *him;* he admitted as much. In fact, I suspect he headed for the creek where Yorky's hut used to be, when he started his search. It's near Guyong, where he told me he stayed—he's a friend of the widow Lister, who keeps the hostelry there. And there's no doubt that Yorky *did* light on a sizable nugget." Johnny shrugged in a resigned gesture. "Dad, I fear it will not be possible to keep quiet about the gold any longer, whatever Deas Thomson said or whatever Governor Fitzroy tries to do. Hargraves isn't going to be easily silenced, and besides, he's not the only man who's come back here from California. They're returning in droves . . . and they're not the best of characters, some of them. It's said that the authorities in San Francisco threw them out."

Justin inclined his head in agreement. "You're right, Johnny. I had occasion to board one of their vessels this forenoon—the brig *Banshee,* registered in 'Frisco. The owner appeared to be a gentleman—he claimed to have been a major in the British Army—but the bunch he had with him was a singularly unpleasant lot. Two of them had served time on Norfolk Island, and they all had come from the Californian diggings. The major—I believe he said his name was Lewis—told me that he had struck it rich in the American fields. But he was evasive concerning his reasons for coming here."

"I wonder whether he knows Edward Hargraves," Johnny said thoughtfully. "I gathered, from what Hargraves said to me, that he talked pretty freely to anyone who would listen when he was at the Californian diggings. It seems he was convinced *before* he left Sydney that the country in the Macquarie Valley was gold-bearing, and that he went to California only to prove his theory—and now he reckons he's done so."

Justin regarded his son anxiously over the rim of his glass. "Is the *Herald* likely to print his story?"

"Not yet," Johnny answered. "I'm to investigate further. I suggested to Mr. Hargraves that he should take me to where he made his discovery, but he wasn't at all keen on that suggestion—even when I offered him a guarantee of complete secrecy. I think he'll wait until he knows how the Governor reacts when Deas Thomson passes on his letter. Not to put too fine a point on it, Dad, but Hargraves is looking for financial reward and maybe some sort of government appointment. Unlike the British major you speak of, he barely covered his expenses in California and his passage home. If there *is* gold in our Blue Mountains, he wants the credit for having found it."

"But you intend to investigate further?"

Johnny's tanned face lit with a boyish grin.

"I aim to, yes, and the paper's keen that I do. Hargraves let slip that he has a couple of lads sniffing around the creeks in the Macquarie Valley—young Lister and a boy named William Tom. Hargraves showed them how to pan for gold. They constructed what he calls a cradle rocker, on the Californian pattern, before he left them. And he seemed quite certain that they would find enough gold to convince the government."

"Does he know what you're proposing to do?" Justin asked. He set his glass down, conscious of a feeling of deep dismay at the prospect of Hargraves's discovery being confirmed. Like Governor Macquarie all those years ago, he feared the consequences of such a discovery. When he put his anxieties into words, Johnny gravely nodded his agreement.

"I know, sir, and I hope to heaven Hargraves is wrong! Indeed, I'll do all I can to disprove his claim. To judge by the situation brought about in California, a gold rush is the last thing we want here." Johnny hesitated. "I'd planned to start for Guyong tomorrow, but . . . there's Mam. I've been away for only a couple of weeks, but I—Dad, I was shocked to see the difference in her even in that time. Did Dr. Munro —" He gulped. "Did he say—"

Justin caught his breath on an unhappy sigh. The boy had noticed, of course; it was inevitable that he would—and Jenny, too. He could not keep the sad truth from them; they both had a right to know, little as he relished telling them. He shrank from admitting it to himself, but . . . "Munro says that there's nothing more he can do for her, Johnny, except try to relieve her pain. It's—oh, devil take it, lad, it's just a matter of time, he says."

"Did he give you any idea of how much time?" Johnny demanded, tight-lipped.

Justin shook his head. "He cannot tell. It could be weeks; it might be longer."

"I hope to God Red gets here in time!"

"That's my hope, too, Johnny." Red's letter, the fact that he was on his way—he must have sailed by now—had given Jessica such joy that perhaps . . . "I think she will find the strength to hold on until Red returns. I pray to God that He will give her that strength. It would mean everything in the world to her to see him again."

"Yes, I know." Johnny was silent for a long moment, avoiding his father's gaze. "Do you think I ought to go to Guyong tomorrow, Dad? I'd have to be away for at least a week, ten days maybe. And I'd not want to leave her if—I mean if Mam needs me, I—" Again he hesitated. "Does *she* know?"

"Munro didn't tell her," Justin replied, his throat tight. "He made a point of it, but— God, Johnny, I believe she knows. But for all our sakes, she'll never admit it, thinking to spare us. So you had better make your trip to Guyong, otherwise your mother might think it strange. I'll tell Jenny— she'll be here—and if it should be necessary, I will send for you."

"Very well, sir." Again Johnny lapsed into silence, and Justin rose, busying himself with the task of replenishing both their glasses, his thoughts such that he could not share them, even with his son.

Johnny broke the silence, deliberately introducing a change of subject. "Red said in his letter that he would be giving passage to a naval engineer, who's to take over command of your dockyard, didn't he, Dad?"

"Yes, I think he did," Justin confirmed, his voice without expression.

"Will you mind?"

"Mind? No, not in the least." Justin shrugged. "Mine was only a temporary command. Officially I'm on the retired list." And it was true, he reflected—he did not mind. He minded nothing now, in the face of Jessica's tragic illness, and in many ways it would be a relief to hand over the administration of the new naval dockyard. Damn it, he thought irritably, he was a seaman, not a—what had Red called his passenger?—a new breed of officer, a naval engineer, a steamship man. "I shall welcome it, Johnny," he added with more feeling than he had intended to reveal.

"You have never been truly ambitious, have you, Dad?" Johnny suggested. "I mean, you were never a glory hunter."

"What makes you think so?" Justin challenged, genuinely surprised. "I held a command at sea for most of my adult life. That was all I ever aspired to or wanted, to be honest. And my commands were all here, for which I consider myself fortunate—Their Lordships might well have appointed me to a ship on the India station or even the Mediterranean or the Channel Fleet." Like Red, he thought, all his service might have been spent twelve thousand miles from his home, but as it was, Their Lordships had left him in Australia, probably because they had granted him his commission reluctantly and . . . His mouth tightened. Because the son of emancipated convicts would have proved an embarrassment to them. But Red, as the third generation—and with Admiral Stirling as his patron—had been freed of the stigma, and, his father reflected proudly, he had made a fine career.

"You could have been Governor of South Australia," Johnny asserted with a certain belligerence. "If you wanted to—you were there with Colonel Light, the surveyor general. And I swear that you would have made a better job of it than Sir John Hindmarsh and the resident commissioner— what was his name?"

"Fisher," Justin supplied. "But Captain Hindmarsh was a most distinguished naval officer, Johnny, with a record second to none."

"Even so," Johnny argued, unperturbed, "he made an appalling hash of his governorship. And after Colonel Napier refused the appointment, you *were* under consideration, weren't you?"

That was so, Justin was forced to concede, although he doubted whether the British Colonial Office would have sanctioned his appointment. In any case, like Captain Hindmarsh, he had not been able to see eye to eye with the South Australia Company's resident commissioner. The endless quarrels over where the new state capital of Adelaide was to be sited, the confusion of land sales to the newly arrived settlers, and the fact that convict labor was barred from the colony—all this had exhausted his patience and strained his tolerance to its limit.

Johnny, Justin saw, was eyeing him in mute expectation, and he said with emphasis, "For the Lord's sake, lad, I was well out of that appointment! Colonel Light had sound plans, and I concurred with everything he proposed. But it's a sad fact that every new settlement in this country suffers when convict labor is excluded. Free settlers can't be counted on to work at arduous tasks such as building roads —aye, and houses, too—or agricultural development. The first free settlers to arrive in South Australia expected to find labor readily available, and Hindmarsh had to have seamen from the *Buffalo* construct shelter for them!" Indeed, Justin recalled, it had taken fifteen years—and the arrival from Germany of Lutheran exiles who were willing to work—for South Australia to reach a reasonably sound financial footing.

The Irish maid, Biddy, came in to announce dinner, and Justin ate his meal without appetite. He and Johnny, by mutual consent, avoided the subject of Jessica's illness, continuing instead to discuss the state of affairs in the country at large. Johnny's views differed only a little from his own; as a journalist he was perhaps more forward-looking, and, Justin thought proudly, the boy was extremely well read, despite the fact that his education had been acquired in Sydney and he had lacked the benefits of an English public school that many of his contemporaries had enjoyed.

Inevitably their conversation returned to Hargraves and the threat to the present mode of life in New South Wales that a gold rush on the California scale would precipitate.

"And it will not only be here," Johnny asserted glumly. "Some of the men from the American diggings are aiming to head for Victoria. Hargraves told me that a friend of his—a character he called Happy Jim—intended to try his luck

there, as soon as he could find a ship to give him passage to
Port Phillip. They're a determined lot, Dad, and they won't
easily be stopped. If Hargraves or those two lads of his find
even one nugget in one of the Macquarie River creeks,
there'll be no silencing him. And you said yourself that you
and Uncle Rick found gold in the river at Pengallon. Add
that to Old Yorky's and Count Strzelecki's and the Reverend
Clarke's and—" He spread his hands in a helpless gesture.
"Did Uncle Rick find any more gold up there, do you
know?"

"I'm inclined to believe he did," Justin began. "But like all
the others, he kept quiet about it. He—" He was interrupted
by Jenny's entrance.

"Dad," she announced breathlessly, "Mam wants to see
you both . . . she wants to settle down for the night. And I
think she will sleep; she managed to take a whole bowl of
broth with only a little persuasion from me. Red's news has
—oh, it's made her so happy!"

And indeed it had, Justin recognized when, with his son
and daughter at his heels, he returned to the sickroom.
Jessica's small, thin face was aglow, her dark eyes brighter
than he had seen them for weeks, and she clung to his hand,
begging him to stay after Jenny and Johnny had bidden her
good night. He seated himself in the chair beside her bed,
retaining her hand in his, and since she displayed no sign of
wishing to sleep, they talked far into the night, as they had
been wont to do in the early days of their marriage, after one
of his long absences at sea.

They talked of Red, of course, since his return was the
subject uppermost in his mother's mind, and of the Mac-
quaries, both of them delving back into memories they had
long supposed to have faded. Justin told her of Edward
Hargraves's discovery and Johnny's decision to go to
Guyong the next day to investigate his claim, and suddenly
Jessica's expression changed, the glow fading, her eyes
brimming with tears.

"Do you remember what your mother said to us as she
caught her first glimpse of the land beyond the Blue Mountains?" She hesitated for a moment, as if she were listening
to a voice Justin could not hear, and then, her own voice

strong and clear, as it had been in her youth, she went on, " 'Think of the flocks and herds this land will sustain, the crops it will grow! Look at it, children, for it is your future spread out down there. This is the prosperous land the Governor has told us shall be called Australia . . . and it is for you to build on!' "

"I remember it well, my dearest love," Justin managed hoarsely. "My mam was always quoting Governor Phillips' promise to me. It was her faith in that promise which dictated her life, and I thank God that she saw it fulfilled. I—"

It was as if Jessica had not heard him. But her fingers tightened about his, and she added in a soft whisper, "But now they will destroy it all in a lustful search for gold! Oh, Justin, *I* thank God that I shall not be here to see it happen and Governor Phillips' promise broken."

She lapsed into silence, and from her quiet, even breathing Justin sensed that she had fallen asleep. He stayed where he was, himself dozing fitfully, to be abruptly jerked back to wakefulness by the sound of her voice.

"Red, dearest son, it is so good that you have come home —so good to see your face again. . . ."

Her voice trailed off, and in the sudden silence, Justin could no longer hear her breathing. He cried out in pain and pity, as Jessica's hand slid limply from his clasp and he knew that she had gone.

CHAPTER VI

"I must take issue with you, Commander Broome," Captain Benjamin Lucas announced aggressively, "on this vexed question of the course you have set. I do *not* subscribe to the theory of great-circle sailing, sir—damme, I do not!"

They were standing in the gun room of the *Galah*, Red Broome's half-finished breakfast still on the long mess table, where Captain Lucas's unheralded arrival had compelled him to leave it. With the patience the eight-week passage in the engineering captain's company had taught him, Red controlled his annoyance. Captain Lucas, he had learned, was habitually critical, and more often than not his complaints were voiced with scant courtesy and based more on prejudice than on knowledge.

Lucas was a small, balding man of stout build, and Red was able comfortably to look down on him from his own impressive height. Like his father, Red was three inches over six feet, with a lean, well-muscled body and a skin that was deeply tanned. The red hair from which his nickname derived was a legacy from his paternal grandmother, and few people were aware that his given name was Murdoch, for he had not used it since his childhood.

"Captain Keppel, sir, under whom I had the honor to serve for four years, was a firm believer in the great-circle principle," he observed politely. "It enabled him to make record passages to the Far East and to Australia." Captain Lucas made to cut him short, but he ignored the attempted interruption and went on, "It is based on an improvement over the Mercator chart, sir, and navigators have used it to advantage for the past hundred years."

"I'm aware of the damned theory, devil take it!" Lucas

exclaimed. "It's how you propose to put it into practice that concerns me."

Red continued to keep a firm rein on his temper. "I intended to make southing until we attain the forty-eighth degree of south latitude. Then I shall set course for Prince Edward Islands, in forty-six degrees twenty-three minutes of south latitude, and—"

"It will be infernally cold that far south," Lucas objected sourly.

"We shall save close on five days on passage. If we followed the old track via St. Paul and Amsterdam islands, it would not be appreciably warmer, and the winds would not be so reliable. Captain Keppel, sir, logged runs of between two hundred and seventy and two hundred and ninety miles between the Prince Edward and Kerguelen islands in the *Dido,*" Red explained with studied patience. "Then, of course, he headed for the Sunda Straits, whereas we shall aim to pick up the prevailing westerly wind in order to make port at Fremantle on the Swan River, and—"

"The sooner Their Lordships abandon sail in favor of steam throughout the Royal Navy, the better it will be from every conceivable angle—speed, efficiency, accuracy, and, yes, damme, comfort!" Captain Lucas asserted. His tone still sour and somewhat hectoring, he added, "Have some thought for the comfort of your passengers, Broome. My wife and her maid are not accustomed to extremes of cold or rough weather, you must realize. In any case, from what I've heard of him, your revered Captain Keppel had a reputation for carrying on, no matter what damage his ships suffered or how many spars were carried away."

Red controlled the impulse to offer an indignant denial. Instead, he answered with restraint, "Captain Keppel is the finest seaman I ever served with, sir. And I dare to suggest that it will be a long time before steam supersedes sail in the service."

Benjamin Lucas glared at him, his rheumy, red-rimmed eyes bright with malice. "We shall see, Commander Broome, we shall see!" He sneezed, robbed momentarily of the powers of speech by the paroxysm of coughing that followed. "Devil take it!" he managed at last. "It's already cold

enough to cause my lungs to be affected, and there's always
the danger of icebergs in these waters. Have you taken account of that?"

"Yes, sir, I have. I—"

"Then think of my wife. Must she keep to her cabin for the
next week or more?"

It was *his* cabin in which Mrs. Lucas would be confined,
Red reflected ruefully. As a matter of courtesy and because
Lucas outranked him, he had given up his spacious stern
night cabin to his passengers, and Lucas had taken possession also of the day cabin, in which normally Red himself
would have taken his meals and entertained his officers,
leaving him to mess with them in the cramped gun room on
the deck below. Or . . . He sighed. If he wished to be
alone, as the captain of a ship had at times perforce to be, he
had to make do with a lieutenant's berth and his food served
on a tray, because there was no headroom for his steward to
stand upright to wait on him.

Lucas's wife, Dora, was in fact his bride. The engineer
captain had married only a few weeks before the *Galah* sailed
for Australia. Possibly, Red suspected, his decision to take a
wife had been dictated by the nature of the appointment he
had been given, which was that of superintendent of the new
naval dockyard in Sydney. A house went with the appointment, as Red had learned from his father, who had filled the
post temporarily during the dockyard's construction, and
Captain Lucas clearly was anticipating a social need that a
bachelor officer would not find easy to fulfill.

Yet . . . Red eyed the stout, red-faced little man in his ill-
fitting uniform with a frown. Lucas was in his fifties, his bride
an extremely pretty girl of just eighteen, and, not for the first
time, Red found himself wondering what could have induced Dora Lucas to accept as her husband one who could
more easily have been her father.

Poverty, perhaps? A desire to better herself? She had
hinted at straitened circumstances when she had talked of
her home to him, Red recalled, evoking his sympathy when
she had mentioned a widowed mother and three sisters of
marriageable age who, like herself, lacked dowries and the
right social contacts. Lucas must have seemed a good pros-

pect, and certainly he had indulged his new wife in the matter of clothes and jewels. He had provided her with a maid, who was traveling with them, and in the *Galah*'s hold were stowed innumerable packing cases and hampers containing furnishings for the official residence they were to occupy when they reached Sydney.

The girl would not lack material advantages from the marriage, but even so, they were an oddly matched pair, and there appeared to be little affection between them. Benjamin Lucas was a domineering fellow; the seamen had already felt the lash of his tongue on several occasions, and he seemed to treat Dora with studied contempt and even with harshness that bordered on cruelty when, as all too frequently happened, the unfortunate girl did anything to displease him. And that, Red thought, was due to ignorance rather than to intent; she had never mixed in naval circles before and was quite unversed in the etiquette. When they had first come on board, she had innocently sought to establish relations with the entire ship's company, including him and his officers, and had earned a public rebuke from her husband when she had requested that young Lieutenant Francis De Lancey might—as she had put it—"show her round the ship."

Francis was a chivalrous youngster, and he had later waxed indignant on the bride's behalf, thereby incurring her husband's severe disapproval and a rebuke more public than that administered to the girl herself—and certainly as undeserved.

Becoming aware that Lucas was still arguing about his decision to set course for the Prince Edward island group, Red made an effort to appear at least to be listening to the diatribe, though he took little of it in.

There had been many matters on which they had disagreed since the *Galah* had left Sheerness, he thought wearily; it was wiser not to listen. Their first clash had come when off the west coast of Africa he had gone to the assistance of the *Leopard* frigate in chase of a slaver. By heading her off, he had enabled the British frigate to bring the chase to a successful conclusion, thus saving the lives of the slaver's unhappy cargo, but Lucas had accused him of dereliction of duty and, damn his eyes, threatened him with court-martial!

But despite his post rank, the engineer captain had never commanded a ship at sea, least of all a sailing ship. The very nature of his previous training and employment had kept him in dockyards ashore, his sea service restricted to the testing of newly fitted steam engines on paddle-wheelers and steam-screw ships.

He— Red stiffened, hearing the mention of Francis De Lancey's name. Jolted out of his simulated indifference, he gave Lucas his full attention and heard him say censoriously, "It has come to my notice, Commander Broome, that Lieutenant De Lancey is paying unwelcome attention to my wife."

"Did I hear you correctly, sir?" Red countered indignantly. "Are you suggesting that Lieutenant De Lancey has given offense to Mrs. Lucas?"

"I am indeed, sir," Lucas returned icily. "I'm aware that you permit more license to your junior officers than I consider desirable. In this instance, however, I trust that it is not too much to ask that you will point out the error of his ways to Lieutenant De Lancey. See to it, please, that he does not offend again."

"I'm quite sure, sir, that if Mr. De Lancey has acted in any way improperly, it was unintentional," Red protested. "I'll speak to him, of course, but—"

"He is a relative of yours, is he not, Commander?" Lucas asked, the implication deliberately offensive.

"He is a cousin." Once again Red had to force himself to reply calmly to the taunt.

"And your first lieutenant—Timothy Broome—is also a cousin? He bears the same surname as yourself, so perhaps he is your brother?"

"He is also a cousin, sir. His father is my uncle, Mr. William Broome, who owns a sheep station on the Murray River in Victoria." Irritated despite his determination not to allow Lucas to provoke him, Red added, "Before you accuse me of nepotism, I should perhaps explain that Their Lordships specifically instructed me to choose my officers from those with Australian connections. My ship, sir, is to remain in

Australian waters for two years. My ship's company are all volunteers, and a number of them have connections with the colony."

Evidently deciding that he had said enough, Captain Lucas adopted a more placatory tone. "Ah, I see," he conceded. "I had not realized that your instructions came from the Admiralty. A wise precaution on Their Lordships' part, in view of the nature of the colony. I—" He caught his breath, and a second paroxysm of coughing prevented further speech. It was so violent that he had to clutch the edge of the table in order to remain upright, gesturing with his free hand to his mouth.

Red summoned the gun room steward and sent him scurrying for brandy. Then, taking Lucas by the arm, he assisted him to a chair. The steward returned with dispatch, and Red took the brandy glass from the tray the man proffered and set it down by Lucas's hand.

"Drink this, sir," he invited. "That's an unpleasant cough you have, and no mistake."

Lucas did not answer, but he accepted the invitation, sipping the strong, neat spirit appreciatively. Red seized the opportunity to excuse himself. After donning his thick watch coat, he took his cap from its hook on the gun room bulkhead and ascended to the deck through the after hatchway. A swift glance aloft showed him that the corvette was still running briskly before the steady northwesterly wind. In these latitudes the wind seemed always to be steady, so that for hours—and even days—on end there was no necessity to take in or reset sail. Keppel, Red recalled gratefully, had taught him this, and for all of Captain Benjamin Lucas's objections, Red intended to carry on until he sighted the Prince Edward Islands.

True, it was cold; already the rigging was ice-encrusted, with the watch on deck, heavily muffled against the prevailing chill, hacking at the frozen shrouds to clear them, their breath misting about their heads as they worked. Timothy Broome was on watch. He drew himself up as he saw his commander emerge from the hatchway and, making to retreat to the lee side of the deck, was halted by Red's raised hand.

Tim was twenty-three; short and muscular like his father, he, too, had inherited their grandmother's red hair and—from what Red had heard of her from his parents—also her courage and stoicism. They had never previously served together and, until Tim had joined the *Galah*, had met infrequently. It had come as a surprise, Red remembered, when he had been told by his father that young Tim had elected to desert the family sheep farm and enroll in the Naval College, with a view to following his own example and making a career in the Royal Navy. There were two other sons—younger than Tim—to work the vast holding on the Murray River, so his family had raised no objection, and Tim appeared to have no regrets concerning his choice of a career. By an odd coincidence he, too, had served under Captain Keppel and had been one of the *Maeander*'s midshipmen when Keppel had visited Hobart and Sydney, as well as China and Sarawak, two years earlier. He had, however, been transferred to the survey ship *Rattlesnake* following the death of her captain and had thus been back in England when the *Rattlesnake* paid off and the *Galah* was fitting out.

Looking at him now, Red was glad that his young cousin had been available. Tim was an excellent first lieutenant, and — He smiled to himself, recalling one of Captain Lucas's disparaging remarks on the subject of naval discipline. Like all of Henry Keppel's protégés, Tim knew how to run a happy and efficient ship, without the floggings Lucas appeared to consider indispensable, even when the ship's company were eager volunteers.

Tim made his formal report with commendable brevity, and then, a worried frown creasing his smooth young brow, he gestured to two figures standing together by the taffrail. Both were as heavily muffled as the seamen of the watch, and for a moment Red failed to identify them; but when he did so, a whistle of dismay escaped his lips.

"Oh, for heaven's sweet sake, is that Mrs. Lucas? And Francis with her, damn it?"

"Yes, sir, I'm afraid it is," Tim confirmed. "And I wasn't sure what I ought to do about them. But I knew Captain Lucas was with you in the gun room, and . . . well, when

the cat's away. Dora said she had to have a breath of air
and—"

"Dora, Mr. Broome?" Red exclaimed sharply.

His first lieutenant flushed. "She told us to call her that,
sir. I'm sorry—it just slipped out."

"Better keep a guard on your tongue," Red cautioned.
"Such familiarity with the wife of a superior officer is liable
to be misunderstood. All right, carry on. I'll deal with Mr. De
Lancey."

He had intended simply to order Francis De Lancey below, but as he strode across to the couple, he glimpsed the
after hatch cover being lifted. Guessing that Captain Lucas
had come in search of his wife, he quickened his pace and
said crisply, "Up to the mainmast head with you, Mr. De
Lancey—look lively!"

"The—the mainmast head, sir?" De Lancey echoed, his
mouth agape.

"That was what I said," Red snapped. "Cut along, lad!"

Dora Lucas had turned, startled, at the sound of his voice,
but she grasped the situation as swiftly as he had. Young De
Lancey went reluctantly to obey the unexpected order, his
booted feet slipping on the ice-covered shrouds, and, ignoring his predicament, Dora turned to Red with a coquettish
smile. Despite the assault of the wind, and although her
small face was pinched with cold, she still contrived to look
singularly beautiful. She tucked her arm beneath Red's, urging him in the direction of the hatchway and continuing to
smile up at him with beguiling innocence.

Seemingly oblivious of the temperature on the open deck,
Captain Lucas had not waited to put on a coat, and he was
coughing thickly when he emerged from the hatch, clinging
to the coaming and unable to find the strength to close the
cover behind him.

To Red's relief, his wife ran to him at once, her arms
outheld and her face the picture of frightened concern.

"Oh, my dearest, you shouldn't have come on deck!" she
exclaimed. "You will make your chest worse, you know you
will. And I would not have been long, truly. I just came up
for a breath of fresh air and—" She turned to indicate Red,

her very blue eyes pleading with him not to deny her claim. "The captain was kind enough to offer me his escort. I—"

Lucas, when he could control his coughing, replied ungraciously. He flashed Red a glance in which suspicion was mingled with puzzlement, and then, evidently deciding that there was nothing to be gained by remaining on deck any longer, he bade Dora go below, his tone brusque, and himself followed her without another word. Tim Broome hastened up to close the hatch cover, and jerking his head up toward the mainmast head, where Francis De Lancey was now uncomfortably huddled, he asked with a hint of a smile, "How long do you wish Mr. De Lancey to, er, to remain on lookout, sir?"

Red did not echo his smile. "Let him stay there till the watch changes. The master is your relief, is he not? Tell Mr. De Lancey to report to me then, as soon as he's back on deck."

"Aye, aye, sir," the first lieutenant acknowledged formally. After a moment's hesitation he added, "I thought you carried off a deuced awkward situation pretty well, sir, if I may be permitted to say so."

"You may not," Red retorted irritably. "Be damned to you, Mr. Broome!" In truth, he thought ruefully, all he had done was to arouse Captain Lucas's suspicions on his own account, and with close on to three months of their passage still to be completed, that was not the outcome he desired. Francis De Lancey was a witless young idiot and should have had more sense than to go looking for trouble. But perhaps another twenty minutes at the masthead would cool his ardor. . . . Red sighed. He waited only to check the log and the course he had set, then went below, where back in the gun room he drank two cups of scalding coffee with the *Galah*'s elderly sailing master, Fergus Macrae, who like himself was an exponent of the great-circle sailing theory and well versed in the advantages to be gained from its practice.

In consequence, Red was in a less irritable mood than he had been earlier, and when Francis De Lancey, shivering and with chattering teeth, reported to him, Red made him drink coffee laced with rum and then dispatched him to his cabin to change his clothing. But when the young lieutenant returned, he kept him standing, subjecting him to a silent scrutiny that clearly had the effect of unnerving him.

The boy was just twenty-one, and he had been commissioned only on appointment to the *Galah*, all his previous sea service having been as a midshipman, most of it in ships of the line, where he had been too junior to be entrusted with the command of a watch. He was a slim, nice-looking young man, with his mother's fair coloring and round features and his father's height. His sister, Magdalen, Judge De Lancey's only daughter, was deeply attached to him, Red knew; that had been one of the reasons why he had gone to considerable trouble to have the boy appointed to his ship.

Red had courted Magdalen De Lancey when she had been in England, eighteen months before, but it had been a brief and hurried courtship, cut short when his shore leave had ended. In the hope that their friendship might be renewed on more favorable terms upon his return to Sydney, he had endeavored to please her by arranging to bring her adored young brother back with him. That end would not be achieved if he permitted Francis to get himself into a scrape with Dora Lucas, so . . . Red eyed the boy sternly.

"Captain Lucas has complained to me concerning the attention you appear to be paying to his wife, Mr. De Lancey," he accused. "He has informed me that your attentions are unwelcome. He—"

"They're not unwelcome," Francis interrupted indignantly. "I assure you they're not, sir. Dora is miserable. Captain Lucas treats her quite abominably. You've seen it for yourself, sir, and heard the way he addresses her. I wouldn't talk to a dog, sir, the way he talks to her—and in public, too. Privately, she says—"

Red cut him short. "I wish to hear no more, Mr. De Lancey," he said angrily. "Captain Lucas is a post captain, and he's my superior officer, as well as yours. He and Mrs. Lucas are passengers on board this ship, and I expect my officers to treat them as such, with proper respect."

"But, sir," Francis De Lancey protested, his sense of outrage outweighing discretion, "Dora Lucas is—sir, she's barely eighteen, a—a defenseless child, and he's an old man. And a cruel bully, with no consideration for her feelings. He

struck her this morning, sir—struck her across the face with
his fist. That was what she was telling me when we met on
deck, and I know it was true because her mouth was badly
bruised. You must have noticed it when you spoke to her,
sir?"

Red shook his head. "I did not. But even if I had, it is no
affair of mine and certainly none of yours, Mr. De Lancey."
This was worse, much worse than he had expected, Red
thought. Francis's chivalrous instincts would land him in
serious trouble if he were allowed to indulge them during
what remained of the voyage. Dora Lucas was not blameless,
of course. It was evident that she had made a strong play for
the boy's sympathy, regardless of the consequences; but her
husband would have to deal with her—he could not. Francis
was his concern; the lad could not be permitted to put his
whole career in jeopardy, and he would be doing so if he
aroused Lucas's jealousy by appearing to be a serious threat
to his marriage.

"For the Lord's sake, Francis," he said, changing tack and
adopting a less accusing tone, "you must control your personal feelings, whatever they are. This young woman is married to Captain Lucas—she chose to marry him, even though
he is so much older than she is."

"But she goes in mortal terror of him, sir," Francis persisted wretchedly. "She did not know what he was like until
she married him. Truly, sir, Captain Lucas does treat her
abominably. I—I can't stand by and watch what he's doing to
her without—without lifting a finger to help her. She's
begged for my help, sir. Nothing drastic—Dora wouldn't ask
that of me. All she wants is to talk to me occasionally, to—to
confide in me. Surely that's not too much to ask of me, is it,
sir?"

Red was tempted to tell him that it was a damned sight too
much in the circumstances, but he restrained the impulse
and tried once more to reason with the boy. For Magdalen's
sake, he thought, he must make the young idiot understand
in what a hopeless position he was placing himself. Lucas
would not spare him if things got out of hand. But his arguments fell on deaf ears.

"I—sir, I *love* her," Francis asserted. "I can't help myself.

I've fallen in love with her. And she—sir, Dora feels the same way about me, I swear she does!"

For God's sake, Red thought, now thoroughly alarmed, Captain Lucas's complaint had not been as lacking in substance as he had supposed when the man had made it. Had he himself been blind, in that he had noticed nothing alarming until Lucas had drawn his attention to it? For how long could Dora Lucas have been meeting Francis in secret without his being the wiser? Tim, as his first lieutenant, would surely have given him warning, if he had been aware of what had been going on. On board a ship of the *Galah*'s size, little happened without most of the ship's company's being aware of it, and—oh, the devil take it! Clandestine meetings between an officer and one of the passengers would not, *could* not have gone unobserved—least of all when the passenger was female and the wife of an officer of Lucas's rank.

Red asked the question, controlling his longing to shout it, and Francis De Lancey hung his head, scarlet beneath the tan of his cheeks. "We've only been meeting alone the past few days, sir. But of course I've seen Dora, watched her, and —and talked to her in company. I—sir, I loved her almost from the first moment I set eyes on her. But I said nothing, not until she—she came to me. On deck it was, sir. I'd had the middle watch, and Mr. Broome relieved me. The captain was asleep, and that was the first time. A week after we left Rio. I'd been ashore with them, sir, and—oh, I suppose she sensed my feelings for her then. And she told me how unhappy she was."

Red frowned. "*Where* have you been meeting?" He hesitated, uncertain what to believe. "Not on deck, surely? You would have been seen."

Francis De Lancey's color deepened and spread. Reluctantly he shook his head. "No, sir. In—in my cabin. I— nothing improper took place, sir, I give you my word. Dora only wanted to talk. We were discreet, sir."

Red's patience evaporated. "Discreet?" he thundered furiously. "Why, you damned young fool, that was not discreet —it was madness! I cannot possibly permit such a state of affairs to continue. Mr. De Lancey, I require your solemn word that it will not. You must give me your assurance that

you will neither seek nor speak to Mrs. Lucas save in public
and in the course of your duties. Is that understood?"

De Lancey faced him defiantly. "I cannot do that, sir. Dora
is—she's counting on me. I can't let her down."

Red's mouth tightened to a stern, angry line. "Then," he
said coldly, "I shall have no alternative but to have you
placed under arrest, with a guard outside your cabin . . .
and I shall have to log my action. In all probability that
would lead to your having to face trial by court-martial when
we reach Sydney. I don't imagine your father would be best
pleased, do you, in view of his eminent position in the judi-
ciary?"

All the color drained from the boy's cheeks. Clearly the
prospect of incurring his father's displeasure was an alarming one, for after a momentary hesitation, Francis swallowed
hard and blurted out miserably, "I'll give you my word, sir. I
haven't any choice, have I?"

"No," Red confirmed gravely. "I'm afraid you don't. Very
well, Mr. De Lancey, that will be all. You may carry on."

Francis drew himself to attention. He started to give the
accustomed acknowledgment when, carrying with ill-timed
clarity from the deck above—from his day cabin, Red's mind
registered—a woman's frightened screams brought both
their heads around.

"Oh, God!" Francis whispered, his voice choked. "That
unmitigated swine is hurting poor, sweet Dora! He has no
right, I—sir, I must withdraw my promise. I cannot stand by
and let him mistreat her, I—you can't ask that of me, sir.
You—"

"I can and I have, Mr. De Lancey!" Red roared. "You will
go to your cabin forthwith and remain there. I am in command of this ship, and I will take whatever action is expedient, do you hear me?"

"Are you placing me in arrest, sir?" Francis asked sullenly.

"I trust that will not be necessary. I shall give you twenty-
four hours to come to your senses. You'll be relieved of your
duties for that time, and to ensure that you obey my order, I
shall post a guard outside the cabin you occupy, but I shall
not log you. Right—on your way. Jump to it, boy!"

Francis De Lancey hesitated and then obeyed him, his

expression still sullen. Red waited, listening, but the screams
were not repeated. He went on deck, to find the master on
watch. Macrae looked at him in apprehensive question;
clearly he, too, had heard the screams, carried above the
thrum of the wind on the taut canvas of the *Galah*'s sails and
the creaking of her timbers, for the day cabin bulkhead was
thin. But he acknowledged without comment the order to
place a seaman on guard outside De Lancey's cabin and gave
Red a sympathetic nod as he watched him make for Captain
Lucas's quarters.

The captain himself responded to Red's knock. He said
curtly, not waiting to be asked for an explanation, "My wife
had the misfortune to slip and fall, but there's no harm done.
She has retired to her cot to rest and recover from the, er,
the shock. I'm sorry you were disturbed, Captain Broome."

It was the first time, Red realized wryly, that Benjamin
Lucas had given him the courtesy title of captain, and the
man looked more than a little shaken. But he said no more,
simply turned his back and retreated into the day cabin, the
screen door closing behind him. Of Dora Lucas there was
neither sight nor sound.

Red did not see her during the twenty-four hours he had
allowed Francis De Lancey to come to his senses. He took
the absent lieutenant's watch himself and, when the weather
worsened, spent virtually all his time on deck, while the
Galah wallowed in mountainous seas and the gale-force wind
compelled him to reduce sail and put two men on the wheel.
But his beautiful Symondite corvette proved herself weath-
erly beyond even her commander's high expectations, and
when the wind at last abated, Red noted with satisfaction in
his log that in one day's run she had equaled Keppel's record, in the *Dido*, of 299 miles—including twelve knots for
eight successive hours before a slashing northeasterly wind.

The Prince Edward Islands came in sight on the weather
bow, snowcapped and inhospitable. The *Galah* passed to the
southward of them, and Red set her course to the northeast,
finding the wind he had hoped for. It was still cold, but they
encountered no pack ice, and the icy squalls were intermit-
tent. At the height of one, the chain bowsprit shroud carried
away, leaving the bowsprit badly sprung. Fortunately the

wind was driving aft, so that the damage was swiftly repaired without the need to alter course. Francis De Lancey, who had returned to duty, was on watch. As if eager to make amends for his previous conduct, he toiled tirelessly with the party of seamen detailed for the task of repair, and to such good effect that Red complimented him on his efforts.

The young watchkeeper flushed but said nothing, and Red began to hope that he had learned his lesson and would give no further trouble where Mrs. Lucas was concerned.

By the time the island of St. Paul was sighted, in the thirty-eighth degree of south latitude, the temperature had risen perceptibly, and the wind, though still strong, steadied and became less blustery. Leaving the deck in the master's reliable charge, Red went below at last, intending to make up for some of the sleep he had lost.

Wearily he stripped off his sodden outer clothing and scraped the two-day growth of stubble from his cheeks, and after draining the beaker of hot rum and chocolate his steward brought him, he thankfully flung himself onto his bunk and composed himself for sleep. For all of Captain Lucas's glum forecasts, the *Galah* would make an exceptionally fast passage to Western Australia, and, he thought, as he drifted into blissful unconsciousness, he was well pleased with her.

CHAPTER VII

It seemed only a few minutes after he had dozed off that Red's peace was rudely shattered. A hand was shaking him by the shoulder, and a woman's voice, distraught and tearful, was calling him by name, beseeching him to waken. He struggled to sit up, blinking in the light from the open porthole, his brain still misted by sleep but every instinct rebelling against the unexpected presence of Captain Lucas's young wife in his cabin.

"For the Lord's sake, ma'am!" he protested wrathfully. "You should not have sought me out here. You could have sent for me. Any of my officers or my steward would have conveyed a message, and I'd have come to you."

Dora Lucas's tears were redoubled. Red, scrambling awkwardly from his bunk, saw that her small, piquant face was blotched and swollen, her blue eyes red-rimmed from weeping. Reluctant to touch her, lest the gesture be misinterpreted, he waved in the direction of the bunk he had vacated, and as he hastily donned his shirt and trousers, he gruffly urged her to sit down.

"Try to compose yourself, Mrs. Lucas, and then tell me what is wrong and how I can be of service to you."

She sat down on the disordered bunk, trembling visibly. "I did try to—to send for you," she defended. "But they told me you were too occupied on deck to—to be disturbed. And Francis De Lancey said there was some damage that—"

"You've been seeing Lieutenant De Lancey?" Red accused, a sharp edge to his voice.

Dora Lucas ignored the question; indeed, Red thought, she did not appear to hear it.

"It's my—my husband, Captain Lucas," she told him, her voice high-pitched and agitated. "He—he is seriously ill, and

I don't know what to do for him. He has a high fever, Captain Broome, and at—at times he doesn't talk lucidly. And I've had no experience of—of sick people, none at all. I simply don't know how to help him."

"We carry a surgeon's mate," Red reminded her. "Jonathan Brown. Did you not send for him?"

Dora wrung her hands despairingly. "Oh, yes, I did. He gave a purge and put leeches on the captain's chest. . . ." She shuddered. "Dreadful, hateful things! But he's worse, and he's rambling more. I—oh, please, will you come and see for yourself the state he's in? I—I'm afraid that he—that he may die, Captain Broome."

Red gave his assent with some reluctance. Although conscientious, the young surgeon's mate was, Red knew, inexperienced and more accustomed to treating seamen's injuries and ills than serious medical conditions, such as that Captain Lucas's wife had described. His fears were confirmed when, a few minutes later, he entered the cabin in which the sick man lay and saw young Brown attempting unsuccessfully to administer a dose to his patient.

Lucas looked terrible. His normally plump red face was devoid of color, his lips were blue, and his breathing was rasping and labored, and despite Brown's attempts to lift him, he seemed to lack the strength even to raise his head. The contents of the cup the surgeon's mate was holding to his lips spilled onto his chest as he turned his head away, and with an angry gasp he motioned the youngster to leave him be.

"Get out," he managed. "I want no more of your—your blasted purges! Let me alone."

Brown reddened in embarrassment as he realized that his captain had witnessed his failure, and he said defensively, "I'm sorry, sir. I've done the best I can for the captain, sir, but he's not responding. He has a very high temperature—his lungs seem to be badly affected. I think it's pneumonia, sir, and I doubt if there's much more I can do. I've been sitting with him most of the night, but"—he shrugged helplessly—"he keeps ordering me to let him alone."

"Very well, Mr. Brown," Red returned. "Go and get your head down. I'll stay with him for a while." Dora Lucas, he

observed without surprise, had not come with him into the
cabin, and he added, "On your way below tell my steward to
make up a berth for Mrs. Lucas in the day cabin, and see if
you can persuade her to take some rest, too. I imagine she
needs it."

"That's been done already, sir," the surgeon's mate
claimed innocently. "Madam's not been in here, save just to
look in once or twice and ask how the captain was faring. She
told me she was afraid he might be infectious, you see, sir."

Again Red felt no surprise. "All right, carry on, Mr.
Brown," he said dismissively, and when Brown had taken
himself off, he drew up the chair the surgeon's mate had
occupied and settled down to his vigil. Lucas, if aware of his
presence, gave no sign of it but lapsed into a fitful doze, his
breathing a little easier. After half an hour, however, he
began to shiver violently. Red piled blankets from the other
cot on top of him and, after summoning his steward, dispatched him for heated stone bed-warmers and, as an afterthought, for a hot rum toddy. When this was brought, he
managed with some difficulty to assist Lucas to swallow most
of it, adding quinine from Brown's medical stores to the
draft. The sick man slept again, and—whether from the effect of the quinine or the rum Red could not be sure—his
sleep was more peaceful, and the violent shivering had
ceased.

Tim came to report a calm sea and a steady, following
wind, and Red instructed him to cram on sail.

"We've got to make Perth with all possible speed, so that
Captain Lucas can receive skilled medical attention onshore," he said. In a lowered voice he added, "He's seriously
ill, Tim, and there's little enough that either young Brown or
I can hope to do to cure him. He'll have to be transferred to
the hospital as soon as we make port at Fremantle."

"And Mrs. Lucas, sir?" Tim Broome questioned.

"She'll have to go ashore with him."

"Yes, sir, I see. Er—" Tim hesitated and then asked uncertainly, "Will you wait to take them on to Sydney, sir?"

"No, I can't." Red was conscious of relief as he said it.
"It'll be weeks before Captain Lucas is fit to continue his
passage—if he recovers. My orders are to relieve the *Falcon*

in Port Jackson so that she can proceed home to pay off. We cannot delay our sailing for more than a few days."

The young first lieutenant nodded his understanding. He again hesitated, for longer this time, as if wrestling with his conscience, and Red, sensing his indecision, urged sharply, "If you've anything to tell me, out with it, Mr. Broome! I presume it concerns Mr. De Lancey."

"Yes, sir, it does. I'm not one to tell tales out of school, but—" He broke off, coloring unhappily.

"They've been meeting, no doubt," Red finished for him. "He and Mrs. Lucas, whilst her husband has been confined to this cabin?"

"I'm afraid so, sir. Francis is a damned young fool, and I told him as much. But it's not entirely his fault. Dora—Mrs. Lucas, I mean, has—well, sir, she's been seeking him out. And Francis is sorry for her, he says. She's worried about Captain Lucas, and—"

"And she has a fine way of showing it," Red put in dryly. He glanced pityingly at the huddled form on the cot, half-hidden under the thick pile of blankets, and wondered what had possessed Benjamin Lucas to marry a girl of half his age. But if they both went ashore in the Western Australian capital, that should be an end to the problem, so far as he himself —and Francis De Lancey—were concerned.

He went into technical matters with Tim before dismissing him. "Ask Mr. Macrae to report to me, if you please, before he relieves you of the deck. And put Mr. De Lancey on watch and watch; that will give him less time to devote to consoling Mrs. Lucas, will it not? Very well, Mr. Broome, carry on please. And send for me if necessary."

"Aye, aye, sir," Tim Broome acknowledged.

Red resumed his vigil. Twice he went on deck, to find all well and the corvette making thirteen knots under a press of sail. The master gave him an estimate of thirty hours to Fremantle, provided the wind held, and satisfied that all that was possible was being done to hasten their arrival, Red returned to Captain Lucas's side. The sick man slept fitfully, waking once, just before midnight, with another alarming attack of shivering, which culminated in convulsions. Red held him as still as he could and, in desperation, administered a second large dose of quinine, having to force it between Lucas's chattering teeth.

Young Brown came, still sleepy-eyed and devoid of any ideas for treatment beyond those he had already attempted. Red enlisted his aid to change the sweat-drenched bedding and refill the bed-warmers and then dismissed him, with orders to remain within call, and, to his intense relief, Captain Lucas finally fell into a deep and restful sleep. He himself dozed off, despite the discomfort of the wooden chair and the ship's at times violent motion, but he wakened at once when, in an almost normal voice, the sick man called his name.

"Sir—" He was instantly alert. "Is there anything I can do for you?"

"I am dying, Captain Broome, am I not?" Lucas's tone was unexpectedly firm, bereft of its usual querulousness. He cut short Red's ineffectual denial. "For God's sake, man, d'you think I don't know?"

"We shall make Fremantle in less than twenty-four hours, sir. Then we can transfer you to the hospital, where you'll be able to receive proper medical attention. You—"

Lucas went on as if he had not spoken. "It is my wife who concerns me. She is young and will be left without means or protection in the event of my death. I am aware of the regard she has for you, Captain Broome. She's made no secret of it."

Taken by surprise, Red stiffened. "I assure you, Captain Lucas, I have done nothing to merit your wife's regard," he began. "Indeed, sir, I—"

"Spare me your excuses," Lucas begged wearily. "She has told me that she has sought your company since this infernal lung affliction laid me low. It's understandable; she is lonely and anxious, is she not? Don't worry—I know you to be a man of honor, Broome. You'll not take advantage of my—my unhappy situation, I'm aware of that. But Dora is a very beautiful young woman, and you are considerably younger than I am, alas! And you are unmarried."

He tried to sit up, and Red, dismayed by the implication of his words, swallowed hard before putting an arm about his shoulders and lifting him into a sitting position. Dora Lucas, he could only suppose, must have lied to her unfortunate husband in order to deceive him and—the devil take her for an unprincipled minx!—in order to hide the truth from him concerning her continued clandestine meetings with young Francis De Lancey. . . .

Unable to restrain his annoyance, he started to protest, but Captain Lucas again ignored the interruption.

"I do not hold anything against you, believe me," he stated earnestly. "You have, I assure you, my complete trust. But I am soon to face my Divine Maker, Broome, and I speak with that most daunting prospect before me. I must make my peace— No, permit me to have my say, for my strength is failing. And I have a favor to ask of you on my poor wife's account."

His voice, which had been quite strong and firm, was indeed becoming fainter. Red bit back the denial he had been about to repeat and grasped the older man's trembling hand.

"Of course, sir," he responded reluctantly. "I will do anything I can, anything within my power to help."

"I want you to give me your assurance that should I no longer be able to care for my wife, you will do so. I—" Lucas's voice was a whisper now, vibrant with emotion. "She is a lovely young creature, Broome—you do not need me to tell you that, do you?"

"No, sir," Red acknowledged with restraint. "But you are a good deal better than you were. I truly think that you have passed the crisis. And as I told you, we shall make port within the next twenty-four hours at most. With proper medical care, sir, there's no reason to suppose that you won't make a full recovery."

"Perhaps," Lucas conceded without conviction. "But if I do not live to make port in Australia, will you take my wife— my widow—on to Sydney with you and see to it that she does not want? You have a family there, have you not—parents?"

"Yes, I have. I—"

"There will be a pension, Captain Broome, but that will take time to come through. And I have money, enough for immediate needs, in my valise. But—" A fit of harsh, dry coughing silenced him, and filled with pity, Red lowered the sick man back onto his pillows once again and pulled the blankets over him.

"Try to sleep, sir," he advised kindly. "We'll get you to Australia, never fear."

By noon the following day the *Galah* came to anchor in Gage's Road, off the port of Fremantle, Western Australia, and Jonathan Brown came on deck to report that Captain Lucas had passed a restful night.

"His fever's abated, sir," the young surgeon's mate added in answer to Red's question. "But I'll be thankful to see him placed under the care of a qualified physician all the same. Will you be arranging for the captain to be transferred to hospital ashore, sir?"

"That I shall, Mr. Brown," Red assured him feelingly, "just as soon as the port health authorities come on board. The pilot has gone ashore, and he promised to warn them that we need assistance."

From the *Galah*'s quarterdeck the distant shore seemed to offer little sign of activity. Its most striking feature was a squat, round tower situated on a high promontory, with a signal flag flying from it. Scattered about its foot were clusters of limestone cottages and a few larger buildings, which appeared to be warehouses and customs sheds, and a wharf, with about a dozen whaling vessels tied up in an irregular line close by.

But, to Red's intense relief, Captain Lucas's transfer was arranged with a minimum of delay. The port medical officer, an efficient middle-aged naval surgeon, cut through the usual formalities on learning the sick man's rank, and within half an hour Lucas was being lowered, muffled in blankets, in a bo'sun's chair, to a waiting boat. He was fully conscious, and when he bade Red farewell, he did so with fulsome gratitude.

"I fancy I owe you my life, Captain Broome," he said huskily, "and I shall not forget it. I understand I'm to be taken upriver by boat to Perth—there is no hospital here for officers and, it appears, no carriage road from the port. This, after the colony has been in existence for more than twenty years!"

His tone, for all his frail state, was critical, and Red offered no comment. The sick man went on, now sounding faintly querulous. "I shall be grateful, Broome, if you will make arrangements for my wife and her maid to follow me ashore as soon as possible, and for Mrs. Lucas's accommodation in, er, the town of Perth."

"That is already in hand, sir," Red was able to tell him. "Lieutenant Martin—the port medical officer, sir, who is accompanying you—has promised to make the necessary arrangements for Mrs. Lucas. He will send a boat to convey her to Perth first thing tomorrow."

The boat was duly sent the following day. It carried a naval crew under the command of a young midshipman. The Lucases' personal baggage was winched into it, the maid waited at the entryport, but Dora Lucas did not appear until a good half hour later. When she did so, it was in tears, her reluctance to leave the ship manifest in each unwilling step she took across the *Galah*'s deck.

To Red, standing stiffly by the entryport, she said accusingly, "You are in haste to rid yourself of me, are you not, Captain Broome?"

"At your husband's behest, Mrs. Lucas," Red returned without contrition. His glance went to Francis De Lancey. The boy had requested permission to accompany Dora Lucas and see her safely installed in the accommodation arranged for her, and Red, against his better judgment, had given his consent, but— His mouth tightened. The fourteen-mile passage up the Swan River to the capital would take about two hours, and Captain Lucas's wife had a right to expect one of his officers to escort her. Perhaps he was tempting Providence by allowing Francis to be that officer.

"You understand that you are to return on board as soon as you have escorted Mrs. Lucas to Perth, Mr. De Lancey?" he added, his tone curt.

De Lancey eyed him sullenly and nodded. "I understand, sir, yes."

"Then see that you do so," Red bade him. "The boat's waiting. Carry on, if you please."

De Lancey obeyed him. He assisted Dora Lucas down the accommodation ladder and into the boat, then seated himself beside her in the sternsheets, his arm resting for a moment protectively about her shoulders. It was as swiftly withdrawn; the boat put off and headed for the shore, and for all his efforts to hide his feelings, Red found himself exchanging smiles with both his first lieutenant and the master.

"A ship of war, sir," Fergus Macrae observed dryly, "is no place for females." He waved a blunt-fingered hand in the direction of Dora Lucas's maid, who had followed her mistress into the boat, demurely enough, and was now perched somewhat precariously on one of the captain's tin trunks. "A sober, well-behaved lass, that one, but for all that, she's leaving a few would-be suitors behind her, including one of my mates. Is it your intention to grant shore leave to the ship's company, sir?"

Red frowned. "They've done damned well, all of them. I don't see how I can deprive them of a run ashore." He sighed. "Do you, Mr. Macrae?"

"Quite so, sir," the master agreed, but he echoed Red's sigh. "I just hope we'll get 'em all back. For how long do you anticipate staying here, if I may make so bold as to ask?"

"No longer than I can help," Red returned uncompromisingly. He looked at Tim, his expression relaxing. "No longer than it will take the first lieutenant to fit a new bowsprit and for me to call on the Governor and visit some of my old haunts in Perth."

Tim's brows rose. "Of course," he said. "I'd clean forgotten that you were here with Admiral Stirling, sir. You'll see a good many changes, no doubt."

In fact, Red decided, when he disembarked from the longboat in the township of Perth later that day, the changes were fewer and less noticeable than he had anticipated. True, the town had grown, but in a somewhat haphazard fashion. Its small, unpretentious houses, each possessing a large garden, bore a closer resemblance to an English village than to the capital city of a new and thriving state. The houses were elegant enough, built in Georgian style, mostly with two stories and pillared entrance porches, their bow windows and timbered fronts adding to the pleasant impression they made. With the exception of St. George's Terrace —a wide boulevard, lined with lilac trees—the streets were narrow and only partially paved, and many of the smaller dwellings and shops had thatched roofs, their gardens devoted to the growing of vegetables and fruit, so that they appeared more practical than ornamental.

Henry Reveley had been the colony's civil engineer and architect in Governor Stirling's day, Red recalled; Stirling, on his way out in the *Parmelia* in '29, had picked him up at the Cape and offered him the appointment, and Reveley had built the Round House tower, as a jail, in Fremantle, as well as the courthouse, numerous administrative offices, and Government House, here in the capital. But none had found favor with either Sir James Stirling or the settlers, and poor Reveley had left for home ten years later.

The *Perth Gazette* had described his Government House as "having more the appearance of a lunatic asylum than of the residence of Her Majesty's representative." Red smiled to himself as he reached the end of St. George's Terrace and caught his first sight of the offending edifice. He had departed from the colony before its completion, but one of the Governor's aides had written to him about it, his description less flattering even than that of the *Gazette*'s editor, if that were possible.

At first sight, however, Red did not find the building displeasing. Like the houses that neighbored it, the Governor's official residence was in the classical Georgian style, with a columned portico at the entrance and rows of leaded windows lining both its lower and upper stories. What seemed to be later additions, in the form of single-story wings, detracted from the original symmetry of Reveley's design, and the spacious garden looked, to Red's eyes, a trifle untidy, although the fruit trees growing there were laden with fragrant blossoms, and the view across the river was enchanting.

He rang the bell at the front door, intending merely to sign the visitors' book and await an official summons; but before he could do so, a small gray-haired woman, casually attired in a gingham dress and a drooping sunbonnet, came from the garden to meet him. She had a boy of about eight or nine with her, to whom she relinquished the basket of vegetables she had been carrying, and having introduced

herself as the Governor's wife, she politely asked Red his
business.

"You are a naval officer, of course—I can see that—but are
you, by any chance, from the newly arrived Queen's ship?
Because if you are, Captain Fitzgerald is most anxious to see
you."

Red removed his uniform cap and bowed, warmed by her
friendly smile and lack of formality. "Yes, ma'am," he confirmed. "My name is Broome, and I am in command of Her
Majesty's ship *Galah*, presently lying in the Gage's Road
anchorage."

"Then come in, do, Captain Broome," the Governor's
lady invited. She touched the boy's shoulder, her smile including him. "Charlie dear, run and tell Papa, would you
please, that Captain Broome is waiting to see him. And then
tell Mrs. Maclusky that there will be one extra for luncheon.
You will stay to lunch with us, will you not, Captain?"

"I shall be delighted, ma'am, if it is not putting you to too
much trouble," Red acknowledged.

"Oh, no, certainly not," Mrs. Fitzgerald assured him. "We
keep open house here. And my husband, as I expect you
know, was in the service. We do not have many naval vessels
calling here. He will welcome you with open arms." She
gestured to a door at the far end of the entrance hall,
through which her sturdy young son had vanished, still
clutching his basket of vegetables. "He's in the room we call
the library, although I'm sorry to say it contains very few
books. Do go in, Captain Broome. Charlie will have told his
father that you are here."

The Governor, Captain Charles Fitzgerald, proved as
friendly and talkative as his wife. He was in his late fifties and
had, Red knew, served in the Royal Navy for thirty years
before being appointed first as Governor of the Gambia and
then, almost three years ago, of Western Australia. He had a
hearty laugh and a ready sense of humor, but Red sensed the
bluff manner concealed a shrewd brain and considerable
ability. He listened attentively to Red's report, questioned
him minutely about his passage, and then said, regarding
him with quizzical eyes, "I understand old Benjy Lucas took

passage with you? And that you had to send him ashore to our hospital as a matter of some urgency. Is he seriously ill?"

Red inclined his head gravely. "He was, sir, yes, whilst we were at sea. But I think he was over the worst when we reached here. I'm hopeful that, given skilled medical attention, which we could not provide, he will pull through. His wife came ashore to be with him—this morning, sir. Lieutenant Martin made arrangements for her to be accommodated at the hospital, I believe." He hesitated. "You know Captain Lucas, sir?"

"Indeed I do," the Governor asserted. His round, tanned face twisted into a wry little grimace. "He was engineer of the *Snake*, the infernal, belching paddle-wheeler in which Their Lordships saw fit to convey me to the Gambia! In all honesty, Captain Broome, I cannot claim that our relationship was particularly cordial—like you, I am a sailing ship man. But you say he's married?"

"Yes, sir, he is. Er—" Again Red hesitated, uncertain of how much it was prudent to reveal of Captain Lucas's matrimonial affairs. Finally, he said, without expression, "His wife is considerably younger than the captain, sir."

"The old dog! I shouldn't have thought it of him. But—" Fitzgerald sighed. "I must pay him a visit. I'd intended to do so today, but my damned paperwork caught up with me. And my wife must call on Mrs. Lucas, too. You say young Surgeon Martin has arranged for her to be accommodated at the hospital?"

"Yes, sir. At the captain's wish, I believe."

"Well, she will be on hand to visit him," the Governor concluded. "And talking of visits, Broome, I should greatly appreciate the opportunity to visit your ship. She's a Symondite corvette, is she not?"

"Indeed she is, sir. Eighteen guns and a crew of a hundred and sixty." Red went into detail, then added, "A visit from Your Excellency will be most welcome."

"Good." Governor Fitzgerald was beaming. "Then tomorrow forenoon, if that suits you. It will give me a chance to exercise my barge crew. Ludicrous, isn't it, that after all these years our communication with the port of Fremantle is still by oared boat on the river? Just as it was in Admiral

Stirling's day! God knows, I'm no lover of steam-powered vessels, but a small paddle-wheeler would be a great convenience. I've repeatedly pleaded with Her Majesty's Colonial Office for funds with which to purchase one, but"—his smile faded—"they are of the opinion that a road would cost less. The trouble is that I've no labor to put to work on it."

"But the colony has applied for convicts to be transported here, has it not, sir?" Red asked with some surprise.

Fitzgerald nodded. "A retrograde step, in the eyes of Sir Charles Fitzroy and the wealthy squatters of New South Wales, I concede. But a necessary, even a vital one for us, Broome. From the outset this colony has been held back by lack of labor. Western Australia's population—in an area almost as large as Russia—is only about five thousand, and it's going down, damme, not up. The initial error, which has since been compounded, was in the type of settlers who were permitted to come out here. They had to be free and possessed of means, and those who proposed to purchase land and farm it were required to bring indentured laborers with them. And so they did, most of them. But with land officially priced at one pound sterling an acre and wages unavoidably high, it wasn't long before the laborers deserted their employers and bought farms for themselves."

With a profound sigh the Governor rose to his feet and started to pace the room, quoting prices, the losses incurred by the sandalwood trade, and a disastrous fall in the price of wool, which, at sixpence a pound, scarcely sufficed to pay the wages of a shepherd.

"When I took office, in February of '49, Broome, I found this colony in a state of depression, stagnation, and despair. We held a crisis meeting, at which it was almost unanimously decided to petition the Secretary of State, Earl Grey, for the establishment of a regular penal settlement. It was authorized by an order-in-council, but to date we have received only two shiploads of convicts, although more have been promised. The first transport, the Indiaman *Scindian*, with seventy-five male convicts on board, made the passage in eighty-eight days and arrived here before word reached us that they were coming! In consequence, the first public work they undertook was the building of a jail in which to accom-

modate them . . . and it is not finished yet. We have a most
industrious young engineer in charge of the work—Harry
Wray, of the Royal Engineers—but we still lack skilled labor.
And our damned Fremantle road has to wait until cottages
for the prison staff are completed and a roof and a second
story are added to the prison itself."

Captain Fitzgerald halted, coming to a standstill facing
Red. "Forgive me, Captain Broome, for airing so many of
my grievances, but"—his smile returned—"it is a relief to
get them off my chest, to a sympathetic listener."

"I was here in '29, with Governor Stirling, sir," Red told
him, "and I served for a year on his staff. So I have some idea
of the problems you have had to face."

"Then you are a sympathetic listener indeed!" The Governor's smile widened. "That calls for a drink, I fancy, before we are summoned to partake of the invariable roast
mutton at luncheon." He crossed to a cupboard and
brought out a decanter and glasses. When two glasses were
filled, he raised his in solemn salute. "To the colony of
Western Australia—may it make progress at last, by the efforts of those men who come out here in chains! Damme, Sir
Charles Fitzroy can say what he likes—without the felons
shipped out in their thousands to Port Jackson, *his* colony
would not be where it is today! And neither would Victoria,
for all Mr. Latrobe's clamor for independent statehood! And
be damned to the editor of the *Inquirer*, who has opposed me
at every turn!"

A soft knock on the door heralded Mrs. Fitzgerald. Enter-
ing the bookless library, she bestowed an affectionate kiss on
her husband's cheek and took the empty glass from his hand.
"Luncheon is served, my dearest," she told him. "And I feel
sure that poor Captain Broome has heard enough of our
troubles for one day. So let us confine our luncheon conversation to the good things, shall we? *I* shall not mention the
damage white ants have done to this house or the fact that
the roof leaks. Instead"—she reached out a hand to take
Red's, her smile courageously cheerful—"we will count our
blessings, starting with the success Mr. Barrett-Lennard has
made of his vineyard. And—oh, yes, we are giving an eve-

ning rout here tomorrow, Captain Broome, to which you
and your officers are most cordially invited."

She led the way into a small, somewhat shabbily furnished
dining room and waved Red to a chair. True to her promise,
she kept the conversation on an optimistic note throughout
a substantial and well-cooked meal and, on learning that the
Governor intended to pay a visit to the *Galah* the following
day, eagerly begged to be allowed to accompany him.

"We shall be honored, Mrs. Fitzgerald," Red assured her.
"And perhaps your son Charlie might care to inspect my
ship also."

"You can have no idea what you are letting yourself in for,
Captain Broome," the Governor warned with a boyish grin.
"But provided Eleanora promises to control him, then thank
you, we shall all three of us look forward to calling on you
and your ship's company tomorrow forenoon."

The meal over, Red took his leave. He called at the small
civil hospital to inquire for Captain Lucas and was told that
the sick man was holding his own.

"I don't know for how long you intend to remain here,
Captain Broome," the principal medical officer said, "but
your passenger is in for a long convalescence, I'm afraid. His
health is likely to cause concern for two or three weeks yet."

Red hid his relief at this news. He paid a brief visit to
Captain Lucas, finding him comfortably installed in an up-
per-story room, with a view across the Swan River and with
few complaints regarding the treatment he was receiving. Of
Dora Lucas, however, there was no sign, but Red was not
unduly worried until, upon his return aboard the *Galah*, Tim
Broome informed him glumly that Francis De Lancey was
still absent.

"He's sent no word, sir," the young first lieutenant grumbled. More cheerfully he added, "Our repairs are completed; we'll be able to sail whenever you wish, sir."

Red nodded his approval. "Well done, Tim. I'll aim to sail
the day after tomorrow, then, if we get all our men back.
Tomorrow, though, we're to have an official visit by the
Governor and his lady, so I'll be obliged if you will do what
you can to make ready for their reception."

"It's short notice, sir," Tim demurred, "and with one

watch ashore, but—I'll do my best. The Governor's a post captain, isn't he?"

"He is—but a very human one, so don't worry." Red clapped a hand on the younger man's shoulder. "And his wife is charming. You will have the opportunity to make their acquaintance socially tomorrow evening. We are invited to a rout at Government House."

Despite the short notice and Tim's foreboding, the viceregal visit was an unqualified success. Captain Fitzgerald, his son Charlie skipping eagerly at his heels, made a lengthy inspection and, when it was over, offered congratulations, which, Red sensed, were at once sincere and a trifle envious.

"I never commanded a Symondite," he admitted. "But, damme, I wish I'd had the good fortune to do so! You are to be commended, Captain Broome—she's a fine ship, with a first-rate ship's company."

Apart, Red thought bitterly, from a missing second lieutenant and five seamen of the port watch, who would have to be rounded up before he could sail. But he accepted the Governor's compliment gratefully, and after entertaining his guests to luncheon in his newly reclaimed day cabin, he ordered the side party to muster, and Captain Fitzgerald, with his wife and son, was piped into his barge with due ceremony.

"Do not forget our party this evening, Captain Broome," Mrs. Fitzgerald said as Red bowed over her hand. "We are expecting you and any officers you can spare from their duties. And I think you will enjoy yourselves. We have a capital pianist—a Mr. Hamersley—who plays most lively waltzes and quadrilles. There is, alas, not much space for dancing, and there won't be until our new reception room is built. But perhaps when you next call here, it will be finished and in use."

It was a valiant hope, Red thought, liking the warm-hearted, friendly woman even more than before. She had much to contend with, but her spirit was unquenchable.

That evening the longboat took him upriver, accompanied by Tim and two midshipmen, in addition to a small party under the master-at-arms, whom he had detailed to round up the missing men of the port watch. He had issued no instructions as to Francis De Lancey, intending himself to seek for him at the hospital when the Government House rout came to an end; but Tim was angry, and as they disembarked at the boat jetty, Red said reassuringly, "Don't worry—enjoy yourself, for God's sake! Our sailing's been notified. The lad will leave it till the last minute, I don't doubt, but he'll be back before we sail."

"I wish I could share your optimism, sir," Tim answered explosively. "But I can't. The infernal young fool has got it badly, and I'm afraid the lady in question has no conscience."

His mood lightened, to Red's relief, when they were ushered into the Government House drawing room, to find assembled there a lively party of some sixty or seventy members of the colony's society, among them a bevy of pretty, smiling young girls and the promised Mr. Hamersley performing at the piano with considerable skill. Dancing was on a carpeted floor and somewhat restricted by the number crowding onto it, but Tim and the two midshipmen swiftly found themselves partners, and leaving them to do the best they could in the limited space, Red went in search of his hostess.

He found her presiding anxiously over a lavish buffet set out in the adjoining anteroom, and she greeted him warmly. "I'm delighted that you could join us, Captain Broome. Alas, the turtle soup I had planned to serve seems to have gone off, or am I imagining it? Be so good as to taste it for me, would you please?" She offered him a spoonful, her plump, charming face flushed and apprehensive.

Red did as she had requested and shook his head regretfully. "I fear you will not be able to serve this, ma'am. It has turned high."

"I was afraid it had. Thank you, Captain Broome." In response to her gesture a servant whisked away the soup tureen, and Eleanora Fitzgerald gave vent to a sigh of exasperation. "One tries, but in this climate it is not easy. Well, I can only hope that our guests will be satisfied with the fruit cup; at least we have fruit of every kind here, and it grows prodigiously. Oh—" She broke off, clicking her tongue apologetically. "I almost forgot. There is a letter for you, deliv-

ered from New South Wales in the mail. Communications
between here and Sydney are few and far between, so it was
fortunate that the letter arrived before you sailed. If you will
come into the library, Captain Broome . . . my husband
left it on his desk to give to you as soon as you arrived."

Red followed her across the darkened hall, conscious of a
feeling of elation. The letter, he told himself, must be from
his mother, who, it seemed, had received the news of his
impending arrival in time to write to welcome him. Mrs.
Fitzgerald put the sealed envelope into his hand and
thoughtfully turned up the oil lamp burning on the Governor's desk.

"I will leave you to read it," she told him. "Come back and
join in the dancing when you are ready."

The library door closed behind her, and Red drew up a
chair and broke the seal on his letter. It was in his father's
handwriting, he realized, as he spread the thin sheet out on
the desk and moved the lamp closer to enable him to read it.
And unlike his mother's lengthy, news-filled epistles, which
usually crisscrossed the pages and occupied the margins
also, this letter was very short.

My dear Red,

It is with great sadness that I write in the hope that
this will find you in Perth. I have to tell you that your
dear mother and my beloved wife died peacefully in her
sleep a week ago, after a long and painful illness, which
she bore with courage and fortitude.

Your letter, with news that you anticipated sailing for
this colony in command of H.M.S. *Galah*, was delivered
the day before she departed this life and gave her immense joy. Your name was on her lips when the dear,
sweet soul breathed her last. I was with her and can
vouch for this.

Without seeking to reproach you for your long absence, I cannot pretend, for her dear sake, that I do not
regret it.

May you have fair winds and make port here very
soon.

The letter was signed "Your affectionate father, Justin Broome." And, Red saw, the writing suddenly blurred and almost indecipherable, the date was April 10, 1851.

He sat for a long time, the letter crushed between his two big hands, trying to control the grief that filled him and regretting, even more bitterly than his father, the fact that he had stayed away for so long. And for what reason? The furtherance of his career? The fulfillment of his own ambitions? He drew a long, unhappy breath and then braced himself as the door opened and Tim came in. The first lieutenant was pale with barely suppressed anger, and he jerked his head in the direction of the improvised ballroom. "Sir, he's here. De Lancey's here, with Mrs. Lucas! And he has the infernal nerve to *dance* with her, if you please!"

Red forced his mind back to the present. "Then we'd best deal with him, hadn't we? Come with me, Tim, and get hold of one of the mids, just in case he tries to make a scene. He can wait in the longboat, under guard, until we're able to take our leave."

Suddenly Red, too, was filled with a cold anger, and his rage increased when, with Tim beside him, he returned to the ballroom and saw with what intimacy the couple were waltzing. Dora Lucas's arms were about her partner's neck, and he, his eyes fixed on her face, looked as if he were aware of no one else in the crowded room. He whirled her around, his body pressed against hers, and he seemed more surprised than alarmed when Red grasped him, none too gently, by the shoulder and brought him to a halt.

"You are absent without leave, Mr. De Lancey," he stated icily. "And we are sailing in the morning. I am placing you under arrest. You will go with the first lieutenant and Mr. Vibart at once and wait, in the charge of the master-at-arms, in the longboat, until I have made my farewells to His Excellency the Governor and can join you. You—"

Dora Lucas cut him short. She objected shrilly, "No—no . . . you cannot take him away! He is staying here, don't you understand? He is quitting the navy and your wretched ship! He promised me—didn't you, Francis?"

Young Francis De Lancey started to echo her protest, his blue eyes bright with defiance. Heads turned, people near at hand stopped dancing in order to listen to what was being said, and, determined at all costs to avoid a scandal for Captain Lucas's sake, Red ordered in a low voice, "Carry on, Mr. Broome—you know what to do." He turned to Dora Lucas, and waiting only until he saw that Tim Broome and Midshipman Vibart had ranged themselves purposefully on either side of their prisoner, he suggested politely, "You have not yet been introduced to Their Excellencies, I take it, ma'am?"

The girl reddened resentfully and drew back a white-gloved hand as if to strike him, but anticipating her intention, Red captured the hand and, drawing her into his arms, swiftly danced her across the room to where Mrs. Fitzgerald was seated with some of the older ladies.

"May I present Mrs. Lucas, Your Excellency?" he requested formally. "The wife of Captain Benjamin Lucas, ma'am, who has the misfortune to be confined in hospital as the result of a severe illness."

With predictable sensitivity, Mrs. Fitzgerald rose to the occasion, motioning Dora to a seat at her side, and the angry girl, compelled to recognize defeat, gave Red a venomous glance and sat down sullenly beside her hostess.

Thankfully, Red took his leave, his last sight of Dora Lucas on the Governor's arm, being escorted gallantly back to the dance floor, a fixed smile on her flushed and angry face.

The return passage downriver in the longboat was a silent one. The missing seamen had been rounded up, and Francis sat, with his head in his hands, saying nothing. Red, his heart heavy, thought of the letter he had received from his father and was glad enough of the silence, his conscience tormenting him anew.

Back on board his command, however, there were other, practical matters to occupy his time and his thoughts, and he flung himself into the preparations for departure, shutting his mind to all else. Soon after first light, the *Galah* hove up her anchors and, under topsails and main course, ran for the open sea before a brisk offshore breeze that carried her swiftly out of sight of Fremantle and the cluster of small white-painted buildings that marked the settlement.

Red set her course southward and ordered Francis De

Lancey on deck to stand his watch. Only then did he go
below and, in the privacy of his day cabin, weep for the
mother whom Fate had ordained that he would not see
again.

Next day, the Great Australian Bight unleashed its fury in
a violent storm, and with the crash of thunder and the
screeching wind in his ears, his conscience gave him ease.
The storm abated after forty-eight anxious hours, and the
Galah once again spread her canvas wings and resumed her
easterly course. Red sought his cot and slept the sleep of the
physically drained. Waking at last, refreshed, he carefully put
his father's letter away and went on deck to find the sun
shining and the sky washed clear of clouds.

CHAPTER VIII

The *Dolphin* swung gently to her anchor in the slight swell, and standing entranced on deck, Mercy Bancroft gazed about her at the calm beauty of New Zealand's Bay of Islands. During the long, leisurely voyage across the Pacific from San Francisco, the *Dolphin*, under the seasoned hand of her owner and master, Claus Van Buren, had called at many picturesque island ports: at Hawaii, which had been the destination of three of the missionary families on board, and at others with such romantic names as Phoenix, Pago Pago, and Tongatapu. But here, on New Zealand's North Island, it seemed to Mercy that she had found paradise.

The last of the missionaries, a young English priest of the Catholic faith, had gone ashore here, accompanied by Claus and escorted by half a score of Maori war canoes, each manned by up to a hundred brown-skinned warriors with hideously tattooed faces. The canoes had surrounded the *Dolphin* even before she had dropped anchor, but Claus, to Mercy's great relief, had assured her that their occupants were friendly. There had been wars, he admitted, pitched battles fought against British settlers and the ships of war sent to protect them, but the missionaries had never been harmed, and now, with New Zealand officially declared an imperial colony, and Captain Grey—elevated to knighthood as Sir George Grey by Queen Victoria—appointed Governor, the fierce Maori tribes and the ever-growing number of settlers were at peace.

As, Mercy thought, they should be, in a place of such unsurpassed loveliness as this. Her gaze took in the vista of rolling hills, their peaks snowcapped in the distance, and the great *kauri* pine trees ringing the shore, their plumed tops dwarfing the squat white-painted dwellings of the little town

of Waitangi—in the Maori language "Weeping Water,"
Claus had told her—where some ten years earlier a treaty
had been signed by the Governor and the tribal chiefs.

Claus had made many voyages to New Zealand—to other
ports and newer settlements in what was known as the Middle Island, as well as to the North Island gulfs and bays. He
was a mine of information concerning the colony's history
from its earliest years, and, Mercy reflected regretfully, she
would gladly have listened to his tales of great Maori chiefs
like Hongi Ika, who had visited England and been received
by King George III, but . . . Luke had cast a damper over
her quest for knowledge.

Luke had grown increasingly impatient as the weeks and
months passed and the *Dolphin*'s course took her to yet another island, where Claus bartered axes and ironware for
copra, pearl shell, sandalwood, and fresh supplies for his
crew.

"The trail will have grown cold," Luke constantly complained. "Jasper Morgan has had too long a start on us. We'll
hear no word of him when we reach Sydney—if we ever do!"

Mercy smothered a sigh. She had never shared Luke's
vengeful zest for the chase, she realized now. Once they had
learned that Jasper Morgan had left San Francisco, she had
never believed that it lay within their power to catch and
bring him to justice. Luke had believed it, of course, and that
had sustained him despite the odds stacked so heavily
against them. He had more reason to continue: the murder
of his brother and that of his two Australian partners
weighed on his mind and fired his stubborn determination
to succeed whatever the cost, while she . . . Mercy repeated her sigh.

Jasper Morgan had wronged her; he had taken cruel advantage of her innocence and her helplessness, but he had
harmed only her pride, her self-esteem. And association
with the missionary families during the long voyage had
restored what he had taken from her. The "men of God," as
Claus always called them, had treated her as a friend and
equal; she had aided them in the care of their children,
talked and prayed with them, and found spiritual peace in
their friendship and liking. Young Father Ignatius—the

priest who had left the ship that morning—had listened to the story of her journey with the wagon train, following her parents' death. He had been appalled by the hardships she had described to him, the strain of the weary journey across swamps and deserts and through the bleak mountain passes to the promised land of California—a journey of more than two thousand miles, covered for the most part at the rate of fifteen miles a day. At the end of her recital, he had given her absolution and, as the others had done, prayed with and for her. Mercy grasped the rail in front of her.

She felt . . . A smile of pure wonder and delight curved her lips as she sought the apt word to describe her present feelings. Renewed, reborn; strong once again in her faith, her lost innocence no longer plaguing her conscience or engendering shame.

Claus, too, had played a major part in her regeneration, she realized. From the outset he had treated her with respect, seeking her company, walking with her on deck when the day's work was done and the ship under reduced sail, and they had talked for hour after hour, as friends talked, of every subject under the sun. She had learned much from Claus Van Buren—about Sydney, about Australia in general, about the islands they had visited and the people who inhabited them, and about the ship, which was his pride and joy.

Luke had benefited from their association also, but— Mercy's smile faded. Initially, Luke had been ready to learn. With time, he had become a competent seaman and, under tuition from both Claus and the *Dolphin*'s mate, he had begun to master the intricacies of navigation, displaying an enthusiasm and an intelligence that had delighted his mentors. But his enthusiasm had waned of late; he went about his duties with more than a hint of sullenness and, when they were alone together, talked of little save Jasper Morgan and the time they were losing as a result of the *Dolphin*'s protracted passage, and the days lost on account of her master's trading activities.

"Captain Van Buren has friends everywhere," he asserted resentfully. "But in order to trade with them, he deems it necessary to visit their homes and their villages, to feast with them and organize races with their canoes. *I* could have bargained for what he has managed thus to obtain at half the cost and in a quarter of the time!''

But without the goodwill, Mercy thought, recalling the reception the Maoris had accorded the *Dolphin*'s master the previous day. A venerable chief, his face tattooed with the record of his daring in battle, a coronet of plumes in his dark hair, and his stocky body wrapped in a feathered cloak, had taken Claus Van Buren into his embrace and, their noses touching, had hailed the new arrival as his son. Later, when the great high-prowed war canoes had departed, Claus had told her that the old chief's name was Kawiti and that he was one of the most revered warriors among the islands' tribes.

"You admire these Maoris, don't you?" she had asked. "Yet are they not can—" She had hesitated over the word, shocked by its hideous implications. "Cannibals? And one of the crew told me they trade in the shrunken heads of their enemies. Is *that* true?"

"Yes," Claus had been forced to concede. "But the missionaries, whom they respect, have converted a great many to Christianity. Such barbaric practices will cease, given time and the influence of the men of God. They are fine, brave people, possessed of great intelligence and a natural nobility of spirit. Their war with the settlers was caused because they were being robbed of their land by unscrupulous white men, who bought great tracts for a few axes and bags of nails. A Maori never sells his land—he only leases it—but the settlers failed to understand this and, of course, claimed ownership in perpetuity, which no Maori could countenance. So they went to war, and they fought on until the British government recognized their just grievances and put them right, insofar as they *could* be put right. Still, many lives were lost on both sides.''

It was hardly a comforting picture Claus had painted for her, Mercy told herself ruefully as she recalled his words. And her first sight of the Maoris had certainly alarmed her, for all their smiling faces when some of them had boarded the *Dolphin* the day before, greeting Claus by name and with evident pleasure at the sight of him. Yet . . . She tensed involuntarily as she watched a procession of war canoes put off from the beach and head toward the anchored ship.

Claus had gone ashore early, and . . . She leaned forward, watching anxiously.

Luke emerged from the forward hatchway and halted beside her, gesturing to the canoes with a thin brown hand. "The captain's coming back. And I reckon—" He broke off, shading his eyes against the glare. "Yes, there's a lady with him, and two young white fellows, can you see? What does that mean, I wonder?"

"Perhaps they are visitors," Mercy suggested uncertainly. "Friends of his, Luke. Old Saleh said he knew the folk at the mission."

"Maybe they are passengers," Luke amended. "There are trunks and some pieces of baggage in two of the canoes. Maybe they're taking passage with us to Sydney." His eyes lit with a hopeful gleam. "I hope to God they are! And I hope they're in a hurry to reach their destination. I couldn't endure another long delay while Van Buren barters with the natives. Jasper Morgan could be to hell and gone before we ever clap eyes on Sydney Town!"

Mercy had been cherishing the hope of what the seamen called a run ashore—Claus had taken her ashore at most of their other ports of call, and she had greatly enjoyed the experience—but, out of loyalty to Luke and their mission, she did not say so, fearing to anger him. Her face clouded over, however, as she watched the canoes approach.

They moved swiftly, skimming over the calm blue water, the strong arms of their paddlers moving in time to a melodious chant, and now, as they came nearer, Mercy was able to see that the white woman, seated at Claus's side in the foremost canoe, was slim and gray-haired. She was soberly clad, in a dark skirt topped by a starched white blouse, and she was hatless, her small, comely face deeply tanned, as if she spent a good deal of her time in the open air or . . . even with the Maoris in their canoes. Certainly she appeared to have chosen to travel thus, for the ship's longboat, in which Claus had left the *Dolphin,* was bringing up the rear of the procession, the sweating seamen at the oars unable to keep pace with the Maoris' skillful paddling.

Of the two young white men Luke had mentioned, Mercy could see little more than the tops of their heads, bleached to corn-colored fairness by the sun and standing out, in vivid contrast, against the dark heads of the warriors surrounding them.

"The captain," Luke asserted, a faint edge to his voice, "seems very friendly with the white lady. Well, maybe she is nearer his age than you are, Mercy."

Mercy flushed resentfully. Of late Luke had been critical of her friendship with the *Dolphin*'s master, and it was true that Claus Van Buren had begun to show her marked attention, seeking her company to walk the deck in the warm moonlit evenings and—after the departure of the ship's other passengers—inviting her to eat with him in the clipper's beautifully furnished stern cabin. Her own cabin, on the same deck, was an officer's cabin, whereas Luke, as a deckhand, bunked with the rest of the crew in the fo'c'sle and messed with them. Of course the two of them had kept up the initial deception they had practiced; to the *Dolphin*'s company, as well as to her master, they were brother and sister, and neither had felt it advisable or necessary to confess to the truth—save, Mercy reminded herself guiltily, to Father Ignatius. She had told *him* the truth, when she had made her confession. . . . She looked up into Luke's face, swallowing her brief resentment.

It was to Luke she owed her presence here. He, by working as a seaman, had paid her passage; he had not abandoned her in San Francisco, as she had feared he might, but had taken her with him, accepting responsibility for her when it would have been easier for him to continue alone in pursuit of Jasper Morgan. He had never professed to love her, never so much as laid a hand on her during the days of their enforced intimacy, but . . . they were linked together by an unspoken bond, stronger, perhaps, than love.

And Claus Van Buren . . . Mercy's smooth brow furrowed. Claus was not, in any way she could recognize, paying court to her. He had never attempted to embrace her, had done no more than offer her his arm when they took their walks on deck together, and they were still on formal terms of address. She was Miss Mercy, and he, of course, was Captain Van Buren, and yet . . . Her color deepened and spread as she met Luke's searching gaze and heard him say in an accusing tone, "You go out of your way to encourage the captain's interest, don't you?"

"No," Mercy denied indignantly. "That I do not! How can you say such a thing?"

Luke shrugged. "Because it's true. And if you want my opinion, I reckon he's showing a pretty strong interest. Or I did until—" He pointed to the canoe. "Until now. Maybe the white lady is the object of his affections." The mate came on deck, shouting to the watch to bestir themselves and rig a winch for hauling the baggage inboard, and Luke hastened to obey him.

The mate, a grizzled veteran of many voyages who, on his own admission, had come out to New South Wales as a convict, touched his faded peak cap and gave Mercy a warm smile. "Passengers, miss," he told her, confirming Luke's guess. "The lady is a Mrs. Yates, from the mission station at Rangihowa—the wife of the doctor there, Simon Yates. Them Maoris think the sun shines out o' the both of 'em, an' that's a fact. I been wonderin', ever since I seen Mrs. Yates in the canoe, what could cause her to want to leave here an' go to Sydney. She an' the doctor, why, they've been at Rangihowa ever since old Reverend Marsden died, an' that's a fair while ago."

"Reverend Marsden?" Mercy echoed, puzzled. "Who was he, Mr. Deacon?"

"It'd take me a month o' Sundays to tell you, miss," Silas Deacon demurred. "But 'twas him as set up the first Christian mission here, an' all the Maori tribes acted like he was the Lord God Almighty Hisself. He had 'em in the palm o' his hand, did old Marsden. Do anything for the old feller, they would, even the chiefs. Funny thing, though—he wasn't well liked by his own kind back in New South Wales. They—" He broke off to yell an order to one of the seamen, and turned back to Mercy apologetically. " 'Scuse me, missy, if you please—I got to make sure that baggage gets safely aboard. You ask Mrs. Yates 'bout Mr. Marsden an' the early days—she'll tell you. An' about the war, too. An ugly business, that were, 'specially when they had to bring the sojers in."

He shambled off, conscientiously testing the winch that

Luke and the others had rigged, and the canoes came along-side. Mercy waited, watching with interest as Claus Van Buren assisted the new arrivals on board, giving Mrs. Yates his two outstretched hands and solicitously helping her rise from her seat in the stern of the canoe and ascend to the *Dolphin*'s entryport. The two young white men followed, and Mercy saw that both were young indeed, the elder perhaps twenty, the other one a few years his junior—smiling, good-looking lads, of imposing physique, clad as simply and prac-tically as their mother.

Summoned to the captain's cabin ten minutes later, Mercy was introduced to Emily Yates and her sons, and to the two Maori chiefs who had accompanied them.

"Mrs. Yates is not coming with us to Sydney," Claus Van Buren explained. He gestured to Saleh, who was standing expectantly behind a table set out with silver tea things and sweetmeats. "She will just take a cup of tea with us and then go back to the mission with Chief Te Marire, whose little daughter is ill and under treatment by the good Dr. Yates. But Rob and Simon . . ." His tone, to Mercy's surprise, became openly critical, even angry, as he went on. "They are bent on joining the new gold rush, which, it seems, is taking place in the Blue Mountains of New South Wales. Or so rumor has it."

"It's true, Captain Van Buren," the elder boy insisted. "Not just a rumor. A man named Hargraves—fresh from the Californian goldfields—discovered gold in the Macquarie River area. And Governor Fitzroy has recognized his claim; he's appointed Hargraves gold commissioner for the colony. And we—" He glanced a trifle shamefacedly at his mother. "Simon and I don't want to spend the rest of our lives here as penniless settlers. We aim to make our fortunes in Austra-lia."

Claus seemed, for a moment, disposed to argue, but Mrs. Yates, accepting a cup of tea from Saleh with a charming smile, put in quietly, "It *is* a fact, Claus. We learned of it in an official announcement by our Governor, Sir George Grey. Since then we have read the reports in the Sydney newspa-pers, which reached us quite recently, and nothing Dr. Yates or I can say will dissuade these two sons of ours from leaving

here to join the gold seekers." She went into detail, but
Mercy scarcely heard what she was saying.

Luke, she thought unhappily, would be wildly elated when
he heard the news, for it would surely mean that Jasper
Morgan was unlikely to have left Australia. If gold had indeed been found there, Morgan would go in search of it, and
perhaps— She drew in her breath sharply. Perhaps, in spite
of the long delay, there was a chance that Luke would manage to pick up his trail and attempt to exact retribution for
his brother's murder. Suddenly she was afraid, dreading the
possible outcome—although, she reminded herself, that had
been the purpose of their voyage halfway across the world,
even if she had been lulled into losing sight of it.

She looked at Claus Van Buren and heard him assert, his
tone still edged with a controlled anger, "If it resembles in
any particular the Californian gold rush, it will be a disaster
for Australia, Emily! Greed, lawlessness, a vast influx of men
from all corners of the globe . . . Dear heaven, I have come
from San Francisco, and I saw what appalling effect it had
there! The harbor was a wilderness of deserted ships, the
town under vigilante administration. God forbid that Sydney
should suffer a like fate!"

"How could that happen, sir?" Robert Yates protested.
"Surely California was barely settled and San Francisco a
mere fishing village when the gold rush started there. New
South Wales has been settled for what? More than sixty
years, with a strong government—a Governor, a Legislative
Council, and a garrison of imperial troops. And the Royal
Navy, sir."

Claus's anger faded. He looked at the young New Zea-
lander almost sadly and answered with restraint, "You do
not know what greed and the lust for gold can do, Robert."

"We shall not be affected," Robert Yates said, with confidence. Smiling, he laid his hand on his mother's shoulder.
"We were brought up in a God-fearing Christian family. For
both of us, it's an adventure really, nothing more. If we
should be lucky and—what do they call it?—make a strike,
we'll come back here and use our gain to good effect. We'll
buy land and stock and settle down, have no fear, Captain

Van Buren. But I hope you'll not deny us the chance to try
our luck."

His younger brother echoed his plea, and Claus said resignedly, "Very well, if your parents are willing to let you
both go, I will not stand in your way." His glance at Mrs.
Yates was questioning, and Mercy, studying her face,
glimpsed the momentary uncertainty in it. But then she inclined her head.

"They will never rest unless they are given the chance,
Claus," she answered.

"Then so be it," Claus acknowledged. He turned to the
two Maoris, who until now had been politely silent, drinking
tea with all the decorum of British gentlemen, their table
manners impeccable but their expressions somewhat puzzled as they attempted to follow the gist of the conversation
and seemingly found it beyond them. Addressing them both
by name and in their own tongue, Claus quickly set them at
ease, causing them to grin broadly at whatever it was that he
had said. The younger Maori replied at some length with
what appeared to Mercy as derision.

"Chief Tamihana says that there is probably gold here, in
the land of Chief Te Tanewha—the man they call Hook-
nose," Claus translated. "And in the Wairu Valley also. But
he asks what need there is for gold, save to fashion orna-
ments for women? It would be better, he believes, to search
for greenstone, in order to make weapons for warriors in the
Maori tradition."

Mrs. Yates, who had evidently understood the chief's brief
tirade, gave vent to amused laughter and, rising to take her
leave, made a pretense of knocking her sons' heads together
before embracing them tenderly.

"You see, Miss Murphy?" she said to Mercy. "They will
not listen to reason. But perhaps your brother—Luke, is it
not?—perhaps he is in the same state. They will learn only
by experience, I fear."

Both men reddened but remained apparently uncon-
vinced. They accompanied their mother to the entryport
and stood there waving until the small floating procession
was lost to sight in the gathering dusk and the chanting of
the paddlers faded into an oddly poignant silence.

Claus lost no time in getting the *Dolphin* under way. The anchor came up and was catted, sail was swiftly set, and the clipper's sharp bow cut through the iridescent water of the bay as she gathered speed and headed for the open sea. Luke was at the wheel, with Claus standing the watch, and Mercy dined alone in the great cabin, waited on by old Saleh, who seemed in a strangely anxious and uncommunicative mood.

"It is not good that they find gold in the Blue Mountains," he said when Mercy pushed away her plate, shaking her head to his offer of replenishment. "You have seen, as have my master and myself, what evil the quest for easy fortune and enrichment can let loose. Even good and sober men can be driven to near madness by gold fever. They will desert their wives and children, their homes and their employment without a second thought, moved only by the desire for riches. I would not wish to witness such a madness taking root in New South Wales, Miss Mercy."

And neither, Mercy reflected, would she, and she shook her head regretfully.

"How can it be prevented, Saleh?" she asked.

The old Javanese spread his brown hands in a despairing gesture. "There is no way, I greatly fear. The two young men, the sons of Dr. Yates, they are sober enough, are they not? Yet they take passage now with us—working their passage, as does your brother Luke—and they will make all haste to the goldfields as soon as this ship comes to anchor in Sydney Harbor. Luke also, I do not doubt."

"Yes," Mercy conceded. "Luke will go to the fields." But not, she thought, to search for gold . . . Luke had a stronger, more compelling reason, and she shivered involuntarily, remembering what that reason was.

Saleh eyed her searchingly, and she found herself wondering whether the wise old servant had somehow guessed Luke's purpose. But it was unlikely that he could have guessed; neither she nor Luke had ever spoken of what had occurred at Thayer's Bend to anyone on board the *Dolphin*. Even to Father Ignatius she had not revealed Luke's desire for vengeance—that was Luke's affair, she had told herself, not hers, and therefore need not be included in her confession. In any event, Father Ignatius was at his mission station in Nelson by this time or on his way there, and to a priest the secrets of the confessional were inviolate.

She met Saleh's shrewd dark eyes and summoned a smile. "Luke worked in the Sacramento River fields, Saleh," she reminded him. "He will have no difficulty in finding employment in the Australian diggings. Men with his experience will be in demand, I am sure."

"Doubtless that is so," Saleh agreed. He paused, continuing to search her face and seemingly seeking for words. Finally, he asked quietly, "And you, Miss Mercy? What will *you* do when the ship comes to anchor in Sydney Cove?"

Mercy felt the color leap to her cheeks, finding his grave scrutiny disconcerting. "I—I do not know," she confessed uneasily. "I—well, I shall hope to find employment. Work in a shop perhaps, or as a servant. I hadn't thought. I hadn't made any plans. There are settlers with large farms, are there not, outside Sydney? I come of farming stock, and I can milk and make butter and care for goats and poultry."

"My master would give you employment," Saleh suggested. "He has a large establishment in Sydney Town. I am in charge of his household when I do not accompany him to sea, but I am an old man, as you can see, Miss Mercy, not able to perform my duties as I did in the past. And . . ." He hesitated. "My master has no wife."

Mercy stared back at him in startled bewilderment, trying to take in what he was implying. "Why," she ventured, seizing on his last, oddly emphatic statement, "Saleh, why has Captain Van Buren never taken a wife?"

Saleh shrugged his bowed shoulders. "There are many reasons why he has not, Miss Mercy. His birth, his color . . . Sydney society is still divided. The gentlefolk, the officers, and the government officials mix more than they were accustomed to in the early days with those they see as their inferiors. But even now those of convict birth or convict descent bear a stigma, however rich and successful they may have become. And those of mixed birth, such as my master, they also bear a stigma, though it is never put into words. My master is a proud man. He asks for no favors. His Excellency the Governor receives him; he is welcome in all the best houses, but not as a husband for the daughter of one such family as I have described."

"I see," Mercy acknowledged uncertainly. The kind of society he had described was beyond her comprehension, and she started to say so, but Saleh ignored her hesitant interruption.

"Many years ago, when my master was only a little boy, his father, the Major Van Buren, would not permit him to claim his kinship. He was compelled to work as a servant, to wait on his father and his father's wife, and both treated him cruelly." Saleh sighed, his face clouding over, as if the memory were still painful to him, for all the lapse of years. "That is remembered by many of the influential inhabitants of Sydney even today, although my master is one of the wealthiest shipowners in the whole of New South Wales. He is respected and envied by many, yet he is not—how can I put it?—he is not fully accepted. Without a wife at his side, he is lonely, Miss Mercy. He should wed and beget sons to inherit what he has built up. I am often telling him so, but he does not listen to my words."

Mercy said nothing. Saleh's words to her held an underlying meaning, she was now certain, and it was not difficult to guess what that meaning was.

"Was there never any woman whom your master wanted to wed?" she asked, and saw the old man's lined face relax in a smile of unexpected warmth.

"A long time ago," he asserted. "When my master was still just a little boy, a young woman convict was assigned to the service of his father's wife, *Mevrouw* Van Buren. My master loved her, and for all his tender years, he promised that he would take her to wife when he was old enough. He aided her escape from our household, but on their way, the two of them fell in with a man of God by the name of Nathan Cox— the Reverend Nathan Cox. Alice wedded him, and together they opened a school in the township of Windsor. My master became one of their pupils, and he remained with them until he was eighteen." Saleh's smile widened. "He has held the image of that good young woman in his heart throughout the rest of his life, but he has never found any woman to equal Alice Cox. Until—" He leaned forward to grasp Mercy's two hands in his. "Until *you* boarded this ship."

Alarmed by his sudden intensity, Mercy drew back, the color rushing anew to her cheeks, his meaning now abundantly clear. Claus had never hinted, never spoken a word concerning his feelings, yet Luke had insisted that the *Dolphin's* master was—how had he expressed it?—showing a strong interest in her.

Saleh said softly, "You resemble Alice Cox so closely that, when we first saw you, my master and I might have been in the presence of her spirit! We both remarked on it." His brown fingers tightened about hers. "Do not fear, Miss Mercy—you have no cause to fear. My master is a good man, an exceptionally good man. Older than you are, it is true, but if he should ask you to wed him, you would be foolish to refuse."

With that he left her, and Mercy spent an almost sleepless night, a prey to conflicting emotions and strange, alarming dreams, in which Jasper Morgan figured prominently.

Next day, Luke sought her out on deck, and as she had anticipated, he was in a state of eager optimism.

"I've been talking to Rob and Simon Yates," he told her. "For half the night, after I came off watch. If their information is true—and they got it from the Sydney newspapers— the gold rush has begun in New South Wales. Morgan will be there, Mercy, I swear he will! I'm going to team up with the Yates boys, and we'll head for Bathurst and the goldfields as soon as we land. I'll find Morgan wherever he is, if it's the last thing I ever do."

"Have you told the Yates boys of your intentions?" Mercy asked, conscious of a sudden coldness about her heart when Luke shook his head. He talked excitedly about the plans he had made with the two young men from New Zealand, but it was not until she asked him what was to become of her when they reached Sydney that his excitement abated. It was evident that he had given the question no previous thought, and he returned, a trifle sheepishly, that he supposed Captain Van Buren would look after her.

"I'll speak to him about it," he offered, but biting back the temptation to reproach him, Mercy in turn shook her head.

"There will be no need, Luke. I can fend for myself."

She walked away from him, her head held high. That evening, with the coast of New South Wales already in sight as a distant blur on the horizon, Claus Van Buren asked her to become his wife. Mercy accepted his diffident proposal, and for the first time, amid the shadows of the moonlit deck, he took her into his arms and kissed her with yearning tenderness.

"I will love and care for you for as long as I live," he promised softly. "You shall want for nothing, dearest Mercy, I give you my word."

Momentarily, Mercy saw his face through a mist of tears, but then she blinked them back and faced him, smiling.

"I will be a good wife to you," she whispered, and lifted her face to his.

CHAPTER IX

Seated at the far end of the long, polished dining table, Red Broome looked about him at the family from whose midst he had been absent for almost fifteen years . . . indeed, he reflected unhappily, for all his adult life.

Ever since his father had come out in the pilot boat, when the *Galah* had brought to off the Port Jackson Heads, they had been at pains, all of them, not to reproach him or cause him to feel that he was a stranger.

His sister, Jenny—grown into a truly lovely, warmhearted young woman—had been particularly welcoming, seeking to bridge the gulf of years and to spare him their father's censure, and he was grateful to her. But Johnny—the brother with whom, during their childhood, he had been on such close terms of friendship and understanding—Johnny, to his chagrin, held somewhat aloof. On the surface he was polite, but beneath it Red sensed a resentment that could not be put into words.

And their father . . . Red felt his throat tighten as he met Justin Broome's searching blue gaze. They had not talked of his mother's death save for the bare details, which Justin had supplied in a flat, expressionless voice.

"Your letter from Sheerness reached her the evening before she died," he had stated, "and gave her immense pleasure. It meant so much to her to know that you were coming back, Red. I'm only desperately sorry that she did not live long enough to see you again."

And so, Red thought, was he—bitterly sorry. But he had not known; none of them had written to tell him how ill his mother was, and she, poor, sweet soul, no doubt thinking to spare him anxiety, had made no mention of her illness in any of the letters he had received from her before leaving England.

Over luncheon they had talked of the influx of gold seekers now flooding the country and of the ill effects of Edward Hargraves's discovery, which was beginning to leave the sheep farms denuded of labor and even Sydney itself hard put to it to retain the services of those employed in shops and stores and in the shipyards. It was a subject on which, as a newspaperman, Johnny was well informed and concerning which both he and their father waxed indignant.

Red, lacking knowledge, had been content to listen to their views—expressed, in Johnny's case, very strongly—but he had seen the mass of idle shipping in the harbor for himself when he had brought the *Galah* in, and had been astounded at the number of different national flags he had been able to identify. Men were coming, it seemed, from all over the world—a great many of them from America—and word had spread that an even richer field than those near Bathurst and Goulburn had been newly discovered in Victoria, between Melbourne and Port Phillip.

"They'll be off to Port Phillip as soon as they can find vessels to carry them there," Johnny asserted. "They're a fickle bunch, most of them—especially the ones who've been in California. Some, of course—those who got in early—have made fortunes in the Macquarie and Turon valleys, but the men that haven't will be off, and Melbourne Town will be in the state we are here, with half the population quitting their employment for the diggings."

"Cannot the government do anything?" Red inquired when his brother finally lapsed into a glum silence. "What about the new immigrants, those who come out as settlers and agricultural workers on assisted passages? There was talk of them in London, and the whole point of sending them out here under indentures was to provide skilled labor for the farms and sheep stations."

"They are free men, Red," his father answered with a rueful shrug, "not convicts, who can be assigned as laborers. Very few, when they reach here and learn that there is gold to be found, are willing to sign on as agricultural laborers— even when they are offered high wages and homes for their families. A good many of the big landowners are having to slaughter their sheep and cattle for lack of men to tend them. If they contrive to shear their sheep, they cannot transport the wool to market—the ox wagons are being used to carry supplies to the diggings. And you cannot buy a horse in Sydney for love or money."

"Some of the landowners are making money," Johnny put in, a hint of disapproval in his voice. "In fact, they're coining it—among them William Charles Wentworth, whose name will not be unknown to you. One of the major diggings is situated on his land in Frederick's Valley, on the road from Orange to Bathurst. In an area of less than a mile along the creek, there were upward of six hundred men digging and panning when I was there a couple of weeks ago. They were living in conditions of considerable discomfort in bark *gunyas* and canvas tents, and most of them were taking two or three pounds' worth—pounds sterling, that is—of gold a day, they told me. One lucky fellow reckoned that he had procured three hundred pounds' worth of nuggets, unearthed from the clay. The largest weighed nearly four pounds troy. I saw it weighed, and he wasn't exaggerating, I promise you. Some of them weren't so fortunate, but—they simply move on, or if they can't afford the prospecting licenses, which cost thirty shillings a month, they hire themselves out to work for those who've struck it rich."

"Good heavens!" Red exclaimed. "Small wonder labor is at a premium on the sheep farms. And what of Uncle Rick, Father? Has *he* found gold on his land? It's in the Macquarie Valley, isn't it?"

"It is," his father confirmed. "And I'm sure he has. But I haven't heard from him recently, Red."

"Weren't you in partnership with him once?" Red questioned, as memory stirred. "The land at—what is it called?— Pengallon, was it not? It was yours originally, surely?"

"The original grant was mine, but I couldn't afford to stock it," Justin confessed. "And then I let Rick buy me out. I was at sea; I'd no time to farm."

"Dad is not an acquisitive man, Red," Johnny asserted, and now, Red noticed, there was a distinct edge to his voice, although his expression, as he looked across the table at their father, was indulgent, even oddly proud. "He doesn't hanker for wealth or honors or even a just reward for his achievements, do you, sir? But *you're* ambitious, aren't you, brother—ambitious enough to make up for it?"

Red turned to him in hurt surprise, but before he could reply, his sister Jenny rose purposefully to her feet.

"I thought we would take coffee in the drawing room," she announced, slipping her arm into that of her elder brother. "And I confess I've heard enough of the gold rush; it is all anyone seems to talk of these days. I want to hear Red's news, news of England and—oh, Red, what of Timothy, our cousin Timothy? You did not bring him with you, but he's one of your officers, isn't he?"

"Yes," Red agreed. "My first lieutenant. He's visiting the Dawsons. He—"

"And Francis De Lancey?" Jenny persisted.

Red smothered a sigh. Francis had been rebellious and intractable ever since the *Galah* had sailed from Fremantle. He had tried, heaven knew *how* hard he had tried, to bring the boy to his senses, but he had failed dismally. Francis had gone about his duties with sullen indifference, and the day before the ship made port, he had sought an interview to announce that he intended to quit the service at the earliest possible opportunity. He ought, by rights, to have faced trial by court-martial, which would almost certainly have resulted in his being cashiered, but for his family's sake Red had decided to deal leniently with him and, in the hope that his father, Judge De Lancey, might exert some influence over him, had given him leave to visit his family.

"I'm sorry to say that Francis wants to end his naval career," he answered guardedly. "And since I could not prevail on him to change his mind, I told him to go to Newcastle and talk to his father. I—"

"But Judge De Lancey is here," Jenny interrupted. "And Aunt Rachel. They've given up their property at Broadmeadows and are living in the house they used to have, behind the judge's chambers in Macquarie Street. They call it retirement, but they are both very active—Aunt Rachel particularly." She glanced at her father, smiling, and he echoed her smile.

"Active is putting it mildly in your aunt Rachel's case," Justin said. "She breeds bloodstock, Red, and has a fine racing stable outside Parramatta. And His Honor Uncle George is on the Legislative Council still, and he's a prominent member of Mr. Wentworth's Pastoral Association, as well as the Committee for Constitutional Reform."

Red accepted a cup of coffee from Jenny and went to seat himself by the window, which afforded a magnificent view of Rose Bay and the harbor beyond.

"Is Magdalen in Sydney, too?" he asked, his tone deliberately casual, addressing his question to his sister.

Jenny was not deceived. Her smile widened, and she said teasingly, "Indeed she is. I met her at Abigail Dawson's a week ago, and she told me that she had seen you in London. I think you must have made an impression, Red, because she seemed very pleased when I told her that we were expecting you back and in command of your own ship. We talked quite a lot about you, as a matter of fact."

"I trust you sang my praises like a loyal little sister," Red returned, matching her light tone.

"*I* could not, since I have not seen you for such a long time. But Magdalen did. She assured me that you had developed into a most personable young gentleman—a credit to Her Majesty's senior service and to Australia."

"Did she indeed?" Red laughed. "That I find hard to believe."

But, he thought, as he sipped his coffee and lent half an ear to a good-humored disagreement between Johnny and their father on the subject of the proposed new constitution for the colony, Magdalen De Lancey had made a deep and lasting impression on him—there was no denying that. She was a singularly beautiful girl, with her father's dark coloring and her mother's—his aunt Rachel's—slim, graceful figure and the Broome blue eyes. Eyes which, he remembered, with a stirring of the pulses, sparkled entrancingly when she was amused or excited.

He had been in London to attend on Their Lordships of the Admiralty after his ship the *Thetis* had paid off, and he and Magdalen had met—quite by chance—at a ball given at the Portuguese Embassy. It had been a memorable affair,

Red recalled. He had owed his invitation to his old captain, Sir Danvers Mundy—who had been of service to the Portuguese government during the *Thetis*'s time with the Mediterranean Fleet—and the last thing he had expected was that he would meet anyone he knew on so formal an occasion. But . . . he had met Magdalen.

She had come with one of her Scottish uncles, a General Donaldson, who was a distinguished Peninsular veteran. The rest of his party had been elderly like himself, and, Red recalled, when the dancing had started, the general had looked around and then summoned him, with an imperious hand, and invited him to partner Magdalen. The revelation of their names had astonished and delighted them both, and for the remainder of his all-too-short shore leave, Red had called almost daily at the Donaldsons' house in Belgrave Square, willing and eager to act as Magdalen's escort whenever she permitted him the privilege.

The general and his kindly, buxom wife had taken them to race meetings at Ascot, to a regatta on the river at Henley, to the theater, and to a reception given by the general's regiment to commemorate one of the famous battles in the Peninsular campaign in which its laurels had been gained.

If they had had more time, the courtship might well have become serious, but . . . his leave had ended, and he had had to go back to sea, Red remembered regretfully. And Magdalen had left Belgrave Square shortly afterward, to take ship for the return voyage to Sydney, their mutual promises to write thwarted by time and distance and the vagaries of the mail service. He had received one letter from her, posted at the Cape, but it had been brief and noncommittal, and— He met Johnny's gaze and reddened.

"I intend to call on the De Lanceys," he asserted defensively. "Quite apart from wishing to renew my acquaintance with Magdalen, there's the question of Francis's notion to quit the service and my ship. I shall have to talk to his father about it."

Justin caught the last remark and asked gravely, "Does the lad have good reason?"

"He believes he has, Father. It involves a woman, with whom the young idiot has become infatuated," Red admitted. "Frankly I shall not miss him greatly if he does quit; I don't think he is cut out for the service. And I have a very promising young master's mate I can promote to acting rank in his place, but . . ." He shrugged. "I feel I owe it to his family to try to keep him, if it's possible."

"It never pays to keep an officer whose heart isn't in his naval career," Justin observed. He started to fill his pipe, and when it was lit and drawing to his satisfaction, he went on. "You said you had left my successor as superintendent of the naval dockyard in hospital in Perth, Red. Was he seriously ill?"

"Captain Lucas was suffering from a lung infection. He was extremely sick before we made Fremantle, but I think he was over the worst when we put him ashore. The doctors seemed hopeful that he would recover, given time and rest, sir."

"And his wife?"

"She stayed with him." Red was at pains to keep his voice even, but Johnny seized on the brief statement, a gleam in his eyes.

"Was *she* the reason for young De Lancey's desire to quit, Red?" he asked. "Is that why—" His father raised an admonitory hand, and he broke off. "All right, Dad, I'm not trying to pry. I was curious, I admit, because—well, we had Francis's elder brother here—on leave from India—a few months ago. Will De Lancey is an officer in Her Majesty's Third Light Dragoons, and I've seldom met a finer fellow. *His* heart's in the right place, though he was in danger of losing it to our little Jenny." He grinned good-naturedly at his sister, who flushed with embarrassment and set down her cup with a clatter. "But that didn't stop him returning to Calcutta when his furlough was up, did it, Jenny?"

"I gave Will no encouragement," Jenny retorted indignantly. "How can you talk like that?"

Johnny seemed disposed to argue with her, but once again their father's raised hand silenced him, and Jenny, her cheeks still pink, rose and picked up the coffee tray. "I have work to do, even if you haven't," she said pointedly, and made for the door. Johnny jumped to his feet and hastened to hold it open for her, bestowing a swift kiss on her cheek by way of apology before resuming his seat.

"Jenny could have any man in Sydney Town she fancies," he told Red. "But the one she *does* fancy spends all his time up-country at Pengallon—digging for gold, probably. At any rate, we scarcely ever see him."

Red frowned, trying to remember. "Do you mean Rick Tempest's son? He and Katie had a son, did they not?"

Johnny nodded. "Yes, that's right—Edmund Tempest. A nice enough fellow but a mite bucolic in temperament, in my humble opinion. Whereas Will De Lancey—now there's a future general if ever I saw one! He covered himself with glory in the recent war against the Sikhs in the Punjab—mentioned in dispatches, personally commended by Lord Gough, and returning to a captaincy without purchase in the Ninth Lancers. Odd that his brother should be so different, but I suppose women can make fools of us all."

"They should never be permitted to take passage on board ships of war," Justin put in thoughtfully. "Least of all on long voyages—it's asking for trouble." He glanced at Red. "I'm presuming that it was—what's his name?—Captain Lucas's wife with whom young Francis De Lancey became infatuated?"

"Alas, yes," Red confirmed. "They're of an age, she and Francis, and Lucas is old enough to be her father."

He did not enlarge on the subject, and his father did not press him. Instead, Justin said a trifle wearily, "So I shall have to carry on at the dockyard for a while longer. Damme, I'd been looking forward to my retirement!"

"You do not look ready for retirement, sir," Red protested.

"I'm nearing my sixtieth birthday, Red," his father reminded him. "And the dockyard is designed to service and repair steamships. In the very near future, steam will supersede sail in Her Majesty's Navy, and engineers like your Captain Lucas will be better suited to command on Cockatoo Island than I shall. Already they are constructing steam paddlers and stern-wheelers for use in coastal and river work and to deliver mail out here. If the new goldfields in the Port Phillip area prove as rich as forecasts suggest, then we'll have steamers coming out from England and the States in their hundreds. There's a rumor that the *Great Britain* may come out—and she's steam-screw and iron-hulled, and of over three thousand tons burden! Three thousand five hundred, I believe. She's also rigged for sail, it's true, but the writing's on the wall, Red. You are fortunate to be in command of a Symondite like the *Galah*."

"What about the American clipper ships, sir?" Johnny asked. "I interviewed a Yankee gold digger for the paper a few weeks ago, and he told me that he had made the passage from New York to San Francisco, round the Horn, in a clipper designed by a man named Donald McKay at a yard in Boston. He claimed that she made the passage in ninety-seven days, when the best the steamers could achieve was something like a hundred and forty. Is that not proof that steam will not supersede sail for a good many years yet?"

"For long voyages, probably," Justin conceded, "and until coal supplies can be made available at every port of call—if the steamers are to carry cargo, they cannot carry sufficient coal for a long voyage in addition." He sighed. "I don't *want* to see the day come when the sailing vessel gives way to the smoke-belching steamer, the Lord knows—and least of all in the Royal Navy. But for all that, I fear it will come."

They argued amicably for a little longer, and then Red, glancing at the clock on the mantelshelf, rose to take his leave.

"I have to call on the Governor, sir," he told his father. "And on Captain Skinner. After that, if there's time and Skinner doesn't detain me, I will try to see Judge De Lancey. And perhaps you, with Jenny and Johnny, will give me the pleasure of entertaining you to dinner on board the *Galah* tomorrow? I'd like to show you round properly and introduce you to my officers, if you can spare the time."

He was rewarded by his father's delighted smile.

"We shall be happy to dine with you, Red. Indeed, it will be *my* pleasure, I assure you. It is good—I cannot begin to tell you how good—to have you back at last."

They bade each other an affectionate farewell, and Johnny walked with his brother to the street door.

"The Governor's in Parramatta, Red," he warned. "You'll

have to call on him there if you want to see him in person.
You know he lost his wife four years ago? They were in their
carriage, leaving Government House in Parramatta to come
here, when the horses bolted. Poor Lady Fitzroy was killed
outright, and His Excellency badly injured—he's somewhat
crippled even now—and it took the heart out of him. He
spends more of his time in Parramatta than he does here and
leaves most of the administration to the colony's secretary,
Deas Thomson, and the Legislative Council. You should try
to see Deas Thomson if you can—he's a very able man, and a
likable one." He stood holding the door, his smile widening.
"As Dad said, it *is* good to have you home again, Red."

"I wasn't sure whether my return was a cause for celebra-
tion in your case, John," Red confessed, feeling the need,
suddenly, to unburden himself to his brother and, if he
could, learn the reason for Johnny's initial resentment. "You
seemed—how can I put it?—a mite offhand."

"Cautious, brother," Johnny amended. "It's been a long
time, and you've been living in a different world from the
rest of us. I was afraid you might have changed and—not to
put too fine a point on it—become more British than Australian. And there was Mam, of course. She missed you so much
and—damn it, you stayed away! Even when she was dying,
poor, dear soul, it was you she wanted by her side. None of
us meant what you did to Mam, you know—not even Dad."

Red felt as if a knife were twisted in his heart. He could not
defend himself, he knew; Johnny's charges against him were
justified. He had let ambition rule his actions, had put the
furtherance of his naval career before family loyalty and the
ties that bound him to the land of his birth.

"I stand convicted," he said regretfully. "And there's
nothing I can do to put the clock back, is there? Not where
Mam's concerned. I can only tell you that I did not know she
was ill, much less dying; her letters never even hinted at it."

"No," Johnny conceded. "She did not want you to know."
He put out a hand to grasp Red's arm. "Look, I'll walk with
you, shall I, and we can talk. Which is your first port of call—
Government House?"

Red fell into step beside him. "Not if the Governor's away.

I'd best pay my respects to our senior naval officer, I think—Captain Skinner."

"Then you're likely to be closeted with him for the rest of the day," Johnny suggested dryly. "Very conscious of the magnitude of his responsibilities, he is, and your *Galah* will be a gift from heaven, since his total command on this station consists of the old *Calliope* and three small sloops. But I'll take you to his official residence. Turn left and head downhill."

They talked as they walked briskly together down the dusty, sunlit street toward Sydney Cove, and when they finally halted outside Captain Skinner's imposing stone-built residence, Red felt that the gulf of years had, at least partially, been bridged so far as his brother was concerned.

At the front door, guarded by a uniformed marine sentry, Johnny held out his hand.

"I take it you'll be calling on the De Lanceys when you get away from here?" He did not wait for Red's reply but wrung his hand warmly, a jesting smile curving his lips. "Magdalen De Lancey is a charming girl, Red. Like our little sister Jenny, she could take her pick of Sydney's eligible bachelors. But for some reason she doesn't seem to have shown a preference for any of them. Could you be the reason, do you suppose?"

Red grinned back at him. "It's to be hoped I am," he admitted. "But I've yet to find that out."

He touched his hat in acknowledgment of the sentry's salute, and the door opened to admit him to the presence of Captain John Skinner.

"Ah, Commander Broome . . ." The stout, red-faced post captain ignored his visitor's tentative greeting and waved him impatiently to a chair, coming without preamble to the point he wished to make. "I had an engagement that prevented me from boarding you when you entered the harbor. But I will not delay my, ah, official inspection. I take it you and your ship's company will be prepared to receive me tomorrow forenoon, will you not?"

Inwardly taken aback by the shortness of the notice, Red contrived to hide his feelings. He would have to repair on board at once, he knew, probably precluding him from making the call he had planned on the De Lanceys, but . . .

"Certainly, sir," he acknowledged with restraint. "If that is your wish, we shall be ready to receive you."

"Good," Captain Skinner approved. He selected a cigar from a box at his elbow, lit it, and settled comfortably back in his chair. "Now, let's hear about your passage, and perhaps you can explain the absence of the new dockyard superintendent you were bringing out—name of Lucas, was it not?— Captain Benjamin Lucas. All right, all right," he said as Red hesitated. "I don't want an official report yet—that'll do later. I only want to know why he's not here. They tell me he was taken ill. Is that so?"

"Yes, sir, that is so," Red confirmed, wondering from whom his interrogator had learned of Lucas's absence—in spite of the fact that a prior, and seemingly more important, engagement had kept him from boarding the *Galah* the previous day. In a flat, carefully controlled voice Red embarked on his explanation.

"Captain Lucas was taken seriously ill, sir, whilst we were still in southern latitudes. He suffered an infection of the lungs and, I surmise, pneumonia. My ship carries only a young surgeon's mate, lacking in experience. He did the best he could, and I assisted him to the best of my ability, but—"

Captain Skinner cut him short with an impatient wave of his cigar. "So you decided to make for Perth, Western Australia, in order that the captain might receive skilled medical treatment?"

Red nodded. "Exactly, sir. In view of the gravity of Captain Lucas's condition, that seemed to me the only course I could pursue. I—" Skinner again silenced him.

"But you decided arbitrarily to set him ashore at Fremantle, with his wife, and contrary to their wishes?"

Red stared at him, frowning, the conviction growing that his new superior had been told a distorted version of the facts, by . . . He stiffened.

"On the advice of the port medical officer at Fremantle, Captain Lucas was transferred to hospital in the town of Perth, sir."

"Against his wishes, Commander Broome?" the captain snapped accusingly. "And those of Mrs. Lucas?" Before Red could answer him, he produced some sheets of paper from a folder on his desk and, selecting one, laid it face upward between them. The writing on it was in the round, childish hand of Dora Lucas, but without permitting him time to read more than the opening sentence, Captain Skinner snatched it up again. "In this letter, which was delivered to me this morning by one of your officers, Mrs. Lucas lays certain damaging charges against you, Commander. These are confirmed, in writing, by the officer in question."

"By Lieutenant De Lancey?" Red offered, his mouth tightening angrily.

"Ah, so you are aware of Lieutenant De Lancey's complaints?" Skinner challenged. "Quite obviously you must also be aware that he is a son of one of our most respected citizens—His Honor Judge De Lancey?"

"I am, sir, yes." Red kept a rein on his growing anger. He had been quite unprepared for Francis De Lancey's action, but in the circumstances, he reflected wryly, perhaps he should not have been. The boy would be afraid to tell his father the truth, and even more reluctant, probably, to confess that he had sought to resign his commission and abandon his career in the navy without good reason. But even so . . . He started to speak, but once again Captain Skinner's half-smoked cigar described a repressive circle.

"It is as well that you decided to call on me here, Commander Broome," he observed. "Here, in the privacy of my office, we can talk the matter over between ourselves, can we not? I'll hear your side of this, ah, unfortunate affair and then make up my mind as to whether or not it will be necessary to hold an official inquiry into it. As I am sure you will realize, serious charges have been made against you, which, if they are proven, will require me to relieve you of your command. I shall not take that decision lightly, you may rest assured . . . and not until after I have made my inspection of the *Galah* and seen for myself the state of, ah, morale of your officers and ship's company. That is why I intend to make my inspection without delay."

It was now with extreme difficulty that Red managed to

refrain from an indignant outburst. Somehow he contrived to do so and to ask in an expressionless voice, "May I know precisely what charges have been made against me by Lieutenant De Lancey, sir?"

The stout little captain hesitated for a moment, riffling through the papers in front of him, a pensive frown creasing his brow. "Well," he said, still frowning, "the most, ah, serious are made by Mrs. Lucas. She claims that you, ah, endeavored to force your attentions on her after Captain Lucas was taken ill and she was without his protection. In consequence, the lady states that she sought protection from Lieutenant De Lancey and, when he attempted to afford her his aid, that you had him placed in arrest." His frown deepened as he turned the page and read on. "Ahem . . . this makes damning reading, Commander Broome, I must confess. Mrs. Lucas writes that you ordered her husband to be put ashore without his consent, and that when she remonstrated with you on that account, you had her put ashore forcibly. You—"

"It was *not* without his consent, sir," Red protested. "And Captain Lucas requested specifically that his wife remain in Perth with him."

"Do you deny her claim that you forced your attentions on her, Commander?"

"Categorically, sir. There is no truth in that whatsoever, I give you my word."

"Hmm—well, I have noted your assurance. The lady is young, is she not?" Captain Skinner paused, looking up from the papers to meet Red's indignant gaze. "Younger than Captain Lucas?"

"Yes, considerably younger, sir. But that does not mean that I—"

"Quite so, Commander Broome. Ah, there is one more charge, if I can find the requisite communication. I . . . yes, here it is. This is a letter in what I take to be Captain Lucas's own handwriting, and it is addressed to the Secretary to Their Lordships of the Admiralty. I must presume that Captain Lucas intended to mail it but, owing to his illness, was unable to do so." Skinner read slowly from the letter, and Red's heart sank. He could make an accurate guess at its contents and realized that, of course, Lucas *had* written it early in the *Galah*'s passage, when Red had first announced his intention of following the principle of great-circle sailing.

He listened, his apprehension increasing as Skinner read on. Lucas had brought up the chase after the slaver as well, and set down thus, in the pedantic style the engineer captain affected, his own actions and the decisions he had made sounded, to say the least, irresponsible. But surely Lucas had not meant to mail his letter; he had written it in the heat of the moment, and Dora must have stumbled on it and seen it as a useful weapon to use against him—probably when she was packing prior to being put ashore.

"Well, Commander?" Captain Skinner demanded. "What have you to say to that, may I ask?"

Red smothered an exasperated sigh. "Only that *I* was in command of the *Galah*, sir, and the decisions I took were proper for me to take. And I would remind you that Captain Lucas was an engineer officer, sir. He had never commanded a sailing ship at sea."

"You have a point there," the captain conceded. "Clearly, if I am compelled to order an inquiry, it will have to be postponed until Captain and Mrs. Lucas arrive in Sydney and can give evidence in person."

"And Lieutenant De Lancey, sir?" Red asked stiffly.

"Ah, yes—De Lancey. The young man informed me that he desires to quit the service." Skinner shrugged. "In the light of that and of the, ah, animosity he clearly bears you, I shall place him on half pay, pending confirmation from Their Lordships that his services may be dispensed with. Unless, of course, *you* wish to bring charges of your own against him, in, ah, rebuttal of his claims?"

"Sir, I . . ." For a moment, as outrage at Francis De Lancey's conduct outweighed discretion, Red was tempted to agree to Captain Skinner's offer. But, he asked himself soberly, what would it achieve? Were he to haul the boy before a naval court-martial, undoubtedly it would lead to a breach between his family and that of Judge De Lancey, who was one of his father's oldest and most valued friends. And there was Magdalen. His courtship would dissolve in bitterness before he had even embarked on it if he became a party to the ruin of her young brother's career and reputation. And the damned young fool was evidently quite determined to quit the navy; probably he had some crazy idea of taking ship back to Perth to rejoin Dora Lucas as soon as he was free. If he did anything of the kind, of course, his charges would no longer hold water, and—

"Well, Commander?" Captain Skinner prompted, with more than a hint of impatience.

"I do *not* wish to bring charges against Lieutenant De Lancey, sir," Red said with emphasis, "for personal and family reasons. If you decide, sir, that an official inquiry is necessary and the parties concerned—including Captain Lucas and his wife—are called upon to give evidence in substantiation of the complaints they have seen fit to make of my conduct, I shall submit willingly. In the meantime, sir, perhaps you will be so good as to reserve judgment until you have made your inspection of my ship and her company."

The stout post captain's brows rose in momentary surprise, and then his expression relaxed, and he got to his feet.

"Very well, Commander Broome, I shall do as you ask. Tomorrow at noon, shall we say, for my inspection? And I take it that you can dispense with Lieutenant De Lancey's services?"

"Yes, sir," Red assured him. "With your permission, I should like to promote my senior midshipman—Master's Mate Dixon—to the acting rank of lieutenant in his place."

"You have my permission, Commander." Captain Skinner stubbed out the stump of his cigar. Almost as an afterthought, he asked curiously, "Are you related to Captain Justin Broome, by any chance? The present commandant of the naval dockyard, I mean?"

"Yes, he is my father, sir. And Judge De Lancey is my uncle." Red drew himself up and saluted, conscious that Skinner's brows had risen once again. But the captain offered no comment, bowed in acknowledgment of the salute, and with a crisp "Until tomorrow, Commander Broome," he resumed his seat, reaching for a fresh cigar.

Red set off briskly in the direction of the cove, where his ship lay at anchor, but after some thought, he made the brief detour that took him into Macquarie Street and thence to the front door of the De Lancey residence, at the corner of Hunter Street. To the smartly liveried manservant who came in response to his summons, he gave his name and asked if Miss Magdalen De Lancey was free to receive him.

"I'm sorry, sir," the man answered, with suspicious promptitude. "Miss Magdalen is not at home."

The door was firmly closed before Red could ask for her father.

When he returned on board the *Galah*, it was to learn, from a puzzled and indignant Tim, that Francis De Lancey had not reported for duty.

"The miserable young rogue!" the first lieutenant exclaimed. "Do you think he has tried to run again, sir?"

"For good this time, Tim," Red told him. "Captain Skinner is placing him on half pay, pending Their Lordships' agreement. Andrew Dixon is to be given acting rank to fill the vacancy." He gave no other explanation; time enough for that, he thought resignedly. If the Sydney squadron commander decided that an official inquiry into Francis De Lancey's trumped-up charges was called for, then Tim could be counted on to bear witness to their complete lack of substance.

He gave his first lieutenant a rueful smile and, clapping a hand on his broad blue-clad shoulder, announced gravely, "Captain Skinner intends to subject us to an official inspection at noon tomorrow, Tim . . . which doesn't give us much time, I'm afraid. So let's make a start, shall we? Pass the word for all officers to assemble in my cabin right away, if you please."

Tim swore under his breath and then, like the good first lieutenant he was, added trenchantly, "Aye, aye, sir. Don't worry—we'll be ready for him, if it takes both watches all night."

CHAPTER X

Jasper Morgan lay in the concealment of a thick clump of brushwood and, his telescope to his eye, studied the activities of three men working a sluice on the riverbank below him.

The older of the three—a tall, good-looking man with iron-gray hair—he recognized, from the description he had been given, as the owner of the great sheep and cattle property known as Pengallon, through which the Macquarie River ran for more than two miles. Tempest was his name, and according to the fellow who had described him, he was a retired naval officer and one of the wealthiest landowners in the colony of New South Wales, whose flocks of purebred merino sheep now outnumbered those of the sons of the late John Macarthur, who had originally introduced the breed.

The other two men were working under Tempest's orders, but neither looked like a paid hand, and from the casualness of their speech and their frequent laughter, Morgan decided that they must be related to him.

He scowled, trying to remember what his informant—a gold digger he had met some weeks ago in a Bathurst tavern —had told him about Tempest's family.

There was a son, in his early twenties, and a daughter some years younger, and— Jasper Morgan's frown lifted.

" 'E's got a nephew," the digger had said. "An 'uge great giant of a feller, what can't 'ear nor speak. Dickon they call 'im. Got the strength o' ten men, that there Dickon 'as, so 'e ain't one ter mix it wiv, though they say as 'e's gentle enough. Part abo, some folk reckon—anyways, 'e understands their lingo an' goes off on walkabout wiv 'em when 'e feels so inclined. An' Mrs. Tempest—why, she's a real nice lady, from all accounts. American, from what I 'eard. Never turns no one from 'er door that's in want o' a meal or a bed for the night."

As he might soon be, Morgan thought sourly, if the ill luck that had beset him since his arrival in Sydney nine months ago did not change for the better. He sighed in bitter exasperation and turned his glass on each of Tempest's two companions in turn.

The son was like his father—tall, well built, and with a frank, open face, which sported a neatly trimmed fair beard. Nothing remarkable about him, Morgan decided, save that he was overly well dressed, in breeches and polished riding boots, for the task he was engaged in. But the man known as Dickon was different. He stood well over six feet—nearer seven, as far as it was possible to judge from the distance separating them—and he worked stripped to the waist, his big, muscular body so deeply tanned that, apart from his height, he might be taken for an aborigine. He, too, was bearded. He wore a cabbage-plant hat, to shield his face from the sun, and worked with prodigious skill but seemingly little effort, transferring great heaped spadefuls of river sand to the sluice with scarcely a pause to draw breath.

Morgan let his gaze linger critically on the sluice. It was of primitive construction and lacked any form of rocker, depending on gravity and what he judged must be a series of filters along its length to trap gold particles as the sand and gravel were washed through it. The men, for all Dickon's energetic toil, did not appear to be finding much gold, and they were losing dust because their filters were too coarse and too easily clogged.

He lowered his glass, cursing softly under his breath. His own finds during the past nine months had amounted to little more. He had reached Sydney very shortly after Edward Hargraves and some other fellow had duly found the gold Hargraves had sworn was there, but the infernal Governor had procrastinated, initially trying to keep the discovery secret, and then—further to hold back the tide—had insisted on the government geologist's making an inspection and a report before any prospectors' licenses were granted. Stutchbury, the geologist, had taken his time, but eventually he had confirmed Hargraves's discovery, and then the rush had started, virtually uncontrolled and augmented almost daily by a fresh influx from overseas.

Morgan's mouth tightened into a hard, angry line as he looked back on the months of frustration he had been compelled to endure. First he had been left cooling his heels, unable to obtain a license and—because there were soon so many crewless vessels in the harbor—unable to sell his brig, the *Banshee*, and recoup the money she had cost him. Back then he had still had money, of course, but the cost of living in Sydney had risen to unprecedented heights, and an unfortunate liaison with a woman he had believed to be honest and trustworthy had greatly depleted his resources, as had the harbor dues demanded for his ship.

At last, however, he had been granted his license, and he had gone first to Goulburn and the Turon River, taking four of the men he had brought with him from San Francisco, who—because they owed him their passage money—had agreed to pay off their debts by working for him. The Turon was a new field, and it had not been overcrowded when he had first started prospecting there; but such a happy state of affairs had not lasted for long. Gold seekers had come pouring in, hundreds more with each week that passed, and they had spread out like a plague of locusts, panning, mining, sluicing, and then moving on as rumors of a fresh find reached the camps. His employees had been tempted by offers of higher wages and had deserted him. True, two of them had paid their debts, but . . . Morgan sighed. He had been left short of money in spite of that, forced to do his own laboring chores, and where other men had made strikes, he had failed, for some reason, to do so.

He had come to Bathurst a week ago, having himself heard rumors that . . . He picked up his glass again and turned it onto the face of Pengallon's gray-haired owner. Rumors had led him to the belief that Mr. Richard Tempest, for many years prior to Edward Hargraves's sensational discovery, had been taking gold from his stretch of the Macquarie River. Illegally, of course, since mineral rights belonged, by law, to the government, not to the owners of agricultural land grants, so that Mr. Tempest had kept extremely quiet about his gold-seeking activities.

Morgan frowned. The idea of blackmail had occurred to him; judiciously applied, it might pay dividends, depending on the sort of man Tempest proved to be, but . . . studying him now, Morgan rejected any such notion. Tempest did not look the type that would yield easily, and in any event, if he had managed to keep his illicit gold digging secret for so many years, it seemed unlikely that, when it was legalized, any threat of exposure would scare him. And doubtless he guarded his stretch of river jealously, permitting only men of his choice to prospect there.

Once again Jasper Morgan lowered his glass in order to mop at his sweating face, on which clouds of plaguey flies were attempting to settle. He needed money and needed it urgently, for he wanted to pay off the harbor dues on the *Banshee*, fill her with trade goods and mining supplies, and make a fresh start in Victoria. Reports from there, published in the *Geelong Gazette* and subsequently confirmed in the Sydney papers, carried news of the opening of rich new fields at Ballarat, thirty-odd miles from Port Phillip, and—the latest and richest—at a place called Mount Alexander, ninety miles from Melbourne.

Experience and the disappointments he had suffered on the Turon River had convinced him that the best chance of making substantial profits lay in being early on the scene, before the rush began. As yet, if the newspapers were to be believed, the Victoria fields were being sparsely worked, and he was determined to get there among the first, if humanly possible.

But to achieve his objective, he had to lay his hands on some ready money, devil take it! And . . . Tempest had money, no doubt of that. If only he could devise some way of parting him from it.

"You're a bad un," the woman who had cheated him had accused spitefully. "And for all your grand airs, *Major*, you're not a gentleman, and I doubt you ever were."

Well, she had been right on that score, Morgan reflected, although he had managed to deceive most people since he had grown to adulthood. He was calling himself Major Lewis now, Major Joseph Lewis, purely as a precaution, lest any miner from the vicinity of Thayer's Bend should chance to

join the exodus from California and remember the name of
Jasper Morgan. He had covered his tracks well, he was confident; the bodies he had left in the mine were unlikely in the
extreme to be discovered, for who would dream of attempting to shift the tons of rock beneath which they had been
buried? It was a pity that the youngster Luke Murphy had
not been with his brother and the two Australians; but the
lad was simple, and whatever he might suspect, without the
bodies he would have no proof that the rockfall had not been
accidental. Indeed, both he and the old fool who styled
himself the *alcalde* of the miners' camp, Ephraim Crocker,
must have been taken in, for there had been no pursuit.
Between them, Morgan felt certain, they would not have
possessed the wits to work out what had really befallen his
erstwhile partners, for he had laid his plans with extreme
care and carried them out meticulously.

And as for the girl—what had she called herself? Mercedes? Mercy . . . Morgan's dark eyes narrowed. A pity his
plans had necessitated leaving her behind. She had been a
pretty, compliant little creature and a more entertaining
bedfellow than the sullen, grasping harlot by whom he had
been so woefully deceived and robbed in Sydney! Had the
circumstances been different, he might have brought Mercy
here with him—indeed, he had seriously considered doing
so—but it would have entailed taking a risk, and throughout
his career he had always been careful to take no risks, if they
could be avoided.

Lord, he thought cynically, how else could a onetime corporal in Her Majesty's 23rd Regiment of Foot have passed
himself off, both here and in America, as a dashing and
distinguished officer, whose decorations included a Spanish
Gold Cross, bestowed on him by Queen Isabella in person
for his services in the Carlist War? And . . . He found himself smiling. A deserter, to boot, who had stolen the cross
from its rightful owner in the course of an armed robbery in,
of all places, Cardiff!

"Time to call it a day, Papa, don't you think?" The voice of
Tempest's son broke into his thoughts, and Jasper Morgan
stiffened and then reached for his glass.

Good, he told himself, they were going, their gold-seeking

over for the day. That would give him the opportunity to examine their sluice. He would note its deficiencies and, when it was dark, retrieve his two horses and ride to the homestead, posing as a benighted traveler in search of shelter. Then he would reveal his California experience and expertise and offer, with well-mannered diffidence, to give Mr. Tempest the benefit of his knowledge. He would ask for no reward, initially—gentlemen were never crude—but he would keep his eyes and ears open and await the first opportunity that arose to turn the situation to profit.

He— The giant Dickon ambled into the range of the telescope, carrying what appeared to be a rock taken from the riverbed. He set it down, a childlike grin playing about his bearded lips, and looked at Tempest in mute question. The older man shook his head and said something Morgan could not hear, whereupon Dickon, still grinning hugely, let the rock slide back into the river, without saying a word. But the big fellow was deaf and dumb, Morgan reminded himself, according to the man he had questioned in the tavern. That meant he was probably a simpleton, even less to be reckoned with than the dim-witted Luke. Morgan crouched down behind the screening brush and watched the men below him gather up their tools preparatory to departure. Dickon led up the three horses, which had been tethered nearby, and the men mounted and rode away.

Morgan gave them ten minutes and then clambered stiffly to his feet, conscious of the chill in the air that had come with the sunset. There was not much daylight left, but it sufficed for his inspection of the sluice, which he dismissed as primitive and badly constructed by Californian standards. He could improve its efficiency, he knew, given the chance, and it should not be too difficult to persuade Tempest to offer him the chance. He started to wade back to the riverbank, caught his booted foot on some unseen obstruction, and, to his annoyance, stumbled and measured his length in the now ice-cold river water.

Rising to his knees in the shallow water, Morgan sputtered and cursed, his fingers closing over the stone or rock that had tripped him; instinctively he raised it to the surface, a sixth sense warning him that it was no ordinary rock. It took both hands and some effort to lift it, and as his find broke the surface of the water, Jasper Morgan was scarcely able to restrain his shout of triumph, for even in the rapidly fading light he glimpsed the soft golden glow emanating from it.

He splashed his way back to the bank and sank down on the soft clay, the better to examine and assess the weight and value of his unexpected prize. It must have lain deeply embedded in the river bottom, he decided, to have evaded discovery by Tempest and his companions. Probably the rock that the deaf-mute Dickon had picked up had pried this one loose from its centuries-old concealment, and blind chance—or a welcome change in his fortunes—had caused it to fall into his hands. Trembling with excitement and oblivious of the chill state of his damp body and sodden clothing, Morgan balanced the nugget in his two outstretched hands.

Worn smooth by the flow of river water, it was almost solid gold, and he judged its weight to be between ten and eleven pounds. At the current price of three pounds sterling an ounce, it was not a fortune, but its sale would suffice to free the *Banshee* and stock her with trade goods, as he had planned, and . . . Morgan's spirits rose. Probably there was more where this nugget had come from, but in the gathering darkness and without the tools he had left on his packhorse, there would be little point in searching for it now.

He sat back on his heels, shivering, while he considered the best way to proceed. He could return to Sydney, cut his losses, and make for Port Phillip in the *Banshee*. A crew and paying passengers would not be hard to find when his destination was known. Or . . . He stared down at the dark surface of the river, reluctant, even now, to leave the scene of his successful find. He could still stick to his original plan, he told himself, play the role of the benighted traveler and seek hospitality at the Tempests' homestead. That, if he played his cards right, would give him a couple of more days here and afford him the opportunity to examine the riverbed more closely and, perhaps, add to the find he had already made.

The mountain cold finally decided him. He would have to make camp for the night if he chose the first alternative, sleep in damp clothing, and run the risk of catching a chill, whereas at the Tempests' he could almost certainly count on a dry bed, a hot meal, and a courteous welcome . . . and the nugget he had discovered so providentially could be concealed in his saddlebag and no mention made of it.

Stiffly Morgan got to his feet, stretching his cramped muscles and shivering anew. It was then that, as he turned, he glimpsed a shadowy figure a few yards away, and he smothered an exclamation of mingled alarm and surprise. It had not occurred to him that he might have been observed; he had heard no sound and had supposed himself alone, but— The figure came nearer, silhouetted against the night sky and revealed as an old aborigine, clad in shirt and trousers. A civilized native, Morgan thought, with relief—an employee of Tempest's, probably, to judge by his garb, and therefore unlikely to be dangerous or obstructive. In any case, he was unarmed. . . .

"Well?" he demanded haughtily, slipping easily into his accustomed role. "What do you want, my man? Why did you creep up on me, eh?" The old man was silent, studying him with bright, birdlike eyes, and Morgan asked impatiently, "Do you speak English?"

The white head was lowered in assent. "I speak and understand your tongue, yes, sir."

"Do you work for Mr. Tempest?" Again there was a nod of assent, and as a ray of moonlight slanted through the trees, Morgan saw that the man's right arm bore a line of scar tissue and appeared to be partially crippled. He relaxed, the tension draining out of him. "I am Major Lewis," he said crisply. "And I am seeking Mr. Tempest's house. Perhaps you can guide me there? My horses are tethered a little way away. You fetch them for me. I'll give you tobacco, I—"

"You find gold!" the aborigine declared. He gestured to the nugget, which, Morgan realized belatedly, he was holding in full view. "Gold belong my master."

Jasper Morgan's reaction was at once angry and dismayed, and he acted without conscious thought. The nugget slipped from his grasp, and the heavy Colt he always carried was out of its holster and in his hand. He brought the butt down with savage strength on the aborigine's unprotected head, felling him instantly, and two more blows were enough to shatter his skull. The old man did not cry out; he lay quite still where he had fallen, the sightless eyes gazing up in mute reproach at his killer, and Morgan, shuddering, turned away, unable to meet them.

After a while he recovered his lost composure and, bracing himself, dragged the body into a thick clump of brushwood some distance from the river. There, he thought, it would in all probability elude discovery, unless a very extensive search were made, and . . . who would bother to search for an old blackfellow, long past his prime, who had simply vanished? Blackfellows went on what they called walkabout, and this one, if he were missed, would doubtless be supposed to have done just that. Tempest would not bother his head about his disappearance—why should he?

The grisly task completed, Jasper Morgan made for the secluded gully in which he had left his horses, to find to his impotent fury that only the packhorse was there. The other —an expensive animal he had purchased in Sydney soon after his arrival there—had slipped its tether and made off, the Lord only knew where. Trying to search for the stray would be useless in the darkness, he knew, and cursing illtemperedly, he unloaded the packhorse and set up his small lean-to canvas tent beneath the shelter of a gnarled gum tree. He lit a fire but had scarcely got it going when a heavy shower extinguished its flickering flames, and cold and disgruntled, he was compelled to retire to his tent, unfed and very conscious of the pangs of hunger gnawing at his vitals.

Nevertheless, once inside the tent and wrapped in a horse blanket, he slept, the nugget he had so providentially unearthed from the riverbed hidden in his saddlebag and the saddlebag serving to pillow his head.

He suffered a rude awakening. A man burst into the tent and, without a word, dragged him unceremoniously from it. Morgan protested angrily, only to recognize the deaf-mute Dickon as his abductor, to whom his protests were inaudible. Outside the tent, however, both calmly sitting their horses, were Tempest and his son, and Morgan unleashed his fury on them.

"The devil take you, sir!" he flung at Rick Tempest, when

he had regained his breath. "By what right do you serve a
law-abiding traveler in this manner? I'd have you know that I
am a gentleman, sir, not some convict-bred scum. Lewis is
my name—Major Joseph Lewis, late of Her Majesty's Household Cavalry. And if this is your land, sir, I am merely passing through on my way from the gold diggings."

His indignant bluster succeeded. Rick Tempest motioned
to Dickon to release him, and dismounting from his horse,
he apologized courteously and introduced himself and his
companions by name.

"Richard Tempest, sir—my son Edmund and my nephew
Dickon O'Shea. I'm extremely sorry Dickon manhandled
you, Major Lewis, but we are seeking the killer of my head
shepherd, an aborigine by the name of Winyara. An old
man, sir, who had been in my employ since his boyhood and
who has been brutally murdered."

So they had found the miserable native's body, Morgan
thought, his heart sinking. Damn them, they must have instituted a very thorough search, since— He glanced skyward,
to see that the sun was high in the blue, cloudless vault
above his head. It was noon. He had foolishly overslept and,
by so doing, had lost his chance to escape. He decided that
to brazen it out would be the best course to pursue, and
summoning all the practiced arrogance at his command, he
proceeded to give vent to his annoyance.

Tempest heard him in politely restrained silence, and
when at last the tirade came to an end, he waved a hand
toward a horse his son was holding.

"Is this your mount, Major?" he asked.

"I—damme, yes, it is!" Morgan had not noticed the animal and was momentarily taken by surprise. "The infernal
creature slipped its tether when I went to the river for water.
That was why I made camp here last night. It was raining,
and I could not go hunting for it in the darkness, of course.
Where did you find my horse, Mr. Tempest?"

"Close to where Winyara's body was lying," Tempest answered. His tone was quiet, betraying no suspicion, and
emboldened by this, Jasper Morgan expressed regret at the
loss of the native shepherd.

"You'll feel his loss, I don't doubt, sir, with so many white farm laborers deserting their employment to join the rush to the diggings. It was the same with the ships that arrived in San Francisco from the East. Their crews deserted, and the ships were left in the harbor to rot for all they cared."

"You were in California, Major?" Tempest asked.

He had taken the bait, Jasper Morgan told himself, and smiled. If he played his cards right, this meeting might well lead to an invitation to a meal, and perhaps the offer of a bed for a night or two. He would accept, of course, partly to make certain that all suspicion regarding the aborigine shepherd was allayed, but mainly because a brief stay would enable him to make a second search of the riverbed in the hope of finding another nugget—or even a number of nuggets—where he had stumbled on the one now hidden in his saddlebag.

He talked knowledgeably of his experiences in California, giving the impression he was always at pains to create concerning his expertise and, for good measure, casually throwing in the mention of his ownership of the brig *Banshee*. Both the Tempests were clearly impressed, and he was duly offered the invitation, which he accepted without undue eagerness.

"A cooked meal and the opportunity to wash and shave and get out of these damp clothes would be most welcome, Mr. Tempest. But if it is inconvenient for you, I will be on my way back to Sydney Town. Do not, I beg you, sir, feel under any obligation to a passing stranger."

"We owe you some recompense for the manner in which my nephew received you," Tempest said. He aimed a playful slap at Dickon's head, and the giant, unabashed, grinned back at him. All three men assisted with the dismantling of the tent, and as Dickon strapped it onto his packhorse, Morgan saw that they had brought the body of the old aborigine with them. Covered inadequately by a coat, it lay across the withers of the deaf-mute's horse, and Morgan suppressed a shudder at the sight of it.

But, he told himself, turning abruptly away, he had had no choice—the infernal blackfellow had observed what he had done and would almost certainly have reported it to his master.

"The poor devil!" he exclaimed, feeling that some comment was called for. "Who would have had reason to kill him? One of his tribe, perhaps?"

"Very unlikely," Tempest answered, suddenly tight-lipped. "We are on good terms with the local blacks, and there hasn't been a raid or an attack in this district for ten years and more, has there, Edmund?"

He appealed to his son, and the young man retorted with what, to Jasper Morgan, was surprising bitterness.

"Old Winyara was the salt of the earth, Major Lewis. No one who knew him would have harmed a hair of his head. But there are a fair number of rogues and ruffians among the gold diggers these days, alas! New immigrants, particularly, who have heard exaggerated tales about our native blacks. They tend to fear and mistrust them, so . . ." He shrugged. "I'd give a lot to get my hands on the man that killed Winyara, I can tell you. I'd gladly break his accursed neck!"

This was a dangerous topic, and Morgan hurriedly changed it. As they rode together toward the distant homestead of Pengallon, he talked of California and of the success he had enjoyed when prospecting in the Sacramento Valley, and then, his tone modest rather than boastful, he went on to describe the differing methods employed by the American diggers in their search for alluvial gold.

"The forty-niners began as they've done here, panning the rivers and streams with anything that came to hand—old frying pans, tin plates, literally anything. But that was soon superseded by more scientific methods of working. Cradle rockers and sluices were introduced, whole reaches of the rivers were dammed, exposing the sandbars, and where gold-bearing quartz was found, mechanical ore-crushing machinery was imported from the eastern states and brought to San Francisco by ships via the Horn. . . ." Jasper Morgan talked on, conscious that both Tempest and his son were giving him their undivided and respectful attention.

By the time they pulled up in the rear of the imposing farmhouse, he was confident that his professional opinion would be sought and that he would be urged to prolong his stay for as long as it might suit him to do so. It would not be for very long, though; two or three days, at most, should suffice for his purpose, and then he would put to sea in the *Banshee* and seek the newer, richer goldfields of Victoria, ahead of the inevitable influx of deserting seamen, fugitive laborers, and new immigrants now swarming in their thousands over the green and fertile farming land of New South Wales.

"I doubt if the licensed prospectors—those who have their claims on my stretch of the river—would stand idly by and permit me to dam it," Tempest said with a rueful shrug as he dismounted. "We have a big mining camp less than half a mile downstream from my own workings. But—" He gave his rein to his son and motioned to Morgan to follow him. "Dickon will bed your horses down, Major Lewis, and I can furnish you with some dry clothing if you wish."

"I have all I need here," Morgan evaded quickly. He unbuckled his saddlebag, shaking his head to Dickon's offer to relieve him of it, and slung its straps over his shoulder. Dear God, he thought, it would never do for Dickon to feel the weight of the infernal thing! He summoned a smile, and Tempest waved hospitably in the direction of his open front door.

"Come in, sir, and make the acquaintance of my wife and daughter. We'll eat as soon as you've washed off the stains of travel and changed out of your damp clothes."

The meal, when it was served half an hour later, was appetizing and substantial, and Jasper Morgan, his bodily comfort restored and his hunger satisfied, permitted himself to relax in what was proving extremely pleasant company. His hostess had, he learned, been born in Boston but had left America when she was only seventeen. A vivacious, handsome woman, she was, he judged, several years younger than her husband and still seemingly devoted to him, the glances they exchanged proof, to his observant eye, that any attempt to exert his predatory charm in her direction would be a waste of time.

The daughter, however, was another matter. Her name was Elizabeth, and she was, perhaps, sixteen or seventeen—a pretty, wide-eyed innocent, with her mother's lovely fair coloring and slender figure and her father's ready smile.

That he had made a favorable impression on her Morgan had no doubt. Probably, he thought, hidden away as she was on this isolated farm, her male acquaintance was confined to uncouth farmhands and the odd passing traveler, and her parents would make sure that she had no contact with the men at the diggings, despite the proximity of their camp.

He smiled and, for her benefit, held forth with practiced erudition on a variety of subjects, addressing her parents but watching the girl, at once pleased and stimulated by her response. His voice, he well knew, was that of an educated man, for had he not spent years perfecting his accent and the musical Welsh lilt that went with it?

Tempest was obviously a gentleman—a onetime naval officer, his informant had said—and Mrs. Tempest, Katie Tempest, was equally well bred. But—Morgan smiled smugly to himself—for all that, they were not hard to deceive. They took him at his face value, and he was careful to assume a modesty he did not often display, hinting at, rather than boasting of, his military achievements and worldwide travels. Indeed, he reflected cynically, because they were gentlefolk, they gave their trust instinctively to one whom they supposed to be of their own kind. It was not necessary to make false claims of the outrageous nature of those he had made so freely in California, in order to win the trust of Luke Murphy and his brother and the two Australians. Only the oafish Dickon continued to scowl at him across the table, but the half-wit, of course, could not hear what was being said, and therefore his hostility could be discounted.

The girl, Elizabeth, said little, but she hung on his words, her blue eyes shining, and Jasper Morgan found himself wishing that circumstances had been other than they were, for he had a weakness for girls of her age, and her fresh, glowing beauty attracted him strongly. But native caution restrained him, and he knew that he dared not linger for long on the Tempest property.

A careless word or a closer inspection of the contents of his saddlebag might all too easily arouse suspicion concerning his involvement in the killing of the infernal old aborigine shepherd, by whom, it appeared, the whole family had set great store. In any event, Morgan reminded himself, he wanted to be on his way to the new goldfields in Victoria before the rush followed in the wake of the recent discoveries there, as undoubtedly it would. Two days—that was the time he had set himself, and he must let nothing, not even the sweet young Elizabeth, turn him from his chosen course.

It took two days to pry three more sizable nuggets from the hole beneath the riverbed where he had found the first. He succeeded in doing so without being observed, but it required all his ingenuity to make an opportunity for his search, for Dickon dogged his footsteps, and only a providential crisis among the sheep in a far paddock enabled him to escape his shadow and rid himself temporarily of the friendly but inhibiting presence of Tempest and his son.

Nevertheless, it was with regret that Jasper Morgan finally took his leave, Tempest's protestations of gratitude for his expert help and advice a sop to his conscience and a relief, after the lingering anxiety he had endured throughout his stay at Pengallon. They would lose less dust in their sluice, thanks to his work on the filters, and the rocker that Edmund and Dickon had constructed, under his supervision, would serve them in good stead—if there was still gold where Tempest had staked his claim.

"We shall miss you, Major Lewis," Mrs. Tempest told him with sincerity when he bade her farewell. "You have been a most entertaining guest. It has been a rare pleasure for us all to hear what has been going on in the world outside, and for myself in particular to have such recent news of my homeland."

Intent on playing his role to the last, Morgan raised her small, work-worn hand to his lips and assured her, with more truth than she knew, that it was he who was indebted to her and her husband. To Elizabeth, listening gravely, he spoke with conscious restraint but had the satisfaction, even so, of bringing the blushes to her cheeks.

Finally, he tore himself away and set off, leading his laden packhorse, to retrace his steps to Bathurst and thence to make the long journey down from the mountains to Sydney.

He had covered only a mile or so from the Pengallon boundary fence, when without warning, the crack of a rifle, fired from close at hand, set his heart lurching. The bullet whistled over his head as he crouched low in the saddle, coming unpleasantly close, and a second shot, following swiftly after the first, was only inches away. Instinctively Morgan reached for his Colt, and he could not suppress a gasp of dismay when he found the holster was empty. He had not cleaned the gun, he recalled belatedly, and the chances were that it must still have borne traces on its pearl-inlaid butt of the blood of the man he had killed.

Cursing himself for his carelessness, he put spurs to his horse, and dropping the pack animal's lead rein, he galloped down the rutted cart track as if the devil himself were after him. There was one more shot, which fell short, and once certain that he was out of range, he pulled up and looked back in the hope of catching a glimpse of his attacker. But both sides of the track were thickly wooded, and he could see no one. An aborigine, he asked himself, a member of Winyara's tribe, bent on revenge, or— Jasper Morgan drew in his breath sharply. Not an aborigine—aborigines did not possess rifles. Whoever had taken his Colt was the most likely suspect. The warmth of the Tempests' farewell must surely exclude all or any of them. Rick Tempest, if he had harbored any doubts, would have voiced them and demanded a denial of culpability; his son Edmund, too, for both were honest, straight-dealing gentlemen, to whom deceit was unthinkable.

So that left the simpleton, the deaf-mute Dickon. *He* owned a rifle and, from the outset, had displayed barely concealed hostility. . . . Morgan scowled down at his empty holster and, taking out his glass, made a careful inspection of the woods lining the track. There was no movement, no sign of anyone that he could see, and there were no more shots. The frightened packhorse caught up with him, and he put the glass back in his breast pocket and secured the animal's rein. He pressed on grimly, abandoning his original intention of putting up for the night in Bathurst, and rode through the darkness at a pace that left both his horses exhausted. But he did not spare them, halting only when he was compelled to feed and water them and cook a scratch meal for himself, the journey made unpleasant by constant heavy rain.

He reached the Nepean River at last, only to find it flooded, with long lines of horse and bullock-drawn drays waiting on both sides of the crossing at Emu Ford.

Morgan did not wait more than the time it took him to sell his packhorse and some of his mining equipment to one of the dray owners—a new immigrant from England—at a worthwhile profit. Then, at first light, he swam his horse across, watched and encouraged by ribald shouts from the stranded wayfarers, a few of the bolder spirits following his example when they saw him emerge safely, but soaked to the skin, on the other side. In the manner of the gold diggers, always generous to one of their own, the onlookers offered him food and drink and a place by the fire to dry his sodden clothes. But he accepted only a glass of raw spirit, and then, shaking his head to suggestions that he must have made a rich strike, he kicked his weary horse into a reluctant trot and continued on his way.

He reached Sydney late on Sunday evening and, first thing next morning, set about putting his plans in train. The nuggets he had taken from the Tempest claim were sold to the Union Bank for a trifle less than he had anticipated, but his gain was sufficient to free the *Banshee* from distraint, and—in spite of rocketing prices brought about by current demand —he was not ill-pleased with the supplies he was able to purchase.

He was in feverish haste to leave Sydney behind him, fearing some attempt by Rick Tempest to follow him and demand his arrest or—perhaps even more cause for alarm— pursuit by the unpredictable Dickon. But the days passed without incident, and his apprehension began to fade.

Finding a crew and paying passengers took time; he wanted to choose carefully the men he signed on, and the old master he had employed to bring the brig from San Francisco—a good man at sea but a hopeless drunkard ashore—proved harder to track down than he had antici- pated, and harder still to restore to sobriety.

But at last his preparations were complete. Eighteen days after his return to Sydney, he ordered the *Banshee* to put to sea, her hold laden to capacity, eleven paying passengers, and an admittedly scratch crew. A second change of name

had seemed to him expedient; the brig's registered owner
was now Captain Jonathan Humphrey, late of Her Majesty's
3rd Foot Guards, and as he stood on the quarterdeck, dis-
coursing with some of the passengers, Morgan found himself smiling, able at last to relax his wary vigilance.

Casually he took his Spanish Gold Cross from the pocket
of his immaculately cut blue jacket, beginning to embark on
the well-rehearsed tale of how he had received it from the
hands of the Spanish Queen, when he broke off in mid-
sentence, aware that his audience's attention had wandered.

All were crowding to the weather rail, exclaiming excitedly at the sight of a magnificent vessel, which, under full
sail, had just weathered the South Head. Although he was no
seaman, Jasper Morgan recognized the unique beauty of
her lines, from her sharp-raked stem to her finely gilded
overhanging counter stern and towering masts. She was
schooner-rigged, and although she was too far away to enable her name to be deciphered, she was flying the British
flag.

"A clipper!" the old master exclaimed, his rheumy, red-
rimmed eyes suddenly bright with pleasure. "A clipper
schooner out o' McKay's yard, I'd stake my oath. An' she's a
real beauty, ain't she, Major?"

"Captain," Morgan reminded him. "Captain Humphrey,
Mr. Jones. And I'll thank you not to forget it."

"Oh, aye, if you say so." Septimus Jones brushed aside the
reproof indifferently. His telescope to his eye, he watched
the newly arrived schooner come smartly about and then
start to trim her sails. "Now, she's the kind o' vessel I'd give
me right arm to command," he observed wistfully. "By God,
she is! An' I reckon I remember her, now I come to think on
it. Made a real fast passage out o' Boston, she did, an' come
into San Francisco only a few days outside o' the *Sea Witch*'s
record. She'd just berthed when we sailed. She's the *Dolphin,*
unless I'm much mistaken, Maj—*Captain* Humphrey. Her
master an' owner's a feller with a Dutch name, Van something, but this is his home port, far as I know. He owns four
or five other ships, an' a grand house in Sydney Town."

"Van Buren," Jasper Morgan supplied, with more than a
hint of envy in his voice. He had heard of Claus Van Buren

and had walked past the fine two-story house in Bridge Street more than once. He lifted his own glass to his eye and moved to the rail as the *Dolphin*'s tack brought her nearer and it was possible to see those on her upper deck with some clarity.

A face came into focus, and he bit back a startled exclamation, for the face was that of the girl he had abandoned in Windy Gully, on the Sacramento River almost a year before . . . Mercedes—Mercy Bancroft. For a moment he was alarmed, but then he shook off his apprehension. A trick of the imagination, he told himself; it could be nothing more. Or his conscience, come to plague him. Smiling easily, he strode across to join his passengers as, in turn, the *Banshee* tacked and the two ships drew apart.

CHAPTER XI

Finding a favorable breeze off the Heads, Red Broome brought the *Galah* into Port Jackson Harbor at first light, to be met by the pilot cutter with orders to berth in Watson's Bay.

The corvette had scarcely dropped anchor when a boat put off from the shore and a keen-eyed midshipman of the watch, spotting Captain Skinner seated in the sternsheets, called out a shrill warning.

"Man the side, Mr. Broome," Red directed his first lieutenant. "It would seem that we are about to receive a visit from the commodore. The Lord knows what he wants of us so urgently at this hour!"

The side party hurriedly assembled, an accommodation ladder was lowered, and to the ceremonious twitter of the boatswain's mates' calls, the Sydney station's senior naval officer was piped aboard.

"So you are back at last, Commander Broome," Skinner observed, a distinct edge to his voice adding to Red's bewilderment. It had been only three weeks since he had left Sydney, carrying a new batch of prisoners to the penal settlement of Norfolk Island—still maintained for the reception of men condemned for crimes committed in the colony—and Red was at a loss to understand his superior officer's evident agitation.

Since the unfortunate incident involving young Francis De Lancey, Captain Skinner had displayed a decidedly critical attitude toward Red, standing on rank and making it humiliatingly clear that he was, in spite of Red's denials, still far from satisfied that the conduct of the *Galah*'s commander in regard to Captain and Mrs. Lucas had been without blame. Indeed, he had aired that opinion openly, Red recalled with regret, causing a rift between Judge De Lancey and himself. And Magdalen, coming loyally to her brother's support, had continued to hold aloof from him, his attempts to renew his courtship—or even to call on her—coldly rebuffed.

On the one occasion that they had met, at a Government House dinner party, Magdalen had behaved as if they were complete strangers, bowing distantly and addressing him formally by his rank when chance had momentarily thrown them together in Sir Charles Fitzroy's drawing room. She, it seemed, had forgotten that he had held her in his arms as a lover, forgotten the happiness they had enjoyed in each other's company and the promises they had made, and on that account he had been glad enough to leave Sydney, although the state of affairs at Norfolk Island . . . Red smothered a sigh, unable, even now, to reconcile himself to what he had witnessed there. It was called the Island of the Damned, he knew, but for all that . . . Captain Skinner was moving impatiently toward the *Galah*'s day cabin, and Red, recalled to his duty, ushered the visitor in, inviting him to be seated and summoning the steward.

"Would you care to break your fast, sir?" he asked politely as the steward hovered expectantly at his elbow. "I can offer you some excellent ham or—"

"No, no—just coffee," Skinner returned ungraciously. He waited until the steward left them and then said, without preamble, "Captain Lucas arrived here from Western Australia ten days ago, with his wife, Broome."

He paused, eyeing Red from beneath scowling brows and clearly expecting some reaction.

"Yes, sir," Red acknowledged, still at a loss to know what reply was expected of him. "Er, the captain is in improved health, I trust, sir?"

"As to that, I'm damned if I know—he looks fit enough. A mite pale perhaps, and his temper's on a very short fuse. But he's after your blood, Broome. In fact, he's demanding an inquiry into your conduct. If it's held and the findings are against you, you'll have to face a court-martial. . . . You realize that, do you not?"

Red stared at him aghast. The last thing he had antici-pated was that Benjamin Lucas would ally himself against him. In spite of all the difficulties of their voyage together, they had parted on the best of terms, with Lucas expressing his heartfelt gratitude for the preservation of his life. True, there had been the request he had made, when he had supposed that he was dying. . . . Sick with dismay, Red recalled the plea and the underlying reason for which he had made it.

"It is my wife who concerns me," he had said. *"She is young and will be left without means or protection in the event of my death. I am aware of the regard she has for you, Captain Broome. She's made no secret of it."*

Dora Lucas, Red thought bitterly, had evidently embroidered the lie, and her husband had believed her. He drew in his breath sharply, becoming aware that Captain Skinner had said something he had not heard.

"Forgive me, sir," he managed, his mouth dry. "What did you say?"

"I said," Skinner retorted testily, "that I have acceded to Captain Lucas's request for an inquiry. I intend to assemble a board, consisting of the four senior officers in command of ships presently on this station, over which I shall myself preside. We shall hear Captain Lucas's com—er, allegations, and you will, of course, be afforded an opportunity to refute them." He again paused, avoiding Red's gaze, and added curtly, "Until the findings of the inquiry are known, you will be relieved of your command. Is that understood?"

Red controlled a wild impulse to rebel. It would do no good, he reminded himself; rather it would go against him, if Skinner reported his outburst to the board of inquiry. He said flatly, "I understand, sir. I take it that Captain Lucas's allegations as to my conduct will be made known to me before the board sits, in order that I may prepare my reply?"

"You'll hear them when Lucas makes them," Skinner said. For a moment he looked disconcerted, but then went on, frowning. "He has not yet put them in writing. All I know is that he is charging you with improper conduct in regard to his wife and insubordination in regard to himself. And—" The steward came with a pot of coffee and cups on a tray, and he broke off, waving the man away when he made to serve the coffee. "I'll pour out. Make yourself scarce."

"Permit me, sir," Red put in, a bite in his tone, "whilst I am still in command of this ship and in a position to offer you hospitality." He picked up the coffeepot, his hand, to his annoyance, not quite steady. "Am I to take it that you wish me to consider myself under arrest?"

Captain Skinner reddened. "It is merely an inquiry, Captain Broome. You will leave the ship, of course. Is your first lieutenant competent to take command in your absence or not?"

"He is competent, sir. But—" Red hesitated and then plunged in. "I shall require to call him as a witness on my behalf. And—" He offered the cup of coffee he had poured, and Skinner accepted it with a brief nod of thanks. "Perhaps I should mention, sir, that Lieutenant Broome is my cousin."

"As also is Mr. De Lancey, is he not?" For the first time since boarding the ship, Captain Skinner permitted himself the ghost of a smile. "That perhaps will even things up." He sipped his coffee and then gave vent to an audible sigh. "This, ah, this unfortunate affair could not have come at a worse time, you know, Broome. A time when I'm driven to my wits' end."

"How so, sir?" Red asked. He poured himself a cup of coffee and sat back in his chair, attempting to relax or at least to appear at ease. But it was a blow, he thought wretchedly, and a blow delivered—if he was not mistaken—by a vindictive Dora Lucas, rather than by her husband. Dora had not forgiven him for ordering her ashore at Fremantle with her ailing husband or, come to that, for having deprived her of Francis De Lancey's company during her enforced stay in Western Australia.

He took a gulp of his own coffee and tried to concentrate on what the commodore of the Sydney Naval Station was saying. It was, he realized suddenly, more than a little alarming.

"Relations between the home government and Russia have worsened, it seems," Skinner told him. "Indeed, the situation could well deteriorate and lead to war. The Governor has received instructions from the colonial secretary to put Sydney in a state of defense. He has only elements of the

Sixty-fifth Regiment here—barely a company—and he's been told he must raise a force of militia to augment them. Easier said than done, with most of the able-bodied males deserting their employment for the goldfields. Deas Thomson says it will take months to raise and train a civilian force, so . . ." The captain's broad, epauletted shoulders rose in an exasperated shrug. "In the meanwhile, His Excellency has seen fit to place the responsibility on *my* shoulders. He has passed the buck to me!"

"You, sir?" Red echoed uncomprehendingly.

"To Her Majesty's Navy, Broome. My squadron is to undertake the defense of Sydney and Port Jackson Harbor, in the event of a Russian naval attack."

"But—" His own unhappy situation momentarily forgotten, Red stared at his visitor in shocked disbelief.

"My squadron, until you rejoined it this morning," Skinner declared bitterly, "consisted of the old *Calliope*, at present in dock for a badly needed refit, and three small sloops—*Herald, Electra,* and *Fancome*—which, as you'll be aware, are under sail and mount thirty-four guns between them. And a recent addition, the paddle-steamer *Acheron* of five. Do you know what the Imperial Russian Navy could send against us, if the Tsar were so minded?" He did not wait for Red's reply, but using the fingers of one hand to enumerate them, he listed the Russian ships. "At Valparaiso—or cruising in the Pacific, no one appears to know which—are an eighty-gun ship of the line and four sixty-gun frigates, plus at least a dozen brigs and sloops. And at Vladivostok, three of the line and fourteen frigates—damme, Broome, they could simply sail into this harbor, and there would be precious little we could do to stop them!"

"But are they likely to sail in, sir?" Red's tone was skeptical, and Captain Skinner glared at him.

"For God's sake, *I* don't know! The Governor considers that it's possible, and the Colonial Office is insisting that we must prepare to defend ourselves. I've had to send the *Electra* to Port Phillip, so that hampers me still further. And now, thanks to this infernal business between you and Captain Lucas, I'm to tie up my senior officers on a damned court of inquiry! I tell you, Broome, it could hardly have come at a worse time."

That, Red thought resentfully, was hardly his fault. He said with restraint, "The court could be postponed, sir, could it not?"

Skinner shook his head. "Captain Lucas won't hear of it. He's senior to me by six months, a fact he does not hesitate to remind me of." He looked at Red, and for an instant his dark eyes were lit with what was undoubtedly a sympathetic gleam. But it swiftly faded, and he went on, making no attempt to conceal his irritation, "The Governor wants a gun battery mounted on South Head, with long thirty-twos, and last night he told me that he thinks we should also mount guns on Dawes Point, George's Head, Pinchgut Island, and Middle Head. But we have no blasted guns, unless we take them out of the ships! And if we do that, how in heaven's name are we to do battle with a Russian squadron, if it appears?" Again he regarded Red searchingly. "The *Galah* and the *Calliope* are the only ships armed with thirty-twos, Broome. And I've already had to take *Calliope*'s bow-chaser for the battery on South Head."

Red met his gaze glumly. "If you take my thirty-twos, sir, the *Galah* will have no teeth. Would it not make more sense to post a guard ship at the Heads—a steamer for maneuverability, perhaps—and let me patrol outside, to bring warning should any hostile squadron be sighted?"

"You, unfortunately, have been relieved of your command," Skinner reminded him.

"Yes, sir, I know. But surely—"

"And if the court of inquiry finds against you, you'll not be permitted to resume your command, save perhaps in the event of a Russian attack, when it might be a matter of expediency." Captain Skinner passed his cup to be refilled, and as he waited, he took his cigar case from his pocket. "Join me," he invited with sudden affability.

Red thanked him but shook his head. "I haven't acquired the habit, sir. I smoke a pipe occasionally, but that's all."

"It helps the nerves," Captain Skinner assured him. "And the temper." When his cigar was lit, he inhaled deeply and returned to the subject of the harbor defenses. "I agree.

What you suggest *would* make more sense. But it's not what Sir Charles Fitzroy wants. I can post the *Acheron* as a guard ship, certainly, and I can back her up with patrol boats. Also, there are, I understand, some old guns of fairly heavy caliber on Dawes Point, so it should be simple enough to construct a battery and fortifications there. But I shall have to take both your long guns if we're to install a battery on George's Head, and *Calliope*'s for that damned island—Pinchgut. In addition, I shall have to deprive you of your gunnery officer and your best guns' crews, if I'm to carry out His Excellency's wishes effectively. I've no choice, have I? As you don't require me to remind you, the lure of the goldfields has denuded Sydney and all the neighboring townships of males of military age, and even if we were able to enlist volunteers, there would be no time to train them in gunnery. So the navy must provide the men as well as the guns, I'm afraid, and it will not be easy. We're faced with an increasing plague of desertions from the ships in port. Seamen run from the ships, and it's the devil's own job trying to get them back from the gold-fields—the infernal miners hide them."

Skinner talked on, almost as if he were finding it a relief to be able to air his anxiety and speak of the problems that beset him, all trace of his earlier animosity gradually fading. Red listened, offering what suggestions he could, and when at last the commodore stubbed out his cigar and rose ponderously to his feet, his manner was the reverse of unfriendly.

"You'll come ashore in your own gig, I take it?" he said. Receiving Red's nod of assent, he held out his hand. "I'll convene the inquiry board as soon as I can, Commander. It will be in everyone's best interests to get it over without delay. I thank you for your hospitality. Ah, you will stay at your father's house, presumably?"

"You will be able to find me there whenever you want me, sir," Red assured him.

"Good," Skinner approved. He reached for his hat but did not immediately don it. Frowning, he added with unexpected frankness, "If it had been left to me, you know, I would have allowed the whole unhappy matter to drop. You're a good officer, with an excellent record, Broome, and

I need you in command of this ship. But Captain Lucas was quite adamant; he would not let the matter drop." He hesitated, subjecting Red to a critical scrutiny, and then said vehemently, "Devil take it, man—*did* you involve yourself with his wife? I want the truth, and it'll go no further, I give you my word."

Red drew himself up. "I did not, sir. I give you *my* word."

"And I'm inclined to accept your word. But . . ." Again the older man hesitated, still frowning. "There was an, ah, involvement during your passage? With one of your officers, perhaps? All right, Commander—" He broke off as Red, in turn, hesitated. "I will not press you on that point, although I anticipate that the inquiry board will have to do so. But since making the acquaintance of Captain Lucas and of, ah, Mrs. Lucas, I confess I'm not surprised. She's a deuced attractive young woman, and he's—damme, he's old enough to be her father! It's asking for trouble to marry a girl like that at his age and then take passage with her in a naval ship."

He sighed, seeming about to say more, then changed his mind and instead donned his cocked hat. Red escorted him to his boat, and he descended the accommodation ladder to the twittering of the pipe, the side party standing punctiliously to attention until his gig pulled away.

Red waited only long enough to acquaint his first lieutenant with the gist of what had passed between him and the station commander and, silencing Tim's indignant comments with a wry smile, told him that he was to be left in command and asked for his gig to be lowered.

"You'll be willing to be called as a witness, I trust, when the court of inquiry convenes . . . if I need you?"

"Of course I will—more than willingly, sir," Tim returned. He added angrily, "I'd like to break that miserable little rogue's neck! We're damned well rid of Francis De Lancey, sir. And if I see him in court, it will be all I can do to keep my hands off him, I can tell you!"

"Between ourselves, I am equally tempted, Tim," Red admitted. "But restraint is essential." His smile widened. "For the honor of the service and all that entails, you understand, I intend to say as little as possible. Perhaps you will be so good as to have a word with our surgeon's mate and warn him that he may also be required to give evidence before the inquiry board?"

"Aye, aye, sir," Tim acknowledged. "I'll do that." He moved toward the entryport. "Your boat's alongside, sir."

The side party formed up once more, the boatswain's mate of the watch put his silver call to his lips, and Red descended to his waiting gig.

Under the lugsail, the small craft skimmed across the blue water of the harbor, and Red observed Lieutenant Robert Fayrer, of the *Herald* brig, on the stone jetty, busy supervising the mounting of twelve-pounder brass guns in his half dozen paddle-wheel patrol boats, Captain Skinner pacing impatiently up and down behind him. Fayrer raised a hand in salute and then as swiftly lowered it. Fayrer, of course, as commander of the *Herald*, would be a member of the inquiry board that was to investigate Lucas's complaints, and, Red thought grimly, it was evident that the lieutenant had already been warned of his duty and of the nature of the complaints.

The gig wended her way up the length of the vast harbor, the various anchorages still crowded with vessels, most of them seemingly devoid of life. At the Van Buren wharf, by contrast with the others, a fine clipper-bowed schooner lay alongside, her upper deck a hive of activity as cargo was unloaded, and Red studied her with interest.

The gig put him ashore at the narrow wooden jetty in Elizabeth Bay, and he walked the short distance to his father's house, the sun pleasantly warm on his back and the scent of flowering shrubs in the well-stocked gardens filling the air.

He found only Jenny at home. Their brother Johnny was, it appeared, on an assignment for his paper at a new gold digging on the Meroo River and could not be expected back for at least ten days. And their father—Jenny's small, sweet face clouded over, the smile with which she had greeted Red's arrival abruptly fading.

"Dad is at the naval dockyard. He should have handed it over to the new superintendent a week ago, but"—she stifled a sigh—"Captain Lucas is making difficulties. He is a very arrogant, disagreeable gentleman, Red, but of course you know him, don't you? You brought him out from England."

"I did indeed," Red confirmed feelingly. "What difficulties is he making, for God's sake?"

"I'm not quite clear exactly," Jenny confessed. "Except that it's about money. Captain Lucas is trying to suggest that Dad misappropriated government funds—Dad, who is the very soul of honesty! It has hurt him very much, and of course there isn't a word of truth in the allegations. How could there be?"

How indeed, Red echoed silently, hard put to it to hide his sense of outrage when Jenny added that Lucas had taken his allegations to the Governor.

"He will get short shrift there. Sir Charles Fitzroy has always thought most highly of Dad, but . . . oh, it leaves a very unpleasant taste in one's mouth, does it not? And when you think," Jenny went on indignantly, "that our dear, honorable father has supervised the building of the dockyard and commanded it for over a year, while he waited for Captain Lucas's arrival, and done all he has done on half pay—it makes one's blood boil!"

Red eyed his young sister ruefully. "I regret to tell you that our dear, honorable father is not the only one to have incurred Captain Lucas's wrath. He is gunning for me also. And . . ." He shrugged, faced with a sudden suspicion. "It's on the cards that he's making trouble for Dad *because* he's my father."

Over luncheon, which they took together, he told Jenny of the commodore's visit to his ship earlier that day, and gave brief details of the pending court of inquiry, careful to treat the affair lightly lest he add to her anxieties.

"So I'm relieved of my command until the board sits. I trust I can count on a bed here until it does?"

"Oh, Red, you've no need to ask," Jenny reproached him. "Of course, there's a bed for you here—there always will be. But you—" She flushed, embarrassed by the question, yet compelled to voice it. "You didn't—that is, Mrs. Lucas is such a shallow young woman, and her manners leave a great deal to be desired. Surely you couldn't have—"

"Fallen for Dora Lucas's doubtful charms?" Red finished for her. "You've made her acquaintance evidently, so I trust you'll believe me when I tell you that I did not. I have more sense than that, Jenny, I assure you."

"But there is—there *was* some reason for Captain Lucas's accusations, surely? Did anyone else—"

"Yes," Red conceded. "Regrettably someone else did fall for the lady. Someone with less sense than I."

The maid entered with their second course, and Jenny waited until, having served them, the girl withdrew. Then she said thoughtfully, "I think I'm beginning to understand. Was it Francis De Lancey? Did *he* fall for—how did you put it? Dora Lucas's doubtful charms, and then lie about it in the hope of involving you? Because if he did, that would explain why Magdalen has been so cold and unfriendly of late—to all of us. And— Oh, Red, she cut you at the Governor's dinner party, just before you sailed, didn't she?"

"Yes, she did." Red could feel the awkward color rising to his cheeks. He pushed his plate away and reached across the table to capture his sister's hand. "Let's say you're pretty near the mark, Jenny. But—"

"I fancy I hit the mark, Red," Jenny amended.

"All right, little sister," Red conceded, releasing her hand. "Provided this conversation is strictly between us, I'll tell you the rest. The young idiot Francis was ready to quit the service on Dora Lucas's account, and I stupidly tried to save him from the consequences of his folly, for his family's sake."

"Or Magdalen's?" Jenny suggested gently.

"Well, perhaps. But I was Francis's commander. I felt I owed it to all of them. I put him under arrest, to stop him from running—that is, from deserting the ship in Perth—in order to stay with Dora. He would have wrecked his career if he'd deserted, and there would have been hell to pay with Captain Lucas, of course."

"And he has repaid you by lying to Magdalen and his parents?" Jenny's eyes were bright with indignation, as they had been when she had spoken of her father's predicament a little while before. "Oh, Red, I'm so sorry! But I'm glad you told me, because it explains why Magdalen has been so strange lately. And Uncle George and dear Aunt Rachel, too." She rose and led the way into the drawing room, where coffee had been set out for them. "I was at a loss to understand why they should have behaved so, even to Dad. And so was he. I think you ought to tell him, Red." She poured the coffee and carried his cup over to him. "It will have to come out at the court of inquiry, will it not?"

Red put down his cup and strode across to the wide window overlooking Elizabeth Bay, seeking to collect his thoughts. "Possibly," he said at last. "Depending on what I decide to tell the court."

Jenny regarded him in some dismay. "But surely you will tell them the truth? Francis De Lancey has left the navy, has he not? You cannot risk your career for the sake of that ungrateful little rogue. Red, you must not! Not even for Magdalen's sake, however much you care for her."

Red was again silent. How much, he asked himself, did he care for his cousin Magdalen? Enough, he knew, to want to see her again, to break through the barrier this unhappy affair had placed between them, and to continue his interrupted courtship. And . . . yes, enough to want her for his wife, if only she would finally consent to wed him.

Staring out across the sun-bright water of the small landlocked bay below him, Red saw Magdalen's lovely, serene face in memory and remembered the warmth of her smile, and how her blue eyes had sparkled when she laughed. They both had laughed often during the all too brief time they had spent together in the glory of an English June, kindly and unobtrusively chaperoned by Magdalen's stout, good-natured aunt. Those had been happy days, the happiest he had ever spent since his boyhood, but . . . Reluctantly he dragged his mind back to the present and the problems that the court of inquiry would pose, not only for himself.

"Jenny," he said awkwardly, "there are others involved, you know. If it were only Francis, I'd let him take the consequences and be damned to him. But it's not. I hold no brief for Captain Lucas, I assure you—in fact, I heartily dislike him, the more so after what you say he's doing to Dad. But if I tell the whole truth, it will wreck his marriage, and he's an old man, a pretty frail one, too. And it would do immeasurable harm to the De Lanceys."

"Yes, but what about yourself? What will it do to your career, if the inquiry finds against you?" Jenny countered.

Red smiled at her. "I can clear myself of any improper association with Dora Lucas. I have a host of witnesses I can call, virtually my whole ship's company. And that will suffice, I believe. Once offered proof that *I* didn't cuckold him, he'll be satisfied, and so will the court, I venture to hope. There's no need to make Francis's infatuation public, and given time, the young fool will probably get over it." He crossed to Jenny's side and put an affectionate arm about her slim shoulders. "Dora has made her bed, now she must lie on it—and I rather fancy she will, when this is over. Lucas may be no great shakes as a husband, but he ranks as a post captain, conferring a certain social prestige, besides a fine official residence and no financial worries. I don't imagine she'll throw all that away, when she's had time to think about it. Besides, what can Francis De Lancey offer her? He's thrown up his naval career—he has no job and no money. And Dora's not entirely a fool."

"I pray you are right, Red," Jenny told him, her voice lacking conviction. "But let's talk of something more pleasant, shall we? Tell me about your visit to Norfolk Island. It's not as terrible a place as it used to be, is it? I know that the government recalled that good Captain Maconochie because he was considered too lenient and because he gave so many of the convicts their freedom, if he believed they merited it. What is the present commandant like? Is he a reformer?"

"If the lash reforms, then yes, I suppose he is." Red helped himself to a second cup of coffee. "I don't know if the subject of Norfolk Island is any pleasanter, Jenny. It is still a hell on earth for the poor, unhappy devils sent there to serve their sentences. True, there are women and children on the island now, but they are the families of the commandant and his staff; convicts' wives are forbidden. And the commandant, John Price, is . . . well, in my view he's a sadist. A gentleman with impeccable manners and cultured tastes, who treats the wretched prisoners with a refined cruelty that horrified me."

He and his officers had been most hospitably entertained, Red recalled; indeed, the Prices had spared no effort to make them welcome, even, on one occasion, giving a garden party for them in the beautifully landscaped grounds of their official residence. John Price was a civilian—the first ever appointed as commandant of the penal settlement. He was a tall, handsome man, who affected a monocle, and his wife, Mary, was a niece of Sir John Franklin, the late Governor of Van Diemen's Land.

Red's brows met in a frown. At first he had been taken in; the penal establishment ran on oiled wheels, its every need supplied by convict labor, and the convicts were docile and well behaved, carrying out their menial tasks with no hint of rebelliousness or even, it seemed, of resentment. But then he had attended a church service, at which all but a handful of convict worshipers had shuffled in, wearing leg fetters, their faces blank masks of suffering and their voices never raised above a whisper, even when hymns were sung by the rest of the congregation.

Later, concerned by what he had seen, he had talked to the chaplain, the Reverend Adam Rogers, and had learned of sickening punishments, floggings, confinements in cells too small to permit the occupants to stand upright, and men spread-eagled in the sun until they screamed for mercy—all this, and more, for the most trivial of offenses.

"Mr. Price was sent here to restore order after the convicts mutinied under the previous commandant, Major Childs," Rogers had told him. "He has done that—there is order here, without a doubt, for the poor unfortunates are too cowed and frightened to rebel. But he has done it with greater brutality than his predecessor ever indulged in, and he is hated more bitterly than even Major Childs was, believe me."

And he had added bleakly, "I am soon to be dismissed from my post, Captain Broome, because I wrote to my archdeacon in Hobart and revealed the truth about this terrible place. Mr. Price refuted all my accusations, and Sir William Denison, alas, has chosen to believe him rather than me. I am, according to Mr. Price, 'too easily disturbed and lacking in discretion.' But judge for yourself, Captain. You have seen the faces of cruelly tortured men in my church this morning."

And indeed he had, Red thought, feeling again the sick pity he had felt during the parody of a service of worship, attended by close to three hundred lost souls, afraid to raise their voices to sing their Maker's praise.

He had accepted no more invitations to garden parties at Orange Vale and had made excuses when Price had suggested a shooting party, to be followed by a picnic on the opposite side of the island. But—

Jenny said, watching his face, "Did you suppose that this country had completely rid itself of its convict heritage, Red? Simply because we no longer accept convict transports here, that does not mean that the—the criminal element has vanished. Those who are sent to Norfolk Island now are classed as incorrigibles. They are guilty of very serious crimes— murder, and robbery with violence, most of them, and persistent lawbreaking."

"They are still human beings," Red demurred. "But Price treats them like animals."

"Well," Jenny told him, "according to reports in our newspapers, there is a possibility that Norfolk Island will be closed as a penal settlement before very long. It is administered by Van Diemen's Land, as you know, not by New South Wales, and the Governor, Sir William Denison, is said to favor the resettlement there of the Pitcairn islanders."

"Good Lord!" Red exclaimed. "Do you mean the *Bounty* mutineers?"

"Their descendants. Apparently there are quite a number of them still living on Pitcairn Island, which is barren and inhospitable. It is a romantic idea really, I suppose, but it seems they are good, deserving folk, worthy of a better home than the one they have."

"Admiral Bligh will turn in his grave!" Red exclaimed. "But I, for one, would be happy to see an end to Commandant Price's hell on earth. Norfolk's a beautiful island, Jenny —truly beautiful, with fertile soil and a mild climate. It deserves better than to be used for—what did you say they

were?—incorrigibles, condemned to a living death. Captain
Cook, you know, described it as an earthly paradise, and I
daresay that is what it could have been, if our government
had used it for normal settlement. We—" He broke off,
hearing the sound of carriage wheels on the gravel drive
outside the house. "Callers, Jenny?"

"No." Jenny jumped up, beaming. "Dad is back. He drives
to the dockyard these days, behind a pretty pair of trotters
he bought from Mr. Edward Hargraves. Hargraves wasted
no time investing in a brougham, you see, as soon as the
governor appointed him commissioner for Crown lands."
Her smile faded, and she eyed her brother gravely. "Red,
you *will* tell him about Francis De Lancey, won't you? He has
a right to know."

"I'll tell him," Red assured her. "If he asks me, Jenny."

But their father was not alone when he came into the
room. His arm was about the shoulders of a slim, dark-faced
man, elegantly dressed in a blue cutaway coat, with Hessian
boots and well-cut white breeches. Red stared at him for a
moment without recognition. Then the stranger wrung his
hand, and Justin Broome said, smiling, "My son Red, commanding Her Majesty's ship *Galah*. Red, this is an old friend
from your boyhood, Claus Van Buren, master and owner of
the clipper schooner *Dolphin*. No doubt you noticed her
when you came in this morning."

"That I did," Red responded. "With my eyes popping out
of my head!" He gripped the new arrival's hand warmly.
"It's been a long time, Claus, a very long time since my
brother Johnny and I hid you in a sail locker to prevent them
shipping you off to—Timor, wasn't it?"

"It was Timor," Claus confirmed. "And thanks be to God
that you came to my rescue!" He studied Red with bright,
inquiring eyes, bearded lips curved in an oddly boyish grin.
"You were a young mid then, wearing your first white patch
and dirk. Then you sailed with Captain Stirling in Her
Majesty's ship *Success*, and we saw you no more. I'm delighted to see you back, Commander!" He bowed and
turned to greet Jenny. "I have issued an invitation to you all
to dine on board my *Dolphin* tomorrow evening, which your
father has accepted on your behalf." He glanced from one to

the other inquiringly and, receiving their nods of assent, added proudly, "I shall have the pleasure of displaying my clipper to you and also of introducing you to my bride-to-be, whom I have brought with me from America."

He received their congratulations with smiling diffidence and then took his leave, refusing Jenny's offer of refreshment.

"I understand that there was an unfortunate occurrence at the naval dockyard this morning," he said, exchanging glances with Justin Broome. "That is how we came to meet . . . although, of course, I'd intended to call on you, Miss Jenny. No doubt Captain Broome will tell you about it when I have gone."

Red ushered him out. He returned to the drawing room to find his father seated in his accustomed armchair, a glass in his hand, and all trace of the pleasure he had displayed in Claus Van Buren's presence wiped from his face.

"What happened at the dockyard, sir?" Red asked with concern. Meeting Jenny's warning glance, he hesitated, recalling what she had told him of their father's troubled relationship with his successor. "Has Captain Lucas—that is, was he—"

His father eyed him somberly. "Captain Lucas collapsed, Red—a heart attack, I imagine, although we shall not know for certain until the doctors have examined him. He came into my office, after lunching at his own house, and started raging at me. I've no idea what about, because he was inarticulate with fury. I could scarcely understand a word he said. But—" He shrugged ruefully. "As Jenny may have told you, we have not been on the best of terms, virtually since his arrival. He has seen fit to accuse me of maladministration, to which—since he could offer no proof—I took exception. But he is so obviously a sick man that I—well, I tried not to make an issue of it."

Red swore under his breath. The devil take Benjamin Lucas, he thought bitterly, but controlling himself, he said without rancor, "You're not to blame, sir. For God's sake, he's brought it on himself, just as he did on our passage out."

"Well, perhaps," his father conceded. He sighed. "We

sent him to the hospital in my curricle. That was how I came
to be with Claus. He met me when I was starting to walk back
here and of course offered me a lift. I brought him in because the maid told me you were here, and I supposed you
would welcome the opportunity to renew your acquaintance
with him. And also, of course," he added with a brief smile,
"the opportunity to look over his fine new schooner, which,
he told me, was built in Boston, Massachusetts, by the ship-
wright who has pioneered these clipper ships, Donald Mc-
Kay."

They talked of the clippers, both men enthusiastic, while
Jenny listened politely, her attention occasionally wandering
when their discussion grew too technical for her to follow.

Their peace was abruptly shattered when the Irish maid-
servant, Biddy, announced a second visitor, and George De
Lancey entered in a state of visible agitation.

All three rose to receive him, and Jenny started to speak
but fell silent when, ignoring her tentative greeting, the
judge announced in a voice vibrant with emotion, "Justin,
Red, I owe you both the most abject apology. My son Francis, to my infinite regret and shame, has run off with Mrs.
Lucas. The infernal young rogue left a note, if you please, in
which he claimed that he and this—this woman are in love
and cannot live without each other! God knows where they
have gone or what they intend to do. Frankly, I do not
greatly care." He paused, two bright spots of shamed color
burning in his cheeks. "I cannot begin to tell you how
grieved I am that my son's lies and prevarications should
have caused a rift between our two families. I . . . and I've
just heard that Captain Lucas suffered a stroke as a result, I
can only surmise, of receiving a similar letter to my son's,
written by his wife." He looked uncertainly at Justin. "Is that
so? Is the rumor correct? Have they taken him to the hospital?"

Red watched with a glow of pride as his father slowly
inclined his head and then, taking George De Lancey by the
arm, led him to a chair.

To Jenny, Justin said quietly, "I fancy your uncle could do
with a glass of brandy, Jenny my dear. Be so good as to pour
him one, would you please?" Then, turning to his stricken

brother-in-law, he went on, still in the same quiet, even tone,
"We all make mistakes, George, particularly where our children are concerned. I'm most infernally sorry for what's
happened, believe me. It must have come as an appalling
shock to you—and to Rachel and Magdalen also."

"It has, Justin," George De Lancey confessed. "It was they
who insisted I must offer you my apologies. Not that it can
compensate, but—" Jenny brought him his brandy, and as
he put out a shaking hand to take it, he met Red's gaze.
"Magdalen charged me to beg that you will call on her, Red,
so that she may express her contrition for the way she has
treated you. I hope that you will find it in your heart to do
so."

Red's answer came without hesitation or, indeed, without
conscious thought. "I shall be happy to, sir," he said. "I—
dear heaven, I'll be more than happy!"

CHAPTER XII

She had not wanted to take the drastic step of running away
with Francis De Lancey, Dora Lucas reflected wretchedly as
she watched the rooftops of Parramatta vanish into the gathering darkness. And she had longed to stay overnight at the
hostelry in the township, so that she might wash and change
her clothing before continuing the journey—a tedious one,
in their heavily laden bullock wagon, with no shade from the
sun in daytime and no shelter from the night chills or any
sudden shower.

But Francis, fearful of pursuit, had insisted that they must
go on. Crouched in the wagon behind him, Dora shivered,
sharing his fear. Her husband, as she well knew from bitter
experience, was a vindictive man, tormented by jealousy, but
even he would surely have stopped short of creating a scene
had he found her in the Parramatta Arms, which was always
crowded. Whereas on the open road, with only Francis to
protect her . . . She drew an unhappy, sobbing breath,
glancing involuntarily behind her and half expecting to see
the dread figure of her husband, galloping after them and
intent on vengeance.

But there was no sound of hoofbeats, no other vehicle on
the long, winding road to their rear. Yet Benjamin must be
aware, by this time, that she had left him. She had penned
her note as soon as he had set off for the naval dockyard, and
had left it propped up on the dining room mantel, where he
would be certain to see it when he returned for luncheon.

Francis had insisted on that, too.

"I want him to know that I am taking you from him," he
had said obstinately when she attempted to argue. "I owe
that, at least, to Red Broome. I've caused him more trouble
than he deserves, one way or another. But he never under-

stood, Dora, he never *tried* to understand that what I feel for you is not mere infatuation. You are the love of my life, my sweet darling, and . . ." He had looked down at her with such tenderness, Dora remembered, holding her in his arms, his strong young body pressed against hers. "Now that you are carrying my child, you cannot stay for a single day longer with that unspeakably vile old man. You are mine, my beloved—you and the child."

Dora shifted uneasily, seeking relief from the jolting of the unsprung wagon. She had made a grave error, she realized now. She should never have told Francis that the baby she had conceived was his. Undoubtedly it was; Benjamin's frequent but futile attempts to get her with child had never succeeded and had only filled her with loathing and contempt for his ineptness. But she *could* have deceived him; he wanted to believe that he was capable of fatherhood, so that it would not have taken much ingenuity to play on his vanity. And she could then have pleaded her pregnancy to spare her from his unwelcome lovemaking, and thus have lived, in reasonable contentment, in the grand official residence allotted to him, freed of financial worries and able to enjoy the social standing she had always coveted.

Benjamin would have been placated, and she could have continued a clandestine relationship with Francis, which, thanks to his father's eminence and his family's loyal support, could probably have gone on for years, quite unsuspected.

But instead . . . Dora's small white hands clenched convulsively at her sides. She had been foolish, she chided herself bitterly. She had permitted her heart to rule her head, and, when Francis had run inquisitive fingers over her thickening belly, as they had lain together on a deserted beach in a joyous prelude to their lovemaking, she had told him the truth, quite unprepared for his reaction to it.

"We will run away, darling," he had decided, in a voice that brooked no argument, for all it trembled with happiness. "I'll buy a wagon and a tent and supplies, and we will go to the goldfields—Lucas won't look for us there. It will mean living rough for a while, I know, but we'll be together, and it is spring . . . it will not be too cold in the mountains,

and in any case I will look after you. You will not need to
sully your hands, because I will do everything. I will take the
greatest care of you, my love, until your time comes and we
will have to seek the services of a midwife. But until then
we'll be free, like traveling folk, with the sky for our roof!
Think of it, my sweet Dora . . . It will be heaven, I promise
you. And who knows?" He had thrown back his handsome
head and laughed, like the boy he was, she remembered.
"Who knows, we might strike it rich, and then all our troubles would be over. I'd be able to buy you a grand house in
Sydney Town, or a squatter's sheep run in the backcountry,
and like the fairy tale, we should live happily ever after, with
our children around us, wanting for nothing save each
other!"

He had painted an entrancing picture, Dora recalled, and
she had let herself believe in it, despite her better judgment
and the sound common sense she had hitherto relied on
when it came to making decisions. But the reality—even at
this, the outset of their journey to the Turon River—was
proving a disillusionment, and at the rate the bullocks traveled, it would take at least a week or ten days to reach
Bathurst. From there the way would lead through the Roch
Forest, along a steep mountain road that was said to be
difficult for vehicular traffic. . . . The wagon lurched, and
Dora cried out in protest.

"Don't worry, my darling," Francis called back with irritat-
ing cheerfulness. "I'll get the hang of driving these wretched
animals soon. Try to sleep, my love, because we have to push
on."

He "pushed on," to Dora's increasing discomfort, for day
after endless day, never quite seeming to manage the bullocks, despite his efforts. The road, after they had crossed
the Nepean River, became heavily congested. Impatient
horsemen squeezed past, leaving clouds of dust in their
wake, and every variety of dray and wagon and horse-drawn
carriage impeded their passage, while men on foot added to
the confusion.

They were from every walk of life—doctors, clerics, and
ship's officers rubbing shoulders with clerks, shopkeepers,
and humble laborers; new immigrants from America, En-

gland, and New Zealand mingling with settlers from Adelaide and Perth and deserters from the ships that had
brought them to their destination. They were almost exclu-
sively male—Dora looked in vain for the sight of one of her
own sex in the motley throng—and for the most part they
were friendly, if impatient of delay in reaching the goldfields
and the fortunes all were convinced were awaiting them
there.

After a while, satisfied that they had lost themselves in the
crowd, Francis relaxed his vigilance and, to Dora's relief,
permitted an overnight stay at an inn on the outskirts of
Bathurst. The inn was rough and overrun by the travelers,
all demanding food and drink and beds in which to sleep,
but a hefty bribe to the landlord secured water in which Dora
could wash and the doubtful privacy of a curtained recess in
his cookhouse, furnished with a single, cramped bunk and a
soiled straw mattress.

After that experience, she ceased to complain about
spending the night in their tent; but as they climbed higher
into the mountains, the cold increased, and the flimsy tent
proved incapable of keeping out the first steady rain they
encountered. Francis was assiduous in his attentions, deeply
distressed by the hardships their elopement had caused her,
and anxious, in any way he could, to spare her discomfort,
but . . . he was not any more fitted for the conditions than
she was, Dora came unhappily to realize.

The bullocks were slow and, in Francis's untutored care,
became increasingly intractable, and Dora suggested he exchange them for horses. Francis finally did so, making the
exchange with a party of rascally fellows returning to Sydney
from Ophir, purportedly with their fortunes made. The gold
diggers got the better of the bargain, for the horses were
worn-out, half-starved creatures whose progress, hauling
the heavy wagon, was little faster than that of the bullocks;
and the bullocks' new owners, to Dora's distress, slaugh-
tered their purchases for food while still in sight and sound
of her and Francis.

They reached the township of Sofala, on the Turon River,
at last, only to find so many people there that they could find
nowhere to stake a claim, save in the dry diggings on a

hillside, where, Francis was told, it was necessary to sink a shaft some forty to fifty feet deep.

"Go on to the Meroo River," he was advised. "It's not above thirty miles distant. Or the Louisa Creek—that's where a lot of folk are heading. Carry on northward, and maybe you'll get there ahead of the rush."

"We'll have to go, my dearest," Francis said, after breaking this news. "There's nothing for us here."

They went on wearily, Dora greatly troubled by morning sickness and alarmed by the rugged terrain through which they must travel. She wept bitterly as they ascended what had appeared to be a gentle rise, with a well-defined track running through the box and gum trees, only to find themselves on the verge of a precipice, with a sheer drop of close to two hundred feet to the river below. In the gully there were men at work, their tents and bark *gunyas* pitched close by, under the swamp oaks at the water's edge, with still more dotted at intervals on the opposite side, where other men were toiling with picks and shovels to dig into the hillside.

"That's the Meroo River," Francis declared, tight-lipped and hard put to it to hide his disappointment. "The rush is here before us, alas! Well, there's nothing for it but to press on, darling. They say that the country round the Louisa is comparatively flat, and there are some farms in the vicinity." He noticed Dora's tear-filled eyes and came to kneel beside her in the back of the wagon. "Oh, my sweet love, what have I done to you, bringing you to this wilderness? I . . . . Dora, heart of my heart, if you say that we should turn back, I'll do so. I will take you back to Sydney and yield you up to your husband, if that is your wish."

But that was a prospect Dora knew she could not face. Benjamin, if he consented to take her back, would exact a terrible price for the humiliation she had caused him, and . . . . there was the baby, her unborn, innocent child, conceived in love, whom he would claim. She looked up at her lover and, blinded by tears, shook her head, finding fresh courage.

"No, Francis, we've come too far. We've been through too much to turn back now."

It had all started lightheartedly, she recalled. When she

had boarded the *Galah* at Devonport, she had already been disillusioned where Benjamin was concerned, repulsed by his fumbling lovemaking, resenting the demands he had made on her, and fearful of his uncertain temper and occasional outbursts of violence. She had been—Dora bit her lower lip, feeling it tremble—she had been ripe for a flirtation, even for a clandestine affair, so that, for her own self-esteem and gratification, she might defy the hateful man she had married and assert herself in the only way open to her. Her small mouth twitched into a wry, pouting smile. Initially she had set her cap at the *Galah*'s commander, but Red Broome had ignored her advances, treating them with cold contempt and adding to her bitter discontent, because he had struck at the roots of her pride.

But Francis De Lancey—handsome, chivalrous Francis—had changed everything. He had restored her self-confidence, made her feel wanted and admired, desirable . . . a woman, not a child. She had not intended to fall in love with him—that had certainly not been part of her plan, for she had always been aware of how much she had to lose if she went too far. Yet, unable to help herself, she *had* fallen in love. The flirtation had become serious, the affair of greater importance than security or the social position she had once wanted so badly.

"We cannot go back now, Francis," she repeated. "*I* cannot!"

Francis held her close, his lips on hers, his arms cradling her stiff and weary body. "I love you, Dora, my dearest girl," he whispered. "I will love you till the day I die, I swear it by everything I hold sacred! We'll go on—there must be somewhere for us in this vast wilderness."

He turned the wagon, whipped the jaded horses into a shambling trot, and they descended the hill to follow a track around its foot. Two more large mining camps lay on their new route, but, when they both were despairing of ever finding it, they breasted a rock-strewn ridge and were suddenly looking down on a green expanse of flat, treeless plain devoid of human habitation, with a creek running through it about half a mile away.

"We're here, my darling!" Francis exclaimed, his voice

elated, waking Dora from a fitful sleep. She joined him on the front seat of the wagon, and he unfolded the rough sketch map he had made, based on information gleaned at their various stopping places. "I think that is a creek called Tambaroora, but I can't be sure. But there are no tents that I can see and no—" He broke off, swearing under his breath. "Oh, the devil take it, we're not the first! Look, there are horsemen down below! Three of them, with packhorses!"

Dora followed the direction of his pointing finger and saw that he was right. There were three mounted men, each leading a packhorse, trotting slowly toward the head of the creek.

"Does it matter?" she asked, an edge of impatience to her voice. "There are only three riders, and it is a big creek. We cannot expect to be alone, Francis."

"No," he conceded. "That's true, darling. We'll go down after them." He plied his whip, and the horses started down the slope, gathering speed as the weight of the wagon impelled them forward. Francis did not attempt to steady them, eager to reduce the distance between the trotting horsemen and themselves, and even as Dora cried out to him to have a care, disaster struck.

One of the horses stumbled, alarming its companion, which kicked over the traces, and then both animals took fright, tearing down the hillside and eluding all of Francis's frantic efforts to control them. The wheels of the wagon on the off side struck a boulder, and the spokes shattered, causing the wagon to crash over onto its side. Dora managed to hold on to the back of the seat, but Francis was flung forward, to fall, with a sickening thud, several yards away. The wagon shaft broke, bringing down one of the horses, and the other, panic-stricken, struggled free and went galloping off toward the creek.

Badly shaken, Dora slithered down from her seat as the wagon discarded most of its load. Fear lent her strength, and, gathering up her skirts, she ran unsteadily to where Francis was lying. Sobbing his name, she fell to her knees beside him, shocked and horrified when he did not answer her desperate cries. He was unconscious, she realized, lying

limp and twisted on the swampy grass, one arm beneath him
and his dark head lolling, as if . . .

"Oh, dear God," she prayed aloud. "Dear kind God in
heaven, let him be alive! Please, Heavenly Father, do not
take him from me! Francis, Francis, my dearest love, speak to
me, tell me you're alive!"

Dora had managed to pillow his head on her lap when,
heralded by the thud of hooves, the three horsemen they
had seen earlier, approaching the creek, pulled up a few
yards from her. The leading rider, a slim, deeply tanned
young man in seaman's duck trousers and a tattered shirt,
jumped from his saddle and, letting his horse go, came to
kneel at her side. Gently he lifted Francis's limp, dark head
from her knee and, murmuring reassuringly, subjected him
to a swift examination.

"I reckon he's only stunned, ma'am," he told her. "But
we'll just make sure he's not broken any bones. Rob—" He
addressed one of his companions. "Help the young lady to
her feet, will you? And then you and Simon right the wagon,
so's we can bring the two of them down to the creek."

Dazedly, Dora accepted the helping hand the youth addressed as Rob held out to her, and she let him lead her to
the shade of an overhanging rock. He left her there and went
to aid in righting the wagon, only to call out, "There's two
wheels busted, Luke. We'll not be able to get the wagon
down the hill until we've mended them. And we'll have to
shoot the horse—both its forelegs are broken, poor brute."

Luke, continuing to give all his attention to the injured
Francis, grunted an assent, and moments later Dora heard
the sound of a shot. She shuddered, and the shorter of the
two young men came to her, offering his arm.

"We're going to set up camp by the creek, ma'am," he told
her sympathetically. "We'll soon have a fire going and the
billy on. I'll take you down, shall I?" He saw her hesitation
and flashed her a friendly smile. "Don't you worry your head
about your husband—Luke and my brother Rob will carry
him if he can't walk. But like Luke said, the chances are he's
only stunned and winded. He came out of your dray at a fair
rate when the horses bolted, so it's small wonder he's out
cold."

On the way down to the creek, he volunteered the information that he and his brother Robert were from New Zealand's North Island, the sons of the Church of England mission doctor at Rangihowa, Simon Yates.

"Luke Murphy's an American, come here from the California goldfields. He was working his passage as a deckhand on the ship that brought us here, the *Dolphin*, and we chummed up on the way to Sydney."

"And now you are prospecting together?" Dora suggested.

The boy nodded. "Rob and I are going to try our luck in the fields, yes, ma'am. We've taken out licenses. But Luke's not looking for gold—he's looking for a man who robbed him, back in California. A Captain Jasper Morgan, who served in Her Majesty's Twenty-third Foot. We had word that he was in these parts, somewhere along the Turon River, but we've not seen hide nor hair of him here. Luke's going to try Bathurst way, soon as he's seen us settled on a claim. I suppose—" Simon Yates turned to look at her inquiringly. "You won't have come across him, will you, ma'am? This Captain Morgan, I mean."

"No," Dora denied. "No, I haven't. We—that is, my husband and I—" She caught her breath, hoping that he would not question her too closely, and then went on resolutely. "My husband and I have come from Sydney, Mr. Yates. We, too, intend to stake a claim up here, but . . . there are so many men searching for gold—thousands of them. We could not, I mean we did not want to join a big camp where there are only men. I . . . it would not be seemly since I am a—a lone female."

"No, ma'am." The mission doctor's son seemed readily to accept her explanation. "Some of the diggers do bring their wives and families with them, but not many. It . . . it's a harsh way of life for a woman. And for a lady born and bred—" He colored, evidently fearing that his words might be misunderstood and taken for criticism. "I admire your courage, ma'am, I truly do."

They reached the creek, a shallow stretch of silvery water bordered by a thick belt of trees and heady with the scent of the mimosa growing on the opposite bank.

Simon Yates, displaying faultless courtesy, bowed Dora to a seat at the edge of the trees, divesting himself of his jacket and spreading it out for her to sit on. Then he excused himself in order to go in search of the packhorses.

"We just let them go, you see, ma'am, when we witnessed your accident, and it looks as if they've strayed. Still, I don't suppose they've gone far. You stay right where you are and rest yourself . . . I'll be back as soon as I've found our horses."

He was as good as his word, returning about a quarter of an hour later with the errant animals. Having secured them, he set about building a cooking fire with what was clearly the skill of long practice, and then, whistling cheerfully, took a smoke-blackened billycan from one of the pack saddles and headed down to the creek in long, loping strides to fetch water.

Dora waited, recovering slowly from the shock of the accident and fighting against the nausea that threatened to overwhelm her. After a while, the sound of voices caused her to look up to see that, at long last, the young seaman named Luke and the older Yates boy were on their way down the steep hillside. Francis, she saw, to her heartfelt relief, was mounted on one of the horses—slumped in the saddle and with Luke leading his horse, but alive and conscious.

She got to her feet and went eagerly to meet them, biting back a cry of dismay when she noticed Francis's right arm was suspended in a sling, fashioned from a belt and the tail of a shirt. He looked white and badly shaken, but was swift to reassure her when she reached his side.

"It's all right, my love. I'm in one piece, thanks to the timely aid these good fellows have supplied. And I don't think my arm's broken—just bruised and a mite sore, that's all. And the wagon can be repaired, they say."

Luke assisted him to dismount. "We've brought your tent down with us, Mrs. De Lancey," he said practically, gesturing to the canvas draped across the saddle of one of the lead horses. "It'll take us only a few minutes to set it up and give you some privacy. And when that fire gets going, we'll cook us something to eat." He glanced about him with evident approval. "Seems a likely spot for game. I'll take a musket and see what I can bag for the pot."

Dusk was falling when, in response to Luke's hail, they gathered around the fire, on which the skinned carcass of a young kangaroo was roasting on a wooden spit, the old black billycan boiling merrily on the embers of the fire. Dora realized suddenly that she was hungry; during their long journey through the mountains, she and Francis had tasted no fresh meat except in Sofala, where, for an exorbitant sum, they had purchased some beef that had soon become putrid. She had never acquired any skills in the kitchen; at home, prior to her marriage to Benjamin Lucas, her mother had attended to all the family's needs, and since they had arrived in Sydney, there had been servants to wait on them, and a well-trained cook.

A trifle shamefacedly, she watched Rob Yates deftly making what he told her was damper, from a mixture of flour and water, cooked to appetizing perfection on an upturned spade, while his brother sliced up the kangaroo meat with equal skill and neatness, using a heavy clasp knife, which he took from his belt and sharpened on a stone. Both the meat and damper tasted delicious, and Dora ate well, her nausea gone.

Later, seated companionably around the fire as the darkness closed in, they talked, the Yates boys of New Zealand and their life there, Dora nostalgically of England, and Francis of his naval service, which, Dora was surprised to learn, had encompassed twelve of his twenty-two years and a war with the Chinese, in which he had been wounded.

Luke Murphy was oddly silent, listening with evident interest but contributing nothing to the discussion.

"Don't you have anything to tell us?" Francis asked him, leaning back, his head pillowed on Dora's lap and his pipe emitting a thin, fragrant cloud of blue smoke. "About California and the goldfields there?"

Luke's expression hardened. "I've told Rob and Simon all that's liable to help them find gold out here, Mr. De Lancey," he defended. "And they can pass it on to you, if you wish. Because I'm moving on, you see, sir, just as soon as I've seen them settled on a likely claim. Tomorrow, maybe, if this creek's as promising as I think it is."

"He is looking for a man who robbed him, Francis," Dora put in, recalling what Simon Yates had told her earlier. "That is so, isn't it, Luke? A man named Captain Morgan, who served in the British Army?"

Luke turned to her, his eyes suddenly bright. "Yes, that's so. Ma'am, do you know him—do you know where he is?"

His face fell and he looked crestfallen when Dora shook her head. "No, Simon asked me that. I've never heard of him, I'm afraid, Luke. I'm sorry if I raised your hopes."

"He *was* here—or someone fitting his exact description. He was working a claim on the Turon but has moved on. Toward Bathurst, one man told me, and he talked of going to Victoria because he had not done good here." Luke leaned forward to poke the fire, the light from it revealing a grim tautness in his pleasant young face. "I have to go after him—to Victoria, if need be."

Francis eyed him in some bewilderment. "But if he robbed you—in California, I take it—would you not be better off staying here? You say this creek is promising; you could make . . . what do they call it? A good strike, which would more than compensate you for whatever Morgan stole from you. If he's a rogue, rogue enough to rob you, what chance will you have of forcing him to repay you? And if he's an officer—that is . . ." He did not complete his sentence, but its implications were plain enough, and Luke reddened.

"Jasper Morgan did not only rob me, Mr. De Lancey," he answered, his tone harsh. "My brother Dan and I were in partnership with him and two Australians, working a claim near the Feather River, and we struck it rich—real rich. More than twelve thousand American dollars the Mint in 'Frisco paid out for the gold we found . . . the gold *I* found. Morgan claimed it; he took the money. He—" Frowning, Luke looked from one to the other of the faces grouped around the fire. He went on, addressing Rob and Simon Yates. "I never told you the whole story. I never told anyone on board the *Dolphin*, not even Captain Van Buren, because I figured it was my business. Mine and Mercy's, because she was there too, in Windy Gully. But I guess I might as well tell you now,

and you'll understand why I have to go after Jasper Morgan,
if it's the last thing I ever do. He's guilty of murder, you see,
and the miners' committee where it happened heard and—
yes, *saw* the evidence with their own eyes, and they found
him guilty and sentenced him to hang. I've come after him to
bring him to justice."

He broke off, and Dora, watching him, saw the glint of
tears in his dark eyes.

"Who did he murder, Luke?" Rob Yates asked, breaking
the silence. "Your brother Dan?"

"Dan, yes, and our partners, Tom and Frankie Gardener. I
went to see Tom's widow when I came ashore in Sydney
Town—his widow and their little kids. It was awful, and it
just about broke my heart, having to break it to her that Tom
wouldn't be coming back. I didn't tell her what really happened, though—I couldn't bring myself to tell her. I just said
our mine caved in and buried the three of them alive, and I
gave her a bag of dust. I didn't have anything else to give
her, you see." Again Luke broke off, his face working.

"*Did* your mine cave in, Luke?" Francis asked him quietly.

"It caved in because Morgan blew it up, Mr. De Lancey,"
Luke told him bleakly. "But he shot all three of them first,
and then he took the gold and made off with it to 'Frisco. But
maybe I'd best tell you how it happened from the beginning."

He told them, in a flat, controlled voice that carried complete conviction, and Dora listened with growing horror as
the ghastly tale unfolded. Francis, sensing her distress,
reached for her hand and held it.

He said emphatically, "Go after him, Luke. Go after the
foul murdering swine wherever he runs to! I don't know
what help I can give you, because—well, my sweet lass and I
have some troubles of our own, and there are reasons why
we had to leave Sydney Town and come up here with the
gold seekers." Dora felt his fingers tighten about hers.
"You'll need money to pay your passage to Port Phillip, if
Morgan has gone there. I haven't much, but you can take
what I have."

Luke shook his head. "No, Mr. De Lancey, I'll not take
your money. It's good of you, but—"

"I'm in your debt," Francis argued.

"No, I—*we've* done nothing that merits reward, sir." Luke smiled and got to his feet. "I'll earn what I need, or work my passage, if I find that the bird has flown. But—" He turned to his youthful companions, his smile warm and affectionate as he looked from Rob to Simon. "These two are good, trust-worthy lads. Join forces with them, Mr. De Lancey, and stake your claim here with them. The rush will catch up with you if you do make a strike, but you're here first, and the four of you could look out for each other. What do you say?"

Francis looked in mute question to Dora. She inclined her head without hesitation. It was, she thought gratefully, a wonderful notion and one likely to benefit them all, pro-vided that she could play her part. Gold-seeking was—as Simon Yates had said—a harsh way of life for a woman. But she had chosen it; she had rejected the chance to return to Sydney and the hateful old man she had married.

"I'll be more than willing, Luke," she said with conscious gravity, "if Rob and Simon are . . . and if they'll consent to teach me some of their cooking skills."

The two boys laughed aloud. "I wish our mama could hear you saying that!" Rob exclaimed. "She always reckoned we were useless layabouts in the kitchen, didn't she, Si? But we'll teach you what we can and gladly. It'll be great to have a wom—that is, begging your pardon, Mrs. De Lancey, a lady's company. It's been a long time since we even set eyes on a female."

"Then let us shake hands on it," Francis suggested. There was admiration in his eyes, Dora saw, as he helped her to rise, as well as the adoration she was accustomed to read there.

The handshakes were exchanged, and Luke said with re-lief, "Then I'll be on my way in the morning. I . . . there's just one question I want to ask, Mr. De Lancey, and maybe you can answer it. Jasper Morgan bought a brig, the *Banshee*, in 'Frisco. A small vessel of about a hundred and ninety tons burden. She wasn't anywhere in Port Jackson when we reached there, to the best of my knowledge, and a wharf laborer told me she'd been impounded by the customs and then sold. He wasn't sure of the buyer's name, but he thought it was Lewis or Levis—some name like that. You wouldn't have heard anything about the sale or about the buyer, would you, sir?"

"No, Luke, I'm sorry." Francis shook his head regretfully. "Not a word."

"It was just a thought," Luke conceded. "We passed an outward-bound brig near the Heads, when we entered Port Jackson, which might have been Morgan's, but she was too far away for me to read her name." He shrugged. "I expect it was coincidence, or maybe I imagined the resemblance. There are scores of small brigs in the harbor."

He bent, from force of habit, to scoop up a handful of earth with which to douse the fire. Dora moved swiftly to intercept him.

"Luke," she said, with a vehemence that surprised even herself, "is that not the cook's job? Please let me do it."

Luke stood aside, smiling, and Dora dropped to her knees beside the pile of glowing embers. Her small white hands were coated with dust and her fingernails blackened, but the fire was extinguished when Francis again helped her to her feet.

CHAPTER XIII

The cattle—about two hundred of them, as nearly as Luke could judge—appeared suddenly through the evening gloom and came charging toward him, an unruly mob with their great horned heads down, bellowing and raising a thick cloud of dust above and behind them.

He reined in, looking about him for a way to escape from their onrush. They were heading for the river, he realized. The Macquarie, a streak of silvery water, lay half a mile or so to his rear, reduced to half its normal breadth and volume by the recent lack of rain. Either the herd had been spooked, or thirst had driven the milling animals to sudden frenzy, and he would, he knew, be wise to remove himself from their path with what speed his tired horse could muster.

He dug in his heels, but his mount responded sluggishly, not yet conscious of danger. Then a warning shout alerted him, bringing his head around, and he glimpsed a rider on a piebald horse, waving at him frantically. There was a slight depression in the ground, he saw, in the direction in which the rider was gesturing, and he made for it thankfully, reaching it just as the herd thundered past. The leader, a huge brown bull with a moon-white face, clearly knew the ground better than he did, Luke thought, for it jinked right, and the rest followed, a single straggler—a half-grown heifer—the only one to contest possession of his refuge. It scrambled out, leaving him unscathed, and tore on after the rest.

His father's farm in California had never boasted a herd of beef cattle; the grazing had been too poor to sustain more than the three or four milch cows needed for their own use. For all that, instinct told him that this herd was heading for trouble, if not for disaster, if it were to hurl itself at its present wild speed down the river's steep and rocky bank.

Where there had been several feet of water there were now boulders, laid bare by the drought. He had observed them, Luke recalled, when he had forded the river lower down and, indeed, had been tempted to stop, in the hope that the receding water might have left exposed a few nuggets, which previously had lain hidden in its bed.

But he had resisted the temptation and gone on, aiming to reach Bathurst before dark. There was no chance of that now, he told himself, so that he could do a lot worse than follow his instinct and try to turn the stampeding cattle or, failing that, slow them down.

Using voice and heels, he urged his horse after them, taking the shortest route through a belt of trees that they had circled, and finally came abreast of them, his horse, excited by the chase, finding its second wind and breaking into a gallop, which enabled him to keep pace with the bellowing mob. But he could not turn them. Yell and beat his saddle flap as he would, the big bull kept on going, refusing to deviate from its chosen path and seemingly deaf to his puny efforts to make himself heard.

A shot rang out, a voice shouted something he could not hear, and glancing over his shoulder, Luke saw to his relief that two other riders had caught up with him. One was the man on the piebald horse who had waved at him, the other a black-bearded giant, with a cabbage-plant hat crammed onto his head, riding a big chestnut. The bearded giant had a rifle to his shoulder, and after jerking his horse to a standstill, he took aim at the bull that was leading the stampede and, to Luke's amazement, brought the animal down with a single shot.

The rush was partially stemmed; more shots, fired into the air from handguns, turned most of the mob and slowed them down, but something like a score of the maddened cattle seemed disposed to continue their dash for the river. He was the nearest to them, Luke realized, and without conscious thought he galloped on, in an attempt to head them off. He had all but succeeded in getting ahead of them when his horse began to flag and, the next instant, stumbled badly and fell to its knees, sending him hurtling over its head. He landed awkwardly and hard on the sun-baked ground, and a black mist closed over him, blotting out sight and sound.

He came to—he had no idea how much later—gasping for breath and with his body racked with pain, to find the piebald horse standing nearby, its rider bending over him.

"I think he's only winded, Dickon," the man called out. "But we'd better see there are no bones broken before we move him." Almost his own words, Luke thought dazedly, when, less than a week ago, he had bent in similar fashion over the injured Francis De Lancey. He attempted weakly to sit up, but the stranger shook his head. "Bide still, lad, till I've had a look at you."

His hands were skilled and gentle as they moved about Luke's body, but even so, when they touched his left shoulder, a cry of pain was wrung from him.

"Dislocated, I fancy. Off your horse, Dickon, and lend me a hand to put the joint back in. Don't worry about the mob; they'll not go far now, and Billy Joe can hold them till we get through here." The stranger's voice was educated and authoritative; he was young—only a few years older than himself, Luke judged—and of fine physique. Even so, he was dwarfed by the black-bearded fellow in the cabbage-plant hat, who, when he slid from his saddle, towered over them both. He grunted something unintelligible and then, giving Luke a smile of singular warmth, grasped his injured shoulder with one huge hand, placed the other in the small of his back, and, with a deft movement that for an instant caused exquisite agony, restored the dislocated joint to its socket.

He sat back on his heels, beaming, and the younger man gestured to him and stated pleasantly, "My cousin, Dickon O'Shea, who has the misfortune to be deaf and dumb. He can read lips, though, so don't hesitate to talk to him. And I'm Edmund Tempest, most gratefully yours for your timely intervention. We could have lost half our beef herd if you had not come to our aid. May I know to whom we are grateful?"

Luke managed to sit up, the now-starlit sky whirling in crazy circles above his head. But it steadied, and he said, "My name's Luke Murphy, Mr. Tempest. From Sacramento, California."

"Ah, a gold digger?"

It was easier to agree than to explain, and Luke cautiously inclined his throbbing head.

"You've come from the diggings on the Turon, I imagine?" Tempest suggested. "Or farther afield, perhaps?"

"A mite farther, sir," Luke agreed. "I'm on my way to Bathurst."

"With your fortune made, I trust." Tempest did not wait for his reply but rose briskly to his feet. "We'll have to get the herd rounded up and down to the river, but that shouldn't take us very long. Unfortunately we've lost all our white shepherds and cattlemen to the gold rush, Mr. Murphy —that's why the beef cattle ran amuck. They broke down two fences before we knew what they were up to, you see." He sighed. "The rain came too early this year, and the drought's hit us badly. Still, perhaps it will break before we lose too many."

He reached for his piebald's rein and, one foot in the stirrup, added courteously, "Bide here for a little while, will you, and then permit us to take you to the homestead. My father will wish to thank you, and the very least we can do is offer you a meal and a bed for a night or two, until you are fully recovered."

Luke, impatient to be on his way, wanted to refuse, but his head was throbbing unmercifully now, and he doubted his ability to stand up, still less to ride a horse. He muttered his acquiescence, conscious that his voice sounded odd, even to his own ears, and when the giant Dickon divested himself of his jacket and placed it, rolled up, beneath his head, he lay back and let himself relax. Minutes later he drifted into an exhausted sleep, and did not stir until Edmund Tempest's deep, pleasant voice once more aroused him.

They rode together through the moonlit darkness, Dickon walking behind his horse, to which was roped the carcass of the bull he had been compelled to shoot.

"At least we'll eat well for a while," Tempest dryly observed. "But my father won't be pleased—he paid a mint of money for that infernal animal. It was bred by the Lees—a red shorthorn-Hereford cross. Luckily we have some of his progeny coming on." He pointed to where, ahead of them, lights flickered from behind a screen of trees, and stifled a weary yawn. "There's the homestead—not much farther now, Mr. Murphy."

Luke scarcely heard him. Wave after wave of nausea swept over him, and the throbbing in his head became well-nigh unendurable. He tried to speak, to explain his predicament, but no words would come, and to his dismay he felt himself slipping from his saddle. Dickon's big hand came out to grasp him as he fell, and he slithered to the ground, once more struggling to draw breath into his lungs and failing to do so. The mists closed in; he could neither see nor move, and Edmund Tempest's voice, harsh with concern, faded into silence as Luke's senses left him.

When he wakened, he was in a big four-poster bed, with sweetly smelling linen sheets covering him and the softest of pillows beneath his head. A woman's voice, with a faintly familiar accent, reached him, seeming to come from a very long way away.

"I believe he's coming round," it said. "Look, his eyes are open. Bring me the bowl of water, Elizabeth dear. I'll put a fresh compress on his poor head."

A younger-sounding, softly musical voice answered the first. "Here it is, Mama. I'll raise his head a little, shall I?" Luke heard the splash of water and felt gentle hands moving about his face and head. He glimpsed a face, its skin like pink and white porcelain, and two deep blue eyes, gazing into his with anxiety mirrored in their dark-lashed depths, and then the bright daylight, coming from somewhere close at hand, caused him such sharp pain that he was forced to turn his head away. His eyelids fell of their own volition, and the vision he had seen abruptly faded.

"He was badly hurt, wasn't he, Mama?" the young voice questioned. "Eddie said he dislocated his shoulder but Dickon put it to rights, and they thought that was all the injury he had suffered. But it must have been worse than they supposed."

"He has suffered a concussion," the older voice answered practically. "But I'm sure he will get over it, after a few days' rest and quiet. There—" Luke felt a blessed coolness pervading his scalp, holding the throbbing at bay, and he let himself sink down into the yielding comfort of his pillows, content to lie there with his eyes closed, lulled by the whispering voices and strangely at peace.

"Let us hope he is not like our last visitor, Mama," the girl's voice declared. "He seemed such a charming gentleman, so—so worldly and so widely traveled. And an officer, who had served in the Household Cavalry! And yet Dickon is sure that he was the one who killed dear old Winyara . . . and for no *reason*. Winyara would have done him no harm."

"People are afraid of the aborigines—those who do not know them, that's to say. The men who have come here from California tend to suppose they are like the red Indians, ready to attack them without provocation, and they react accordingly. And"—the mother's voice took on a sharper note—"Dickon took a strong dislike to Major Lewis, you know, Elizabeth."

"Dickon is usually right, Mama. Because he cannot hear or speak, he has other ways of judging people—ways the blackfellows taught him. I'd trust his judgment anywhere." There was a pause, and then the girl's voice added quietly, "Dickon likes *this* young man. I could tell by the way he carried him in after he had fallen from his horse. He took so much care not to hurt him."

She was talking about him, Luke realized, and felt heartened by her words. But . . . the earlier part of her conversation with her mother ought, he was reasonably certain, to have had some significance for him; only he could not call to mind what the significance was. They had spoken of a major, who had served in the British Household Cavalry—a major named Lewis—but the name meant nothing to him. It seemed strange that Dickon should suspect Major Lewis of killing an aborigine and that—what was the girl's name? Elizabeth, that was it—Elizabeth's mother should pour scorn on the idea. He puzzled over it and then dismissed it.

The voices ceased, there was a faint click of a door closing, and Luke drifted back to sleep, his mind again blank and untroubled.

The girl's voice wakened him. He opened his eyes and saw that she had placed a lighted oil lamp on the table by his bedside and that she was carrying a steaming bowl in one hand and a spoon in the other.

"Mama thought that you must be hungry, so I've brought you some broth. Do you feel well enough to take it, Mr. Murphy?"

The contents of the bowl smelled very appetizing, and Luke tried to sit up, surprised and more than a little embarrassed when the effort proved beyond him, and the girl had to set down her bowl and come to his aid.

"I—I'm sorry," he stammered awkwardly. "I seem to be as weak as a kitten."

"That is not to be wondered at," she assured him, picking up the bowl and seating herself on the edge of the bed. "You were rather badly hurt, you know, and Mama says that you have a concussion. I'm Elizabeth Tempest, by the way. And you're Luke Murphy, my brother says."

"I guess so, Miss Elizabeth." She was a beautiful girl, Luke saw, studying her by the light of the lamp. Tall and slim, with wide-set blue eyes and a mass of corn-colored hair, braided very neatly about her head. Her dress was simple—blue, echoing the color of her eyes, with a starched white collar and matching cuffs, worn with a white pinafore over it, presumably because she had been at work in the kitchen. He took the bowl from her, holding out his hand for the spoon.

"I can feed myself," he asserted, anxious to regain some measure of masculine independence.

"Are you sure you can? Mama said I should feed you if you couldn't manage it yourself. She thought you might still be experiencing vertigo."

Luke shook his head and was deeply chagrined to find that the vertigo persisted, the ceiling of the room suddenly seeming to be rising and falling and the end of his bed describing odd gyrations for which he could not account. But he clung obstinately to the spoon and, by the exercise of stern willpower, managed to drink a few sips of the cooling broth.

Elizabeth Tempest watched him gravely. "You really should let me help you. Your hands are shaking badly, you know, and you'll spill it if you're not careful. Besides, I'm really quite good at it—I feed the calves and any sick animals on the farm." Her lips twitched, as if she were trying to suppress a smile, and suddenly Luke found himself laughing at the absurd comparison.

"All right, then." He yielded up the bowl, still laughing. "Pretend I'm a sick calf."

She joined in his laughter and was setting about the task of feeding him when her mother came in.

"You must be feeling much better, Mr. Murphy," she said approvingly, "to be able to laugh like that. I'm so glad. For a while we were quite worried about you. Could you manage to take some more broth, do you think? Or tea and cake, perhaps?"

"Nothing more, thank you, ma'am."

"You slept for a long time," Mrs. Tempest told him. "Almost twenty-four hours. You were on your way to Bathurst, were you not, when you stopped to help Edmund and Dickon?"

To Bathurst, Luke thought—*had* he been on his way to Bathurst, and if he had, for what purpose was he going there? He could not remember; the past was a blank. "I—yes, I guess so," he managed. "I must have been."

Mrs. Tempest eyed him uncertainly and then, with a warning glance at her daughter, said sympathetically, "Do not worry if your memory has failed you. Concussion has that effect sometimes. It all will come back to you in a little while, I'm quite sure."

But nothing came back to him, not even his name, although, since the Tempests addressed him as Luke or Mr. Murphy, he supposed that must be his name, and he answered to it readily enough. Within another twenty-four hours his physical ills had greatly subsided, and realizing that his hosts were short of labor, he offered his assistance, which was gratefully accepted. The Pengallon holding was extensive and well stocked, with several thousand merino and crossbred sheep, as well as the beef herd, and there were hundreds of acres of arable land, now starting to show signs of neglect.

Apart from Tempest himself—who worked as hard as any of them—only Edmund and Dickon and an aborigine called

Billy Joe were left to cope with the stock and the day-to-day chores, and Luke's help was welcomed. To his own surprise he found that he possessed some skills: he was able to milk the house cows, could handle a plow with inbred competence, and required no instruction in either the blacksmith's art or that of the sawyers and carpenters, who had abandoned their employment to join in the search for gold.

In normal times, Pengallon must have been as self-contained as a small village, he realized. It was well supplied with cottage homes for the laborers and their families; there were stables, paddocks for the stud mares and the foals that were bred there, granaries and sheep pens, a large shearing shed, and a beautiful garden containing fruit trees, vines, and close to an acre devoted to vegetable cultivation. A small, fenced-in lawn, surrounded by shade trees, grew a variety of flowers and sweet-smelling flowering shrubs native to the area, and Mrs. Tempest, whose province this was, had had a pretty wooden summerhouse built there, where guests were entertained and visiting children happily played.

Not all the women had left with their men; five or six, with young families, had remained, and Elizabeth, Luke discovered by chance, regularly took a class for Bible studies and the basics of education, which most of the children attended in the now-empty granary.

He spent as much of his time as he could in her company. It was not much, for he toiled on the land from dawn to dusk, but he came increasingly to savor the brief interludes when they were able to be together: walking by the river just before dusk, or sitting by her side at mealtimes and later, when the whole family gathered in the pleasantly furnished living room; listening to her pretty, tuneful voice as she sang to her mother's accompaniment on an old but lovingly preserved upright piano. Such moments, and the fact that the Tempests had accepted him almost as one of their own, brought him a warm glow of happiness, which, he began fervently to hope, might continue into the foreseeable future.

He no longer worried about his lost memory or asked himself why it was that he had been on his way to Bathurst when he had encountered the stampeding beef herd, for it seemed no longer to matter. Edmund had tried, once or twice, to jog his memory by talking of the goldfields on the Turon, whence he had supposedly come, but Luke knew that he had little interest in gold-seeking now.

The diggers who had camped on the Pengallon stretch of the river had moved on, with their tents and their tools, seeking more promising sites on the Louisa, the Meroo, and the Pyramil, and the sluice the Tempests had worked had, of necessity, to be neglected, if the valuable merino flocks were to be kept alive until the drought broke. Luke took only a passing interest in it, recognizing simply that it was of sound and skillful construction, for which, Edmund told him, they had Major Lewis to thank. Dickon had scowled darkly at the mention of that name and walked away, his face like thunder.

"He will have it that Lewis murdered an old aborigine shepherd we had here—a fine old fellow called Winyara, whom we all loved," Edmund explained. "But there wasn't a shred of proof, except some bloodstains on a Colt revolver that Dickon unearthed from God knows where. It could just as easily have belonged to one of the diggers as to the major, and in any event, what possible reason could he have had for killing the old man? He was a British Army officer; he fought in the Carlist War in Spain—he would be unlikely to panic at the sight of a frail old blackfellow, even if Winyara had crept up on him in the dark. And besides, Lewis stayed with us for a couple of nights, which, I'm sure, he would never have done if he *had* battered the poor old fellow to death with a Colt six-gun."

"A Colt six-gun?" Luke echoed, mildly puzzled because he had a sudden vision of a holstered Colt revolver coming, or so it seemed to him, from nowhere.

"Yes, that's right," Edmund confirmed indifferently. "It's an American handgun, which fires six shots from a revolving chamber." He grinned good-naturedly. "You're an American, or so you told us when we first picked you up. You must have seen dozens of them."

And most probably he had, Luke told himself; men would have carried such weapons in the California diggings for protection . . . and worn them in holsters, no doubt, as western cowhands wore them, ready to hand.

"Ask Dickon to show you the one he found," Edmund suggested. "Who knows? It might trigger that lost memory of yours!"

Luke nodded, but, he asked himself, what would it profit him if he did recover his memory? Life at Pengallon was simple and uncomplicated, and even if the work was hard, Rick Tempest was an appreciative and generous employer, and Edmund and Dickon were his friends now, as well as his workmates. And there was the sweet young Elizabeth, with whom, if the truth were known, he was already more than a little in love. It would be a wrench to leave them, and had they not all insisted that they did not want him to go? True, he was penniless—his gold-seeking in both California and on the Turon appeared to have shown no return—but he could earn a living as a farmhand here or anywhere else. He could support a wife, and if Elizabeth should look upon him with favor and her father give his consent, then the last thing he wanted to do was resume his journey to Bathurst. Or—

"Can you take water out to the broodmares in the far paddock?" Edmund asked, breaking into his thoughts. "It would appear that we have visitors." He pointed to a small procession approaching the homestead from the direction of Bathurst, and Luke was able to make out a curricle, drawn by a pair of bay horses, with two mounted men trotting, in leisurely fashion, behind it.

"Visitors?" he questioned.

"Yes, indeed," Edmund confirmed, sounding suddenly elated. "And if my eyesight isn't failing me, they are most welcome visitors, Luke my boy. The Broomes from Sydney Town—Captain Justin Broome, his daughter Jenny, and, I think, his son John. Yes, I'm sure that's who they are."

He was off at a gallop, waving his hat excitedly in the air and shouting an enthusiastic welcome. Luke stared after him and then, mindful of his duties, went to water the broodmares.

Over dinner that evening, he was introduced to the new arrivals, who, it was evident, were friends of long standing, on intimate terms with all the Tempests. Their exchange of news went on throughout the meal, and Luke listened with a polite pretense of interest, although little of what they said had any meaning for him. But he studied them as he ate, watching each in turn and liking what he saw, for all they were strangers and their concerns outside his ken.

Justin Broome was a retired naval post captain, of some distinction, he judged—probably a contemporary of Rick Tempest's, or even a onetime shipmate in his youth, for it was apparent from their conversation that they knew each other well and had memories in common going back many years. His son, whom the Tempests addressed as Johnny, was a tall, bearded fellow and a newspaperman, recently returned from an assignment for his paper in the new Victoria goldfields.

The daughter, Jenny, was a few years older than Elizabeth, a charming, vivacious young woman, with bright auburn hair and a most engaging smile, in whom, it became increasingly clear as the meal progressed, Edmund Tempest had a keen and proprietary interest.

Evidently there was another son—a naval officer, like his father—who had arrived in Sydney comparatively recently, in command of Her Majesty's ship *Galah*, and who was referred to as Red.

Jenny spoke of him with affection and, it seemed to the listening Luke, with a measure of pity when she mentioned that he had been relieved of his command.

"For God's sake, why?" Rick Tempest demanded. "I heard that Commodore Skinner was throwing his weight about over some quite incredible threat of a Russian attack on Port Jackson by the Tsar's Pacific Fleet. They were supposed to be mounting the attack from Valparaiso or something equally absurd. Did Red point out the absurdity of the notion or what?"

Captain Broome shook his head. "That scare blew over, although the home government took it seriously enough to order Sydney to be put into a state of defense. Skinner had all the long guns taken out of the ships and set up at strategic points onshore—South Head, Middle Head, Bradley's, Pinchgut, and even Dawes Point. Then he had to remove them back where they belonged." He shrugged. "That wasn't what put Red ashore. He had had the misfortune to be ordered to give passage to an engineer captain named Lucas, who was appointed in my stead as superintendent of the Cockatoo Island dockyard. An awkward gentleman, Benjamin Lucas, and that is no exaggeration, I give you my word. He took exception to the manner in which his wife was treated during the voyage from England—the implication being that Red had alienated her affections toward her husband, you see—and Skinner, of course, jumped in regardless of the consequences. He ordered a court of inquiry and relieved Red of his command, pending the court's findings. But then Lucas's wife left him and ran off with young Francis De Lancey, who was one of the *Galah*'s officers, and—''

Luke stiffened. The name was one he had heard, and heard quite recently, he was sure. He had not taken in more than a few words of what Captain Broome had been saying, but he listened intently now, trying to recall where or when the name had been mentioned or what possible significance it could have.

"George and Rachel's younger boy?" Rick Tempest exclaimed. "Oh, the damned young fool! The De Lanceys will be heartbroken."

"Indeed they are," Justin Broome confirmed gravely. "Luckily the boy had quit the service within twenty-four hours of the *Galah*'s making port, so at least he's not posted as a deserter. But the unfortunate husband, Captain Lucas, collapsed with a heart attack when he learned what had happened—at the dockyard, Rick, and in my presence, poor devil! I did not greatly care for him, but even so, I would not have wished that on him, even to spare Red the court of inquiry."

"But surely Red does not have to face a court now, does he?" Tempest asked, frowning.

Everyone at the table had fallen silent, Luke realized, hanging on Broome's reply. He gave it wryly.

"Alas, he does. Lucas died without regaining consciousness and without, of course, withdrawing the charges. But he made them in writing, and Commodore Skinner insists that the court must hear them, so Red remains kicking his heels onshore, and the commodore has given temporary command of the *Galah* to one of his staff! It is a damnably unhappy state of affairs. In the hope of being able to put matters right, Johnny and I decided to come up here in search of the two fugitives—young De Lancey and Dora Lucas. Rumor has it that they are somewhere on the Turon goldfields." He glanced across the table at his daughter. "We'll go on tomorrow to start our search, if you will be so kind as to put Jenny up for a week or so."

The assent to this suggestion was immediate, and it was voiced enthusiastically by Edmund, bringing the color rushing to Jenny Broome's cheeks, as his mother said, smiling, "Of course—we shall be more than delighted to have you, Jenny my dear."

Luke found his tongue at last, the memories flooding back. The two fugitives, as Captain Broome had called them, were the two he had encountered on the hill above Tambaroora Creek, the two calling themselves Mr. and Mrs. De Lancey—there could be no doubting that. Had not De Lancey admitted to having served in the navy? And he had called his wife Dora.

"Sir . . . ." He hesitated, reluctant to betray the young couple if his information as to their whereabouts should lead to trouble for them. "I believe I can tell you where to find the two you are searching for. But might I first ask what you would require of them? I do not think that they would wish to return to Sydney Town, sir."

Edmund turned from his rapt contemplation of Jenny's pink, embarrassed face to look at him in pleased surprise.

"Luke," he began, "you've remembered—you—" and then broke off, as if fearing he had said too much.

Justin Broome looked relieved. "You will save us a long search if you are able to tell us where they are, Luke. And I should not ask them to return to Sydney. That will not be necessary, provided they are willing to give me a written deposition which my son can put before the court of inquiry. I don't know whether or not you have understood the nature of the charges made against him, but clearly they are false, and they should have been laid against Mr. De Lancey."

"I understand, sir," Luke assured him. He hesitated no longer, confident that Captain Justin Broome was a man of his word, who could be relied upon to keep it. With only minor difficulty in remembering, he succeeded in giving the necessary directions, adding that he had left the two who had called themselves Mr. and Mrs. De Lancey with his own two companions, Simon and Robert Yates, preparing to search for gold in Tambaroora Creek.

"That's what it is called, to the best of my knowledge, sir. It is between the Turon and the Pyramil, and it runs into the Macquarie about five or six miles below the junction with the Turon."

Captain Broome thanked him with grateful sincerity. "Mr. Tempest tells me that you have suffered from amnesia since being thrown from your horse. Have I perhaps said anything that jogged your memory?"

Luke exchanged a swift glance with Edmund and then inclined his head. "Yes, you did, sir. The name De Lancey. I —it came back to me, and I remembered where I'd heard it. I'd come from the Tambaroora Creek, you see, sir."

"Ah, yes, I see." The gray-haired captain subjected him to a lengthy scrutiny. "Let us endeavor to jog that memory of yours still further, shall we? Your name is Luke Murphy—is that right?"

"Yes, sir, I believe so."

"Good. Then I fancy I can fill in some of the gaps. You worked your passage from San Francisco to Sydney on board the clipper schooner *Dolphin,* owner and master Claus Van Buren."

"I—" Luke stared at him. Van Buren, the *Dolphin* . . . As before, he realized, everyone at the table was silent, waiting for his reply. And the names had a meaning. They were familiar, as that of De Lancey had been, emerging as if from the mist that had shrouded him. He saw in memory Claus Van Buren's darkly bearded face, and that of a girl. A girl of Elizabeth's age, whom he had claimed to be his sister. Mercy, with whom he had made the journey from Thayer's Bend, on the Feather River, to San Francisco, in order to track down the man who had murdered his brother Dan and the two Australians, Frankie and Tom.

He drew in his breath sharply. *Jasper Morgan*—Captain Jasper Morgan. *That* name was etched into his memory. How could he possibly have forgotten it or lost sight of the purpose that had brought him halfway around the world in search of Jasper Morgan?

"I think you're starting to remember, are you not, Luke?" Captain Broome prompted quietly. To the others, he said, "Claus Van Buren brought a splendid clipper schooner back from America and, for good measure, a sweet young bride—Luke's sister Mercy. Their nuptials are shortly to be celebrated. But"—he turned to Luke again, smiling—"they will both be bitterly disappointed if you are not there to give the bride away, Luke."

Luke sought vainly for words as Edmund rose from his seat to wring his hand. "By all that's wonderful, Luke my boy!" he exclaimed delightedly. "You remember now, don't you? Good Lord, you can't have forgotten that your sister is to wed one of the wealthiest shipowners in the colony—and one of its finest men? Claus Van Buren—you must remember him!"

"Yes," Luke managed. "I remember Claus Van Buren." Elizabeth, he became aware, was looking at him, her blue eyes wide, and he instinctively averted his own gaze, bitterly conscious that his time at Pengallon was over, and with it all hope that their brief and tentative friendship might develop into . . . what had he hoped? He wanted suddenly to go to her, to fall on his knees beside her and plead for her indulgence, if not her understanding. But with all her family present and the Broomes, he knew that he could say nothing, and the fear grew that, even if they had been alone, he would have been unable to find the words he longed to say to her.

He expelled his breath in a long-drawn sigh, letting the tension drain out of him, forcing himself to speak calmly. "It's all coming back, Edmund. But I—it's something of a shock. I had not realized that the wedding—that Mercy and Captain Van Buren would set any store by my presence at their wedding."

"But of course they do!" Mrs. Tempest offered kindly. She glanced at her husband, the glance at once questioning and pleading. "We must let him go, Rick. Obviously Luke was on his way to Sydney when our cattle stampeded, and perhaps, if he leaves at once, he will be in time to give his sister away.''

Or, Luke thought dully, in time to pick up Jasper Morgan's trail again. He was reminded suddenly of the visitor the Tempests had entertained—the major, who had claimed to have served in the British Army. Lewis, the man Dickon had suspected of killing the Tempests' old aborigine shepherd—dear God, why had he not seen the link, the coincidence?

As if from a long way away, he heard Mr. Tempest agree to his wife's suggestion. "Certainly you must continue your journey, Luke, now that we know your destination, my boy. But you will always be welcome here at Pengallon. There will be a job for you whenever you want it.''

Luke thanked him, ashamed of the deception he must practice. He could not bring himself to look at Elizabeth, even when, the meal over, she followed her mother and Jenny Broome from the room, passing close to him, her hand lightly brushing his.

Dickon never stayed to smoke and drink port with the male members of the household; he rose, as he was wont to do, bowing his lofty head in Rick Tempest's direction, and on impulse Luke rose, too, mumbling his excuses.

"Dickon," he said when they were standing in the yard, out of earshot, "the Colt revolver that belonged to Major Lewis—do you still have it?''

Reading his meaning from watching the movement of his lips, Dickon scowled, as if at a memory he did not relish, and nodded.

"May I see it?" Luke asked. The nod was repeated, and Dickon led the way across the yard to the room he occupied on the far side of the main house. His room was in meticulous order, the bed neatly made, his clean clothes for the next day laid out on a chair, and those he had discarded, after the day's work, rolled into a bundle ready to be washed. A wardrobe and a tallboy completed the sparse furnishing of the room. Dickon went without hesitation to the tallboy, pulled open a drawer, and took out an object, wrapped in an old linen kerchief, which he unrolled to reveal the handgun.

Luke eyed the weapon with revulsion, for the pearl-inlaid butt still bore unmistakable signs of dried blood and a few fragments of skin. He did not touch it, but Dickon, as if sensing his reluctance, closed his own big hand about it and lifted it high in the air, to bring the butt down with simulated savagery on the piled blankets of his bed.

"Did Major Lewis do that?" Luke asked. "Was this his gun?"

Dickon nodded solemnly.

"Did you see him kill the blackfellow—what was his name? Winyara?"

This time a regretful headshake answered his question, and Luke motioned to the gun. "All right, Dickon, you can put it away. Thank you for letting me see it." He sighed audibly. "Damn it, I wish you could talk! I wish you could tell me what Major Lewis looked like . . . but you can't, can you? There's no way you can tell me. For all that, though, I'm sure it was Jasper Morgan."

Dickon returned the Colt to its hiding place. He rummaged in another drawer of the tallboy, and to Luke's surprise he returned to curl up on the bed, a sketch pad and some pieces of what appeared to be charcoal in his hand. Swiftly he started to draw, his big, blunt fingers moving with practiced skill, now blurring a line, now tracing one in sharp relief across the paper, his eyes narrowed and his concentration unwavering.

Luke waited, controlling his impatience and not supposing that, with such crude materials, Dickon would be able to create a recognizable image. He was unable to suppress a cry of mingled astonishment and admiration when, a little later, the sketch was passed to him and he found himself looking at what was unmistakably a portriat of the man he was seeking.

Jasper Morgan looked back at him from the sheet of coarse white paper. The supercilious smile, the heavy mustache, the jet-black hair with its powdering of gray at the temples, the cold, dark eyes—all were there, just as he now remembered them. Dickon O'Shea might not be able to talk, but his portrait, acutely observed, talked for him, each and every detail reproduced by those big, seemingly clumsy hands, even— Luke held the paper nearer to the flickering light of the oil lamp. Yes, even the flowing cravat Morgan had affected, with its distinctive gold stickpin.

"Dickon, this is Jasper Morgan to the life!" he exclaimed excitedly. "And you were right not to trust him, because I'd stake any odds that it *was* he who murdered your old aborigine! He had blood on his hands when he came here—my brother's blood, God rot him for the foul, murdering devil that he is! Captain Jasper Morgan, that's who he is."

Dickon eyed him reproachfully and shook his head. Taking the sketch again, he slowly scrawled beneath it, "Major Lewis." Luke let that pass. "All right, but where did he go when he left here, Dickon, do you know?"

Dickon attempted to answer him in the odd, grunting sounds that both Rick and Edmund Tempest seemed able to interpret, but realizing that Luke could not, Dickon had to resort to the sketch pad again. In painstaking capitals he wrote "Sydney," and then, with a few deft strokes, he drew the outline of a ship under sail, with the name *Banshee* beneath it.

That, Luke decided, was probably the extent of his knowledge of the self-styled major's movements. The *Banshee,* if Morgan had not sold her, had almost certainly taken him to Port Phillip and the new goldfields in the state of Victoria. Indeed . . . Memory stirred sluggishly. The wharf manager he . . . had questioned had said that a Major Lewis had bought the brig and that she had left Sydney—oh, dear heaven!—about the time that the *Dolphin* had made port, seven or eight weeks ago. His throat tightened. While he had been searching the goldfields in the Ophir and Turon area, Jasper Morgan had been on his way to Port Phillip. As always, his quarry was ahead of him, and all he could do was follow after him in the hope that, one day, they might again come face to face.

He made to take his leave, but Dickon gripped his arm, shaking his head vigorously. He had made a second sketch, Luke saw, and was offering it for inspection. This was much less detailed than the one he had done of Morgan. A smudged blur suggested trees bordering the road; a figure on horseback, leading a second animal, was sketched in below the trees, and . . . Luke bit back a gasp of surprise as Dickon's charcoal-stained finger jabbed at the outline of a man's figure, crouched low down among the trees, which he had initially overlooked. There was a rifle in the second figure's arms, raised to the level of its shoulder and aimed, beyond possibility of doubt, at the rider below.

Dickon bared his teeth in a mirthless smile and pointed first at the figure with the rifle and then at himself.

"You?" Luke questioned in some bewilderment. "And the major, Major—what did you call him? Lewis?" Dickon nodded. "Because you were certain that he killed your old aborigine and—" Understanding dawned. "No one believed you?"

Again a vigorous nod of assent, and for a moment Luke's hopes rose. If Jasper Morgan had been wounded, then perhaps . . . "Dickon," he demanded sharply, "did you hit him?"

Dickon shook his head disconsolately, making signs that appeared to mean that his target had been too far away and too fast-moving for accurate aim.

"Don't worry, Dickon," Luke offered with grim determination. "I'm going after him, and I won't rest until I find him, I give you my word."

Dickon hesitated for a long moment, as if deep in thought. Then, finally coming to a decision, he went to the tallboy and again took out the Colt in its linen wrapping. He thrust gun and wrapping into Luke's hands, smiling his familiar, guileless smile, and since there was no mistaking his meaning, Luke accepted the unwelcome gift, but with a reluctance he could not hide.

"This is between our two selves, Dickon," he cautioned. "We will not speak of it to your people, either of us, you understand? There is no need for them to know."

And it was best that they should not, he thought; Jasper Morgan was his affair, not theirs—and least of all Elizabeth's. To his relief, when he rejoined the Tempests and their guests and announced his intention of leaving Pengallon, they appeared to take it for granted that Mercy's wedding to Claus Van Buren was the reason for his departure. He did not contradict their assumption.

"Come back to us, Luke," Rick Tempest invited, "when the festivities are over. There will always be work for you here and, I promise you, a warm welcome from us all."

Luke reddened as he heard Mrs. Tempest echo her husband's kindly suggestion. "It's likely that I shall have to go to Victoria, to the new goldfields," he evaded, anxious not to carry his deception too far, yet more reluctant than ever to admit to the truth. He sensed Elizabeth's eyes on him and hated himself for being the cause of the disappointment he read in their candid blue depths. "There is a—a man I have to find," he went on awkwardly. "One with whom I was in partnership in California. I was looking for him when I came here—I'd heard he was somewhere on the Turon. But he had gone. I—that is, I have a debt to settle with him, and I cannot be free until the debt is settled. I know now that the likelihood is that he has sailed for Port Phillip. If he has, then I must go after him."

"A debt of honor, Luke?" Edmund questioned, an odd note, almost of doubt, in his voice. "Or something else that you've just now remembered?"

Luke had a sudden, sickening vision of Dan's dead face and then of the bodies of his two young Australian partners, uncovered from the wreckage of their mine at Windy Gully. A debt of honor, he thought—oh, yes, surely it was that! His conscience would give him no rest until he paid it, and he knew, in that moment, that if he found Jasper Morgan, he would kill him. Perhaps with the Colt Dickon had given him —the weapon Morgan had used to take four lives.

"A debt of honor," he echoed hoarsely, seizing on Edmund's words like a drowning man clutching at a straw, and hoping that somehow they would carry conviction. He met Elizabeth's gaze, his own mutely pleading, and then turned back to her father. "If you will bear with me, Mr. Tempest— if you will permit me the time I need, sir, I should like nothing better than to enter your service. I've been happy here, happier than I have ever been in my whole life. You have all been more than good to me. I—I'll come back, I—I swear I will, however long it takes."

Elizabeth said nothing; she lowered her gaze, leaving her father to answer for her, and he did so with typical generosity.

"You know your own business best, Luke, and if it is a question of honor, I will not seek to dissuade you. My offer

stands. Take what time you need, and come back when your
debt is paid. You've money due to you in wages, and there
will be a bonus for your help in saving my beef herd. I'll
square up with you before you leave us."

For all that, her family closed protective ranks about Elizabeth. Luke was not permitted a moment alone with her, and
when he prepared to ride off the next morning, her mother
stood at her side, an arm resting lightly about the girl's slim
shoulders. She waved, as they all did, to him and to Justin
Broome and his son, who set off in the opposite direction,
heading for Tambaroora Creek to complete their own
search.

Luke's heart was heavy as he turned his back on Pengallon
and kneed his horse into a trot. It would take him five days,
at least, to reach Sydney, and he found himself wondering, a
trifle belatedly, whether he would be in time for Mercy's
wedding to Claus Van Buren, his flagging spirits lifting a
little at the prospect.

He was in sight of Bathurst Town when, without warning,
the drought broke in a slashing rainstorm that soaked him to
the skin. In the midst of it Dickon caught up with him, as
drenched as he was, to jerk his big horse to a standstill in a
flurry of churned-up mud.

Beaming, he took a folded scrap of paper from inside his
shirt, gave it to Luke, and motioned him to take shelter
under a tree in order to read it.

The note was brief, but Luke could scarcely restrain himself from shouting his happiness aloud as he read it.

"Please do come back, Luke," the note read. "I shall be
waiting for you, however long it is."

The signature was blurred by a sudden gush of rainwater
from the leaves above his head, but it was still decipherable
as "Elizabeth."

He could not reply to it, for he had neither pen nor paper,
Luke realized, and he was tempted to abandon the chase for
Jasper Morgan and turn back. But Dickon, still smiling at
him benignly, offered his sketch pad and a lump of charcoal.

Luke, his throat tight, contrived to scrawl the words that
came from his heart: "I love you, Elizabeth. I will come
back."

Dickon took the pad from him, thrust it into his saddlebag, and made off, the sodden cabbage-plant hat lifted in a farewell salute.

Luke waited only to read Elizabeth's note once again and then rode on, his heart singing.

CHAPTER XIV

Mercy felt as if a great weight had been lifted from her shoulders. Confession had not been easy, but the presence of the Reverend and Mrs. Nathan Cox—invited to Sydney so that Mr. Cox might conduct the wedding ceremony—had helped her unburden herself.

She could not have married Claus with such a secret on her conscience, she had told herself, yet again and again she had put off telling him, dreading that were he to learn what her past had been, he might decide that she was unworthy to be his bride.

But instead of the bitter condemnation she had feared, Claus had shown compassion and a wonderful measure of understanding, taking her gently into his arms to assure her that he loved her.

"You are all I have ever dreamed of in a woman, my sweet Mercy. Believe that, for it is the truth! And if the world treated you cruelly, and if a callous and evil man took advantage of your innocence, how could I blame you for it? We are none of us perfect, I least of all."

He had looked at Alice Cox, serene and beautiful, for all her graying hair and work-bowed shoulders. "Alice will bear me out, will you not, my dear? When we first knew each other, I was virtually a slave in this house, whipped and humiliated. And Alice had been sent here to serve a sentence of seven years for borrowing a few yards of lace from her employer! We made our escape on a carriage horse, purloined from the stables under cover of darkness, both of us in infinite danger of being apprehended as runaways and flung into jail. We owed our salvation to our providential meeting with my good friend and longtime mentor, Nathan, on the road."

"Where I," the Reverend Nathan Cox finished for him,
"had lost control of the recalcitrant animal I had hired to
convey me to my destination, and was far from certain where
my destination was. Claus, who was then about twelve years
old, informed me solemnly that he intended to wed Alice, so
that she might thus obtain her freedom!" He smiled across
at his wife. "I became instead her bridegroom, and when
eventually I was appointed to the church school at Windsor,
Claus enrolled as one of my pupils."

"The brightest and best," Alice put in fondly.

"Indeed, yes," her husband agreed. "As you may see and
judge for yourself, Mercy, the good Lord took pity on us and
intervened in our favor. He gave me my beloved wife and six
fine sons and daughters, and Claus an inheritance, from
which he has built a great trading enterprise. Now, as final
proof of His beneficence, He has brought you to share our
lives and become wife and helpmate to Claus. The manner
of your coming and what went before it are of small account,
my child. Suffice it that you are here."

He had spoken lightly, even humorously, yet with an underlying gravity that gave substance to his words, and she
had taken comfort from them, Mercy recalled. Now, with
Claus entertaining Nathan and a number of his male friends
and associates on board the *Dolphin*, she was with Alice in the
house in Bridge Street, the night before her wedding, and
they had talked long and earnestly together, like old friends
rather than strangers, the difference in their ages and back-
grounds offering little impediment.

Alice had spoken of her early days in the colony and—
without either bitterness or self-reproach—of the time when
Nathan had been appointed chaplain to the penal settlement
on Norfolk Island, when, in the words of the Governor of the
period, "punishment short only of death" had been the lot
of all who had been sent there as convicts.

"The women were ordered to evacuate the settlement,"
she said, and for all the lapse of years her eyes filled with
tears at the memory. "The officers' wives, as well as the
wives and children of the poor wretches serving their sentences on the island. I was with them when they were taken
away, and all of us were brokenhearted, because the women

had been the one civilizing influence, the children the one source of joy and hope. I rebelled when I was back in Sydney. . . . I permitted a newspaper to publish the diary I had kept. It cost Nathan his appointment—that was inevitable, of course. But he never blamed me, and thanks be to God, the Governor's lady arranged for him to be given the living in Windsor and the church school, which was in need of a teacher."

"And you are still there?" Mercy questioned.

"Not at the same school. Thanks to Claus—our dear, generous Claus—Nathan is head of two schools now: the grammar school, and a fine school for the native children, founded originally by Governor Macquarie—the Native Institution at Parramatta." Alice stifled a sigh. "Governor Macquarie's intention was to found an independent settlement for the aborigines in the bush, where they could be educated and instructed in husbandry and stock raising, yet be free to come and go as they pleased. It was to be called Macquarie City, but . . . it failed for many reasons, and for years there was no native school of any kind. Ours is an attempt to carry out the old Governor's wishes and those of the Reverend Robert Cartwright, who originally planned it. Nathan first worked with Mr. Cartwright in Windsor, you see, and it was he—God rest his soul—who married us. I like to think it would please him, and I hope against hope that it won't fail."

She spread her hands in an odd little gesture, almost of resignation. "So many of our good intentions meet with failure here, Mercy. Looking back, I find myself wondering whether we have made progress at all. Sometimes I despair. The dark people are still badly treated, robbed of their land and even persecuted, and although transportation has ceased, Norfolk Island still exists, and conditions there are only a little better than when I wrote my diary. True, the other terrible penal settlement at Moreton Bay is closed and the land opened for agricultural settlers, but in Van Diemen's Land there is another hell on earth for convicts—Port Arthur. And now the gold seekers have come, in their thousands, to despoil the pastoral prosperity built up with such effort and sacrifice over so many years."

"Claus told me that there is talk of closing the Norfolk

Island prison," Mercy offered, thinking to console her, "and giving the island to the *Bounty* mutineers' descendants from Pitcairn."

"Yes, I have heard the talk," Alice acknowledged. "And I pray that it will be translated into action." Her smile returned abruptly, and she took Mercy's hand. "Dear child, I should not have permitted my tongue to run away with me. This is your wedding eve, and that is a time for hope and good cheer. You will be marrying one of the best and finest men I know, Mercy. Claus has waited a long time to take a wife, and for his sake I am truly glad that he has found you. Make him happy, Mercy, for he deserves happiness."

"I shall do everything in my power to give him happiness," Mercy promised. "I—I know how fortunate I am. But—" She hesitated, looking into Alice Cox's unlined and still youthful face. "Saleh told me once that Claus loves me because I resemble *you*. I—I hope I do, Mrs. Cox, and that I can be like you. But—"

"Oh, my dear!" Alice exclaimed. "That simply is not true. Saleh, for all his age and wisdom, is quite wrong. I was a mother to Claus when he had no one else who cared what happened to him. A mother or an elder sister, perhaps, since I was not much older . . . and he was only twelve when he offered to wed me. You are different; you are to become his wife and, I am quite sure, in your own right and because you are *you*. Do not, I beg you, try to be anyone else, Mercy. As Claus reminded us, we are none of us saints, you know. Certainly I'm not. I rant and rail against the fortune hunters and the gold diggers and weep for the harm I fear they will do to this land, but two of my sons are among them. The elder was to have taken holy orders, like his father. He left for the Turon three months ago."

"That is where Luke went," Mercy began. "The Turon. He—"

"Oh, yes, Luke—the young man who is *not* your brother." Alice Cox's gently mocking tone robbed her words of any malice, but her smile faded. "He is seeking not for gold, but for the man named Morgan, you said, did you not? The man who wronged you and who he believes was responsible for the death of his brother and others?"

"His brother Dan," Mercy supplied. "And their partners, Tom and Frank Gardener. And it's not just that Luke *believes* Jasper Morgan killed them, Mrs. Cox. It was proved, proved beyond doubt." For Luke's sake, and anxious to clear up any misunderstanding, she told of the trial before the miners' committee at Thayer's Bend. "I was there. I gave evidence. The committee brought a formal charge of murder against Jasper Morgan and ordered that he stand trial. Luke swore to find him and bring him to justice. He will not rest or even seek for gold on his own account until he does find him."

"Can he not be dissuaded, child?"

Mercy shook her head. Nothing, she reflected ruefully—not even her wedding to Claus Van Buren—would turn Luke from his purpose. His brother Dan had meant everything to him—more than his parents, certainly more than herself—and his meeting with Tom Gardener's widow, soon after the *Dolphin* had reached Sydney, had served to harden his resolve. Tom's widow and his two fatherless children . . . That meeting had upset Luke greatly, she recalled. He had given them every penny he had and, in consequence, had left for the Turon possessed of nothing save his horse and the clothes he stood up in, pledged to work for the two young New Zealanders from the Rangihowa Mission in return for his keep.

"No," she stated with conviction. "Luke won't be dissuaded. Claus offered him employment—here in Sydney or at sea in one of his ships—but Luke refused. He will go on searching for Jasper Morgan until he finds him, Mrs. Cox. I'm sure he will, even if it takes him the rest of his life."

"And if he does find him, Mercy?" Alice persisted. "Will he take the law into his own hands, do you suppose?"

"I don't know," Mercy confessed uneasily. Luke had only ever spoken of bringing Jasper Morgan to justice, she reminded herself. But clearly it would be difficult, if not plain impossible, for him to take Morgan back to Thayer's Bend— or even to America itself—with his limited means and after so prolonged a lapse of time. Claus might help, but he was in no way bound to support Luke's cause. "I suppose," she added, feeling that an answer was required of her, "it will depend on whether or not the authorities here are willing to act on Luke's testimony and mine. They might *not* be willing. It would be Jasper Morgan's word against ours, would it not? And since he claims to be a British officer—'' She broke off, suddenly afraid to give voice to her thoughts.

"*A life for a life,*" Luke had once quoted. "*An eye for an eye, tooth for tooth . . . wound for wound,* that is what the Holy Bible teaches. Morgan put his life in jeopardy when he killed Dan and the Gardeners, and he must pay with his life." Mercy shivered, avoiding Alice Cox's anxiously searching gaze. She *did* know, she thought; she knew with harsh, cold certainty that if the Australian authorities refused to take action against the self-styled Captain Morgan, then Luke *would* take the law into his own hands, regardless of the consequences to him or anyone else. But she could not tell Alice Cox, who was the wife of a member of the clergy— Claus's most revered "man of God." In that respect, Luke had a right to her silence.

"I don't know, Mrs. Cox," she repeated, continuing to avert her gaze. Alice Cox did not press the point. Old Saleh was on board the *Dolphin,* but another servant brought them coffee, and as if by mutual agreement, the subject was changed.

"We caught a glimpse of Claus's fine new vessel on our way here," Alice said. "I know little of ships, but Nathan was quite excited when he saw her. You will be going to sea in her again after your wedding, I believe?"

"Yes," Mercy confirmed. "Claus is sending two of his ships to Port Phillip with mining supplies, but we are going to New Zealand on board the *Dolphin,* his new ship. She is a truly beautiful ship, and I am overjoyed to be going back to Wellington and the Bay of Islands. I had hardly any time ashore on the voyage out here. New Zealand is a wonderful country, everyone says, and I should like to see more of it. And of the Maoris. They—" She lapsed into embarrassed silence, realizing that Alice Cox's expression was inexplicably unhappy.

"Forgive me," the older woman begged, "but we lost a very dear and good friend in the recent war against the Maoris, and I tend to think of them, somewhat uncharitably perhaps, as cruel and vengeful savages. Oh, I know that there have been faults on both sides and that some of the settlers who have gone out there have tricked the native inhabitants out of their land. But Michael Dean was not a man of that stamp. He was a soldier, it is true, yet all his endeavors were directed to keeping the peace and ensuring that the Maoris were treated justly. In spite of that, they ambushed and killed him when he was on his way to negotiate with one of the chiefs who had sued for peace. I heard the story only at second hand, so I know few details, but I knew Captain Dean very well." Alice Cox smiled, blinking back the tears that had welled into her eyes. "He left his mark on this colony. He was largely responsible for the closure of one of the worst penal settlements here, at Moreton Bay, and, as I did, he initially drew public attention to its evils in the columns of the *Australian*. And he explored and surveyed much of the country beyond Bathurst in the early days, and later joined the expeditions led by Captain Sturt and Mr. Hume. And yet"—her smile widened—"it was rumored, after his death, that Michael Dean was once a highwayman! Frankly, I do not believe that he could have been, but if he was, I can only say that he redeemed himself out here a hundred times over."

Mercy stared at her in puzzlement but did not offer any comment, and Alice Cox put down her coffee cup and rose.

"I think," she said, "if you will excuse me, Mercy, I will go to bed now. And you should have an early night, too, for tomorrow will be your great day—yours and Claus's. You must not skimp on your beauty sleep, child."

"No," Mercy conceded dutifully. "No, indeed."

She accompanied the older woman to her room, bearing their two candles, but after bidding her good night, she found herself unable to settle down to sleep. A shower of pebbles striking the windowpane sent her rushing across the room from her bed, and the shadowy form she glimpsed, standing below her window, resolved itself into Luke's travel-stained person, waving to her to let him in.

Joyfully, Mercy hastened to answer the summons, and Luke hugged her.

"Am I in time for your wedding?" he asked.

"You are just in time." Mercy could not quite keep the

reproachful note from sounding in her voice. "It is tomorrow."

"I'm sorry. I came as soon as I knew. Captain Broome and his son told me that you and Claus had fixed a day. But I wasn't sure—you see, I . . . Oh, it's a long story, Mercy. I've been chasing shadows all along the Turon."

Mercy took his arm. "You must be tired and hungry, Luke." One of Claus's Javanese servants came in response to her call, and she sent him scurrying to the kitchen, then escorted Luke through the double glass doors into the parlor. "There is a room prepared for you. By the time you have washed, Abdul will have your meal ready and—" A second houseboy appeared, holding a candle and rubbing the sleep from his eyes. "Go with Kassim. He will bring you anything you need."

"You are already mistress of this great household!" Luke exclaimed admiringly. "What a change from the old *Nancy Bray* and Jemmy Kemp's beef stew and taters! You play your role well, little sister."

"Our deception is finished," Mercy warned. "I could not wed Claus with so much on my conscience—I could not, Luke! He has given me everything—his love, his trust. I—"

"You told him that I'm not your brother?"

"Yes, I did. I—I had to."

Luke's dark eyes narrowed. "And about Morgan? Did you tell him about Morgan?"

Mercy met his alarmed gaze with a reassuring smile. "Yes, I told him everything."

"And clearly he did not send you packing," Luke observed. His momentary dismay faded, and he echoed her smile. "I'll clean myself up, and then we can talk. I'm glad I'm in time to see you wed, Mercy. So very glad."

"So am I," Mercy told him. "I hoped so much that you would be. Because it's the end of—of our chase, isn't it, Luke? It is for me. You said you had been chasing shadows along the Turon, and that—that must mean that you didn't find him, you didn't find Jasper Morgan?"

Luke's expression hardened. "No," he admitted, tight-lipped. "But I found his trail, with another killing to mark it. Morgan has gone to the new goldfields in Victoria. He sailed from here in the *Banshee*, calling himself Lewis, before we made port here."

"Then—" Mercy held her breath, her heart thudding. "Then you—"

"I'm going after him," Luke said with harsh finality. "Just as soon as I've seen you wed. I've a debt to pay—it's a debt of honor now, and if it kills me, I'll settle the score." The harshness faded from his voice, and he quoted softly, "Eye for eye, tooth for tooth, wound for wound. A life for *four* lives it's become, Mercy. And I'm not about to give up."

He turned his back on her, permitting Mercy no chance to plead with him, and Kassim hastened after him, the flickering flame of the candle he bore almost extinguished as the parlor door slammed shut behind them.

CHAPTER XV

Her Majesty's ship *Huntsman*, of twenty guns, signaled her arrival off the Port Jackson Heads on the morning of October 10. Red Broome, who had spent the previous two days as a guest on board the *Acheron* steam survey vessel, on guard ship duty in Watson's Bay, watched her bring to to receive the pilot. As she sailed past the anchorage, he listened to the speculation concerning her expressed by the *Acheron*'s officers.

His own ship, the *Galah*, had, to his intense chagrin, been dispatched to Hobart under the temporary command of Commodore Skinner's nephew, and he himself was still officially unemployed, waiting—with ever-increasing impatience—for the long-delayed summons to appear before a court of inquiry. Skinner had continued to postpone the convening of the court until the missing Dora Lucas could be traced.

"Her evidence is essential, whether it is given in person or in writing," the commodore had informed him, brushing aside Red's objections and, indeed, permitting him little chance to voice them. "In view of Captain Lucas's unhappy demise, the court must afford his widow a hearing. Even you, Commander Broome, must see the justice of my decision."

He had attempted to do so, Red reflected resentfully, but with conspicuous lack of success. Now all he could hope for was that his father and Johnny would manage to track down young De Lancey and his paramour and, at the least, obtain a statement from them that would satisfy both Skinner and his court.

"Perhaps she's bringing Skinner's relief," Red heard the *Acheron*'s commander, John Stokes, suggest. His tone was guarded, but from the expression on his thin, austere face, it was evident that he hoped his guess might prove correct. "The *Huntsman*—any of you know who's commanding her?"

Heads were shaken regretfully. The *Acheron* had been on the East Indies station for four years, engaged in survey duties in New Zealand waters, and she was due to return to England to pay off. Overdue, in fact, Red remembered, according to John Stokes, but Commodore Skinner had detained her, giving the purported threat of attack by a Russian fleet as his reason for delay. The commodore had attained post rank in 1838, Stokes eight years later, and Skinner had, as usual, pulled rank, effectively putting an end to argument and pleas alike.

"Perhaps she's *our* relief, sir," the first lieutenant, Adam Elliott, offered.

"The commodore still would not permit this ship to leave," Stokes countered glumly. "He remains convinced that a steamer is an essential part of the defense of Port Jackson." He expelled his breath in an exasperated sigh. "Here we are, permanently at anchor, with all our scientific instruments and our highly trained ship's company deteriorating from lack of use. Not to mention," he added, with a wry gesture toward the master, Frederick Evans, "one of the Royal Navy's most experienced surveyors, recently honored by the fellowship of the Royal Geographical Society *and* that of the Royal Astronomical Society! Honor and glory will deservedly be his, if only we can arrange his passage back to England . . . is that not so, Mr. Evans, sir?"

The slight, ruddy-cheeked master waved a deprecatory hand. Under the command of Captain Francis Blackwood in H.M.S. *Fly*, he had, Red knew, charted the Great Barrier Reef, on Australia's eastern coast, and been responsible for the erection of the great stone beacon that, seventy miles offshore, marked the eastern extremity of the reef. Evans's Edifice, as it was termed, had saved countless vessels from shipwreck on the treacherous coral fangs of the reef.

"I'm in no hurry to leave here, Captain Stokes," he answered gravely. "After all, sir, I can work on my charts undisturbed and at leisure, and I have been made free of the observatory. This anchorage is perhaps a trifle inconvenient, but apart from that I've no complaint, none at all."

Stokes groaned in mock despair. "You see what he's like, Broome—honor and glory are of no concern to him. Whilst the rest of us chafe at our unaccustomed idleness, Mr. Evans calls it leisure! And you, I am sure, have still more reason for complaint, with the commodore's precious nephew—who has never previously held or merited a command—now vanished with your *Galah* into the deep blue yonder. But I have an idea. We are tied here, all shore leave denied us, but you are not. You are attending a wedding in Sydney Town this afternoon, you said?"

Red nodded. "Yes, sir, I am. At the Church of St. James, I—" He hesitated, anxious lest Stokes might seek to disrupt his plans. Magdalen had consented to his being her escort to the church, and nothing would induce him to forgo that privilege. Of late she had become more responsive to his courtship, and— He added quickly, "It is the wedding of a boyhood friend of mine, Claus Van Buren, and I've promised I'll attend."

"Then of course you must, my dear fellow," the *Acheron's* captain acknowledged readily. "But it's early. You've the whole forenoon before you. Time enough, surely, to call on Captain Skinner and ascertain what tidings the *Huntsman* has brought? The breeze is nor'easterly and brisk; your cutter can whisk you back to the hub of things, and the chances are that you'll find the *Huntsman's* commander closeted with the commodore by the time you present yourself. Damme, if our sailing orders have come, I want to *know!* And you can send your cox'un back with a note, if the *Huntsman* has brought any news of interest to us—you don't have to come yourself. Come, be a good fellow, Broome. It's not too much to ask of you, is it?"

"No, sir, of course not," Red assured him. "A small return for your hospitality and for permitting me to study Mr. Evans's charts." He drew himself up. "If Mr. Elliott will be so good as to call away my cutter, I'll take my leave now. And I hope I'll be able to send you the news you want."

The cutter—on loan to him and manned by a crew of veteran seamen from the dockyard establishment—made good use of the lively breeze, and a little more than an hour later Red was admitted to Commodore Skinner's official residence.

As John Stokes had shrewdly forecast, the newly arrived ship's captain must have come ashore as soon as his vessel had dropped anchor off Sydney Cove—no doubt in response to an imperious signal from the commodore, who, of late, had shown a marked preference for summoning his subordinates to him by means of the semaphore mounted on his roof, rather than exert himself by going out to meet them when they entered the Heads. For once, however, Red observed, Skinner was in an extremely affable mood, deferring to the tall officer seated facing him across his littered desk and addressing him with exaggerated courtesy as "My dear Sir James."

The newcomer wore gold epaulets on both shoulders, denoting that he had held post rank for more than three years, but at first glance he appeared too young to be of the same rank and seniority as the Sydney squadron's commander. About his own age, Red decided, or at most a year or two older. He was dark-haired and of a thin but wiry build, and there was something oddly familiar about him when he turned his head in response to Skinner's introduction.

"Permit me to present Commander Broome. This is Captain Sir James Willoughby, Broome, who has just brought the *Huntsman* into port, as doubtless you'll have observed. You have called at an opportune moment, since—"

Sir James Willoughby cut him short. Rising to his feet, he went to meet Red with both hands eagerly extended.

"Red, my dear chap, how good it is to see you again! It's been a long time—the Woosung River in '42, wasn't it? You were with that incredibly brave firebrand Captain Henry Keppel, in the *Dido*, and I was acting first of *Inflexible*. Your gig took the admiral ashore, and we met in the wreckage of the town. On the anniversary of Waterloo, I seem to recall."

"Indeed it was," Red agreed, pleased beyond measure at the unexpected encounter with so old a friend. James Willoughby was the son of Rear Admiral Sir Francis Willoughby and had inherited the baronetcy after the admiral's death, in place of his elder brother, who . . . Red stiffened, remembering. Good Lord, of course—Robert Willoughby had come out to Australia to farm, and had lost his life in an encounter with a party of bushrangers! James had inherited his brother's land grant and his stock; he had quit the navy with the intention of remaining in the colony to farm and— Red warmly wrung the young post captain's hands.

"I really regretted giving you my place in the *Success*'s midshipmen's berth," Willoughby said, as if Red had spoken his thoughts aloud. "Lord, it took me only a couple of months to discover that I wasn't cut out for farming, Red. So I went back to the service and was fortunate enough to be taken as supernumerary by Captain Clement Lowe of the *Lapwing*. I went home in her, and then . . ." He talked on, filling in the gaps, which, in the awful carnage of Woosung, there had been neither time nor inclination to fill. Captain Skinner listened with ill-concealed irritation and finally broke in, a distinct edge to his voice.

"Gentlemen, you will have ample leisure to discuss your respective naval achievements at some later date, I feel sure, and no doubt in more, ah, congenial surroundings than my office can provide."

"So we will," James Willoughby conceded imperturbably. "I must beg your indulgence, Captain Skinner. I let my tongue run away with me. But it is not very often that I encounter a friend of Commander Broome's standing in my esteem, and as you'll have realized, we haven't met since the China war." He smiled, seemingly amused by Skinner's indignation, and the commodore's color deepened. "But of course, sir," Willoughby went on smoothly, before his superior could speak, "you will be anxious to acquaint Broome with the news of your new appointment."

Skinner accepted the proffered olive branch with a bad grace. "I'm to command the *Monarch*," he announced coldly.

"A line-of-battle ship!" Red exclaimed. "My congratulations, sir." It was, he was well aware, a considerable step up; the commodore's last command had been the *Havannah* frigate, and the *Monarch* was an eighty-four-gun three-decker of the second rate.

"Thank you," Skinner acknowledged, his tone a trifle warmer. "It means, of course, that I shall be leaving this station and handing over my responsibilities to Captain Willoughby." He glanced down at the scattered papers on his desk and released a sigh. "The *Acheron* is ordered home to pay off. I shall take passage in her as soon as she can be prepared for sea."

John Stokes would be over the moon, Red thought, but he hid his smile and avoided Skinner's eye as the commodore went on. "Ah, I shall take my nephew, Lieutenant Frazer Skinner, with me, of course, since he's under my patronage." He hesitated, still continuing to avoid meeting Red's gaze.

"Lieutenant Skinner is presently in Hobart, is he not, sir?" Red prompted with well-simulated innocence. "In acting command of the *Galah?*" He had the satisfaction of witnessing Captain Skinner's obvious discomfiture and added, without heat, "Pending the result of the court of inquiry into my relationship with the widow of the late Captain Lucas?"

"Quite so," Skinner conceded. "Ah . . ." He made a show of searching among his papers, his color deepening. James Willoughby, clearly puzzled by this exchange, looked across at Red with raised brows but said nothing, as Skinner cleared his throat and said reluctantly, "Ah, Judge De Lancey has intimated that, in his view, you are blameless, Commander Broome. He, ah—that is, he has approached me with the stated intention of giving evidence to the court on your behalf, whilst admitting his son's, ah, culpability. In the light of that, I have decided that an inquiry will not be necessary."

"I'm glad of that, sir," Red responded evenly. When, he wondered, had the commodore made his decision to forgo the court of inquiry? But aware that to ask as much might well provoke an outburst, he restrained himself and questioned deferentially, "Am I restored to command of my ship, then, sir?"

"Certainly you are," Skinner answered. "The whole, ah, unfortunate affair is best forgotten, since it is evident that the charges against you were based on a series of untruths, perpetrated by—well, we need not go into that now, I think, in Captain Willoughby's presence. No." With a return to his accustomed, blustering tone, the commodore added,

"You'll accompany me to Hobart on board the *Acheron,* Commander Broome, where you will relieve Lieutenant Skinner of command of the *Galah.*"

"Aye, aye, sir," Red acknowledged. Again meeting James Willoughby's mutely questioning gaze, he shook his head and rose. "If that's all, sir, I'll leave you with Captain Willoughby. I imagine you'll have much to arrange and—"

But Willoughby rose with him, smiling. "Nothing that cannot wait, my dear fellow," he asserted easily. "You must permit me to offer you luncheon aboard the *Huntsman,* if you can spare the time. We've the gap of years to span, have we not? Then, by your leave, Captain Skinner—" His leave-taking was brisk and unceremonious, and once outside the commodore's house, he clapped a hand about Red's shoulders and asked curiously, "What the devil was all that about, Red? A court of inquiry, for the Lord's sake, charges based on—what did Skinner call them? A series of untruths? And your command given to his precious nephew?"

"It's quite a long story, sir." Red flushed, seeking to evade the question. "And past history now."

"I have all the time in the world to listen. And damme, Red, don't stand on ceremony, I beg you. I'm Jamie Willoughby, remember, and we were mids together in the old days. I was made post only three years ago, and that by fortunate chance, when an uncle of mine hauled down his flag and wasn't enamored of any of my seniors." Willoughby gave vent to an amused and faintly cynical laugh. "It pays to have patronage in the Royal Navy, as doubtless the younger Skinner will have cause to appreciate one of these days. Come on, tell me the story, however long it takes. You can lunch with me, can't you?"

"I have to attend a wedding this afternoon," Red told him. He consulted his pocket watch. "It would be cutting it a mite fine, if I came out with you to the ship. But I'm living ashore at present, in my father's house, which is ten minutes' walk from here. Why do you not lunch with me and—yes, of course! Attend the wedding with me? It is that of another old friend, whom you may perhaps remember. Claus Van Buren."

James Willoughby's brows met in an effort to remember.

"Claus Van—oh, Lord, yes, I do recall that name, and with reason! My brother fought a duel with Major Van Buren soon after he came out here."

"The late and unlamented Major Van Buren," Red supplied. "Claus was his son from a marriage with a Javanese woman. He had a wretched childhood, but Van Buren acknowledged him before he died, and Claus inherited a couple of trading vessels. From that beginning he's built up a very prosperous enterprise. Indeed, he is one of the colony's leading shipping merchants now. His latest acquisition is a Boston-built clipper schooner, the *Dolphin*, which you may have noticed at her moorings when you came in."

James pursed his lips in a silent whistle. "Yes, I did. And it's his wedding you're suggesting I should attend?"

"That's so, Jamie, yes. You will be welcome, I'm sure. He is wedding an American girl, whom he met in San Francisco." Red waved a hand at the road ahead. "My father's house is in Elizabeth Bay—a white two-story house, perched on the hill overlooking the bay. As I said, it's only ten minutes' walk from here, but if you'll excuse me, I have a message to give to the cox'un of my cutter." He gestured to the waiting boat and, after taking a used envelope from his pocket, scribbled a few words on it, smiling as he did so. "For John Stokes of the *Acheron*. You brought the news he's been waiting for."

"His orders to sail for home?"

"Yes—they are long overdue." Red folded the envelope. "The *Acheron*'s been out here for well over four years, on survey duties. But we had a recent scare concerning the possibility of war with Russia and a rumored attack by a squadron of the Russian Pacific Fleet. The Governor was advised to put Sydney in a state of defense, and Commodore Skinner would not permit the *Acheron* to go. She's under steam, you see, and he's kept her as guard ship in Watson's Bay. I—excuse me, if you will."

James Willoughby waited until Red had entrusted his missive to the cutter's coxswain, and then, as they fell into step together to breast the slight slope, he said gravely, "The possibility of our being drawn into war with Russia is more than a scare, Red, although I doubt whether you will see any

Russian warships here. The most likely naval confrontations will be in the Black Sea and the Baltic—particularly the Black Sea and the Bosporus. The Tsar is said to be casting acquisitive eyes on Turkey. . . ."

He went into carefully reasoned detail as they strode briskly through the Government Domain, and Red listened in shocked surprise. The twelve thousand miles that separated Australia from the mother country formed a barrier of both time and distance, he reflected, and news of impending conflict in Europe was always slow in reaching the colony, since the ships that bore it were subject to the vagaries of wind and weather. James Willoughby's frigate had made a comparatively fast passage, but even so . . . "Do you believe that war is likely?" he asked.

"It's on the cards, Red, no doubt of that. Lord Aberdeen's government will do all in their power to prevent it, that goes without saying. Our fighting forces are overstretched—in India, China, and even New Zealand. But we and the French have treaties with Turkey, and any act of aggression by the Tsar would drag us in, however reluctantly." Willoughby sighed. "I was in two minds about coming out here, when I was offered the appointment. But it's for only two years, and I think we'll have that long before anything drastic happens. I hope so, anyway. I want to pay a visit to New Zealand—I've three sisters at the Rangihowa Mission, in the Bay of Islands."

Again he went into detail, speaking with warm affection of the sisters he had not seen since his midshipman's days.

"I moved heaven and earth to have myself sent out during the trouble with the Maoris on North Island six years ago," he confided. "But Their Lordships had other ideas. The *Inflexible* went there from China, as I expect you know, but I'd been invalided and sent home, and when the surgeons finally released me from their clutches, I had to be thankful that my uncle applied for me to join him in the West Indies. It gave me my step, but—" James shrugged. "Anyway, Red old friend, I'm here. Now, indulge my curiosity, won't you, and tell me about the court of inquiry that Skinner has decided not to hold."

Over luncheon, in the house overlooking Elizabeth Bay,

Red told him of the events that had led up to his being
relieved of his command. James heard him without interruption and, when the brief recital had ended, shook his head in
disbelief.

"Somewhat autocratic, our friend the late commodore, is
he not?"

"A trifle so. But the evidence against me was conflicting,
to say the least, and poor Lucas's death ill-timed. It placed
Skinner in an awkward position," Red defended, his tone
resigned. "I had supposed, though, that when Dora Lucas
eloped with young De Lancey, he would at least have given
me the benefit of the doubt."

"And he did not?"

"No, he did not. He insisted that he must have a statement
from Mrs. Lucas. That's why my father isn't here; he's gone
up to the goldfields in search of the two of them, in order to
obtain a statement. But that is no longer needed, thanks—"
Red smiled across the table at his guest. "Thanks to your
providential arrival. And to Judge De Lancey's intervention,
I suppose."

"De Lancey . . . Are the judge and your delinquent
young lieutenant related to the beautiful Miss De Lancey—
Miss Magdalen De Lancey—whom I met, all too briefly, in
Scotland?" James Willoughby's tone was thoughtful, the expression on his thin, sensitive face suddenly eager, as if the
memory Magdalen's name had evoked were one he had long
treasured, and Red stiffened instinctively. Of course it was
possible that he and Magdalen had met; they would have
moved in the same circles and attended similar functions,
dinner parties, balls, and the like. Magdalen had relatives in
Scotland, on her father's side, Red reminded himself. There
was an aunt, after whom she had been named, with whom
she had stayed while waiting for her return passage to Sydney. She had gone there after her visit to her kin in London,
where he himself had met her. Where he had met and fallen
in love with her, if the truth were known . . . His mouth
tightened.

"Yes," he confirmed guardedly, in answer to James's question. "Her father and younger brother. The judge is an

American but of Loyalist descent. He served with the British Army under the Duke of Wellington and was at Waterloo."

"Ah, that explains the connection. Magdalen was staying with the widow of a Waterloo veteran, at Dunglass Castle, and I attended a ball they gave there. By heaven, Red, she is a charming girl—charming, as well as incredibly beautiful! Dark hair and blue eyes, the most delightful contrast imaginable. I confess I lost my heart to her." James was smiling as he helped himself to cheese. "I made her a proposal of marriage after only two dances—the most impulsive thing I ever did in my life! I'd no idea who she was, only that she'd been born out here and intended to return to Sydney." His smile faded, and he gave vent to a deep sigh. "Oh, she turned me down, of course. Who could blame her? She didn't believe that I was serious, and perhaps I was not, at the time. But that was another reason for coming out here, Red. I wanted to see her again. She is here, is she not? She did come back to Sydney?"

"Yes, she came back," Red confirmed woodenly.

He hesitated, conscious of an unreasoned anger, and James asked, with smiling casualness, "Is she married, Red? I imagine she must be—a girl like that. Lord, at the Dunglass ball she was almost under siege!"

Red shook his head. Fool that he was, he chided himself, to have conducted his courtship of Magdalen at so laggardly a pace. He had been obsessed with the threat to his naval career posed by Commodore Skinner's miserable court of inquiry, but, damn it, the threat no longer existed! His pleasure at the unexpected reunion with Jamie Willoughby abruptly faded, and he said, a distinct edge to his voice, "No, Magdalen isn't married, Jamie. But that doesn't mean that she's not—how did you put it? Under siege."

To his annoyance, Jamie Willoughby threw back his head and laughed uproariously. "Do I sense rivalry? A prior claim?"

"You do indeed," Red managed wrathfully.

"On your part, Red?"

"Certainly on mine, yes." Reluctantly Red added, "And you will meet her again very soon, as it happens."

"I shall be delighted to meet her again. But how so?"

"I had arranged to escort her to the church this afternoon, for Claus Van Buren's wedding."

"To which you also invited me, all unsuspecting? Oh, Lord, that is rich!" Jamie Willoughby's tone was amused but, relenting, he offered seriously, "Your invitation need not hold, my dear fellow. I'll go back to my ship if you wish to withdraw it, and no hard feelings. But I cannot promise not to offer you a challenge, unless Magdalen is already affianced to you. Is she?"

"No," Red was compelled to admit. He rose to cross to the sideboard, ashamed of the jealousy he felt. "You'll take a glass of port?" he invited. "Or brandy, if you prefer it . . . and a cigar? And of course I shan't withdraw my invitation, Jamie. Half Sydney will be at the wedding. Only the diehard elitists will stay away, and there are not too many of them left, I'm glad to say." He went back to the table and laid a brimming glass of brandy at his guest's side. "I must go and change, if you'll excuse me. The carriage I've hired will be here in half an hour."

"A toast before you go, Red." Jamie was mocking him, Red sensed, but good-humoredly and without even a hint of malice, and he responded to it with a good grace.

"To Magdalen De Lancey," he said, and raised his own glass, echoing Jamie's smile.

They drank the toast together.

Half an hour later, the hired carriage bore them to the De Lancey residence, and Magdalen herself received them. She was looking more beautiful than ever, Red observed, slim and graceful, in a dress that matched the blue of her eyes, and with a beribboned bonnet that shaded but did not conceal the glowing loveliness of her small, piquant face.

To his secret relief, she did not at first appear to recall her previous meeting with his guest, but then, when Jamie himself reminded her of it, she exclaimed amusedly, "So that's who you are! Of course, I remember now. You were exceedingly merry at my uncle's ball. Merry to the point of recklessness, Sir James. We were dancing an intricate reel, with which neither of us was familiar, and—" She glanced at Red, her eyes bright with laughter. "And would you believe it, Red, he asked me to marry him!"

"I take it you rejected his overtures," Red prompted, eager to make a jest of it.

"I could scarcely do otherwise," Magdalen answered lightly. "He was a complete stranger, on whom I had never set eyes, and I don't think we had been properly introduced. But"—her smile was warm—"now that Red has introduced us, I am delighted to renew our acquaintance, Sir James."

Jamie bowed. "Your devoted admirer, Miss Magdalen," he declared. "No longer reckless but, I assure you, no less determined." Forestalling Red, he offered Magdalen his arm, and they went out together to the waiting carriage.

The church was already crowded when they reached it and were ushered to a pew on the bridegroom's side, with Magdalen seated between them. In the foremost pew, Claus Van Buren and his best man were seated, Claus with his head bowed, seemingly deep in prayer, and so he remained, looking at no one, until the organ—a recent acquisition, gifted by the congregation—burst into a joyous warning of the bride's arrival.

The girl came in a trifle hesitatingly, her eyes behind the enveloping veil darting anxiously this way and that, until they lit on Claus, who was on his feet and turning to look at her. Then, as if his welcoming smile had reached out to touch her, she lost her initial hesitation and advanced with oddly moving dignity to his side, on the arm of a slight, dark-haired young man in what, Red guessed, must be a borrowed velveteen jacket, tailored for one both taller and heavier than he.

Claus, he recalled, had talked of a brother who, like most of the new arrivals in the colony, had gone to the gold diggings but now, evidently, had returned to Sydney without the fortune for which they had all come to search . . . and who must have returned very recently, for his thin young face bore the unmistakable traces of a freshly shaved beard. But he looked happy enough and bore himself well, despite the borrowed finery, standing quietly aside to enable Claus to take his place beside his bride.

The clergyman, a gray-haired man whom Red did not recognize, stepped forward, prayer book open in his hands, to intone the opening address of the marriage service.

"Dearly beloved, we are gathered together in the sight of
God and in the face of this congregation, to join this man
and this woman in holy matrimony, which is an honorable
estate, instituted by God in the time of man's innocency,
signifying unto us the mystical union that is betwixt Christ
and His Church. . . ."

Red listened, conscious of a swift surge of emotion engendered by Magdalen's closeness to him in the narrow pew. He
ventured a sidelong glance at her, but she was seemingly
unaware of him, her own gaze fixed on the two standing in
front of the altar.

". . . which holy estate Christ adorned and beautified
with His presence and first miracle that He wrought in Cana
of Galilee," the gray-haired priest read on, in a clear, deep
voice. "It is commended of Saint Paul to be honorable
among all men and therefore is not by any to be taken in
hand unadvisedly, lightly, or wantonly. . . ."

Wishing that it might have been Magdalen and himself
standing there, Red closed his eyes, visualizing the scene
and permitting his imagination free rein. If Jamie Willoughby could propose to her on impulse, then surely he
could do no less? She was the woman he wanted for his wife,
heaven knew, and since the carefree, happy time they had
spent together in London, no other woman had occupied his
thoughts or found a place in his heart. What did ambition or
his career matter? What did life hold, if it were lived only for
these and lived alone?

"Claus Karimon," he heard the priest ask, "wilt thou have
this woman to thy wedded wife, to live together after God's
ordinance in the holy estate of matrimony? Wilt thou love
her, comfort her, honor and keep her in sickness and in
health and, forsaking all other, keep thee only unto her, so
long as ye both shall live?"

Claus's answer, given firmly and with deep feeling, woke
an echo in Red's heart. Once again he looked down at Magdalen, and this time her gaze met his, and he saw that her
blue eyes were misted with tears. She looked swiftly away,
but when he reached for her hand, she made no attempt to
withdraw it, and he felt her shoulder brush his.

"Mercedes Louisa, wilt thou have this man to thy wedded

husband, to live together after God's ordinance in the holy
estate of matrimony? Wilt thou obey him and serve him,
love, honor and keep him in sickness and in health and,
forsaking all other, keep thee only unto him, so long as ye
both shall live?"

The words seemed to be coming from a long way off, and
the bride's answer was a whisper of sound, scarcely audible
to the listening congregation. Red did not hear it; he did not
consciously hear the rest of the service as he stood, clasping
Magdalen's small hand in his, his heart thudding and his
mouth dry. He had forgotten Jamie Willoughby's presence
and his threatened rivalry, and as Claus and his bride rose
from their knees to follow the tall figure of the priest to the
vestry, the organ pealed and, all about them, voices rose in
the singing of a hymn.

"Magdalen," he said, lips close to her ear, "I love you. I'll
love you till the day I die. Will you marry me, my dearest
love?"

The dark head beneath the ribbon-trimmed bonnet was
bowed in assent. "I will, Red," she whispered softly, and, for
all the lusty singing on all sides of them, Red heard her
answer. He bore the hand he held to his lips, heedless of who
might be watching, and then, as he lowered it, realized that
Jamie had observed the gesture.

That he had also understood its significance became evident when, the service over, the congregation started to file
out of the church in the wake of Claus Van Buren and his
bride. Jamie, smiling, stood aside, permitting Red to offer
Magdalen his arm, and as they walked out into the sunlight,
Jamie bowed to them courteously and was gone.

CHAPTER XVI

Dora's pains started when she was filling a water cask at the creek bank. She doubled up in agony as they tore at her, causing her to cry out with pain and shock. But there was no one to hear—the gold seekers had moved on farther downstream, Francis and Rob and Simon Yates with them, to where now they were digging gold-bearing quartz from the hillsides. An enterprising organization, styling itself the Great Nugget Vein Company, had set up expensive machinery on the lower reach of the Louisa Creek for crushing the quartz, and in common with the rest, Francis and his partners had decided that it would pay them to take advantage of it.

Dora drew a deep, sobbing breath, and as the pain subsided, she reached again for her cask. It was only half full, the water it contained brown and muddy, but it would have to do, she decided, for she had not the strength to refill it. The pains were premature, she told herself chidingly, for had not the doctor, whom she had consulted when she and Francis had gone to Sofala to be wed, had not that kindly, highly skilled man assured her that her child would not be born before November? And it was still only October—October the tenth, if her calculations were accurate, although perhaps they were not. Time passed her by these days, when each day had a sameness that dulled thought.

True, her belly was greatly swollen and distended, the child in her womb alarmingly active at times, but that, surely, did not mean that its birth was imminent? Had either of them supposed that it was, Francis would have stayed with her, ready to harness the horses to their wagon and drive her back to Sofala, where—even if the doctor had moved on—

there would be a midwife and other women, mothers themselves, who would care for her.

So . . . the pains had to be premature, or possibly a fig-
ment of her imagination. She had never borne a child before
and therefore could not judge whether or not the severity of
the spasm that had just passed ought to be taken as a warning. And the spasm *had* passed. Dora clambered awkwardly
to her feet and, holding her half-filled cask as firmly as she
could, started up the bank toward the small log cabin that
her husband and the two young New Zealanders had built
for her with such care. But the creek bank was slippery from
the heavy rain of the previous week, and as she felt her feet
slipping, the pain came again, and she dropped to her knees
in the mud, unable to stifle the shriek that rose unbidden to
her lips.

As before, the awful gripping of her stomach muscles
gradually eased, and, really frightened now, Dora hauled
herself up the bank on hands and knees, dragging the water
cask after her with obstinate courage. In the past months she
had learned to endure hardship and isolation; she had
worked as she had never supposed she could work, ready
each evening with a hot meal for her weary menfolk, and up
at dawn each morning to light a fire, brew tea, and see them
on their way to the distant diggings, each provided with
clean linen and dry socks and a package of whatever food
was available for their midday break.

And she had been happy, Dora thought with sudden wonder. Francis was her adored husband and lover; his strength
of purpose and his determination to succeed had sustained
her and kept her hopes alive, even though, day after endless
day, there had been little tangible reward for his toil. In his
arms, lying on their bed of boughs and canvas in the warm
darkness, she had been fulfilled, worshiped, and wanted,
secure in the steadfastness of Francis's devotion and daring
to believe that, when he made his strike, they might return to
civilized living with their heads held high and no sense of
guilt left to be purged.

She had given Commander Broome's father the written
statement he had asked for, and he, to her intense relief, had
told her that Benjamin Lucas's death had left her free to wed

the man she loved. Somehow—looking back now, Dora wondered how she had managed to overcome the shame she had felt—she and Francis had broken it to the Yates boys that they were runaways, not the respectable married couple they had pretended to be. But both boys had taken the disclosure well and had offered neither reproach nor criticism. For all the strict upbringing they had had in a missionary household, neither of them had uttered a word of censure, but had continued to treat her with respectful courtesy, and Francis with something approaching veneration. Nowadays they were on terms of warm affection, all four of them, and—despite her anxiety, Dora managed a shaky smile—it was as if she had acquired not only a husband, but two splendid brothers as well.

She gained the cabin at last and went inside, its well-scrubbed neatness affording her a feeling of pride. It was primitive enough, in all conscience; a structure of rough-hewn logs and an earthen floor, with a shingle roof, shaped and fitted together most skillfully by Rob Yates from tree bark, after a pattern, he had told her, devised by the first settlers before bricks or slates had been available.

There were two rooms—hers and Francis's, and the boys' sleeping quarters, which doubled as a living room for them all—and her kitchen, a lean-to at the rear with a stone fireplace.

Dora set her water cask down by the door, too spent, after the bouts of pain, to carry it to the kitchen. As always, there was work to be done: clothes to wash, worn garments to be patched or darned, bedding to be aired, and preparations for the evening meal to be begun. Simon had caught two sizable fish the day before; he had gutted them for her, but . . . the thought of having to touch them nauseated her. She would lie down for a little while, she decided, try to sleep, perhaps, in the hope that the child she carried might, after all, settle down and wait for its proper time to be born.

But the pain came again, more severe than it had been before, and lasting longer this time. Lying on her back in the bed, Dora writhed in helpless agony, her body drenched in perspiration. When at long last it eased, she knew instinctively that her baby was clamoring to make its entry into the world and that there was nothing she could do now to postpone its coming. But she had to have help; she could not give birth alone—she was too ignorant of all that was entailed, too afraid that she might commit some terrible error that would deprive her child of its life.

"Labor, in a first confinement, can be of many hours' duration, Mrs. De Lancey," the Sofala physician had told her, in response to one of her nervous questions. "The pains come initially quite a long time apart. When they are virtually continuous, then that is the end of the first stage, and the passage of the child through the birth canal will commence with what, in layman's terms, is called the breaking of the waters."

As yet the time between the pains was, as nearly as Dora could judge, fifteen to twenty minutes, which should permit her a little leeway. Not long enough for her to try to walk to the diggings, but sufficient, in all probability, for her to signal her need for help. If she lit a fire in the open, on the highest part of the creek bank, the rocks would prevent it from spreading, and the smoke—if she piled damp grass or brushwood on it—would rise above the screening trees. And surely Francis or one of the Yates boys would see it and understand its significance. They would know that her kitchen fire was never lit until late in the afternoon. . . .

Controlling her rising fears, Dora dragged herself from the bed and then out to the kitchen. Another spasm racked her as she sought materials with which to start the fire, but she endured it stoically and, when it ceased, started to make her way at a shambling run toward the site she had chosen.

But she did not reach it. Halfway up the slope, the sound of voices brought her thankfully to a halt, and she cried out, praying that whoever was there, hidden from her by the trees, might hear her faint cries and come to her aid. It seemed that they had, for the voices faded into silence and then sounded again, and she heard footsteps approaching her and the voices coming nearer.

"Oh, thank God!" she whispered, and sank down on the muddy ground, her strength ebbing away. "Thanks be to God!"

Her relief was cruelly short-lived. Three figures emerged

from the concealment of the close-growing gums, and Dora
shrank back in terror when she saw that they were blacks,
seminaked, and that two of them, their faces hideously
daubed, were carrying spears. The third was a woman, with a
small child clinging to her back.

There had been no trouble with the aborigines in this
area, Dora knew; they were there but were seldom seen, for
they avoided the vicinity of the diggings and only occasionally descended on an isolated farm, to beg for food or ask for
seasonal work, if the owner was known to them. In spite of
this, she was afraid, the warlike appearance of the two men
adding to her fear, and, unable to restrain herself, she
started to scream her terror aloud.

The men came to a halt, exchanged a swift glance, and
then, with one accord, turned their backs on her and started
to lope away. The woman, however, recognized her predicament and stood her ground, looking down at Dora with
pitying eyes. After a brief hesitation, she called out to the
men, set her child down, and moved to Dora's side, a finger
to her lips. She was short and squat, of indeterminate age,
and her dark-skinned body, with its pendulous breasts, was
liberally plastered with dried mud, which exuded a musty
odor. But she bared two rows of white teeth in a disarming
smile, and her hands were gentle as she laid them on Dora's
straining belly, whispering something that, for all it was
unintelligible, was at once kindly and reassuring.

The two men stood silent, keeping their distance, but one
of them—evidently in response to a call from the woman—
moved a few reluctant paces and picked up the child. That
done, they waited, squatting down and leaning on their
spears, with the child between them.

Dora was conscious of an agonizing pain, longer and more
excruciating than those that had gone before. Her teeth
closed convulsively over her lower lip in a vain attempt to
suppress the cry that was wrung from her. The woman
turned her firmly onto her back, thrusting her legs into a
bent position, and she felt the warm rush of fluid and knew
that, as the Sofala doctor had told her, the waters had broken and her child's birth had begun.

She had no strength to resist, and the aborigine woman

took charge, loosening her clothing, pressing something hard into her mouth for her to bite on, and then, with strong, sure hands, aiding her to bear down when the pains came, somehow—without words that Dora could understand—making her meaning clear and telling her what she must do.

Even so, the birth was not easy, and Dora's agony lasted for a long time. The sun was sinking in a ball of crimson fire behind the distant tree-clad hills when at last it was over and the baby's first, feeble cries were borne to its mother's ears, bringing a joy whose like Dora had never before experienced. The woman was beaming at her, she saw, sharing her pleasure and her relief, the dark eyes aglow.

"Allira," she said, and repeated the word several times. *"Dandaloo?"*

A low-voiced command from one of the men distracted her; she gave him no answer but rose with sudden haste, her smile wiped abruptly from her round black face and fear replacing the delight her eyes had reflected a moment before. The baby, wrapped in the petticoat Dora had been wearing, was placed gently in her arms—a tiny bundle, with a crown of black, silky hair.

"Kateena," the native woman whispered. She raised Dora into a sitting position and, giving her no time to utter her thanks, took to her heels and ran, to snatch her own child from the bearded man who held it.

All four vanished into the gathering darkness, merging like ghosts with the gnarled trunks of the gum and stringy-bark trees in which they had sought concealment, leaving Dora to wonder if they had ever been. Then the reason for their swift and unexpected flight became clear as she heard Francis frantically calling her name and Rob and Simon echoing his call.

"She's gone," she heard Francis say. "She's not in the cabin! In God's name, where can she be? Dora—Dora my love, answer me!"

Dora attempted to respond, her voice a thin whisper of sound that did not carry, and it was the baby's sudden, lusty crying that guided the searchers to where she was. Her husband was the first to reach her, and he flung himself down beside her, gazing in stunned bewilderment at the tiny, bawling infant in her arms.

"God in heaven, it's born! And you were alone. Oh, my sweet darling, I should never have left you! Rob said he spotted some abos, two men with spears, and I—darling, I was so afraid. I feared they might have harmed you."

Dora shook her head, summoning a tremulous smile. "They didn't harm me, dearest. There was a woman with them . . . she helped me."

Francis rose, his face reflecting his concern, and then, bending quickly, he picked her up in his arms and started to carry her back to the cabin. The baby's sobs were stilled; Dora held the tiny creature close to her heart, and with her free hand she drew the crumpled linen covering aside. The child was female. She said softly, "We have a daughter, Francis—a lovely little daughter."

Francis, intent on picking his way over the rough ground, did not answer her at once, but Rob Yates, catching up with them, offered his warm congratulations.

"Have you thought of a name for her?" he asked. "Or is it too soon?"

Dora turned to look at him. He was carrying his hunting rifle, she observed, shocked; but of course, that must have been why the aborigines had run away—they would have seen and feared an armed pursuit.

She hesitated, going over in her mind the words the black woman had said to her. *Allira, dandaloo,* and . . . yes, *kateena.* She did not know what they meant, but they were musical words, words that would remind her, if she were ever likely to forget, how much she owed the dark-skinned young mother, who had left her own baby in order to help a white stranger in the hour of her need.

"I shall call her Kateena, Rob," she said decisively, savoring the word as she uttered it. "Kateena . . . unless her father wishes it otherwise."

Francis looked down at her. He was smiling, but she saw that his eyes were moist. He nodded and did not speak until, reaching the cabin, he set her carefully down on the bed they shared. The cot he had fashioned, some weeks before, stood at its foot; he picked up the small bundle that was his daughter and laid it in the cot.

"There, Kateena," he said, a catch in his voice. "You're home, safe and sound. Sleep in peace, little daughter." Almost as an afterthought, he added quietly, "This will not have to be our home for very much longer. We struck a rich gold-bearing vein today, Dora my love. It will take us a week or two to work it out and have the ore crushed. After that we can go back to where we belong—all of us."

He did not know whether Dora had heard him, for when he looked at her, she had fallen asleep.

Tenderly, Francis pulled the blanket over her, and after tucking it in, he bent to kiss her white, exhausted face.

"It will not be easy, going back," he said, more to himself than to his sleeping wife. "But with God's help, we'll face up to it, darling. That I promise you."

In the adjoining room, Rob was cleaning his rifle, and he asked, as Francis joined him, "Is it true—did Dora say the blackfellows *helped* her?"

"That was what she said," Francis confirmed. "I've no reason to doubt it. There was a woman with them, it seems."

Rob Yates shrugged his broad, muscular shoulders. "Odd, that—seeing the folk here reckon they're all savages. What they did was worthy of our Maoris." He returned the rifle to its rack on the wall and added wryly, "It was lucky I didn't pull the trigger when I had them in my sights. But when we found that Dora wasn't in the cabin, I was afraid, Francis. Scared out of my wits."

"So was I, Rob," Francis confessed. "A hell of a lot more scared than you were! I had a nightmare vision of becoming a rich man without the one woman in all the world I want to share it with me."

"Shall we be rich men?" Rob questioned. "Do you really think the seam we've struck is that good?"

"That remains to be seen. I *think* it is. But if it's not—" Francis sighed. "I'm still going back to Sydney, Rob. It's not fair on Dora and the child to keep them here. And I might be able to eat humble pie and persuade Commander Broome to let me serve under him again. He could take me as a mid, if he were so minded. What about you and Simon?"

Rob grinned. "Oh, we'd soldier on here, I reckon. I promised Dad I'd make enough to build him a new mission hospital, you see. And"—his grin widened—"that I'd follow in his footsteps and go to medical school. I'm not sure what Simon will do."

Simon came in at that moment, carrying a plate of cooked fish. Hearing his name, he said gravely, "I'd like to go to sea. Serve my apprenticeship in a clipper, like Captain Van Buren's *Dolphin*, and then do what he did. Have Mr. McKay of Boston build me one of my own." He set his plate down on the roughhewn wooden table. "Supper's ready, and if you two aren't hungry, I am."

CHAPTER XVII

Jasper Morgan sat down in the entrance to his tent, lit his pipe, and permitted himself to relax. A few yards away, the two young brothers he had engaged to join him in partnership—Angus and Lachlan Broome—busied themselves with preparations for the evening meal, talking in low voices to each other.

They sounded happy—almost, Morgan thought cynically, as happy as he himself felt . . . and with good reason, for his luck had changed since his arrival, ten months earlier, in the state of Victoria. He leaned back, drawing with conscious pleasure on his pipe, the thin blue cloud of tobacco smoke effectively warding off the assault of the flies and other stinging insects that plagued the campsite.

There were other men, hundreds of them, and a veritable forest of tents and ramshackle shelters in the valley a quarter of a mile away, their cooking fires lighting the gathering darkness like so many fireflies. And they would be quarreling among themselves, Morgan knew, grumbling incessantly about the price of food and the exorbitant charges made by the government for the monthly licenses they were compelled to take out before they were allowed to begin their search for gold. Most bitterly, though, they would be complaining of the brutality of the Victoria police, trading stories of armed raids and arbitrary arrests, of beatings and heavy fines, and cursing the man who ordered these things— the local police inspector, whom they had nicknamed Basher Brownlow.

Brownlow—Lieutenant Leonard Arthur Brownlow, to give him the name and rank he claimed were his—was not, Morgan reflected, a man he either liked or trusted, but he was undoubtedly one with whom it was expedient to keep on good terms. He was a tyrant, and he was corrupt, and it was unlikely that he had ever held commissioned rank in the British Army. Unlike himself, Len Brownlow made no effort to appear to be of gentle birth; his accent was uneducated, his language coarse, and his manners were uncouth. But he ruled his police troopers with a rod of iron, and they—many of them recruited from the Van Diemen's Land convict establishments—respected and obeyed him without question, their high-handed treatment of the gold diggers more a reflection of their superior's attitude than a manifestation of their own.

Morgan's thin lips curved into a satisfied smile. Soon after staking his claim in the Ballarat field, he had come up against Lieutenant Brownlow, and they had struck a mutually advantageous bargain for which, he was forced to concede, he was now more than glad. The diggers were an unruly lot, particularly in the region of Ballarat, where the worst of them seemed to have congregated. There were Irishmen, Americans, English, Italians, and native-born, and an even higher proportion of ex-convicts than were serving in the police, and—inevitably, with so volatile a mixture of races—there was unrest, coupled with hardship and heavy drinking, often culminating in riots and pitched battles.

He had been in a position where he had been able to give Brownlow warning of impending trouble, and the police inspector had shown his gratitude in more ways than one.

He had had only to ask, Morgan recalled, and his gold had been sent to Melbourne under police escort; troublemakers of whom he had complained had been promptly arrested and taken off to jail; and when one of his horses had contracted some equine ailment and died, Brownlow had replaced it from the government pound, gratis and without question.

"Captain Humphrey!" Young Angus Broome's voice broke into his thoughts, and Jasper Morgan reluctantly tapped out his pipe and stood up.

"Yes, what is it?"

"Meal's ready, sir," Angus told him, jerking his head in the direction of the campfire. "Lamb chops." He grinned. "Bundilly lamb. Don't let it spoil."

"I won't," Morgan assured him, pleasantly conscious of hunger. He had been uncommonly fortunate in his choice of companions this time, he was aware. Angus and Lachlan were of a very different stamp from the two dour Mormon farm boys and the Australian seamen with whom he had been in partnership in California.

They were young, scarcely more than boys, it was true, but they were well educated and articulate, as well as hard and diligent workers, putting to shame the hired men he had initially employed to sink his mine shaft. Their father, William Broome, was a wealthy sheep farmer, whose station, Bundilly, was only fifty miles away, on the Murray River . . . and he saw to it that they did not starve.

At the outset, the elder Broome had been adamant in his determination not to allow his sons to succumb to the all-prevailing gold fever and go prospecting, but . . . Morgan smiled to himself as he hunkered down beside the glowing ashes of the fire and accepted a brimming plate from seventeen-year-old Lachlan. He had used his persuasive charm to some effect, and the boys' eager pleading had done the rest. They had been entrusted to his care, and their father's visits —ostensibly to ensure that they were supplied with fresh provisions—had become less frequent. Latterly, because the wet season had caused flooding over his vast acreage and he was short of labor, William Broome had not come in person but had sent their supplies by carrier, and the two boys had claimed proudly that this was a tacit admission that he considered them adult and able to take care of themselves.

As, in fact, they were—too adult, and rapidly becoming more than able to take care of themselves. Enjoying his meal, Morgan studied them covertly, conscious of a faint but growing anxiety. He was loath to part with them, yet he knew parting was inevitable, once they started to gain knowledge and ask questions. It had been easy at first to pull the wool over their eyes; they knew nothing of gold mining and, obedient and trusting, did as he bade them, toiling with pick and shovel to sink their mine shafts twenty, forty, even seventy or eighty feet through the layers of earth, red sand, and quartz, till the bluish clay marl was reached and a gold-bearing vein —if one existed—was revealed.

He had left the boys to load the marl into sacks and barrows, cart it down to the creek, and wash tons of it through the cradle rocker, to take as reward for their labor a few ounces of glittering dust, while he himself, whenever he could contrive to be alone, sought for and found the mine's real treasure, in the form of lumps, chiseled skillfully from the gold-impregnated rock. In the shaft's darkness, and in their ignorance, his partners remained unaware of the finds he made, and he kept them well hidden.

And so, Jasper Morgan reflected with regret, it might well have continued, with the profits from their enterprise paying for their living expenses and affording each of them a wage. But as luck would have it, young Angus had inadvertently made the strike of a lifetime when, wielding his pick a trifle carelessly, he had brought part of the wall of the mine shaft crashing about his ears. After the rubble had been cleared and the lad, shaken but not seriously hurt, had been extricated, the gold was there: seven of the largest and purest nuggets any of them had ever seen, worn smooth by the water in which, hundreds of years before, they had lain, unnoticed and deemed without value by the primitive people who had then inhabited this land. The smallest had weighed thirty-five pounds; the largest, ninety-eight.

The find—worth at least twenty thousand pounds—had gone to Melbourne, escorted by Brownlow's mounted policemen, and, on Morgan's instructions, had been lodged, in his sole name, at the government Treasury Office. He held the official receipt for it, of course, but . . . Leaning forward to pour himself tea from the blackened billycan on the fire's embers, Morgan smothered an exasperated sigh. Added to his own secret plundering of the shafts they had sunk on their claim, it was a small fortune waiting to be paid over. Enough to keep him in comparative luxury for the rest of his days, provided he was able to keep it for himself. Divided into three, it would not suffice, and the young Broomes were now constantly talking of making the split, to enable them to return to their father's station and take up their lives as sheep farmers once again.

The tea was scalding hot, and Morgan swore softly as it burned his lips. Once again, he thought resentfully, he was facing the situation he had faced at Windy Gully, back in California. But this time the same solution to the problem could not be contemplated, for a variety of reasons—the boys' wealthy and influential father, for one, plus the fact that here at Ballarat all the diggers lived cheek by jowl—an estimated ten thousand miners in this area alone.

He leaned back, sipping his tea more cautiously while listening to the boys' cheerful chatter, and his dark brows knitted in a frown. They were accustomed to his moods and did not question or seek to break his silence, but as he took in the gist of their present conversation, his irritation grew.

Damned young fools, he thought contemptuously. Better educated and infinitely superior to the Mormon pair—what were their names? Murphy—Daniel and Luke Murphy, but . . . the Broomes were no more ambitious than the Murphy brothers had been.

"We could stick together, Lachie," he heard Angus say. "Our two shares would be ample to buy—what? Ten thousand acres between us, and Pa would let us have the stock, enough to start us off, anyway. He'd lend us a couple of merino rams, I'm sure he would."

"Yes, of course he would," Lachlan agreed. "Because we wouldn't have to quit Bundilly. We could buy out old Abel Knight's holding—he'd let it go if we made him a fair offer—and then we could squat, like Pa did. And we could still work for him when he needed us."

"I'd want to do that," Angus said forcefully. "After all, Pa let us go, didn't he? He let us come here, even though half the men went off to the diggings, leaving him short. We owe Pa, Lachie. I reckon we're agreed on that point."

"Yes, we're agreed." Sensing Lachlan's eyes on him, Jasper Morgan closed his own, feigning weariness, but Angus, undeterred by the subterfuge, leaned across to grasp his booted leg, shaking it gently.

"Captain Humphrey, sir," he said politely. "My brother and I—we're grateful for all you've done for us, all you've taught us. But we've talked it over for quite a while now, sir, and we both reckon we've been away long enough."

"Do you?" Morgan challenged, an edge to his voice. "You're making a mistake, you know. One should never quit when one's on a winning streak, and we are, boy! We could double or even treble what we've got."

"We figured we have all we need, sir," Angus argued with characteristic obstinacy. He waved a hand in the direction of the forest of tents below them. "We've been lucky so far. There are men here who've worked harder and longer than we have, with nothing to show for it. Some poor devils can't raise the price of their licenses—you know that, sir, and you know what the police do to them if they can't. Besides"—he glanced at his brother—"we're afraid that before much longer there will be trouble, like there was in Bendigo, and frankly, Lachie and I want no part of that. Pa wouldn't like it if we were mixed up in any sort of confrontation with the police. He's a magistrate, sir. It would go against him, you see."

Jasper Morgan took out his tobacco pouch and his pipe. He took his time filling and lighting it, but both boys continued to wait, eyeing him expectantly, and finally he was compelled to attempt to refute Angus's argument. He did so with easy fluency, denying any possibility of trouble, for all he was acutely aware that it was there, simmering beneath the surface. The Governor of Victoria, Charles Latrobe—torn, it was said, between the rights of the farmers and landowners and the ever-increasing influx of gold seekers, who demanded the right to search wherever they pleased—had recently increased the license fee from thirty shillings to three pounds a month, and as Angus had said, a great many of the Ballarat diggers were unable to raise such a sum. The gold commissioner at Forest Creek had been besieged in his tent when he had posted the new decree, and throughout the goldfields there were rumbles of discontent, culminating in a proposal, put forward by a number of the Ballarat miners, to form some kind of union for the protection of their rights, which had been so brutally denied at Bendigo, Beechworth, and Castlemaine.

Indeed, he himself had been approached by two of the men involved and invited to join, Morgan recalled, and he had given serious consideration to the suggestion. Nevertheless . . . He smiled in friendly fashion from Angus Broome to his brother and reiterated his firm belief that they would be risking little if they delayed their return home for a few more weeks.

Angus, however, to his annoyance, remained adamant.

"We've made up our minds, Captain Humphrey," he asserted. "There's no point in your trying to persuade us otherwise. We'd leave you the claim, sir, with no strings attached—that goes without saying. But—"

"But what, lad?" Morgan broke in, vainly trying not to show his irritation. "What do you want me to do?"

"Come back to Melbourne with us, sir," Angus returned uncompromisingly, "cash in the gold, and pay us our share. That's all we're asking."

The prospect of going back to Melbourne held singularly little appeal for Jasper Morgan. The invasion of thousands of men, women, and even children, compelled to halt there on their way to the goldfields, had brought chaos in its wake. The flimsy wooden houses, built by the first settlers, were insufficient to accommodate even half the newcomers, and conditions in the tented camp that had sprung up were unsanitary and unhealthy. There was no street lighting, robberies were commonplace, and the roads, after rain, were a sea of mud, in which wheeled vehicles quickly became bogged down. People on foot had no choice but to wade through the morass, often knee-deep in the glutinous mud.

He had been fortunate in that he had managed to sell his brig *Banshee* to a speculator, after disposing very profitably of his cargo, and, Morgan reminded himself, the vessel was now tied up alongside the jetty at Liardet's Beach, serving as a lodging house for those better-off new arrivals who could afford the present owner's sky-high charges.

He forced himself to adopt a quiet, placatory tone, drawing deeply on his pipe and meeting young Angus Broome's challenging gaze with a hint of a smile. "Well, if you're sure that is what you both want, Angus," he conceded, "then I'm willing. But give it another week or ten days, will you? I've some matters to attend to here before I can leave."

Having won his point, Angus readily acceded to the brief delay. A week, even two weeks, might not be enough, Morgan knew—but there was always Brownlow. The police inspector might, if offered a bribe, be willing to detain one or both of the young Broomes on some trumped-up charge, at least long enough for him to go to the Treasury Office ahead of them. And Brownlow need not be told why. . . .

"We'll turn in now, sir," Angus Broome said. He paused to damp down the last flickering embers of the fire and then gestured to his brother. "Lachie's almost asleep on his feet, aren't you, kid? But it's Sunday tomorrow. We'll go into the township and mail a letter to Pa, to tell him we're coming home. Then it won't be such a shock to him when we show up as men of substance, in the market for grazing land and a flock of prime merinos!" He grinned good-naturedly—the slight animosity he had shown earlier swiftly forgotten—bade Jasper Morgan a courteous good night, and, an arm about Lachlan's thin shoulders, made for their tent.

Morgan was about to follow their example when he saw two dark figures approaching from the track leading to the main camp. Both of them called to him by name, and by the light of the lantern one was carrying, he recognized Peter Lalor, the man who had first broached the suggestion of a union for the protection of the diggers' rights. With him was a slim, dark-faced Italian with flaming red hair, who introduced himself as Rafaello Carboni.

"We'd like a word with you, Captain Humphrey," Lalor said, "if you can spare us half an hour. It's a matter of some gravity, otherwise we would not have disturbed you."

Lalor was a young man, still in his early twenties, who hailed from Ireland and had graduated from Trinity College, Dublin, as a civil engineer. He had come out only the previous year, Morgan knew, and initially had worked a claim at the Ovens diggings without success. The Italian was older, a handsome, engaging fellow, who had worked as a language teacher in one of the government schools before he, too, had deserted his post in search of gold.

Lalor seated himself and came to the reason for his visit in a few crisp, telling words. "You will recall, I feel sure, sir, the tragic death of one of our number in a brawl at the Eureka Hotel—James Scobie, sir, who was brutally murdered by the rogue of a proprietor?"

Morgan nodded, making an effort to remember the incident. Scobie had borne a good character, according to his friends; the proprietor of the hotel, on the other hand, had not. An ex-convict, who had served many years in Van Diemen's Land's worst prisons, his name was . . . Banbury, no, Bentley—that was it. The diggers hated him, suspecting him of cheating and overcharging them, but since the Eureka Hotel was the only hostelry within easy walking distance of the camp, most of them had continued to frequent the place, for all the drunken brawls that broke out there.

Scobie's death, though, had outraged them, and on the evidence of Scobie's brother and a number of others, the police had arrested Bentley and charged him with the murder.

"They brought Bentley before Magistrate D'Ewes's court earlier today," Peter Lalor went on. "Rafaello and I were present at the hearing, hoping to see justice done. But Police Sergeant Milne botched up the evidence—deliberately, in our view, eh, Rafaello?"

His companion nodded emphatically. "Yes, indeed, Captain Humphrey, that is so. Commandant Brownlow did not call any of the witnesses who could have proved Bentley's guilt. The trial was—oh, it was a travesty!"

"Do you mean that Bentley escaped conviction?" Morgan asked, startled. "And his roustabout Farrell?"

"That is precisely what I mean," Rafaello asserted. "Bentley and Farrell were acquitted, and they're now back at the hotel, celebrating their escape."

Brownlow had run true to form, Morgan thought dispassionately; no doubt the owner of the Eureka Hotel was now entertaining him in a back room, delighted by the turn events had taken and by the aid he had received.

"Well," he said, feeling that some comment was called for, "the result is clearly to be deplored. But why have you come to me? What can I possibly do about it?"

"We intend to take organized action," Lalor told him. "I am making the first move. We shall form a committee and press for a fresh prosecution. A meeting is to be called for the night of the seventeenth in the hotel, and we shall summon Bentley before us." He saw that Morgan was frowning and added, "Frederic Vern, Tim Hayes, and George Black are with us, Captain Humphrey. We have come to you, sir, in the hope that, as an influential member of our community, you will join us."

Morgan's frown deepened as he considered the records of the men the young Irishman had named. Vern, he knew, was a Hanoverian, a practiced rabble-rouser with a golden tongue, who was wont to wax eloquent in defense of the rights of the common man. A man, it was true, of passionate convictions, but somehow lacking in substance. Black, on the other hand, was an Englishman of considerable learning and intelligence. A man of few words, by contrast with Vern, but when he expressed an opinion, others listened with respect. Tim Hayes he knew little about, save that, like Peter Lalor, he was Irish and was believed to have republican sympathies.

"Presumably you are expecting trouble?" Morgan questioned at last.

"We are not looking for it," Lalor assured him. "But feelings are running high where the villain Bentley is concerned. When the magistrates' verdict is known, they'll run a good deal higher, I'm afraid. And if our demand for a fresh trial is rejected, well—" He shrugged in a gesture of helplessness. "I, for one, can't answer for the consequences. Much will depend on the attitude of the police. If there should be an outcry and Basher Brownlow sends his troopers in, the situation could turn dangerous, no doubt of that."

It could also, Jasper Morgan recognized, turn to his advantage. Apart from anything else, if he were to join Lalor's proposed committee, it would provide him with a plausible excuse for delaying his return to Melbourne with his two young partners. Like Frederic Vern, Angus Broome harbored sympathies for the downtrodden and the oppressed, and James Scobie, the murdered man, had been one of a number who had been hard put to it to raise the price of his mining license.

His frown lifted. "I will certainly attend your meeting, Mr. Lalor," he said. "The seventeenth, you say? And at Bentley's hotel?"

"Here at the camp first, sir," Lalor qualified. "To elect a delegation and make clear our aims. Having done that, we shall confront Bentley and endeavor to extract a confession from him." He added thoughtfully, "It's said that the new Governor has arrived—Captain Charles Hotham, of the Royal Navy. I've no idea what manner of man he is, but rumor has it he's likely to be more liberal in his views than Latrobe. That would present few problems, admittedly, but —well, Captain Humphrey, we none of us want to take any action that might set His new Excellency against us. So I do not believe that you need worry that we shall cause trouble."

For all that, Morgan decided, he would have to take the first opportunity that presented itself to meet with Brownlow and offer him a warning. The opportunity came the day before the planned meeting. The police inspector rode into camp, and after being closeted for half an hour with the gold commissioner in his tent, he made the short detour that took him past Morgan's and then trotted off into the bush, closely followed on foot by two of his black trackers. Allowing a discreet interval to elapse, Morgan saddled up and went after them, to find Brownlow dismounted and awaiting him at the bottom of a steep gully ablaze with the golden, sweet-scented mimosa that grew freely everywhere in the vicinity of the diggings.

The police inspector—who preferred to be addressed as commandant—was a big man, heavily built but now past middle age. His once-powerful muscles, Morgan noted, were deteriorating into unhealthy fat, and he was sweating profusely in the midday heat, plying a fly whisk irritably about his moist red face as he waited.

But he greeted Morgan civilly enough and even exchanged a few coarse jests with him before pronouncing, with an abrupt change of tone, "The Jackass"—his nickname, Morgan knew, for the gold commissioner—"the Jackass tells me there's to be a diggers' meeting in town tomorrow night. Of course he's not the faintest idea what it's about —just the usual malcontents, he reckons, getting on their soapboxes to protest about the price of their blasted licenses. That's why I wanted to see you, Captain Humphrey. I figured you'd know what's riling them."

"Yes, I know," Morgan confirmed. He explained with

elaborate care and saw a slow smile spreading over the inspector's face as he listened.

"Can you get into the meeting?" Brownlow asked, still smiling.

"I've been invited," Morgan said with smug satisfaction. "They want me to stand for election to their committee."

"And you will?"

"I think so, yes."

"Good! And you'll keep me informed?"

"I'll do my best, Mr. Brownlow, certainly."

Brownlow took out a large handkerchief and mopped his sweating face. "God, it's hot out here, ain't it? And about this sodding meeting. Will they make trouble, d'you suppose?"

"It depends on Bentley, in my view. If they obtain a confession from him, then—"

"They'll not get a fresh trial, I can promise you that. But—" The big policeman caught his breath. "You don't imagine they'll try to lynch him, do you?"

Morgan shrugged. "I have no idea, my friend. It's possible, but . . . oh, I think it's unlikely they'd go that far."

"You'd warn me, if they should? I'll have my men under arms and standing by, that goes without saying. If there *is* trouble"—Brownlow's smile was unpleasant—"I'll send them in and arrest the ringleaders. You can name 'em, can't you, Captain?"

"I think I'll leave your men to pick them out," Morgan evaded. "Except—" An idea occurred to him suddenly, and he found himself echoing Brownlow's smile. "Let's say there is one young hothead who'd bear watching. Angus Broome."

"One of your lads?" Brownlow exclaimed, puzzled. "Well, I don't doubt you'll have your reasons, Captain Humphrey, and—one good turn deserves another, eh? You keep me posted, sir, and I'll see my troopers know one of the troublemakers, at least. Let's see now—young Broome's a redhead, ain't he? A thin, wiry lad, nigh as tall as I am?"

"That's the one," Morgan confirmed. He looked about him, anxious to make sure that no one had observed his rendezvous with the police commandant, and satisfied that they were alone, he pulled his horse toward him and swung himself back into the saddle. He took his leave, only mildly disconcerted when, as he started downhill, one of the black trackers emerged from a nearby clump of trees to grin at him insolently, then loped off to rejoin Inspector Brownlow.

The meeting, when it took place the following evening, was attended by several hundred miners. Morgan took both the Broome boys with him, and though he had intended to keep carefully in the background, Lalor insisted on calling him to the makeshift platform and, after a brief speech, introduced him as a candidate for election to the committee, together with Rafaello Carboni, Black, and Hayes.

All, with Lalor himself, were duly elected. The meeting was conducted in a brisk and businesslike manner, its purpose soberly explained, and when a vote was taken, the decision to demand a new trial for the innkeeper Bentley was unanimous. Frederic Vern, speaking from the floor, made the suggestion that the delegates should proceed to the Eureka Hotel and there interrogate its proprietor.

"If we can obtain from this vile and wicked man a full confession, witnessed by us, then the Governor will have no choice, save to assent to our demand," the German declaimed gutturally. "He has foully murdered one of our own people, as we are all aware. Let justice be done, my brothers! Let us go now to the hotel!"

A loud chorus of voices supported him, and an American miner excitedly discharged his pistol into the air, calling for Bentley to be hanged, a suggestion that also met with vociferous approval.

Peter Lalor called them to order. "No, my friends," he shouted. "No! We are law-abiding people, and we cannot, whatever the circumstances, take the law into our own hands. There will be no shooting. Leave any weapons you possess behind you. Your elected representatives will conduct the interrogation on your behalf and, having done so, will draw up a petition addressed to Governor Hotham in our joint names."

They obeyed him, to Jasper Morgan's dismay, but he said nothing and, with young Angus Broome at his side, joined the long and orderly procession that formed up preparatory to marching the short distance to the Eureka Hotel. Lalor was still marshaling them when a cry went up from some men on the fringe of their ranks.

"The police! The bloody police are coming, boys! They'll try to break us up—they'll try to stop us!"

Within moments, the hitherto peaceable gathering became a mob of angry, vengeful men. There were only half a dozen troopers, Morgan realized, sent, no doubt, to observe and report on the progress of the meeting. As soon as the mob turned on them, they fled, a yelling crowd hard on their horses' heels. Reaching the Eureka Hotel, they re-formed in line with the police detachment that was already in position outside the flimsy wooden building and, together with their fellows, attempted to ward off the miners' attack.

They might as well have tried to hold back the sea, Jasper Morgan thought, his excitement growing as he watched. Although well armed, the troopers were heavily outnumbered, and their musket fire, directed over the heads of the mob, failed to deter all but a handful of fainthearts. Peter Lalor shouted in vain for order; he was ignored as the angry diggers pressed forward, screaming for Bentley to show himself. He failed to do so, and the leading ranks, egged on by those to their rear, pressed forward, cheering triumphantly as the police troopers fell back before them.

Losing sight of Angus in the melee, Morgan, too, fell back, contenting himself with the suggestion, made to several of the men in his immediate vicinity, that they should burn down the murderer's miserable hostelry. His words were echoed at once by a score of voices, and within minutes of his having uttered them, the windows were smashed and the hotel set ablaze. Barrels of beer and kegs of spirits were hurled out through yawning gaps where the windows had once been, and the mob seized them, still deaf to Lalor's frantic pleas, gleefully splitting them open as they fell.

It was several hours before order was restored and the mob of diggers began, at last, to disperse. Led in person by Inspector Brownlow, the police took the opportunity to make three arrests. Two of the men—apprehended with stolen liquor in their possession—were unknown to Morgan, and the third was Angus Broome.

In the following weeks, Jasper Morgan was foremost in urging that action should be taken to plead for the release of the three miners. The two men who had been caught with stolen liquor had, on the sworn testimony of Brownlow himself, been convicted of leading the riot; but to Morgan's secret delight, it was Angus Broome—charged, in addition, with arson—who had received the heaviest sentence, that of six months' imprisonment with hard labor. Twenty-five days after the arrests, at a meeting convened on Bakery Hill, Morgan found himself elected a member of the committee of the Ballarat Reform League. By common consent, he was chosen, with three others, to present a petition to Governor Hotham in Melbourne, demanding that the convictions be quashed and the men released.

On the eve of the delegation's departure for the state capital, Lachlan Broome came to him in tears.

"I'm going home, Captain Humphrey," the boy said. "Back to Bundilly. Maybe Pa can help to have Angus released." He passed a shaking hand over his eyes, ashamed of the unmanly tears. "You'll get our money for us, won't you, sir, when you're in Melbourne? And perhaps you'd better hold it until Angus is free or until I can come back here to fetch it."

Although the boy's decision to leave the diggings had taken him by surprise, Morgan's hesitation was brief. He would have to stay and see the Ballarat crisis resolved, he thought uneasily, since he had allowed Lalor and the others to involve him so prominently in their committee and their infernal reform league. Simply to vanish, after presenting the petition to the Governor, would arouse suspicion; and in any event, he might have to wait for weeks in Melbourne before he was able to take passage in a homeward-bound ship. It was easier and wiser to finish up his business here than to risk being tracked down in Melbourne. Like Sydney at the start of the gold rush, Port Phillip and its neighboring anchorages held only crewless vessels.

He laid a hand on Lachlan's thin young shoulder and forced a reassuring smile.

"Don't worry, lad," he said gently. "Our gold is safe

where it is. Time enough to sell it and take our profit when Angus is back with us again. I'd not want the responsibility of holding a large sum in cash here at the diggings—not all the folk here are honest, you know. I could easily be robbed."

"Yes, sir, but—" Lachlan began. "I—"

"Off with you, Lachie," Jasper Morgan bade him. "The sooner you go, the sooner you'll be back and, it's to be hoped, your brother, too. I'll do all in my power to persuade Governor Hotham to order his release. Trust me, boy."

"Oh, I d-do, sir," Lachlan stammered. "T-truly, sir, more than anyone in the world—apart from my own family, that is."

His avowal was oddly moving, and for once Jasper Morgan could find no words in which to make reply.

Part Two

A DEBT OF HONOR

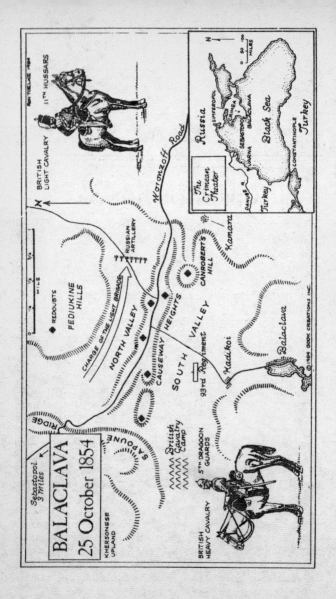

BALACLAVA
25 October 1854

Sebastopol
3 miles

KHERSONESE
UPLAND

SAPOUNE
RIDGE

British
Cavalry
Camp

5TH DRAGOON
GUARDS

BRITISH
HEAVY CAVALRY

FEDIUKINE
HILLS

REDOUBTS

CHARGE OF THE LIGHT BRIGADE

NORTH VALLEY

RUSSIAN
ARTILLERY

CAUSEWAY
HEIGHTS

SOUTH VALLEY

93rd Regiment

CANROBERT'S
HILL

Kamara

Kadikoi

Balaclava

Woronzoff Road

N

MILE

BRITISH
LIGHT CAVALRY

11TH HUSSARS

RON TOELKE 1984

The Crimean
Theater

Russia

SIMFEROPOL
CRIMEA
BALACLAVA
SEBASTOPOL
VARNA

DANUBE R.

Turkey

CONSTANTINOPLE

Turkey

Black Sea

N

MILES

© 1984 BOOK CREATIONS, INC.

CHAPTER XVIII

Mail from England had arrived, and Jenny Broome glanced in some surprise at the letter her brother Johnny held out to her, a quizzical smile playing about his bearded lips as he did so.

"From William De Lancey, according to the signature franking it," he observed. "I thought he was in India with his regiment, but this came out in the *Merton Castle.*" His smile widened, and he added teasingly, "Well, open it, why don't you, little sister? No doubt the gallant William is still carrying a torch for you . . . Edmund won't be pleased by that, will he?"

Jenny flushed indignantly but made no reply to her brother's taunt. She took the letter from him and, ignoring his suggestion, thrust it unopened into the pocket of her dress. She had spent almost three weeks at Pengallon awaiting her father's return from the Turon Valley, and a further week after that before they had gone back to Sydney, yet . . . for all the attention he had paid her during her stay, Edmund Tempest had not committed himself to a proposal of marriage.

Not that he could be blamed for that; the blame lay with her, Jenny readily conceded. She had been reluctant to place their relationship on an irrevocably permanent basis and, to that end, had carefully evaded Edmund's diffident attempts to lead up to a proposal.

He had made more than one attempt, but . . . She stifled a sigh. She had sensed his intention and had been at pains to distract him from it—tactfully, of course, for she was genuinely fond of him and flattered by his evident affection for her. But that was all it was—affection. They had been brought up together, had been companions and friends since childhood, for Edmund had been educated in Sydney and, while school was in term, had boarded with her family, establishing as close an intimacy with them as he had enjoyed with his own. In consequence, he held no surprises for her, no . . . Jenny's brow furrowed. No romantic mystery. And . . . there was William. Her fingers closed about the letter in her pocket. There was William and the dream she had had about him . . . a dream, no, rather a nightmare, from which she had awakened with a cry on her lips and her cheeks wet with tears.

Jenny glanced across at her brother, but he was absorbed in a letter of his own, forgetful of her presence, and she moved to the window, to stare out across the blue, sunlit waters of Elizabeth Bay with eyes that saw nothing of its beauty, as memory of her nightmare returned.

Vividly, in the dream, she had seen William in a hussar's blue, gold-frogged jacket and scarlet overalls—a uniform she did not recognize. He had been mounted on a small, shaggy horse, quite unlike a British cavalry charger, and he had been slumped in the saddle, as if severely wounded, his face white as death and his saber dangling limply from his left hand. Behind him, seemingly in pursuit, had been two strange-looking horsemen in fur caps, their lances couched, and even as she had reacted in shocked bewilderment to the vision, she had heard the distant rumble of gunfire and then the sharp, staccato crack of a pistol, discharged from close at hand. William had called her name, his voice slurred and despairing, and the sound had lingered even as the dream faded and she returned to wakefulness.

She heard it again now, her heart heavy with foreboding. India was at peace, she knew, and that knowledge had added to the bewilderment the vivid dream had engendered; but William's letter had not come from India. Johnny had said, a few moments ago, that it had come from England in the *Merton Castle.* Jenny drew in her breath sharply, wishing that she could seek the privacy of her bedroom in order to read the letter. But it was lunchtime; her father would be in very soon, and there were several letters awaiting his attention. He would think it odd if she absented herself from their meal, for he liked to comment on the news he received when

mail came in, and if she opened William's letter now, both
he and Johnny would expect to be given at least the gist of
whatever news it contained. Perhaps Johnny would forget it;
she hoped he would. Certainly his own letter appeared to be
of singular interest to him, for he was rereading it, a frown
of concentration drawing his brows together.

Their father came in while Jenny was still undecided, and
making an effort to hide her feelings, she bade him a smiling
welcome and busied herself with the preparations for the
meal.

"It appears that Captain Skinner was right, sir," she heard
Johnny say, gesturing at his letter. "There *is* going to be war
with Russia, according to Frank Mercer of the *London Mer-
cury.* You remember him, don't you, when he was here, reporting on our gold rush?"

"Yes, I remember him," their father responded. He left
his own mail untouched, regarding Johnny with gravely
searching eyes. "What does he say? Is the British government coming in on the Turkish side?"

"It seems they'll have to," Johnny confirmed bleakly. He
spread out the pages of his letter and read from it, in a low,
concerned voice. " 'On November thirtieth last year, a small
frigate squadron of the Turkish Navy, overtaken by a severe
storm in the Black Sea, was compelled to put in to the Bay of
Sinope for shelter—' Sinope, Mercer explains, is a little town
situated midway between Constantinople and Trebizond, a
hundred and fifty miles south of the Russian naval base of
Sebastopol, on the Crimean Peninsula." Johnny's frown
deepened as he read on. " 'Despite the fact that war had
been declared between Turkey and Russia a little over a
month before, the Turkish commander, Vice Admiral Os-
man Nari Pasha, anticipated no danger to his small fleet, in
spite of his proximity to Sebastopol.' "

"Why should he suppose anything of the kind?" Justin
Broome questioned.

Johnny shrugged. "Mercer says that both the Tsar and the
Sultan had announced that, although reluctantly compelled
to settle their differences by force of arms, each intended to
confine himself to the defensive and that an unofficial truce
existed between their two navies, which hitherto had been

scrupulously observed by both sides. But then"—his tone,
Jenny heard, was suddenly indignant—"under cover of fog,
six Russian line-of-battle ships, each mounting between
eighty and a hundred and twenty guns, entered the harbor
of Sinope and attacked the Turkish ships at anchor. Within
an hour, all had been sunk or set on fire, and then the
Russian admiral, Nachimov, opened his fire on the town.
The wretched Turks lost more than four thousand men,
women, and children before Nachimov called a halt to the
slaughter."

"Good God!" Justin exclaimed, visibly moved.

"Mercer says that when news of the outrage reached London, it roused a storm of public feeling, culminating in repeated demands in Parliament for the Mediterranean Fleet
to be sent into the Black Sea to protect the Turks from
further unprovoked attack." Johnny turned the pages of his
letter.

"Has war been declared?" his father asked.

"No, apparently not. Lord Aberdeen's still seeking to
avert a war, if he can. But a combined British and French
fleet is on its way to the Bosporus—eighteen sail of the line,
with escorting frigates and steamers, under the command of
Vice Admiral Deans Dundas."

Jenny's heart plummeted, as she heard her father observe
grimly, "Then it's evident that they mean business. It can
only be a question of time, I fear."

"That is Mercer's opinion, too, sir," Johnny agreed. He
read on, but Jenny was no longer listening. Her dream, she
thought uneasily—her nightmare vision of William De
Lancey seemed suddenly all too real a possibility, as if, for
no reason she could understand, she had been allowed a
glimpse into a hideous future. If there were to be war with
Russia . . . William was a cavalry officer, and he was in
England. Since a British fleet had been dispatched to Turkish waters, it was logical to suppose that British troops would
also be sent to the Sultan's aid. Perhaps even now William's
regiment had received orders to embark, and his letter, still
unopened in her pocket, was to tell her so.

A wave of nausea swept over her, and she pushed her plate
away. Her father was opening one of his own letters, she saw,

exclaiming as he read an extract from it that contained the
same alarming news that Johnny's had done.

"This is from Frederick Evans—you remember, the naval
surveyor? Like your friend Mercer, he seems to think that
war is inevitable. The fleet is mobilizing, new vessels being
fitted out and commissioned in every dockyard in the country, for service in the Baltic and the Black Sea. Sir Charles
Napier has been appointed to command in the Baltic, and—
damme, Johnny, Skinner's been given a steam-screw of the
line! The *Orion*, of ninety guns. He timed his return well,
didn't he?"

"And what news of Mr. Evans, sir?" Johnny asked.

"He's expecting to be sent on a secret survey mission to
the Gulf of Finland. He—"

Jenny did not wait to hear more. She excused herself, and
her father nodded abstractedly, continuing to discuss the
grave implications of the news with Johnny, his food also
untouched and growing cold on his plate.

"Red won't have heard, or James Willoughby, come to
that, unless he's received dispatches from Their Lordships.
I'll go out to Watson's Bay this afternoon, because I suppose
this raises the question of a possible Russian attack on Sydney, if war is declared. Although I don't honestly think
. . ."

Jenny slipped away, closing the door behind her, Sydney's
fate of less concern to her than that of William De Lancey.
She had had no dream of Russian warships sailing, with guns
blazing, into Port Jackson, as they had sailed into the Turkish
harbor of Sinope. But William—dear God, the Russian armies included Cossacks in their ranks, didn't they? Savage
horsemen in fur caps, mounted on small, rough horses like
the ones she had seen so vividly in her dream. Her fingers
trembling in their haste, she broke the seal on her letter and,
flinging herself full length onto her bed, spread out the
closely written pages on her pillow and started to read.

My dearest Jenny,

I am penning these few lines to you because there
seems every likelihood that by the time you receive
them, I shall be going to war. The ghastly, merciless

massacre of a small squadron of Turkish frigates in a Black Sea port by the Russians has aroused public feeling to such a degree that it seems all England is demanding that war should be declared and we should dispatch naval and military aid, forthwith, to Turkey.

You will no doubt be surprised to learn that I am presently in England, serving as a captain in the 11th Hussars—a regiment recently commanded by the Earl of Cardigan, an officer of somewhat infamous repute, now promoted to the rank of brigadier general and appointed to command of the Light Cavalry Brigade.

A British Expeditionary Force of 30,000 men is being formed, with Lord Raglan, master general of the ordnance and a distinguished veteran of the Peninsular campaign, named commander in chief. As soon as transport ships can be provided, this force—which will include a division of cavalry—will embark for Gallipoli and Constantinople. Already battalions of the Foot Guards have marched through London on their way to Portsmouth, and my regiment is eagerly awaiting orders to follow them.

War has not yet been declared, but I think that it is inevitable and that it will come very soon, for it is reliably reported that a Russian army is massing on the Danube River, preparatory to marching on Constantinople. The Turks can offer little resistance; their defenses consist of a few ill-manned mountain fortresses, dependent for their supplies on a port called Varna, which may be unable to hold out against superior Russian naval squadrons based only a short distance away at the Black Sea port of Sebastopol.

It is rumored that Varna will be our eventual destination, but as yet this is only rumor, and our regiment, with its horses, is expected initially to be conveyed to the island of Malta.

As you may imagine, Jenny, great excitement prevails throughout our ranks. Our cause is a just one; the Tsar's desire to add Turkey to his vast dominions by armed assault and brutal slaughter, as evidenced at Sinope, must be opposed at all costs.

War is a soldier's calling, and I am a soldier. I pray only that I may do my duty without thought for my own life, should my country demand this sacrifice of me. I know the bitter realities of battle—I experienced these in India—and in consequence, I view the prospect of once more going to war more soberly than do some of my fellows in the regiment. But if I may ask this of you, sweet Jenny, think of me sometimes, pray for me, and of your goodness, write to me, giving me news of yourself and our two families and of my homeland. Letters, directed to London in care of the British Expeditionary Force, will be forwarded, we are told. I entreat you to write as often as you can, and I sign myself, as ever, your devoted friend and admirer,

William De Lancey

He had added a postscript, Jenny saw, but she was barely able to read it, her vision blurred by tears.

We have just been informed that Major General the Earl of Lucan has been appointed to the command of the cavalry division—that is, the Heavy Brigade and ourselves, who form the Light Brigade of hussars and lancers. The Heavies are dragoon regiments, with the famous Scots Greys included.

Those in the know fear that Lord Lucan's appointment augurs ill; he and Lord Cardigan are on very bad terms and have not exchanged a civil word for twenty years, although they are related by marriage. However, to balance this, our fine Indian commander, Sir Colin Campbell—one of the best generals living, in my humble view—is to be given one of the infantry brigades. He, at least, possesses more recent experience of active campaigning than the majority of our generals.

Jenny dabbed at her tear-filled eyes. Why, she wondered, had the terrible dream come to her, all unbidden and before she had known that William was about to go to war? Should she—dare she tell him of the vision she had seen? He had begged her to write to him, and of course she would; but it would be far too late, by the time a letter from her could reach him, to attempt to offer a warning. Probably by this time he would be already in Turkey. . . .

Making an effort, she blinked back her tears and, after folding the letter, placed it once more in the pocket of her dress. She would write at once, she decided, warmly and affectionately, promising that, as he had requested, he should be always in her prayers and her thoughts. But she would not mention the dream, lest it sap his resolution and his courage. William was a soldier, as he had reminded her, and war was a soldier's calling; he must go where and when he was ordered to go.

She breathed a silent prayer for his safety, recalling with a pang the brief, happy hours they had shared during his leave in Sydney, and then, after crossing to her desk—the desk that had been her mother's—she reached for quill and paper and started to write.

William De Lancey sat in his tent in the Light Cavalry Brigade camp before Sebastopol, and, a blanket wrapped about his shoulders to ward off the bitter chill of evening, he read, for the twentieth time, the letter he had received two days ago from Jenny Broome.

It was the first and only letter that had reached him since his arrival in the Crimea with the British Expeditionary Force; but she had written to him once before, when he had been in Varna, in Bulgaria, and he had replied immediately and at length. The mails, he knew, took weeks to reach England, and from there a lengthy interval must elapse before they could be consigned to a Sydney-bound vessel. He would have to learn patience. The letter in his hand bore the date of May 10, 1854; it was now October—October 24, if his memory served him right.

It was possible, William reflected resignedly, that Jenny—in common with his parents in Sydney—might not be aware that the Allied forces of Britain, Turkey, and France had crossed the Black Sea in a vast armada of ships, to land on the Crimean Peninsula just over a month ago, and that they were now conducting a siege of the great Russian fortress and naval base of Sebastopol. . . . He sighed and leaned forward to turn down the wick of his oil lamp, which was smoking vilely.

War had been officially declared on March 28, but by that time the combined fleets of Britain and France had already entered the Black Sea, and he had been on his way to Malta, with two squadrons of his regiment, on board the transport *Henry Wilson.* Thereafter had come a period of intense frustration, when the troops of the expeditionary force had been sent via Gallipoli to Varna, and—with never a sight of the enemy—a severe outbreak of cholera had taken hundreds of lives, and morale had been at a very low ebb.

The decision to attempt the capture of Sebastopol had come as a relief, and initially all had gone well. The Allied armies, with their guns and horses, had landed at last on Russian soil. They had won a splendid victory at the Alma River and had found themselves within sight of their objective, the enemy fleeing in disarray before them and offering no opposition.

Recalling his first sight of the Russian stronghold, from a summit overlooking the valley of the Balbec, William repeated his sigh. It had looked peaceful in the afternoon sunlight, a beautiful town of dazzling white buildings, surmounted by domes and cupolas of green copper and cut in two by its harbor, across the entrance to which blockships had been sunk to deny entry to the Allied fleets.

There were forts with gun embrasures facing north and south, as well as out to sea, and of these, the great star fort had seemed the most formidable. But there had been few signs that the town was defended in strength or that the guns were all manned. The beaten Russians, fleeing in disorder from the Alma, did not appear to have rallied behind Sebastopol's crumbling walls, and the sunken blockships, lying submerged in the harbor mouth, possessed no guns. Indeed, William remembered wryly, it had been rumored that the commander of the British Fourth Division, General Cathcart, had assured the commander in chief, Lord Raglan, that he could walk into the town and take it, then and there, with scarcely the loss of a single man.

Lord Raglan had been in favor of an immediate assault, but the French would have none of it. Their commander in chief, Marshal St. Arnaud—who, although no one had known this at the time, was dying of the cholera—had obstinately insisted that both armies must march inland and around their objective, establish themselves on the southern heights and, seizing the ports of Balaclava and Kazatch, land their siege trains and subject Sebastopol to a prolonged bombardment before any attack could possibly be launched.

Raglan had yielded reluctantly, and in the weeks that followed the ludicrous flank march, the great guns of the invading forces had been landed and dragged into position on the heights of the Khersonese Upland. The Russians had taken advantage of the respite this had given them to pour thousands of troops into the town and build up their neglected defenses, repair their forts, and send in their own great guns.

It had been stalemate, William reflected moodily, and St. Arnaud's successor to the French command, General Canrobert, had proved as obstinate in his concept of how war should be waged as had the man he had replaced. To the British soldiers he was known, derisively, as Robert Can't. It was an apt nickname, the Lord knew, and with the bitter Crimean winter in imminent prospect, optimism among the besiegers was at a premium.

William shivered. He drew his blanket more closely about him and, opening his small leather dispatch case, looked in it for writing materials with which to pen his reply to Jenny's letter. She had written happily of her doings in Sydney, of picnics and dances, of gay garden parties hosted by mutual friends and acquaintances, and of races on the course that Governor Macquarie had originally designed and at which two horses of his mother's breeding had triumphed. Whereas he . . . God in heaven, what could he write of this inglorious war? He—

"Sir—" The voice was his servant's, and almost with relief William bade him enter. Private Robert Bubb had been his groom in India and had transferred with him from the 3rd Light Dragoons to his present regiment. Bubb was a quiet, sober Yorkshireman, of exemplary character and an excellent horseman, and William held him in high esteem. He set a steaming mug of black coffee at his officer's elbow, careful not to disturb the writing materials scattered about the flimsy portable table. Coffee beans in their raw, unroasted state had been delivered to the camps by the hard-pressed commissariat, but Bubb contrived, by some means known only to himself, to produce a drinkable beverage each morning and evening, for which service alone, William thought, he was worth the small extra sum he was paid as a batman. He was also a reliable news gatherer, seeming to hear every whisper and rumor and able, usually, to separate fact from supposition.

He said diffidently now, as William sipped his coffee, "They say a Turkish spy has come in an' given warnin' of a Russian attack on Balaclava, sir. Twenty thousand infantry, wiv guns an' strong cavalry support, this feller reckoned."

There were always dire warnings from Turkish spies, William reflected; Rustem Pasha, the Turkish commander, was the source of most of them, and three days earlier he had issued a similar forecast, which had proved to be without foundation—although not before a furious General Cathcart had brought his division down from the upland and had then been compelled to march them back again, in a state of exhaustion.

But any threat to Balaclava had to be taken seriously. The small harbor was packed to capacity with shipping; through it, all stores, ammunition, food rations, and water for the infantry divisions and the naval gunners on the Khersonese Upland had to be taken, and the wounded brought down by the same route to the ships lying offshore. And the port was thinly defended. Under the command of Sir Colin Campbell, a single infantry regiment, the seven-hundred-strong 93rd Highlanders, was positioned at the village of Kadikoi, at the head of the gorge a mile above the harbor, supported by a single troop of horse artillery.

Spread out in a semicircle behind them were two battalions of marines with artillery and, across the South Valley, guarding the Causeway Heights and Woronzoff Road—the main line of communication with the upland—fourteen hundred Turco-Tunisian auxiliaries, manning six redoubts, as yet only partially completed.

"What has been the reaction to the spy's warning, Bubb?"

William inquired. "What have your informants to say about it?"

Clicking his tongue disapprovingly, Private Bubb bent to pick up the heavily mud-coated boots William had discarded after that morning's picket duty.

" 'Twill take me a month o' Sundays to get these back in shape, sir," the batman said glumly. He added, without a change of tone, "They do say as Lord Raglan is of the opinion that it's just another false alarm, but that Sir Colin disagrees wiv him. He's worried about them Turks on the Causeway Heights; he doesn't reckon as they'll 'old if they was to come under an 'eavy attack, you see, sir. An' who's to say they would? When all's said an' done, the poor sods is cut off—there's nigh on a mile atween some o' their positions, and they ain't been given all the guns they was promised. Some of 'em only have a couple o' six-pounders."

That was true, William realized. The ships of the fleet had been stripped of their heavy guns weeks before to arm the upland siege batteries; their commanders, understandably, were loath to part with the few that were left to them. Least of all did they want to entrust them to the Turks, of whose fighting qualities they were in doubt.

"Lord Lucan's been 'aving a confab wiv Sir Colin seemingly, sir," Bubb went on, referring to the cavalry's divisional commander, General the Earl of Lucan. " 'Twill be us or the 'eavies as will be called out to 'elp them Turks if they do come under attack, I fancy. Leastways, sir, that's what 'is Lordship's orderly was sayin' in the canteen."

"He should know," William said dryly. "If anyone does." He set down his cup, regretting that the coffee was finished. "And let us hope he is right, Bubb. It's time our men were given the chance to show what they can do. Is reveille at the usual time?"

"Aye, sir. Inspection an hour afore daybreak, like it always is. But Lord Cardigan won't be there—gone back to 'is yacht, he has, an' taken Private Ash wiv 'im. So *he* can't be expecting no attack, can 'e, sir?" Bubb cleared his throat noisily and gestured at the boots. "I'd best see what I can do wiv these, sir, so's you can wear 'em in the morning. Wouldn't do to go into action against the Ruskies wiv dirty boots, would it, sir?" He grinned. "*If* we go into action, that's to say. I dunno about you, sir, but speakin' for meself, I'm a mite tired o' being called a gilded popinjay by a bunch o' bloomin' foot soldiers!"

And so, William thought sourly, was he, for all he was aware that the reason for it was that Lord Raglan was so deficient in cavalry that he would not—*dared* not—risk the few regiments he had in major conflict. He needed the Light Brigade for outlying picket duty and intelligence gathering, and time and again—most memorably at the Alma—when a charge might well have turned the tide in the Allies' favor, the order had come for them to withdraw. Small wonder, therefore, that the infantry soldiers, who had borne the brunt of the fighting and suffered many casualties in consequence, should mock the men of the lancer, hussar, and light dragoon regiments in their brilliant uniforms and deride them as popinjays.

Edward Nolan, aide-de-camp to General Airey, Lord Raglan's chief of staff, and an acknowledged expert in cavalry tactics, had openly and angrily criticized the British commander in chief's failure to make use of the Light Brigade.

"What is the use," he had demanded scornfully, "of possessing the best-trained, best-disciplined, and best-mounted light cavalry regiments in the world and keeping them in a damned bandbox?"

It had been Nolan, William recalled, who—one evening in mess, when he had imbibed the 11th's brandy somewhat freely—had bestowed the uncomplimentary nicknames of Lord Look-on and the Noble Yachtsman on the cavalry's two commanders. It was, perhaps, deserved in Lord Cardigan's case, since, disliking the rigors of camp life, he spent much of his time on board his private yacht in Balaclava Harbor. Lord Lucan, however, had been left with little choice, save to obey the orders he had been given by his commander in chief—and as divisional commander, he would have been held accountable had he sent the cavalry into action and suffered heavy casualties as a result.

And whatever Nolan might think of them, neither nobleman lacked courage. It was an unfortunate fact that—as he had told Jenny in one of his letters—relations between them had always been strained; it was even claimed that they had not spoken to each other during the past thirty years. They did not do so now, except when necessity demanded that they should, and Cardigan's invitations to dine on board the luxurious yacht *Dryad* had, apparently, never once included his immediate superior.

Private Bubb tucked the boots under his arm, picked up William's empty mug, and drew himself smartly to attention. "They do say, sir," he offered, his expression carefully blank, "as Sir Colin Campbell's ordered the Ninety-third to sleep in line tonight, under arms, an' that he's keeping the Turks at their guns. But I can't rightly swear to the truth o' that, seein' it were only what one o' our younger lads 'eard at second 'and like. Will that be all, sir?" Receiving William's nod of assent, he pulled back the tent flap and vanished into the misty darkness.

Left alone, William moved the flickering oil lamp nearer and picked up his pen. If Bubb were right about the impending Russian attack, it would be well to write his letter now, so as to make sure it was ready to be added to the post corporal's bag in the morning, for he did not want Jenny Broome to find him remiss as a correspondent. And certainly he did not want her to forget him, for since his arrival in the Crimea, she had been constantly in his thoughts . . . at times almost obsessively so.

He wrote busily for more than an hour, first replying to points she had raised and then attempting to describe the position occupied by the British forces in general and the cavalry division in particular, adding a small sketch map to illustrate his meaning. If such warlike matters were not of interest to Jenny, then probably her brother Johnny, who was a newspaperman, would appreciate the description.

The oil lamp was smoking and close to extinction by the time he had filled two closely written pages. Stifling a weary yawn, William read through the final page, fearing, as he did so, that Jenny might find it dull and lacking in feeling.

We are under canvas in the plain of Balaclava, at the head of what is termed the South Valley, with the infantry divisions and the naval siege batteries on a plateau behind us—known as the upland—which overlooks our objective, the town and naval base of Sebastopol.

From there a heavy bombardment is kept up on the town, often for twenty-four hours at a time. But Sebastopol has been substantially reinforced and its defenses have been rebuilt since we caught our first glimpse of it after our victory at the Alma. Now the Russians reply from forts and from the remaining ships of their fleet in the harbor, which is heavily defended by a number of great stone-built forts at the entrance. These defy all attempts by our fleets to penetrate the harbor, and both our navy and the French have suffered many casualties in a brave effort to battle their way in.

Another act of folly, William recalled grimly, had been the order to pit wooden-walled ships against those mighty Russian sea defenses. Heroically though the seamen had worked their guns, they had made virtually no impression on the immensely thick stone walls and casemated batteries of Fort Constantine, which had been the British fleet's objective.

He yawned again and, his eyes smarting from the smoke of the lamp, read on.

Here on the plain, where our cavalry division camp is situated, two parallel valleys—North and South—are divided by a narrow ridge of high ground, known as the Causeway Heights. The causeway carries a road, which I have marked on my sketch map in its Russian name—the Woronzoff Road. This issues into a gorge, leading to the coast and the port of Balaclava, from where all supplies for the siegeworks must be taken, after being landed from the ships.

William frowned. It was an infernally dull description, he decided, and not very easy to follow, although perhaps the sketch map would take it clear, should Jenny be sufficiently interested in it—and in him—to take the trouble to study it. He had made the sketch a couple of days before, from the upland, when he had been sent to Lord Raglan's command post in a farmhouse on the ridge overlooking the plain, from

which it was possible to see quite clearly across both valleys,
but . . . His frown deepened. Depicted thus, the causeway
appeared flat, whereas from the cavalry division camp, its
grassy slope effectively obscured all sight of the North Valley.

Well, it would have to do; he was too tired, and the light
too dim, to make another sketch. He rubbed his red-
rimmed, watering eyes and read on.

The rest of the letter consisted of an account of his daily
doings, which were dull enough—or they seemed so, when
set down on paper. He had no stirring deeds of valor to
report; as Bubb had reminded him, the Light Cavalry's record until now had been less than glorious, their losses not in
battle but resulting from cholera and exposure, and— William gave vent to an exasperated sigh.

Campaigning in India had been very different from this
static warfare. Here all that mattered were the great siege
guns on the upland and the supplies of ammunition that
must reach them daily, even if fodder for the cavalry's horses
had to be left to rot on Balaclava's congested wharves. William was conscious of a tightening of the throat as he remembered the first battle in which, as a young cornet newly
arrived in India, he had fought. His regiment, the 3rd Light
Dragoons, had charged the Sikh guns at Moodkee, carrying
all before them to a historic victory, won against all the odds.
True, they had lost almost half their number, killed or
wounded, but Edward Nolan had cited their charge as an
example of what, properly commanded, light cavalry could
achieve. And they could do it again, Nolan had asserted,
granted the chance and a commander worth his salt, in place
of the overcautious Lord Look-on.

Controlling an almost irresistible desire to close his eyes
and drift into sleep, William drew the sketch map toward
him and added the symbols denoting the redoubts on the
Causeway Heights, which, in the light of what Bubb had told
him, had assumed a new importance.

There was one, separated from the other five, on a hillock
at the far end of the South Valley, near the village of Kamara,
armed with six-pounder naval guns and held by the Turks—

Canrobert's Hill, it was called. William's frown returned as he penned in the name.

If the Russians did attack, marshaling their forces in the Chernaya Valley, they might well catch the Turks on Canrobert's Hill unprepared and, yes, unsupported, unless some, at least, of the cavalry could reach them in time. Certainly none of the infantry divisions could do so; the descent from the upland to the plain was an arduous one, taking at best more than two hours.

He folded the sketch and returned his attention to the letter, to swear softly as he read its final paragraph. It was not the kind of letter he had intended to write to Jenny Broome. The devil take it, he told himself . . . since meeting her again in Sydney on his last leave, he had been haunted by her memory; her small, sweet face had come to him all too often in his dreams, and he longed to see her again. Not by one word in this parody of a letter had he given her any hint of his feelings, yet suddenly he was acutely aware of what she meant to him—she, more than anyone else.

He had known other women—some he had known intimately and made love to, but . . . Jenny Broome had a quality, a charm no other woman had held for him. Sitting there in the cold, lamplit darkness of his tent on the Balaclava Plain, he let his thoughts wing back to the time he had spent with her in Sydney, remembering the picnic from which, on account of her mother's illness, she had returned prematurely. He had wanted then to tell her that he was falling in love with her, but it had not been possible, and the ball to which he had invited her, given by the garrison regiment, had been marred by her mother's death. Because she was in mourning, she had had to refuse, and he had had to go back to India without telling her how he felt. And in Calcutta, on his return, there had been the widow of a company nabob, with whom he had drifted into an affair he had not really wanted and had not enjoyed.

Now, however, it was as if suddenly he had a premonition of what was to come, and his heart quickened its beat. Picking up his quill, William wrote the words he had not said when he had left Jenny at the door of her parents' house in

Elizabeth Bay—the words scrawled, crisscrossing the lines of those he had already written, because he had no more paper.

"I love you, Jenny—I love you with all my heart. Wait for me, I beg you, for I have had my fill of war and soldiering. When this is over, I'll come home. Please wait until I come to you."

He added his name, folded and sealed the letter, and, leaving it ready for Bubb to take to the post in the morning, gathered his blanket around him and, not troubling to undress, flung himself onto his camp bed, to fall almost instantly asleep.

CHAPTER XIX

The cavalry division turned out, as usual, an hour before daybreak, in accordance with Lord Lucan's practice of inspecting them at this hour. Lord Cardigan, on the plea of an attack of dysentery, had slept late on board his yacht, and in his absence, command of the Light Brigade devolved on Lord George Paget, to whom William, this morning, was acting as aide.

The inspection over, the men started to walk their horses back to the lines to be watered and fed, grumbling in low voices, for the early morning stand-to was unpopular with the entire division. Lord Lucan led his small cavalcade in the direction of the Turkish-held positions on the Causeway Heights, and when Lord George indicated his intention of accompanying the divisional commander, William fell in at the rear.

It was still dark and cold, and a thick mist swirled and eddied about them as they trotted down the valley toward the most easterly of the redoubts, on Canrobert's Hill. Despite the previous night's premonition and Bubb's warning, William had no sense of impending disaster, yet as the first gray light of dawn brightened the eastern sky, he saw, with a sudden quickening of his pulses, that something unusual was afoot. Two flags, instead of the single crescent and star, flew from the flagstaff behind the redoubt, and uncertain of what this signified, he was about to draw attention to it when his commanding officer also observed the strange signal.

Reining in his horse, Lord George Paget pointed in the direction of the flagstaff and exclaimed in a puzzled voice, "Hullo—there are two flags flying. What does it mean?"

One of Lord Lucan's aides replied, "Surely, my lord, it means that the enemy is approaching!"

"Are you sure—" Lord George began, only to break off as his question was dramatically answered when a gun in the redoubt opened fire. It was met by a thunderous cannonade from the high ground to the right, and a round shot came hurtling toward the little group of officers, to pass between the legs of William's horse.

Lord Lucan took in the situation, after a moment of shocked dismay, and started to issue swift orders. An aide was sent galloping back to warn Sir Colin Campbell and the 93rd at Kadikoi, and a second dispatched to Lord Raglan's farmhouse headquarters six miles away, urgently requesting infantry support. As the mist began to disperse, a very large body of Russian infantry could be seen, advancing in two columns to the south of the Woronzoff Road. They were preceded by skirmishers, with cavalry on both flanks, escorting their guns.

William, hard put to it to calm his startled horse, dismounted to make sure that the animal was unhurt, and above the now-continuous thunder of gunfire, he heard Lord Lucan say bitterly, "Since Lord Raglan failed to act on the communication sent to him yesterday by Sir Colin Campbell and myself, and since he has left us here altogether without support, I consider it our first duty to defend the approach to the port of Balaclava. The Turks will have to do the best they can—we are in no position to help them, and they have their guns. The defense of the harbor will, of course, depend on my cavalry, so that I shall be compelled to reserve them for that purpose."

When the commander of the Heavy Brigade, General Scarlett, started to voice a protest, Lucan shrugged. "I will see whether I can accomplish anything by a feint—we may, at least, delay them. Lord George, I am placing the Light Brigade in reserve. General Scarlett, you will mount your brigade at once, if you please. I shall require one dragoon regiment to escort two troops of the horse artillery— Maude's and Shakespeare's—as soon as you can get them mounted."

"De Lancey," Lord George Paget snapped, "back to our lines as fast as you can ride! Give the alarm and get our men mounted—then rejoin your regiment!"

William needed no second bidding. He swung himself into the saddle and was away at breakneck speed across the rutted grass of the plain.

Ten minutes later, Paget's order delivered, William sat his mount and watched as the trumpeters sounded "Boot and saddle!" and the men responded with a rousing cheer that set the hot blood coursing in his veins.

It was true that their divisional commander had decreed that the Light Brigade was to be held in reserve, but if the Turks were overrun and failed to hold the enemy's advance, then it could not be long before they, as well as the Heavies, were called into action.

And the Turks *were* being overrun. Even as the two troops of horse artillery galloped forward, unlimbered, and opened fire, an unruly mob of Tunisian auxiliaries could be seen leaping and scrambling down the slope from Canrobert's Hill, their brief resistance at an end. After them came a troop of Cossacks in relentless pursuit, hacking the Turks down as they vainly sought escape, while Russian infantry, in close-packed ranks and with bayonets fixed, advanced on the vacated redoubt and swiftly occupied it. Within a few minutes they had turned the abandoned guns around and were firing them into the next redoubt. From there, too, after replying with one ragged volley of musketry, the Turks fled with shrill screams of terror. As before, the Cossacks cantered after them, with lances and pistols used to terrible effect, and few escaped the savage slaughter.

Finally, with Lord Lucan returned and at their head, the Heavy Cavalry Brigade rode out of camp, advancing along the valley to positions below and to the right of Canrobert's Hill. Lord George Paget led the Light Brigade after them, bringing them to a halt below Redoubts Three and Four on the causeway, which were still occupied by the Turks and putting up at least a show of resistance.

The two troops of horse artillery were giving them what support they could, William saw, but were themselves coming under withering fire, their six- and nine-pounder guns no match for the enemy twelve-pounder fieldpieces with which they found themselves engaged. After a while they received the signal to withdraw to extreme range, but as they

limbered up, a Russian shell exploded in their midst, killing
or wounding a number of men and horses. In spite of this,
they completed their withdrawal, covered by two squadrons
of the North British Dragoons—the Greys—and having sent
their wounded to the rear, they once again resumed firing.

Still the Russian infantry came on, slowly and inexorably,
flanked by two large bodies of cavalry. They were not
deceived by Lord Lucan's feint. The order came for both
British cavalry brigades to fall back, and as this was obeyed,
the Turks in all save one of the redoubts, believing themselves abandoned and about to be sacrificed, beat a hasty
and disorganized retreat. Those in Number Four, however,
still held out, delivering a rapid and accurate fire into Number Three as the Russians entered it, then bravely disputing
possession of their own redoubt until a bayonet charge, in
overwhelming numbers, sent them rushing for safety, pursued, as before, by Cossack lancers. But they were made of
sterner stuff than their comrades, and William joined the
cheers as a handful of them fought off their pursuers and
found sanctuary across the narrow valley, in the ranks of Sir
Colin Campbell's Highlanders.

At this juncture, Lord Cardigan made his belated appearance. William had held no brief for him when he had commanded the 11th Hussars, but as he rode up on his big
chestnut charger to take his place at the head of the Light
Brigade, the men raised a cheer, in which, for all his personal
reservations, William found himself also joining.

Certainly James Thomas Brudenell, seventh Earl of Cardigan, made an impressive figure. Long legs encased in the
cherry-colored overalls he had chosen for the regiment
when he had been their colonel, he sat bolt upright in his
saddle, his blue, fur-trimmed pelisse swinging from his
shoulders, and his head, in its crimson and white plumed
busby, held arrogantly high as he fired rapid questions at
Lord George Paget concerning the position and the orders
he had been given. It was evident from his scowl and the
tone of his voice that he did not like the replies he received
from his second-in-command, and he gestured angrily toward the redoubts that the Turks had abandoned; but when
an aide-de-camp galloped up to deliver a second order from

Lord Lucan to fall back, he obeyed it. Both cavalry brigades were now within musket range of the Russians occupying the redoubts, so that a withdrawal was necessary if casualties were to be avoided.

For all that, William could hear the men about him expressing their dissatisfaction at the move, and when their withdrawal brought them into their own 93rd's line of fire, even the officers began to voice their anger. Yet Lord Lucan, after a hasty consultation with Sir Colin Campbell, led them still farther back, until they were finally halted in front of their campsite in the South Valley.

"In God's name!" a youthful cornet exclaimed, his voice shaking. "Are we to abandon the Ninety-third as we abandoned the wretched Turks? If the enemy cavalry attack them, what chance will they have?"

Other voices echoed his dismay.

"Lord Look-on is playing his usual role, isn't he? Avoiding battle, the devil take him!"

"The infernal Russians were a stone's throw away, and we had to retreat from them!"

"I suppose he's waiting for infantry support from the damned upland, so that the foot sloggers can fight our battles for us. Well, it will be hours before they get here, and by that time God knows what will have happened!"

But for all his own disappointment because the chance of action had again been denied, William, looking about him with experienced eyes, recognized that strategically the move was a wise one. Posted as they were, facing the slopes of the Causeway Heights, the cavalry division was in a position from which—should Sir Colin Campbell's force fail to hold the expected Russian attack—they could launch a counterattack on the enemy's flank.

He tried to say this but was met with scorn.

Lieutenant Alexander Dunn, with whom he had been on terms of close friendship since joining the 11th, observed cynically, "Such tactics may have succeeded against the Sikhs, Will—I don't doubt they did—but the Russians are a different breed, you know. They attack en masse and don't give a damn how many men they lose—you saw them at the

Alma. And quite apart from anything else, my dear fellow, I've always believed that attack is the best form of defense."

William shrugged and did not argue. Their withdrawal down the full length of the South Valley had been well handled, their retreat by alternate regiments in accordance with accepted cavalry tactics, but it *had* been a retreat, and the vital Woronzoff Road along the causeway was now in the hands of the enemy, with only Sir Colin Campbell's Highlanders and the marine gunners to dispute possession of the port of Balaclava. If the Russians passed Kadikoi, then . . .

"I wonder . . ." It was the young cornet who had spoken so emotionally a few moments ago. "I wonder what Captain Nolan is making of our craven maneuvers. He'll be up there on the Sapouné Ridge with Lord Raglan and his staff, and they'll see everything from there, right over our heads!"

The 11th's commanding officer, Lieutenant Colonel Douglas, silenced the angry boy with a frigid glance. But the cornet was right, William thought wryly. From the lofty vantage point of his command post on the Sapouné Ridge of the upland, Lord Raglan was able to overlook both the North and South valleys, spread out like a relief map six hundred feet below him—he had seen that for himself when he had ridden up there and made his sketch. And Nolan would be there, with the rest of the British staff, doing duty as aide to General Airey, the quartermaster general and chief of staff. Edward Nolan, who had stoutly maintained that British light cavalry was invincible when properly commanded. . . . William's mouth tightened. What, he wondered despairingly, was Lucan intending to do?

Colonel Douglas rode forward to speak to Lord Cardigan and, on his return, announced flatly, "Gentlemen, the order to position the cavalry division here came from the commander in chief, but his orders, unfortunately, owing to the distance they must come, are taking upward of half an hour to reach us. I understand that we are instructed to cover Sir Colin Campbell's left flank and await the support of infantry, which has been ordered to advance on two fronts."

His announcement was greeted with groans and glum faces, but no one spoke until Lieutenant Palmer exclaimed suddenly, "My God, look! Enemy cavalry—advancing in strength on the Ninety-third's position!"

His hand was shaking as he pointed, and with a sinking heart William saw that a body of Russian cavalry, some six hundred or seven hundred strong, was starting to move down the causeway slope in the direction of the hillock behind which the two thin lines of Highlanders crouched waiting, as yet unseen. So they had lain all night, he knew, wrapped in their plaids and greatcoats, their muskets beside them. . . . He drew in his breath as an aide on a lathered horse galloped up to where Lord Lucan was positioned.

That he had brought another order from Lord Raglan became apparent when Lord Lucan, his face like thunder, signaled the division to commence a further withdrawal. This was accomplished, officers and men protesting loudly now, until, reaching the foot of the Sapouné Ridge, the two brigades turned in line to find themselves facing east, looking out along the South Valley.

"Well, this passes my comprehension," Alexander Dunn confessed bitterly. "If Sir Colin's fellows cannot hold, then Balaclava is lost. The poor devils of Highlanders will be overwhelmed, and we are precluded from going to their aid."

But to the heartfelt relief of the watching British cavalry division, the 93rd held. The approaching enemy horsemen advanced at a brisk trot, without scouts or skirmishers, clearly supposing that they were faced with no opposition and that, save for the marine guns at the head of the gorge, the way to Balaclava was clear. Then, as the jingling line of lancers came within musket range, the Highlanders rose as one man to their feet, to stand with bayonets fixed to oppose them. To the Russians, William thought, his spyglass to his eye, the red-coated soldiers, with their towering feather bonnets and the menacing steel-tipped muskets, must have appeared to have materialized out of the ground. The first volley of musketry abruptly halted the Russian advance, and they seemed for a moment to be about to retreat; but then they rallied, and half-hidden from his gaze by eddying gun smoke, the whole force gathered speed and thundered once more into the attack, only to be met by a second volley. By the time the gun smoke cleared, the Russians were seen to be withdrawing, the Highlanders and the marine gunners firing into their retreating backs.

As word of their defeat was passed from man to man, the British cavalry broke into cheers, their own frustration temporarily forgotten.

"They've done it—God be thanked, the brave fellows have done it!" Palmer cried, a catch in his voice. "They've saved Balaclava!"

"With no help from us," Dunn reminded him as the cheering faded. "But look—" His tone was suddenly harsh. "Some of the Heavies are being sent into action—see them, Will? Now, what in the world can *that* portend? And for the Lord's sake, isn't that General Scarlett going with them?"

It was, William registered. Led by their brigadier, several squadrons were detached from the Heavy Brigade, and with the gray horses of the North British Dragoons in the van, they set off in the direction of Kadikoi.

"Belated aid for the Ninety-third?" he suggested.

"Perhaps." Dunn was frowning. "I wonder where in hell the rest of the Russian cavalry has got to? There were several thousand of them when we first caught sight of them earlier, covering the infantry's attack on the redoubts. But only about seven hundred tested the Highlanders. Hard to tell at this distance, I know, but they looked to me like a single regiment of lancers—and now they've vanished. What are they up to, do you suppose?"

William considered the question. "I'm damned if I know," he admitted. "But—" His gaze went to the wide, undulating ridge of the Causeway Heights. "Since we lost the redoubts, they would meet with no opposition if they crossed the Woronzoff Road and entered the North Valley. That's what I would do if I were commanding them. They would have a clear field, and—" Struck by a sudden, alarming realization, he put his glass to his eye. "Lord Raglan could have sent Scarlett's squadrons into trouble, if that's where they are, Alex. The order came from him, did it not?"

"Y-yes. But our view is obscured by the causeway—Lord Raglan's is not. If the Russian cavalry *have* entered the North Valley, he'll have seen them. Besides—" Alexander Dunn broke off, his frown returning. "Heavens, though, I was forgetting—his orders are taking more than half an hour to reach us! So that—"

"Quite," William put in grimly. "But General Scarlett is no fool—he's seen the possibility. Look, those are the two Indian aides attached to him: Colonel Beatson and what's his name—Elliott. He's sent them up to the causeway to reconnoiter."

He had his glass on the two horsemen, watched them breast the southern slope of the causeway, and then saw them pause and, wheeling their mounts almost in unison, gallop back to where Scarlett waited. A massive column of Russian horsemen appeared over the crest barely a minute later, and beside him Dunn breathed a startled oath.

"God in heaven, you were right, Will! There they are!"

A second column followed the first, and both started to descend the slope. The sight was at once imposing and alarming, although it was evident, from the way they rode and the fact that they had no scouts on either flank, that the Russian commander did not suspect the proximity of the British cavalry, any more than Scarlett, until that moment, had suspected theirs.

They trotted downhill in two lines, the light blue uniforms and splendid horses identifying the two leading regiments as hussars—the cream of the Russian cavalry. William watched them, his stomach churning. The last vestige of mist had dispersed, and the sun drew glittering reflections from weapons and accoutrements as the great mass came steadily on. There were, as nearly as he could judge, between three and four thousand of them; below, even now passing through the tents and horse lines of their own camp, were a scant five hundred British dragoons, quite unprepared to receive an attack from so overwhelming a force.

From the distance that separated them, William could not see the expression on General Scarlett's face, even with the aid of his glass, but he saw Lucan's, as the divisional commander shouted an order to Lord Cardigan.

"The Light Brigade is to be held in reserve! I shall order General Scarlett to charge them with the Heavy Brigade. Do you understand, Cardigan?"

Cardigan lifted his hand in acknowledgment, and Lucan galloped over to where Scarlett, anticipating his order, had wheeled his squadrons into line facing the causeway, halfway down which the Russians had halted. The Heavy Brigade's other squadrons were hurrying to join their comrades, and as Lord Cardigan led the Light Brigade to take up position on the flank, William saw that Scarlett's officers, their backs turned to the enemy, were sitting their horses as if preparing for a peacetime review, meticulously completing the dressing of their ranks.

The Russians also started to change their formation, seeming in no haste to descend from the commanding position they occupied on the slope. The Heavies, William thought apprehensively, outnumbered as they were, would suffer the added disadvantage of having to charge uphill. After what appeared to be a heated altercation between Lord Lucan and General Scarlett, a trumpeter sounded the charge, in obedience to an order from Lucan.

The clear, high notes echoed and reechoed from the enclosing hills; but the white-haired Scarlett's raised sword restrained the British line, and not a man moved until, satisfied at last with his alignment, the brigadier ranged himself at their head and, turning in his saddle, ordered his own trumpeter to sound the call. Then, setting spurs to his horse, with two aides and his orderly at his heels, he rode straight at the Russians. The scarlet-clad line of the leading squadrons of Greys and Inniskillings broke into a trot, quickening their pace as soon as they were free of the tents, and thundered after their old commander.

"My God, Will," Alexander Dunn said in a shocked voice, "they're going to their deaths! And look at Scarlett—he's going at them alone!"

For several agonizing minutes the watchers could see little for dust and smoke, as the Russian cavalry, still motionless in their close-packed ranks, discharged their pistols at their attackers. But when the smoke cleared, William saw to his stunned relief that the first line of red-jacketed British dragoons had cut and hacked their way through the enemy center and, led by Scarlett, were beginning to emerge on the other side.

With a wedge driven into their center, the Russians were wavering. When the second line of Inniskillings and 5th Dragoon Guards, still keeping their splendid alignment, hurtled into the melee at full gallop, the enemy broke formation, and the remaining regiments of the Heavy Brigade, charging in their turn from the flanks, completed the rout. The great mass of Russian cavalry, with startling suddenness, was driven back, reeling and thrown into confusion by the disciplined assault of the courageous Heavies.

Within a few minutes they were in headlong flight, reascending the ridge in complete disorder, pursued by a handful of Scarlett's men. A great cheer went up from the rest, whose horses were too blown to join the pursuit, as they watched the beaten enemy streaming away over the Woronzoff Road and across the causeway, in a panic-stricken bid to gain the shelter of their guns in the North Valley.

All the while, the Light Brigade had been positioned in full view of the action, fewer than five hundred yards away, every man ready and eager to launch his own attack on the flank and waiting impatiently for the order. But it had never come; now, as Lord Cardigan continued to sit his horse, seemingly intending to remain immobile, an angry group of officers left their regiments to surround him, pleading for permission to pursue the beaten Russians.

William and Alexander Dunn, as disappointed and angry as the rest, added their voices to the urgent pleas, but Cardigan shook his head at them.

"Gentlemen, I am as anxious as you are to join the pursuit of the enemy. I was ready to attack their flank in support of the Heavies. But I received orders to post the Light Brigade where it now is and none—*none*, I say, gentlemen—from either Lord Raglan or Lord Lucan to bring the brigade into action. Do not blame me, devil take it! I am simply obeying the orders I was given."

"But the enemy are being allowed to escape, my lord," Captain William Morris, who was in temporary command of the 17th Lancers, protested furiously. "I beg you to permit me to take my regiment after them. Sir, I will take the consequences. I—"

Icily, Cardigan cut him short. "I wish to hear no more.

Captain Morris. I cannot permit you to disobey orders. Return to your posts, gentlemen, at once."

They did so reluctantly, continuing to protest among themselves, and Morris, his face dark with rage, wheeled around in front of his regiment and, in a display of bitter frustration, slapped his overalled leg with his drawn saber, swearing aloud.

The Light Brigade stayed where it was. The Russian cavalry, with their horse artillery intact, gained the far end of the North Valley unmolested and established themselves there, behind their unlimbered guns. The officers and men of the Heavy Brigade, whose brave charge had succeeded against seemingly impossible odds, watched the fruits of their hard-won victory slip away from them and—many of them in tears—counted their dead and carried their wounded slowly back to their tents, to be delivered to the surgeons' care.

CHAPTER XX

The order came for the Light Cavalry Brigade to take up position at the western end of the causeway, facing down the trough of the North Valley, with the re-formed Heavy Brigade drawn up on the slopes of the Woronzoff Road, behind them and to their right, so as to occupy the ground their earlier charge had cleared.

Thereafter nothing happened, and sensing his men's growing frustration, Colonel Douglas rode over to seek enlightenment from Lord Lucan. Joined in his quest by Captain Morris of the 17th Lancers and followed by Lord George Paget, he conferred at some length with the cavalry division commander, only Lord Cardigan holding wrathfully aloof from their discussion.

When Douglas returned, his officers besieged him with questions, but he could only shake his head despairingly.

"His Lordship is satisfied, after talking to Sir Colin Campbell, that the enemy have been pushed back from Balaclava and that the threat to the harbor has been countered," he told them curtly. "As to ourselves, Lord Raglan has sent an order for the cavalry division to await the arrival of the First and Fourth Infantry divisions, which are now on their way down here from the upland. With infantry support—when that reaches us—we are to use our best endeavors to recover the captured Turkish redoubts on the causeway." He repeated his shrug, controlling himself with a visible effort. "That is all I know, gentlemen. But in view of the time the infantry divisions are taking to descend to the plain, Lord Lucan has given permission for both brigades to stand easy. Be so good as to pass that order to your men."

Thankfully, the men of the Light Brigade dismounted, to lean against their horses, the officers sipping rum or brandy

from their flasks, and those who had them eating hard-
boiled eggs and biscuits. Some of the men lit their pipes but
were sternly reprimanded for smoking in the face of the
enemy—a reproof that provoked wry laughter.

William had been provided with refreshment by the far-
sighted Bubb, but he felt so sickened by the earlier events of
the day that he found himself unable to eat, and most of his
brother officers were in a similar state.

"We had the chance of a lifetime, and we had to let it go,
for God's sake!" Lieutenant Palmer grumbled bitterly.
"This campaign has been nothing but frustration for the
Light Cavalry—frustration and humiliation!"

"I know, Roger," Alex Dunn agreed, his tanned face taut
with resentment. "I could have wept as I watched the Heavies come back in triumph this morning. They deserved their
triumph, heaven knows—theirs was a truly gallant achieve-
ment. They went in like heroes, every man jack of them,
whilst we—" He choked on the biscuit he was eating and
flung it from him in disgust. "Damn it, *they* can hold their
heads high, but we must bow ours in shame! Those Russian
lancers were beaten, they were routed and running. All we
had to do was go after them. We'd have driven them all the
way back to Simferopol, with their tails between their legs!
But we had to stand fast and let the swine escape."

"Cardigan blames Lord Look-on," young George Houghton observed. He leaned his dark head against the saddle of
his big chestnut charger despondently, hiding his face. "And
so do I, the devil take him!"

"He had his orders, George," William defended.

"He could have used his discretion! He was on the spot—
he saw what ought to have been done. No one would have
censured him if he'd done it, least of all Lord Raglan. And
we were ready to go, by heaven we were!"

"The day is all but over," Dunn rasped irritably. "And
what are we offered? According to the colonel, we're to be
given the chance to support the infantry, which is conspicuous by its absence. So we wait, and the infernal Cossacks jeer
at us when we encounter them. . . . Even our own infantrymen call us gilded popinjays and worse. If this goes on,

I'll sell my commission and make tracks for home. Or for one of the colonies.''

And so, William thought glumly, would he. The humiliation they all had endured had bitten deep; the men, talking in low voices among themselves, felt it just as deeply—the Indian veterans, like Bubb and himself, perhaps most of all.

They continued to wait, fretting at the delay as another half hour passed without sight or sound of the expected infantry divisions. From where they had halted, they could see the line of Russian guns at the far end of the North Valley and the troops massed behind them, and they watched in futile anger as a field battery ascended the hill to their left front and turned its guns toward them.

But suddenly a horseman in hussar uniform was seen descending from the upland at breakneck speed. He was easily recognized as Edward Nolan, for, scorning the circuitous track previous gallopers had followed when carrying Lord Raglan's orders to the plain, he plunged straight down the steep hillside, waving excitedly, only his consummate horsemanship saving him from disaster.

He reached level ground only a few minutes later, and sinking his spurs into his horse's sides at the foot of the escarpment, he crossed the intervening space at full gallop. As they watched his approach, the officers and men of the Light Brigade guessed, from his reckless haste, that the order he carried must be of extreme urgency, and their spirits lifted, for the order could be intended only for them.

The aide-de-camp's route took him close to their lines, and as he thundered past, William heard Captain Morris of the 17th Lancers—his closest friend—call out eagerly, ''Nolan, what's going to happen?''

Nolan, without slackening speed, shouted back triumphantly, ''You'll see, you'll see!''

He jerked his lathered horse to a standstill beside Lord Lucan—who was waiting, with members of his staff, between his two brigades—and thrust the order into his hand. The officers, catching the young aide-de-camp's excitement, crowded closer as Lucan read it, but his expression, when he had done so, was one of shocked perplexity.

''Find out what it's about, De Lancey,'' Colonel Douglas

growled, and William reached the group gathered about their divisional commander in time to hear him read aloud the order Nolan had given him, his tone one of incomprehension.

" 'Lord Raglan wishes the cavalry to advance rapidly to the front and try to prevent the enemy carrying away the guns. Troop of horse artillery may accompany. French cavalry is on your left. Immediate.' " He paused, eyeing General Airey's aide-de-camp as if wondering whether he, as well as the commander in chief, had taken leave of his senses. The only guns in any danger of being carried away by the enemy, of which Lord Lucan or the cavalry under his command were aware, were those at the end of the North Valley, behind which the defeated Russian cavalry had established themselves—in a defensive, rather than an offensive position—and William, listening as the order was read, found himself as bewildered as the rest of those who heard it.

Lord Raglan, he thought in stunned disbelief, could surely not wish the attack to be made on *those* guns, without infantry support and with only one troop of horse artillery and possibly belated aid from the French Chasseurs d'Afrique, somewhere on their flank. Not, that was to say, unless he wished for the annihilation of the entire British cavalry division . . . William's heart sank. The men of the Light Brigade had longed to be ordered into action, but this—this was madness! He choked down the bile that rose into his throat as he heard Lord Lucan put into puzzled and irritable words his own unvoiced doubts as to the meaning of the order.

Edward Nolan cut him short. He said in a deliberately insolent and peremptory tone, "Lord Raglan's orders, sir, are that the cavalry are to attack immediately!"

Lucan, visibly taken aback, stared at Nolan. He must be aware, William thought, that Nolan disliked him; and in common with the rest of the division, he knew that in the past Nolan had openly criticized him for the hesitancy he had shown in his handling of cavalry in the field. But as a lieutenant general, Lucan was certainly not accustomed to being addressed so disrespectfully by a mere captain—even if that captain was an acknowledged expert on light cavalry tactics and a favorite with the commander in chief.

There was a moment's shocked silence, and then Lucan turned on the arrogant young aide-de-camp with barely controlled fury.

"Attack, sir?" he shouted, his words carrying to all the officers in his vicinity. "Attack *what*, for God's sake? What guns, sir? What enemy am I to attack?"

Indeed, the word "attack" had not been mentioned in Lord Raglan's order, and it was far from clear on which front the commander in chief required the cavalry to advance; still, all of Edward Nolan's contempt for the man he had nicknamed Lord Look-on exploded suddenly. He flung out his arm in a gesture that embraced the North Valley, where the Russian cavalry waited behind their guns, and answered, with a provocative scorn he made no attempt to conceal, "There, my lord, is your enemy! There are your guns!"

To those who watched him, whether or not they were in earshot, Edward Nolan's outflung arm could indicate only one thing—the Light Brigade's objective lay at the end of the North Valley. The guns they were ordered to attack were indeed those sheltering the Russian cavalry. Numbly, William swung his horse around and rode back to report to Colonel Douglas.

After all the talking and speculation, a strange, unearthly silence had fallen. The men spoke in whispers, as the news passed from regiment to regiment, from squadron to squadron, from man to man, and its import sank in. Their hour had come, and there were few who failed to realize the immensity of the task that lay ahead of them.

Douglas received his brief repetition of the wording of the order in tight-lipped silence and, without comment, waved William back to his squadron, his face grimly set.

"Look at Cardigan, Will," Alex Dunn urged softly, as William pulled up beside him.

Lord Cardigan, sitting his horse a few yards from them, was reading the written order that Lord Lucan's aide had hurriedly copied and passed on to him. An expression of incredulity was on his florid face, transcending Lucan's own when he had received the orders from Edward Nolan. As

they all did, William thought, Cardigan knew that for cavalry
to attack guns in battery without infantry support was contrary to every accepted rule of war—and the North Valley
was shut in by hills, which were the site of other batteries,
besides those at its far end that the Light Brigade had now
been ordered to charge.

Still obviously bewildered, Cardigan sent his own aide,
Fitz-Maxse, to remonstrate with Lord Lucan before attempting to comply with the order.

Lucan rode over to him, the commander in chief's original
order in his hand. Coldly, he read its contents aloud to the
indignant Cardigan and then instructed him to advance
down the North Valley with the Light Brigade, while he
himself followed in support with the Heavy Brigade.

Cardigan brought down his saber in formal salute and
replied, with equal coldness, "Certainly, sir. But allow me to
point out to you that the Russians have a battery in the valley
at our front and batteries and riflemen on each flank. It will
be a costly attack, sir."

"I know it," Lucan returned with bleak resignation. "But
Lord Raglan will have it. We have no choice but to obey."

Cardigan repeated his formal salute. "Advance very steadily," his brother-in-law commanded. "Keep your men well in
hand."

There was the same icy acknowledgment. Then Cardigan
wheeled his horse and, in a harsh undertone that could
clearly be heard by those grouped about him, muttered to
himself, "Well, here goes the last of the Brudenells!"

His throat tight, William watched him as, preserving an
outward calm, he trotted across to Lord George Paget, who,
with the second-in-command of his regiment, the 4th Light
Dragoons, was dismounted and smoking a cigar.

"Lord George, we are ordered to make an attack to the
front," he announced without preamble. "You will take command of the second line, and I expect your best support.
Mind—your *best* support!"

The last sentence was repeated, and Lord George red-
dened resentfully. He glanced at his companion, Major
Halkett, and then responded gruffly, "Of course, my lord.
You shall have my best support."

Captain Nolan rode past, and William called out to him in anxious question. The aide-de-camp smiled. "Back to the upland? Oh, no, my dear fellow. I intend to charge with the Seventeenth." His smile widened. "Death or glory, what? I trust I shall see you again."

The trumpets were sounding now in shrill succession.

"Stand to your horses!"

"Mount!"

"Officers, take post!"

Watched by their commander, the Light Brigade formed up and wheeled into line. The first line, from right to left, consisted of the 13th Light Dragoons, the 17th Lancers, and, slightly to their rear, the 11th Hussars. The 4th Light Dragoons and the 8th Hussars formed the second line. With half a squadron of the 8th acting as Lord Raglan's escort, the brigade had paraded that morning 675 strong. Lord Lucan, looking down the valley, apparently saw that their wide deployment would be too exposed for the coming attack and ordered Colonel Douglas to move the 11th back, so as to take position to the rear of the 17th Lancers, thus forming the second line, with the 4th and 8th now acting as the third.

Lord Cardigan rode forward, to take his place at the head of the right squadron of the 17th Lancers, his expression inscrutable, but his head, as always, carried arrogantly high. The dressing of their lines completed, the shouted commands of the troop officers died away, and once again there was a strangely pregnant silence. William, with Alex Dunn a few yards away to his left, waited tensely. Then Cardigan raised his voice and, exhibiting neither excitement nor apprehension, gave his orders, his saber raised.

"The brigade will advance. The first squadron of the Seventeenth Lancers will direct. Walk march!"

The three lines of the Light Brigade started to move slowly down the North Valley, followed several minutes later by the Heavy Brigade, led by Lord Lucan.

To the watchers high above them on the Sapouné Ridge there was, at first, no indication that Lord Raglan's order had been misrepresented by the man entrusted to deliver it. It was not until the leading ranks had covered some two hundred yards and then, instead of inclining right, in the

direction of the captured Turkish redoubts on the causeway
—as the commander in chief had intended them to—continued to advance at a trot straight on down the valley, that the
terrible truth began at last to dawn. But by the time Lord
Raglan realized how appalling was the error that had been
made, it was too late—much, much too late to correct it. The
order had been given; all unaware, the officers and men of
the five regiments of light cavalry obeyed it.

Even the Russians occupying the redoubts had assumed,
until that moment, that the naval guns they had captured
were the objectives toward which the British cavalry was
advancing. They hurriedly formed up to receive the expected charge, momentarily abandoning their efforts to dismantle the cumbersome iron cannon preparatory to removing them. Similarly, their gunners and sharpshooters across
the narrow valley, on the Fediukine Hills, as well as those on
the forward slopes of the causeway, did not at first divine the
purpose of the steady advance of the brilliantly uniformed
regiments of the Light Brigade. They held fire, expecting
the line of horsemen to wheel and escape from the trap
before its jaws closed on them . . . but they did not.

At an unhurried trot, with superb precision and in perfect
alignment, the Light Brigade came on. Fifty or sixty yards
separated their first line from the second; the third was
about the same distance behind the second, the gap gradually widening. At their head, alone, rode the tall, striking
figure of their brigadier general, the gold frogging on his
blue and cherry-red hussar uniform glistening in the sunlight. He led them into the range of the enemy's flanking
guns as if he were either unaware of their presence or else
supremely indifferent to the terrible threat they offered to
himself and the men who followed him.

The Russian gunners stared at him in stunned surprise;
the infantrymen sighted their rifles but did not fire. Then the
first numbing shock of surprise passed. Officers bellowed
frantic orders, and one after another the batteries on the
Fediukine Hills opened up, hurling a deadly flanking fire of
grape and round shot and canister upon the slowly moving
horsemen below.

As the first battery started firing, a single rider detached himself from the 17th Lancers' leading squadron and galloped frenziedly across its front toward Lord Cardigan. Captain Edward Nolan passed ahead of him—an unforgivable breach of military etiquette, which Cardigan observed with outraged astonishment.

Nolan was waving his saber and shouting at the pitch of his lungs, as if, at the eleventh hour, he had just realized Lord Lucan's mistake—a mistake that had been prompted by his own careless taunt. Seeking desperately to halt the brigade's advance toward the wrong objective, Nolan called out to Cardigan, but his voice was inaudible above the crash of gunfire and the drumming hoofbeats of the Light Brigade's horses, and the commander wrathfully waved him back. To Cardigan it seemed as if the young upstart aide-de-camp who fancied himself a cavalry tactician was dissatisfied with the speed of advance and was attempting to take over the leadership of his brigade, and this, quite properly, he could not allow.

Then a shell burst to Lord Cardigan's right, and a splinter from it struck Nolan in the chest, killing him instantly, so that—by an ironic twist of fate—he who was the cause of the tragic misinterpretation of Lord Raglan's order became the first to pay the price of it.

The saber fell from his hand, but the hand remained raised, high above his head, and a ghastly scream burst from him, echoing above the thunder of cannon fire and the crackle of musketry. Yet even in death, Edward Nolan did not fall from his horse. The animal wheeled around in terror, and although Nolan's body slumped, it was still in the saddle as his charger passed through the ranks of the oncoming dragoons, slipping from it only after the last line of the Light Cavalry Brigade had passed by.

The advance continued, its pace quickening a little now as, from both sides, the awful hail of fire opened great gaps in the ranks, mowing down men and horses, who had no defense against it. William felt his heart turn to stone as the shells burst among the men of the 11th. Every man's instinct was to end the unendurable ordeal by speeding up the advance, but Lord Cardigan sternly restrained them, aware that to do so now would be disastrous. They still had almost

three-quarters of a mile to cover before they reached the
guns they had been ordered to charge, and to gain their
objective on blown horses would be to court defeat.

They came, at last, within range of the guns at the valley's
end, and in a frenzy to come to grips with the gunners who
were wreaking such havoc among them, the 17th Lancers
began to press forward. Cardigan, without looking around,
laid his saber across Captain Morris's chest and called
out, above the din, "Steady . . . steady, Seventeenth!"
Abashed, William Morris dropped back.

"Close to your center! Look to your dressing there, men!"
the troop commanders shouted. "Close in! Close in to the
center!"

This was now the most frequently repeated order, and
William instinctively shouted it, as the screams of the
wounded men and horses all around him increased and the
charging line narrowed, becoming more ragged and un-
evenly spaced. Riderless horses added to the confusion. Instinct and training impelled them to seek the familiar formation and to return to the squadron lines after their riders had
been killed. Wounded men, too brave to seek safety in retreat, endeavored to keep up with their unwounded comrades and found that their bravery was just not enough . . .
and they fell back, bringing further disorder to the line behind them.

It had not been like this against the Sikhs, William
thought, a sick sensation in the pit of his stomach. This slow
advance under such an inferno of fire was the greatest ordeal
that he, and the men with him, had ever been called upon to
endure. The Heavies' charge had taken a scant ten minutes.
It had been mercifully short, their casualties relatively few,
for they had come instantly to grips with the enemy and had
been able to meet that enemy on equal terms, man for man,
if not in equal numbers. And they had won a significant
victory.

But the Light Brigade could not achieve victory. They had
no weapons with which to answer the ghastly hail of shot and
shell that rained down upon them. Only courage and discipline kept the men from breaking ranks and dashing forward
in disorder to attack the guns with their sabers and lances.

Theirs was a matchless courage, and as he watched the men about him fall and their horses go down, William felt a glow of heartbreaking pride in these soldiers who were his flesh and blood, if not his countrymen, and in whose company, it seemed, he was about to die.

For a fleeting moment, he let his thoughts stray to his homeland—to Sydney, to his father's house, and to his family. To Jenny Broome and to the letter he had written to her the previous night, and he drew a rasping breath as, beside him, George Houghton slumped over his chestnut's lathered neck, struck, as Nolan had been, by a bursting shell splinter, his young mouth open but no audible sound issuing from it.

Would Jenny Broome ever know how he had died, he wondered, or how much he had loved her and wanted her for his wife? He had a vision of her face, as it had come to him when he had read through his letter, and now it seemed to be floating ahead of him, just for a moment blotting out the straining blue-uniformed backs of the lancers riding into the swirling smoke from the Russian guns, now only twenty yards away.

The vision faded, a dream, William knew, existing only in his imagination, a long way from reality. Reality for him, and for the pitifully few survivors of the Light Brigade's first two lines, were the Russian guns, shrouded in smoke and dust, belching forth flames.

The charge became a wild gallop. The Russian gunners fired their last salvo and then, in terror, fled or crawled beneath their guns. The 17th, just ahead, lances couched, were in among them now, William's own regiment close on their heels. Conscious of neither fear nor pity, William tore through the battery, hacking and slashing at the enemy gunners as he went, with Alexander Dunn shouting madly at his side and Colonel Douglas's broad, blue-jacketed back glimpsed through the gun smoke ahead.

Behind the line of guns was ranged a daunting, motionless mass of Russian cavalry. A group of these, in lancer uniform, started to form up to their right, and Douglas, expecting reinforcements and having no orders to retire, flung over his shoulder an urgent command to rally to him and charge.

Wearily the eighty men of the 11th—all, it seemed, that were left—realigned themselves and charged. The Russians broke and retreated before them, and they galloped on, still in the belief that reinforcements from the Heavy Brigade must be following them.

But none came. They could not see that Lord Lucan had halted the Heavy Brigade when, coming under heavy fire from the Fediukine Hills, they had suffered severe casualties, with Lucan himself wounded in the leg. He ordered his trumpeter to sound the halt and withdrew out of range of the Russian guns, grimly prepared to cover the Light Brigade's eventual and inevitable retreat when it came.

Unaware of this, the 11th drove the Russian lancers back until, realizing at last that the expected reinforcements had not appeared, the 11th's commanding officer decided that the time had come to break off the attack and retire. They had silenced the guns with their charge but had neither the men nor the means to capture and carry them off.

But now Cossacks dashed in to attack them on the flank, firing their pistols with deadly effect, and a second regiment of lancers loomed up on their left to harass their retreat. Joined by Lord George Paget, with the remnants of the 4th Light Dragoons, the 11th continued to fall back, until William heard Bubb's voice yelling out a warning and, turning, saw that they were about to be taken in the rear.

"My lord!" he shouted at the pitch of his lungs, shocked at the feebleness of his cry, but Lord George heard it and called on his small, exhausted handful of men to make a stand.

"Halt—front!" he bade them hoarsely. "If you don't halt front, my boys, we're done!"

The men of both regiments obeyed him, officers mixed with their men and Bubb at his side, William saw, his gaunt, smoke-blackened face grimly set. Faced by a resolute line, the lancers and Cossacks who had been pursuing them halted as well, and finally—inexplicably—drew off. There remained the newly arrived squadrons of lancers in their rear, which now started to form up, as if with the intention of taking the offensive and cutting off their retreat, and Lord George said, with admirable calm, "We are going to have to fight our way out of this, I fear." He turned to his trumpeter, only to see that the man lay dead at his feet, killed by a Cossack pistol shot, and once again shouted an order to them to form up and charge to their rear.

In response to the urging of their few surviving officers and NCOs, the men of the two regiments, now reduced to a total strength of fewer than fifty, faced about and again formed as compact a line as they could. Their charge was delayed when Alexander Dunn broke ranks to go to the aid of a sergeant of his squadron, who had been cut off and was under attack by three of the enemy lancers. Both rejoined, the sergeant's horse lamed, but leaving the attackers unhorsed and wounded to the rear.

"Charge, boys!" Lord George Paget bade them. "One last effort, and we'll be out of here!"

The men raised a defiant cheer and spurred their tired horses at the lancer regiment blocking their retreat. Their charge met with little resistance. The lancers wheeled away, evidently reluctant to meet it, and they galloped past, almost unscathed, halting only when they reached the now-silent line of guns against which the brigade's original charge had been made.

But now they, with the other shattered and cruelly depleted regiments of Lord Cardigan's Light Brigade, had the mile-long gauntlet of the North Valley to run a second time. Weary and wounded, many of them on foot, others leading lame and bleeding horses, they must once again brave the Russian cannon fire, although this had been rendered less effective by the attack of the French Chasseurs d'Afrique on the Fediukine batteries, which they had charged and silenced to aid their British allies' retreat.

Nevertheless, for William De Lancey, as for many of the other survivors, the return through the valley was to prove the worst part of their ordeal. The guns on the Causeway Heights still dealt out their awful carnage; the riflemen, on the slopes to either hand, poured down a hail of minié balls from safe concealment, and roving bands of vengeful Cossacks rode down the lame and the unhorsed, the wounded and the disarmed, showing them no mercy.

The whole valley was a shambles, the ground strewn with

dead and dying men and hideously mutilated horses, their
agonized cries audible even above the crash and thunder of
the guns. Ahead of them, as the 11th Hussars began their
painful retreat to their own lines, small groups of men, their
uniforms so spattered with mud and blood as to be almost
unrecognizable, straggled back, some stumbling blindly
over the rough ground, barely able to keep their feet, some
leading a horse, miraculously unscathed, on which a badly
wounded man clung weakly to the saddle. Others, just able
to hobble themselves, dragged a dying mount that they refused to abandon and sought, even in their own extremity,
to save.

William heard a strangled cry coming from close behind
him and turned to see that his servant Bubb had been hit in
the chest by a sharpshooter's ball. The man fell from his
horse, which staggered a few yards and then collapsed almost beside him, its entrails spilling out in a gout of blood.

"Go on, sir," Bubb urged. "I'm done for—save yourself!"

But that, William knew, he could not do. They had been
through too much together, he and Bubb, in India and now
here, in the dank wilderness of the Russian Crimea. He
dismounted and, with infinite difficulty, for there seemed to
be no strength in his arms, picked up his servant and somehow got him onto his own horse's back. It was then that he
realized, for the first time, that he had also been wounded.
His right arm was stiff, the sleeve of his tunic soaked in
blood, and he lurched along, clinging to his horse's stirrup,
in a state of dazed half-consciousness and well-nigh unendurable pain.

He had no warning of the Cossacks who attacked him, his
attention distracted by the sight of Major Halkett, the 4th
Light Dragoons' second-in-command, falling suddenly from
his horse as an exploding shell struck him in the back. Attempting to assist the stricken major, William stumbled and
lost his grip of his own horse's stirrup leather, and the Cossacks were upon him, three of them, evidently bent on taking
him prisoner.

One of them, approaching at a trot, thrust his lance tip
into poor Bubb's side and sent him crashing to the ground,
and then William found himself surrounded and fighting for

his life. His sword arm was useless, but he managed some-how to fend them off, his weapon in his left hand. He lunged at them blindly and, by a lucky chance rather than skill, succeeded in unhorsing the nearer of his assailants. But that was the end of his resistance. A Cossack lance struck his left arm, knocking his saber from his grasp, and he went down under a blow from a pistol butt, delivered by the man he had unhorsed.

His senses reeling, he lay where he had fallen, dimly aware that a fight was taking place close at hand. He could hear the clash of steel and heavy breathing, punctuated by cries of pain, and was then dimly aware that hands were grasping him by the shoulders and attempting to drag him along the ground. The hands were not ungentle, and he was aware of an English voice, close to his ear, apologizing for the manner in which he was being manhandled.

"We drove them Cossack swine off, sir, so don't you worry no more on their account. And we'll get you back. . . . It's not much more'n a quarter of a mile now, and there's a couple o' squadrons o' the Heavies coming out to meet us. You'll be all right, sir, once we get you back."

"Major Halkett," William managed, through tightly clenched teeth. "And Private Bubb of ours, of the Eleventh. Are they—"

"They're dead, sir, both of 'em," the voice answered with bleak finality. "Them bloody Cossacks did for them. Now, if you can sit a horse, sir . . ."

But William knew that he could not sit a horse. He tried to shake his head, to tell these men who had saved him from the Cossacks that they must leave him and go on to seek safety themselves. Just as Bubb, good soldier that he was, had told him, a long time ago. Seemingly they did not hear him, for he found himself being bundled into the saddle of a Cossack horse and held there by two of them, when they realized that he could not sit upright unaided.

He recognized one of his rescuers as a crony of Bubb's, whom he had recently had occasion to reprimand for a mi-nor breach of discipline; the others were men of Halkett's regiment, the 4th Light Dragoons, and strangers to him. They were talking of poor Halkett, and he heard one of them

say, "Told us to take his money, the major did, afore he died.
For the married families left at home, he said."

"And did you take it, Bob?"

"Aye, I did. And I'll see it goes to them he wanted to have
it, if 'tis the last thing I do. He were a good bloke, Halkett."

"And so's this one," the trooper of the 11th put in. "De
Lancey, they call him—Captain De Lancey. Comes from
Australia. Poor old Bubb thought the world of him, but—
d'you think he'll make it, Sar'nt? He's hurt pretty bad, by the
looks of him."

"We'll take him back," the unknown sergeant returned.
"Then it'll be up to the bloody sawbones." His tone
changed. "They say Cardigan came back without a scratch—
one o' the Heavies said so."

"He led us well, though, Sar'nt, didn't he?" the 11th man
defended. "Never flinched, never turned his face from them
guns—just rode straight at 'em."

"Oh, aye," the sergeant conceded. "But they never ought
to have sent us to charge them guns—not just the brigade on
its own. Still," he added philosophically, "no one can call us
gilded popinjays now, can they? What's bleedin' left of us,
that is."

William attempted to straighten his aching body, but the
effort proved too much. He slumped forward, numb fingers
losing their grip of the pommel of the Cossack's saddle. The
men's voices and the now-distant roar of the guns became a
meaningless blur of sound, drowned in his pain.

William De Lancey remembered little of the days that
followed the Light Cavalry Brigade's charge into the Valley
of Death.

He came perilously near to death himself but was unaware
of it and did not know—for the surgeons had no time to tell
him—that they had amputated his right arm at the elbow.

He had been conscious of the agony but without realizing
its cause, for the 11th's young assistant surgeon, Henry Wilkin, who had returned unwounded from the charge, was
skilled and well practiced in his work, and the amputation of
an arm, the muscles of which were already half-severed, took
him only a few minutes to complete. There were other

wounds, too—lance thrusts, which had had to be sutured, and an ugly contusion on the forehead, where the Cossack's pistol had descended with savage force.

But this, as Surgeon Wilkin explained to Alexander Dunn, when he came to the forward dressing station to inquire for wounded comrades, was a blessing in disguise.

"There's a degree of amnesia in Captain De Lancey's case. We're evacuating him, with the rest of the severely injured men, to Scutari by steamer in the next few days. I'm afraid it won't be a pleasant voyage, but he, at least, won't know much about it."

And William did not. The hours he lay on the wharf at Balaclava with the other casualties passed as a bad dream; the days, in the overcrowded lower deck of a paddle-steamer, fighting its way through a vicious Black Sea storm, were a nightmare, to be endured and then forgotten.

On November 6—eleven days after the battle—he was lowered into a *caique* and rowed to a rickety landing stage outside the great, imposing bulk of the barracks hospital at Scutari. From there, after a lengthy delay, a stretcher party of Turks, indifferent to the suffering their jolting progress caused, carried him, with a score of others, into the hospital.

From outside, the hospital presented the magnificent appearance of a Sultan's palace. Inside, it was dank and dark, a maze of long, echoing corridors and vast, badly ventilated rooms, the walls cracked and streaming with damp, the floors unswept. The whole place was filthy and verminous and, as a hospital, deplorably inadequate to care for the thousands of sick and wounded men who were now crowded into it. Destitute of furniture, lacking medical supplies, drugs, comforts, and proper cooking facilities, it was also short of physicians and surgeons and staffed by untrained, overworked orderlies recruited from invalid battalions.

The arrival, a few days earlier, of Miss Florence Nightingale and her band of forty officially appointed nurses—twenty-four of whom were Catholic and Anglican sisters—had not been welcomed by the surgeon superintendent, who had informed them that he considered female nurses in a military hospital "an unwise indulgence, unfavorable to military discipline and to the recovery of the patients." They were permitted in the wards only when under the superintendence of a doctor and might not dress wounds until the patients had been examined by a member of the surgical staff.

In consequence, the sick lay in long lines, half-naked, on the floor, the majority without bedding, cholera and dysentery sufferers lying cheek by jowl with those injured in battle, and it was often several days before they were examined or had their wounds dressed by a surgeon. Miss Nightingale, although she had been appointed superintendent of the Female Nursing Establishment of the British General Hospitals in Turkey by the Secretary of War, was compelled to restrict her activities, and those of her nurses, to attempts to clean the wards and improve the diet of those who occupied them.

William's bearers had deposited him, none too gently, on a pile of reeking, verminous straw, spread out thinly over the cracked tiles of the floor. The fact that this narrow corridor was designated an officers' ward made little difference as to the conditions—they were no better than those of the other ranks in the huge, barnlike rooms beyond. There were fewer officers, that was all; but to compensate for this, there were fewer orderlies to attend to their needs. At present there was only one—a wizened, unshaven old pensioner, who had found the fresh influx of casualties from the ships too much for him. After fortifying himself in the canteen, he had crawled away to seek temporary oblivion in sleep, deaf to the pitiful pleas for water from those for whom it was his duty to care.

William was as parched as the rest, but he did not cry out, too far gone to care now whether he lived or died. He lay where the stretcher-bearers had set him down, a ten-day growth of stubble on his cheeks, the stump of his right arm wrapped in a blood-soaked bandage, and his frogged hussar jacket torn and tarnished, the sleeve cut away to expose the arm the surgeons in the field hospital had taken off. He saw it and recognized what they had done, no longer caring about that either, since he believed himself doomed.

Night fell, and he drifted into an exhausted sleep, only

occasionally disturbed by the moans and cries of those near to him.

The vision of Jenny Broome's face, which had come to him at intervals and momentarily sustained him, came again as he slept, bringing him fresh hope. But when he wakened, it was gone, and with it his hopes and the fading remnants of his courage. "Father in heaven," he whispered brokenly, "I beg thee to let me die. I have no strength to go on."

Then the sound of a slow, measured footfall reached him, and the rustling of the straw scattered about the floor of the corridor. William looked up, to glimpse the faint, flickering light of an oil lamp and, silhouetted behind it, a woman's slight form, clad in a starched white dress and apron. He watched as she bent over one of his fellow sufferers to hold a cup of water to his lips, heard her voice, speaking very softly, and as she moved on to the next in the long row, he struggled to sit up, raising himself with infinite difficulty on his one good arm and willing her to come to him.

She came at last, a woman with a plain, pale face and darkly pitying eyes, the lamp in her hand dispelling the shadows in her immediate vicinity and casting its muted light over his gaunt, unshaven face.

The cup of water was held to his parched lips, her free hand steadying him, as she set the lamp down. As if she had read his thoughts, she whispered gently, "Do not lose hope, dear young man. Pray that you should live to return to your homeland and those who love you. I shall join my prayer to yours."

And then she was gone, passing like a ghostly angel of mercy down the long, dark corridor, her lamp shining like a beacon in the foul-smelling dimness of the wretched ward and its rows of sick and suffering men.

William lay back and closed his eyes.

"Dear God," he prayed silently, "of thine infinite mercy, grant that I may live to—to return to my homeland. Please, Lord, give me the courage to live and to go back . . . to Australia!"

CHAPTER XXI

In the sprawling canvas town of Ballarat, with its polyglot population of some ten thousand, its miles of gold diggings, its crowded drinking dens, bowling alleys, and brothels, the situation was deteriorating with each day that passed. The diggers reacted with bitter fury to the police "license hunts" and the arrests that inevitably followed their biweekly invasion. Inflammatory articles in the *Ballarat Times* and the new *Melbourne Age* encouraged defiance and discontent; the Chartist *Diggers' Advocate* went even further, calling for manhood suffrage and democratic reform, with social and political rights and an end to police persecution.

Even Jasper Morgan was alarmed to observe the change when he, along with George Black and Thomas Kennedy, returned to the diggings from an unsatisfactory visit to the new Governor in Melbourne. Driving back on the Geelong road, the three emissaries passed through a main street plastered with posters, then arrived in camp to be ushered before a meeting of the reform league, attended by virtually every member of the mining community. It was convened in the open on Bakery Hill, and when Frederic Vern rose to speak from the makeshift platform, the angry murmurs that greeted him made it evident that news of the failure of their appeal to Sir Charles Hotham had preceded the deputation's return.

Vern, however, convinced of his own powers of oratory, embarked on what he intended to be a lengthy speech.

"My friends, we have won some concessions," he asserted in his strong German accent. "His Excellency appointed a commission of inquiry. The archscoundrel Bentley and his creature Farrell were tried by the Supreme Court in Melbourne, found guilty of the manslaughter of poor Jim

Scobie, and given three years apiece. Magistrate D'Ewes has been removed from the bench, and Sergeant Milne discharged from the police. The commission found them both guilty of corruption. In addition—"

"What about our lads?" a voice from the crowd demanded aggressively. "The poor devils they locked up after we burnt down the bloody Eureka Hotel? Young Broome and Andy Macintyre and Yorky Westerby? Weren't you sent to demand their release?"

"I, personally, was not," the wordy Vern was compelled to admit. "I will call on George Black, who led our deputation. Unless . . ." He glanced inquiringly at Jasper Morgan. "Unless Captain Humphrey, as secretary to our committee, wishes to speak?"

Morgan hastily refused the invitation, and Black, a sober, dignified figure in his dark frock coat, rose somewhat reluctantly to his feet.

"The Governor received us courteously," he began, as the shouts died down. "He is a well-spoken gentleman, with a fine record in the naval service—they say he distinguished himself in naval operations against Argentina a few years ago. He has something of a—well, what I can only describe as a quarterdeck manner, in that he is inclined to bark questions at one. In fact, he—"

"Did he listen to the answers?" a man at the front of the crowd interrupted. He added, amid ribald laughter from those about him, "We don't need you to tell us what New Chum Charlie did before he came here or what he's like. We had the doubtful pleasure of a visit from His bleeding Excellency when he first got here, didn't we?"

George Black smiled. "Ah, I was forgetting that," he said, without rancor. "Thank you, sir, for reminding me. And as to your question—yes, he listened. And we did all in our power, all three of us, to convince him of the injustice of the sentences imposed on the so-called ringleaders of, ah, what he was pleased to call the riot at the Eureka Hotel."

"Sure, and were you after tellin' him that swine Bentley deserved all we gave him?" an Irish voice asked pugnaciously.

"Aye, and that he was one o' the accursed Sydney ducks,

out in 'Frisco?" another put in. "A bloody murderer ten
times over?"

Other voices echoed these demands, and it was with difficulty that Timothy Hayes, as self-appointed chairman, restored the meeting to order. "Mr. Black is trying to tell you
what took place, boys. Let him speak!"

"I imparted every scrap of information I had concerning
Bentley," Black protested indignantly, losing a measure of
his calm. "And I told him—we all told him—that the police
were to blame for the fracas at the Eureka. They began it;
they fired on us—I told His Excellency all that."

"Well, did he *listen?*" the first man who had spoken repeated his question impatiently. "Or is he only giving cre-
dence to Brownlow's lies, and that rogue Milne's, like Latrobe did?"

"His Excellency's disposition seemed to be to favor the
people," Black insisted. "But he is surrounded by injudi-
cious advisers, as you rightly suggest."

"What about our poor lads in jail?" someone else asked.
"Is he goin' to release them or ain't he?"

Black started to flounder. "The great objection His Excellency entertained against your representatives was that we
were sent not to petition for the release of the prisoners but
to *demand* that they be freed. His Excellency regarded this as
lack of courtesy on our part. Indeed, gentlemen, the word
'demand' was the stumbling block. It—"

There was an outcry, and Jasper Morgan, losing patience,
raised a hand for silence and stated coldly, "The Governor
refused to commute the sentence imposed on my young
partner Angus Broome, who, as you are all aware, played no
significant part in the riot. And he was adamant as far as the
other two were concerned. I understand, however, that
Angus's father—a landowner and magistrate—will make a
personal appeal on the boy's behalf."

A chorus of enraged shouts greeted his announcement,
but, Morgan thought with satisfaction, what he had stated
publicly concerning Angus would free him of any possible
suspicion of complicity in his young partner's arrest. And
Brownlow would not talk; the police commandant had too
much to lose if he failed to keep a guard on his tongue.

The meeting continued for another two hours, but it eventually broke up in confusion, the men's fury aroused to fever pitch when Tom Kennedy told them that Governor Hotham had threatened to send in troops if there should be any repetition of the Eureka Hotel riot. Hotheads in the crowd howled down attempts by Black and Lalor to smooth things over, and there were renewed complaints of the ever-rising cost of prospectors' licenses.

"A lot of us *can't* pay what the bloody government's chargin'," a black-bearded giant yelled bitterly. "We ain't takin' out enough for our grub, let alone three quid a month to the soddin' gold commissioner! An' we gotta eat to stay alive, ain't we? We gotta eat to have the bloomin' strength to sink shafts sixty, eighty feet down an' work 'em when we have!"

"If Mr. Hotham sends troops in," one of the Americans said grimly, "he'll regret it, because then there *will* be a riot, and there are a heck of a lot more of us than there are of them. And we're armed!"

The reform league committee met briefly after the crowd had dispersed, but beyond expressing anxiety should the Governor decide to send in troops, they made no decision as to their own future action, the fiery arguments of Rafaello Carboni being countered by those of the young Catholic priest, Father Smyth, who begged for restraint.

Next day, in response to a message from Brownlow, passed on discreetly by Rede, the resident gold commissioner, Morgan rode out into the bush to meet the police commandant at their accustomed rendezvous.

"Good morning, Inspector," Morgan said uncertainly. "I understand you wanted to see me?"

"I have to confess I'm worried, Captain Humphrey," Brownlow admitted, without responding to the greeting. "The mood here is downright ugly, and it's growing worse— you can see that with half an eye, can't you? I've orders to check for unpaid or expired prospectors' licenses daily, and however little the infernal diggers like it, I'm bound to do it. What worries me is that they have arms—too bloody many of 'em have Colts and muskets."

"I'm aware of that," Morgan returned unhelpfully.

"But will they use 'em?" Brownlow asked, scowling.

"They may. I'd say they're likely to, if Governor Hotham does send the troops in."

"You think the redcoats would inflame 'em, do you?"

Morgan's answer was flat and uncompromising. "Yes, I do. I tried to tell Sir Charles Hotham that, but he paid no heed. The diggers are fomenting rebellion, he said, and must be taught a lesson."

"And are they, Captain Humphrey?"

Morgan shrugged. "Well, last night's meeting was an angry one, as no doubt you know. You had men spying on it, didn't you? Tom Kennedy said you had."

Brownlow ignored the question. "I have reinforcements coming in," he volunteered. "But they'll be mostly raw recruits. We're under strength, and I asked for more men, as a matter of urgency. If I had twice the number of mounted troopers, there'd bloody well be no need for the soldiers. But with recruits—hell, I don't know. We could be in for trouble. And mounted men can't come by steamer—they'll have to ride here."

Morgan hesitated, wondering how he could turn this information to his advantage. Trouble—if it were sufficiently serious—might cause the new Governor to continue to hold Angus Broome and his fellow rioters in prison, and it would certainly discourage the boys' father from allowing Lachlan to come back to Ballarat. More important, it would create confusion, and in that confusion he himself might be able to slip away unnoticed, claim the sale price for the gold deposited at the Treasury's assay office in Melbourne, and take passage in any ship leaving Port Phillip . . . no matter what its destination, so long as it took him out of reach of his erstwhile partners and their wealthy father. And, of course, out of reach of the members of the reform league . . .

"Do you want trouble, Inspector?" he questioned bluntly.

For a moment Brownlow seemed indecisive, as if he, too, were weighing the possible advantages against the drawbacks posed by his lack of men, but finally he nodded.

"Why not?" he suggested dryly. "I thrive on trouble. And I could get a promotion, if I deal with it expeditiously—a commendation from His Excellency, even. Whilst it's true

the diggers have arms, they don't know how to use 'em, and
my troopers do. Granted I get my reinforcements, and if the
soldiers are ordered to stand by to give me support should I
need it . . . then, yes, Captain Humphrey. Let 'em rip! But
I'd be counting on you to keep me informed of every move
the blasted diggers make—*before* they make it."

"You can count on me, Mr. Brownlow," Morgan assured
him. "Provided you can ensure that I can be safely out of
range once the trouble starts."

"A police escort to Geelong, you mean? Or right through
to Melbourne?"

"That would be a fair return for my services, I think, yes."

Brownlow mopped his moist red face with his neckerchief.
His eyes held a gleam of suspicion as he turned to study his
companion from beneath furrowed brows.

"You've got your reasons for wanting to light out, I suppose? Seeing you're on the blasted committee of the—what
do they call themselves? The Ballarat Reform League."

Jasper Morgan met his gaze unsmilingly. "Yes," he conceded. "I have. I simply cannot walk out on them at this
stage. Too many questions would be asked."

"About young Broome, for instance?" the police inspector pursued. "I don't mean the one who's safely locked up in
jail. His kid brother's the one I mean. I heard tell he was
back."

"Lachlan—here in Ballarat?" That took Morgan by surprise, and his tone was sharp. "I've not seen him."

"One of my fellows met him on the road this morning.
He'd put up at Watson's Inn—reckoned his horse was lame,
and he was waiting for the Cobb's coach."

Morgan recovered from his surprise. Lachlan's unexpected return might complicate matters, but he could find a
way to rid himself of Lachlan, too. If there was trouble, with
the police or the soldiers, it would not be too difficult to see
that Lachlan became embroiled in it. The boy had always
been friendly with the American diggers, and they had filled
him up with their republican ideas and the rubbish most of
them preached about the rights of the common man. He
would join in any battle with authority, and with his elder

brother already jailed as a rioter . . . . Morgan's expression relaxed.

"All right, Inspector Brownlow," he said easily. "You shall have your trouble. It will flare up without my lifting a finger, if the Governor does send the troops in. And if he doesn't, there will be other ways."

The troops marched in, two hours after Lachlan's arrival, and Morgan watched his forecast become reality. The advance guard, under the command of a youthful subaltern, entered Ballarat by the Geelong road with bayonets fixed, to be greeted by catcalls and jeers from the mob of diggers lining the way. They suffered no worse and reached the government camp, a mile and a half distant, without incident. But their arrival spread alarm, and shouts rose from the miners. "There are more coming! . . . Hotham's sending cannon to blow us to kingdom come! . . . It'll be martial law—they'll take our license money at the point of the bayonet, the bloody lobsterbacks!"

By the time the main body of men of the 40th Regiment, under an arrogant captain named Wise, reached the outskirts of the camp, thousands of diggers had gathered and the whole town was in a state of uproar. In an attempt to keep the peace, Peter Lalor requested a parley but was brusquely waved away, the captain informing him coldly that he did not parley with rebels.

His words, passed from man to man, inflamed the diggers even more. Before Wise knew what was happening, the mob was upon him. He was dragged from his horse, his men were swiftly scattered and overwhelmed by sheer weight of numbers, and two of their baggage wagons were overturned and their cargoes set on fire. The soldiers withdrew in disarray, carrying half a dozen of their number wounded by stones and brickbats, to take refuge in the government camp with the advance guard and Brownlow's police. Brownlow persuaded them to remain there, holding themselves in reserve, and promising that his troopers would restore order. "We'll give 'em till tomorrow morning to simmer down," he decided. "My reinforcements may be here by then, and that will put me in a stronger position, because they'll be

mounted. Licenses are due for renewal tomorrow. I'll send
in a strong party and make as many arrests as I can, just to
show the rebellious swine what's what."

But the diggers were in no mood to simmer down, as
Jasper Morgan observed with increasing satisfaction. They
had won an unexpected victory over the soldiers, and the
fact that they had done so renewed their confidence. At
Morgan's suggestion, several hundred of the more militant
of the men gathered outside Peter Lalor's tent, demanding
that another meeting be called at once. "A council of war,
Mr. Lalor," one of them asserted gravely. "That's what it will
have to be, whatever Father Smyth says. If the bloody Governor dubs us rebels, then so be it—he shall have his rebellion.
We've stood enough."

Lalor was reluctant to give his agreement, but Morgan,
sensing his indecision, urged him to comply. "The men
won't rest until you give them what they ask," he insisted.
"And it's surely best if we are organized and under proper
leadership. A stone-throwing mob will achieve nothing."

Vern, Hayes, and Carboni backed up his argument, and a
raid by the angry Captain Wise to recover his baggage wagons decided the issue. Shots were exchanged, Wise ha-
rangued the diggers and again accused them of planning
rebellion, and the harm was done. Despite misgivings on the
part of Lalor and some other members of the committee, a
meeting was called for the following day. As before, virtually
the whole camp attended, the hotheads much in evidence,
their anger fueled by a second raid, at dawn, by police and
troops, which had resulted in a score of arrests and a charge
by the mounted troopers.

Fiery speeches from Rafaello Carboni and Frederic Vern
won thunderous applause.

"I say," Vern concluded his address, "that every miner
here should burn his license and that we pledge ourselves on
oath to do so here and now. And that we swear to unite and
protect any man whom the police attempt to arrest for having no license. Is that agreed?"

There were few dissenting voices, and Lalor's plea for
time in which to renew negotiations with Commissioner
Rede for the release of the prisoners taken that morning was

howled down. Morgan did not speak; with young Lachlan Broome at his side, he was content to leave the shouting to others, satisfied that the boy had been caught up in the frenzied excitement and was giving his pledge with the rest.

Bonfires were lit; although some of the men drifted away, most of them took out their licenses and gleefully consigned them to the flames. It was dawn when the last piece of government vellum had been destroyed, and when a squadron of mounted police made their appearance to conduct a license hunt, they were greeted with catcalls and volleys of stones.

The youthful Commissioner Rede attempted to read the Riot Act, but he, too, was howled down. "There is not a man here who has a license, Mr. Rede," Lalor informed him gravely.

"You are in breach of the law," Rede threatened, "for which you are liable to arrest and imprisonment."

"Very well, sir," Lalor challenged. "Arrest us. The whole camp will surrender to you. All or none, sir."

The gold commissioner paled, losing his bombast. "You must know that I do not have a sufficient force to hold all of you in arrest, Mr. Lalor." He flinched before the angry faces and menacing attitude of the men surrounding him and reined back his horse.

"Then, sir," Lalor answered levelly, "I beg you to retire. You will be in no danger from us if you will do so and take the police troopers with you. I myself will escort you. You may wish to release the prisoners you took this morning—on bail, if you require it."

Commissioner Rede admitted defeat. He agreed to bail his prisoners, and with Lalor and two others of the committee walking beside him, he left the camp to the jeers of the men standing by—the police troopers, commanded by a sub-inspector, following sullenly at his heels. Brownlow, Morgan observed cynically, had not seen fit to accompany his men—a prudent decision on his part. Clearly, he was waiting for his reinforcements.

"You have not heard the end of this, Lalor," the commissioner found the courage to say, when they reached the edge of the miners' campsite. "You have committed an act of open rebellion. I shall inform His Excellency the Governor, and you need have no doubt he will at once send a large force of troops to restore order here. The penalty for rebellion against Her Majesty's government, sir, is death."

Peter Lalor released his hold on the bridle of the commissioner's horse. He drew himself up and returned, with dignity, "We are not in rebellion against Her Majesty's government, sir, I give you my word. All we are asking is justice—an end to excessive license fees and police persecution, and the release of three of our people, who have been wrongfully convicted. We are ready at any time, Mr. Rede, to send a delegation to wait on His Excellency Governor Hotham in order to put our case to him. If there is armed conflict, it will be of your making. But if we are attacked, we shall defend ourselves."

"I will see you hanged, Lalor," Rede retorted furiously. "You and those who support your outrageous demands! You are a traitor, sir, to your Queen and your country, and by heaven, you shall take the consequences—that I promise you!"

Motioning his police escort to follow him, he kicked his horse into a canter and made off.

Lalor said wryly, "Well, it would seem that we have burnt our boats, as well as our licenses, in a vain quest for justice, my friends. Now there's nothing left to us but to resort to force of arms, I fear. So we had better call another meeting."

Studying his face, Morgan became aware of a subtle change in the man who had hitherto preached restraint and negotiation and deplored violence. Peter Lalor was roused to a deep, abiding anger; he would fight, and because of his intelligence, his courage, and his genuine sense of grievance, he would prove a formidable opponent.

At a hasty rendezvous with Brownlow, Jasper Morgan expressed his fears, which were in no way placated when the police commandant pooh-poohed them.

"My reinforcements will be here in a few hours, Captain Humphrey, and Captain Wise, of the military, is hopping mad at the way his soldiers were set on by that blasted mob of rebels. *He's* sent for reinforcements, too. The bloody diggers won't last five minutes against us, once we get organized—you can take my word for it."

Morgan shrugged. "I shouldn't be too sure of that, Mr. Brownlow. The diggers are really up in arms, and they mean business, believe me."

"There ain't that many of 'em," Brownlow countered, refusing to be convinced. "A hell of a lot moved out of Bendigo and Castlemaine and even Beechworth, didn't they, when the malcontents there were shown what's what? It'll be the same here. I think you'll find that support for their precious reform league will crumble, when the sensible fellows realize what's afoot. They'll light out for places like Mount Korong and Omeo, on the upper Murray, where they know there'll be less chance of us getting at 'em. You know what they're like—it'll be up-stakes and on their way when it comes to the crunch. They'll be a pushover if they do take up arms against us."

That might be so, Morgan was forced to concede. Of late, there had been an exodus from Ballarat, caused partly by fear of the coming confrontation, but mainly as a result of stories of richer strikes being made elsewhere. The fortune hunters were always susceptible to such tales, always ready to move on in the hope of easier pickings, and they moved in their hundreds, virtually overnight, taking their tents and their wagons with them.

He repeated his shrug. "They've called another meeting for tonight. That will decide whether they fight or run—but I still think the majority will fight."

"Aye, but how many?" Brownlow sneered.

"I can't tell you that yet. At least five hundred, maybe twice as many. They all burnt their licenses, you know," Morgan cautioned uneasily.

"More fools them," Brownlow retorted with unconcealed contempt, "because they'll all have to pay up for 'em again or face being arrested." He spit on the dry, sandy ground at his feet and climbed once more into his saddle, jerking his horse's head from the sparse grass it had been cropping. "Come on, you big brute, you've eaten enough." He tipped his cap at Morgan in farewell and added, before starting to move away, "You'll tell me what happens at the meeting, Captain Humphrey?"

"I'll tell you," Morgan assured him. He mounted his own horse, frowning. "I fancy," he called after the retreating police commandant, "that I'll be on the move pretty soon after it, Mr. Brownlow. And I shall expect you to keep your promise."

"You may have to earn your escort to Melbourne," Brownlow called back over his shoulder. "I reckon you'll have to ride with us, if it comes to a showdown." He put his horse into a canter without waiting for Morgan's reply.

Vaguely uneasy, Morgan waited until Brownlow was out of sight before heading back to the camp. Much would depend on the outcome of the diggers' stand, he thought. Certainly, if they made a stand, it would cause all the confusion he could possibly want; but if he were seen to be on Brownlow's side, riding with the police, he would be branded a traitor by the members of the reform league, with consequences too hideous to bear thinking about.

On the other hand, he dared not ally himself openly with a bunch of rebels in defiance of government authority—that would be to risk ruin, if not his life. Morgan drew a long, apprehensive breath as he trotted through the closely growing screen of blackwood and stringybark trees, to emerge by the gravel pits and the road that led to the government camp, with its jail and its fortified stone buildings. He would attend tonight's meeting, he decided, since failure to do so would undoubtedly arouse suspicion; but after that, if it came to a battle, he would seize the first chance that presented itself to slip away—even without the promised police escort. All he need do was to ensure that young Lachlan Broome threw in his lot with the diggers—and that should present little difficulty.

The meeting was attended by fewer than half of those who had previously pledged their support to the reform league, many pointedly staying by their claims or in their tents. In marked contrast with previous gatherings, it was sober and well ordered, speeches from the platform by Vern, Carboni, and George Black being listened to without interruption, considered carefully, and then voted on. And the vote was for action, as outlined in the speeches.

Vern, claiming previous military experience in Austria, put himself up for election as commander in chief, but by an almost unanimous vote Peter Lalor was elected in his stead. The young engineer took his stand beneath a blue flag, adorned with the stars of the Southern Cross, and invited those present to take a solemn oath to "stand truly by each other and fight to defend the rights and liberties of all."

Although many had already drifted away, a hard core stayed to take the oath, following which the committee gathered in a store tent on Bakery Hill to organize resistance to the attack they knew must come.

"Let it be understood, gentlemen," Peter Lalor warned them solemnly, looking up from the rifle that lay across his knees, his bearded face grimly set, "we take up arms for no other purpose than for our defense. The battle is for our liberty and independence and to right the wrongs that we, as honest, hardworking men, have for so long endured at the hands of a corrupt authority. Let us proceed at once with our preparations to defend ourselves."

By first light the following morning—Friday, December 1 —an area of about an acre on the Eureka lode had been enclosed with piled-up mining props, building material, and timber. Close to five hundred miners were hard at work, improving and strengthening the barricades. A German blacksmith, working with half a score of eager helpers, began the task of fashioning pikeheads, and those who possessed firearms set about cleaning them and sorting out supplies of powder and shot. Thomas Kennedy set off for Creswick to enlist the support of the diggers there, while others formed themselves into companies and drilled in front of the stockade or went out in foraging parties to gather weapons and commandeer stocks of food.

In a last and somewhat despairing attempt to avert conflict, Father Smyth and George Black led a deputation to the commissioner, demanding that he keep his promise to release the recently arrested men on bail, which he had failed to do, and give an undertaking that the license hunts should cease. Lachlan Broome was also a member of the deputa-

tion, and he returned to report glumly that Commissioner
Rede had rejected these demands.

Black nodded in somber agreement. "He's singing a different tune from the last time we talked to him. Very cocky,
he was. 'These men were taken in riotous assembly,' he said,
'and will be taken before a magistrate. I cannot interfere
with the course of justice.' Young Lachie spoke to him as
nice as you please, but he just ranted on that our wanting the
licenses abolished was a cloak to cover a damned socialist
revolution and he had his duty to do. Then he told us to get
out. We're going to have to stand and fight, Peter, or we'll be
back where we were, with that miserable scoundrel Brownlow arresting anyone he has a mind to. We've no choice."

There was an angry murmur of agreement from the
others, and Rafaello Carboni exclaimed excitedly, "We'll
give as good as we get, by heaven we will! We have fifty men
with rifles or muskets, the Californian Rangers have revolvers, and Jim McGill, who is a West Pointer, is leading them,
two hundred strong."

"Aye," Timothy Hayes agreed, "and we've a division of
Irish pikemen, led by Mike Hanrahan. Some o' them have
muskets, and there'll be the lads from Creswick, when they
get here. Brownlow's bullies and old Wise's redcoats will
have their work cut out to dislodge us, so they will!"

Then, to Jasper Morgan's dismay, came the question he
had dreaded. It came from George Black, in his accustomed
quiet, polite tone. "And what of Captain Humphrey, if I may
ask? You held commissioned rank in Her Majesty's Foot
Guards, did you not, sir, and have in your possession a
medal for valor in Spain? Should you not be in command of
a unit of our volunteers, instructing them in how to conduct
themselves?"

Morgan's cheeks drained of color. But he swiftly recovered his composure. "I've not been approached, George,"
he answered. "And it is a long time since I followed the
profession of arms. But naturally, if I am needed, I shall be
only too ready to make myself available."

He was saved from having to make good his offer by news
that some four hundred diggers from Creswick had come in,
drenched to the skin by a storm they had encountered in the

hills, and it appeared they were without food, dry clothing, or arms. Led by Peter Lalor, the committee left the store tent to welcome them.

Alone there, Morgan wiped the sweat from his brow, his mouth suddenly dry. The time had come, he knew, for him to make his getaway, if he did not want to be dragged into the coming battle. Brownlow would have to do without his services as informant; he would leave young Lachlan to fight and, at the first opportunity, slip out of the diggers' stronghold. There were a number of men who, like Kennedy, had absented themselves in quest of supporters from neighboring fields or of arms and provisions for the stockade.

Despite the prominent position he occupied as a member of the reform league's committee, if he chose his moment carefully, escape should present no real problem. And the gold—a fortune in gold—awaited him at the Treasury in Melbourne. It would be his, and his alone, when he went, with his receipt, to claim it. . . . Morgan found himself smiling as he moved about the defenses of the stockade and waited for an opportunity to run.

The opportunity came next evening, when Tom Kennedy's volunteers from Creswick, finding neither food nor water in the stockade, left in a body to go in search of what they needed. Their example was followed by some of the Ballarat men, many of whom, however, progressed no farther than the nearest grogshop, where they paused to refresh themselves from the strenuous exertions of the day. Lachlan was on sentry duty, and satisfied that the boy would not desert his post, Morgan quickly packed what he could into his saddlebag and set off for the Geelong road.

He had covered only a few hundred yards when a huge figure loomed up in front of him and he found himself looking into the barrel of a leveled Colt.

"Not so fast, Captain Humphrey," the owner of the Colt warned. In the dimness, Morgan stared at him in frank bewilderment, finally recognizing him as a miner named Goodenough, who was more often drunk than sober.

"Don't be a damned fool, Goodenough!" he exclaimed impatiently. "Out of my way!"

"*Trooper* Goodenough," the big man corrected. "Of the

police." He grinned unpleasantly and put out a massive hand to grasp Morgan's rein. "Inspector Brownlow said you'd try to light out, and he told me to bring you in if you did. Are you coming quietly, or do I have to make you?"

Morgan's jaw dropped; he attempted bluster, but the trooper merely continued to grin at him, and the Colt was still aimed at his heart. At last he asked resignedly, "Where do you want me to go?"

"Why, to the government camp, of course—to Inspector Brownlow. And maybe we'd better walk, all friendly-like, just in case anybody spots us. Get down off that horse, Captain Humphrey, will you? That's better." The supposed drunk laughed at his captive's discomfiture as Morgan sullenly dismounted. He added, as they fell into step together, the horse between them, "Played my part pretty well, didn't I? You weren't Brownlow's only spy. I've been reporting to him, too, see, 'cause he didn't trust you."

Morgan lapsed into angry silence. On reaching the government camp, they found Brownlow at the jail, the camp a fortress, and the troops and police standing to under arms.

The police commandant dismissed Goodenough with a brief word of praise and a whispered injunction that Morgan did not hear. When the man had gone, Brownlow waved Morgan to a chair in the small, badly lit office.

"You did not see fit to tell me that the blasted diggers' stockade was virtually undefended, did you, Captain Humphrey?" he accused coldly. When Morgan did not answer, he went on, with an abrupt change of tone. "I had an idea you'd try to make a run for it before things came to a head, and without waiting for the escort to Melbourne I promised you. And that don't suit me, you know. It don't suit me at all, because *I'm* counting on acting as your escort. But of course I can't leave here till we've settled the diggers' hash—not that it'll take long. We're going to attack them in a couple of hours' time, if it's of any interest to you."

"What in God's name do you mean, Brownlow?" Morgan flung at him. "And why in hell should you want to be my escort?" But the ugly truth was starting to dawn on him, and he cursed his own stupidity for having put his trust in a rogue.

"I worked out what your game was awhile ago," Brownlow said. He leaned back in his chair, his thick lips twisted into a parody of a smile. "That gold my men took to the Treasury for you—for you and your partners, I mean—there was a hell of a lot more than you let on, wasn't there? More than those Broome lads ever knew about, and you weren't intending to give them their share, were you?"

Shocked, Morgan could find no words to answer him, and the policeman's smile widened into one of genuine amusement. "No," he said, answering his own question. "Of course you didn't mean to share it . . . and I've only just managed to find out what it's worth. Well, Captain bloody Humphrey, you're going to share it after all. You're going to share it with *me*. When tonight's business is finished and those Chartist swine in their stockade have been given a taste of cold steel, you and I are going to Melbourne, to the Treasury, with your receipt and your proof of identity. Do you get my meaning?"

His hands clenching into impotent fists, Morgan stared back helplessly, conscious that he had been deceived, out-witted, and driven into a corner by the man he had for so long considered to be his own inferior in intellect. And . . . yes, in cunning. There was now, he recognized, nothing he could do save allow Brownlow to call the shots and appear to acquiesce in his demands—until a chance to escape from him should arise. And perhaps it would. Much could happen in the next few hours.

He lifted his trembling hands in an elaborate gesture of surrender. "I understand," he managed, controlling himself with difficulty. "I'll do whatever you want. I'll share the gold with you. We'll go to Melbourne together when this is over." He hesitated, watching the other man's face. "And now? What do you propose to do with me?"

Relishing his triumph, Brownlow laughed aloud.

"Well," he observed gloatingly, "I'll give you a choice, shall I, eh? You can ride with my troopers when we go in to drive your former friends out of their miserable stockade . . . and take a chance that they'll spot you. Aye, and maybe kill you for betraying them. Or I'll lock you up here in my jail. Either way, I want your receipt from the Treasury."

Jasper Morgan's face drained of its last vestige of color. His life was at stake, he knew, whichever choice he made. If he decided to stay in the comparative safety of the jail, Brownlow could accuse him of rebellion and have him hanged with the rest of the reform league's leaders when they were defeated—as clearly they would be, with so few of them left to defend the stockade they had so painstakingly erected. But—— The sweat broke out on his brow, and his hands were suddenly clammy. If he rode with the police and the troops, he would have at least a slender chance of survival, perhaps of escape, if he could contrive to make a run for it in the darkness and head for the hills, for Mount Korong or Omeo. That would mean starting again, it was true, but there was always the hope of a rich strike. The Omeo lode was said to be promising. . . . He made a great effort to regain his lost composure.

He would *have* to escape. Whatever Brownlow said, once possessed of the Treasury receipt, the rogue had no intention of going with him to Melbourne or sharing the gold he had deposited there. He would be kept in jail. . . .

"Well?" Brownlow prompted. He took out his pocket watch and glanced at it pointedly. "Time marches on, Humphrey. Which is it to be?"

"I'll ride with you," Morgan gritted, his lips stiff with contained fury.

"Very well." The police commandant rose to his feet, his hand outheld. "The Treasury receipt, *if* you please."

There was no help for it. Shaking with the intensity of his feelings, Jasper Morgan took the precious scrap of paper from his breast pocket and put it into the hand of his tormentor.

Brownlow flashed him a pleased smile. "Thank you," he said, with cynical courtesy. He thrust the receipt into his own breast pocket and opened the door. Goodenough was waiting in the outer office.

"All right, Captain Humphrey," Brownlow said, "you can go now—but not far. Remember, you'll be under my eye. If you run, I'll brand you a fugitive from justice and have you hunted down. Either way, I wouldn't stake a lot on your chances."

Outside, a grinning Goodenough mounted up, then motioned Morgan to take the rein of his own animal.

"It's off to the barracks for us, for a little nap," he said, then added, in what purported to be a conspiratorial whisper, "There's fewer than two hundred diggers in the stockade, Captain Humphrey, and most of 'em are asleep. The rest are all out foraging—or drinking themselves footless! I reckon by tomorrow morning you'll find you chose the right side after all."

Morgan ignored the thrust. He climbed stiffly into his saddle, feeling for the stock of his rifle. The rifle was gone, but the Colt he had purchased from one of the Californians was still in his saddlebag. He took it out and slipped it into his waistband, unobserved.

CHAPTER XXII

Luke had been in Melbourne for six long and frustrating weeks before necessity drove him to volunteer for service with the Victoria Mounted Police.

With the quadrupling of its population as a result of the gold rush and the steady influx of men from the diggings who had struck it rich and wanted only to spend their fortunes on drink and women, the once small and peaceful settlement had become the worst of boomtowns. To Luke, it seemed almost indistinguishable from San Francisco, with its gambling and drinking dens, its muddy, unpaved streets, roistering inhabitants, and sky-high prices. Substantial brick buildings were springing up, owned by speculators and erected by the labor of disillusioned and unsuccessful diggers—lavish restaurants and hotels, which charged exorbitantly for the services they provided; the nucleus of a railway system; banks sailing on a wave of sudden prosperity, thanks to the gold they had purchased; and a veritable host of houses of prostitution.

The Canvas Town, as it was known, provided squalid accommodation for new arrivals. Lacking street lighting, passable roads, and sanitation, it nonetheless demanded high prices for those unfortunate enough to have nowhere else to go. Luke sampled its hospitality for the first two weeks and then gravitated to a dirty wooden hut near Liardet's Beach, with no heating and scant protection from the rain, surrounded by piles of undisposed garbage and overrun by rats and seemingly ownerless pigs, hens, and dogs.

But he found the *Banshee*, almost unrecognizable in her new, sad role as a hulk doing service as a rooming house, and learned, at last, from her new owner that the man he sought—now going by the name of Captain Humphrey—

had equipped himself for the gold diggings and was believed to be in Bendigo or Ballarat.

He would have set off at once in pursuit, but even while he was engaged in bargaining for a horse and supplies, his much depleted savings had been stolen from him one black dark night by a pair of footpads, whose faces he did not see and whose identities he could only guess at. Afterward he had sought employment, ready to tackle any job, however menial, in order to raise the money he desperately needed, and for the next three weeks worked as a dishwasher at the Criterion Hotel, in Collins Street, owned by a fellow American by the name of Moss. It was an affluent establishment, popular with all his countrymen, at which the new Governor and his lady were several times entertained as guests of the elegantly dressed proprietor and where another enterprising young American named George Train was frequently to be seen, when not engaged in the profitable business of running coaches to the goldfields.

Luke marveled at the commercial success they enjoyed but did not envy them, his search for Jasper Morgan ever uppermost in his mind. He managed to save enough to buy a ticket on one of Train and Cobb's coaches to Ballarat, but later that day made the mistake of displaying it in the squalid eating house to which hunger had driven him.

"I'm on my way to the field at last," Luke told the proprietor, unable to hide his jubilation, "and I'm booked on Mr. Cobb's coach, too! All the way to Ballarat!"

A pretty but shabbily dressed young woman, whom he had noticed with no more than casual interest as he had passed her table, rose suddenly to her feet with a strangled cry. Gathering her threadbare shawl about her shoulders, she abandoned her meal and came to stand in front of him. Her eyes, Luke saw, were moist, her smile by contrast warm and ingratiating, and she plucked nervously at her shawl, baring shapely shoulders and disclosing more of her swelling bosom than strict propriety normally permitted.

Embarrassed by her proximity and the attitude she had adopted, Luke stood up. He asked uncertainly, "Can I be of service to you, miss?" Young women of easy virtue thronged the Melbourne streets, he was aware, but their quarry were the diggers who had struck it rich, and few spared so much as a glance for those who, like himself, were patently too impoverished to show them the good time they were seeking. He shuffled his feet awkwardly. "I don't have any money. I've not been to the goldfields yet. I—"

She cut him short. "Ah, now, 'tis not your money I'm wanting, and don't I know what it's like not to have even a farthing to be made!" Her voice had an Irish lilt, musical and beguiling, and as if by instinct sizing him up, she swiftly drew the shawl closer about her, hiding the charms she had—seemingly inadvertently—exposed. "But you could do me the greatest service any man ever did, should you have a mind to, and that's God's truth, so it is." She held out her hand. "I'm Patsy O'Dowd—Mrs. O'Dowd, wife to Seamus Michael O'Dowd. May I—" She gestured to the empty chair facing Luke. "May I join you, mister?"

It would have been churlish to refuse. Luke accepted the proffered hand and, forcing a smile, introduced himself and pulled out the chair for her. "What of your meal, Mrs. O'Dowd? You're not finished eating—"

"Ah, 'twas just tea and a mess of potato stew," Patsy O'Dowd assured him indifferently. "I've no appetite. A body can't eat when she's sick to the heart with worry, can she, now?" She seated herself, her big, tear-filled dark eyes meeting Luke's gaze confidingly. "You've the look of a good, kindly young fellow, so you have, Mr. Murphy. I was after noticing that when I seen you come in, and I made up me mind then and there. 'Ask that young fellow to help,' I says to meself. 'He'll not refuse when he hears the terrible trouble I'm in.' And seeing you have the one thing I'm in desperate need of, Mr. Murphy—why, the Lord and His Blessed Mother surely sent you here this night!"

Luke stared back at her uncomprehendingly, all his chivalrous instincts aroused by her evident distress. She was sobbing now, mopping vainly at her eyes as the tears fell unchecked.

"Please," he besought her, "don't upset yourself. How can I help? I've nothing, like I told you, ma'am, I—"

"You've a ticket on the coach to Ballarat," Patsy O'Dowd reminded him, "and I've not the money to buy one. 'Tis a

matter of life and death, Mr. Murphy. I *must* get there."
Before Luke could protest that for him, too, getting to Ballarat was of primary importance, she had launched into her
tale . . . and a moving one it was, described in graphic
detail in her lilting Irish voice.

Her husband, it seemed, had met mysterious injury in a
fall into one of the deep mine shafts in the Eureka lode at
Ballarat. His leg was broken, they had told her, and maybe
his spine as well. His need of her to nurse him back to health
was dire and urgent. But—the tears came again, threatening
to overwhelm her—short of selling her body, she had no
means of making the journey to his side.

"I'm a good woman and a faithful wife, Mr. Murphy," she
added pathetically. "But sure, if the price for your coach
ticket is that I betray me marriage vows, 'tis not too high a
price to pay, I swear it! Just so I can get to poor Seamus,
there's nothing I'd not do, so help me God!"

His conscience pricking him, Luke gave her his precious
ticket, assuring her hastily that he would set no price on it.
Patsy O'Dowd called the blessing of the Holy Mother of God
and all the saints on his head and bent to plant a moistly
grateful kiss on his cheek. Then she left him, a whiff of a
cheap perfume in his nostrils and the first, unhappy dawning
of doubt in his mind.

The doubt was turned into certainty when he went to
settle his check for the meal.

"Up to her old tricks, Patsy was," the old proprietor said
gruffly. "Took you for your coach ticket, did she? Pah,
should've warned you—but truth to tell, I figured you had
more sense. She's been wanting to get to the goldfields for
quite a while, has Patsy. Well, now she's got her wish. Leastways she'll not trouble me no more, so that's an ill wind! You
could report her to the police, if you've a mind to, but she'll
be well on her way before they can lay hands on her."

Luke took this advice, and a not very sympathetic police
sergeant confirmed that he had been duped.

"We can't pick her up just on your say-so. She'll be on the
coach with a valid ticket—no reason to pull her in for that.
But if you're so anxious to get to Ballarat, lad, there's one
way that won't cost you a penny. You could sign on as a

police trooper. There's trouble brewing there." The sergeant eyed Luke's tanned face and now well-muscled body with a speculative smile, taking in his worn clothing and the stained moleskin trousers. "Been at the diggings before, ain't you?"

"Yes," Luke confirmed. "In California and in New South Wales, Sergeant."

"Then you'll know the way things are. An unruly lot, the diggers, bent on making trouble for the government. Some say they're revolutionaries, tryin' to set up a bloody republic here. Are you one o' that kind, lad?" The question was grave.

"No," Luke assured him. "I'm not. But I want to go to Ballarat. There's a man there I have to find. He . . . that is, I was in partnership with him in California. He calls himself —well, his name is Humphrey, Captain Humphrey."

"Humphrey?" The sergeant's eyes narrowed. "Ah, now there's talk about a Captain Humphrey—they call him Jonathan Humphrey. Seems they've formed what they're pleased to call a Ballarat Reform League, and he's in it up to his neck. Come here a few weeks back, with a bloody deputation, to try and persuade His Excellency the Governor to release three o' their men sentenced for leadin' a riot." He went into brief details, still watching Luke's face, as if uncertain whether or not to trust him. "They went to Toorak House, His Excellency's official residence, making all kinds o' demands, they were. I know, I was on duty there, as it happens, and I seen an' heard 'em. This Humphrey, now, the one you're lookin' to find—is he a gentlemanly kind o' cuss, Welshman by his accent, with a dark mustache?"

Luke was conscious of a surge of excitement.

"Yes, sir, that's him. You say you saw him when he called on the Governor?"

"Large as life, lad. Him and a big, surly Scotchman name o' Kennedy and a decent enough feller they called Black. Old Quarterdeck—" The sergeant stopped himself, swearing beneath his breath. "That is, His Excellency, he gave 'em short shrift, an' quite right, too, in my humble opinion. So they went off back to Ballarat and started to stir up trouble." He hesitated, again searching Luke's face. "Why do you want to find Captain Humphrey, lad? You said you was his partner in California. Does that mean he's a friend o' yours?"

Luke hesitated in his turn, wondering whether to reveal the truth. He decided on the half-truth he had fallen back on before. "No, Sergeant, he's no friend of mine. He robbed me of my strike in California."

"Ah, then, that figures, don't it?" The sergeant frowned. "We're looking for recruits for the police—they're sendin' for reinforcements for Ballarat, and there's not that many decent lads as are willin' to volunteer. Plenty o' bad types, ex-convicts like, there always is. Can you ride a horse, boy?"

"Yes," Luke assured him. His excitement increased. It would be one way of getting to Ballarat, he told himself, and . . . for God's sake, a pleasant change from dishwashing.

"Got any references, have you? Character references, I mean?"

"I . . . ." Luke considered the question. "I suppose Mr. Moss of the Criterion would give me a character, Sergeant. I've been working for him. Or there's Captain Claus Van Buren. He's known me longer—I came out from San Francisco in his clipper schooner, the *Dolphin.* And he married my—that is, he married my sister two months ago, in Sydney."

The sergeant's expression relaxed. He said, beaming, "Ah, now you're talkin', lad! If you're related to Captain Van Buren, no need to question you further. Very well respected is Captain Van Buren." He shuffled among the papers on his desk and found a form, which he pushed across for Luke to read. "Terms o' enlistment as a trooper in the mounted police—read it through. If you want to volunteer, I can attest you right here an' now."

Luke glanced at the form without taking it in. "Could I be sure of being posted to Ballarat, sir?"

"Aye, pretty sure, if you make out all right in the trainin'." The sergeant searched for quill and ink, eyeing Luke with kindly, approving eyes now. "I can put it on your papers that you're volunteerin' for Ballarat, and it's for Ballarat we need the men at the present time. You'll get there, lad—I can almost guarantee it." He added with wry mockery, "And I reckon you've learned a lesson, ain't you? You won't be fallin' for no more soft-spoken young women with hard-luck stories, will you?"

"No, sir," Luke assured him, reddening. "I won't." He signed the enlistment forms, and the old sergeant swore him in.

Next day he reported to the mounted police depot, was given a cursory medical examination, issued with a smart blue uniform, a saber, a carbine, and a horse, and, following a fortnight of training, found himself on the way to Ballarat with some thirty others, as reinforcements for the goldfield police, under the command of Senior Inspector Brownlow.

His comrades, Luke quickly discovered, were anything but the "decent lads" the sergeant had considered desirable. There was a hard core of older men who had served time in the notorious prisons of Van Diemen's Land—now officially called Tasmania, they told him, and spit as they did so. These men were tough, hard-bitten individuals who had taken part in battles with the diggers in other goldfields and had little sympathy for them.

"A bunch of bloody malcontents and revolutionaries," a balding, heavily bearded trooper asserted. "And the damned Yankees are to blame for much of it. Came out here to spread their republican ideas, as well as make their sodding fortunes. And the Scotchmen are nearly as bad—Chartists, they call themselves, stupid puritanical bastards, every last one of 'em. But the Irish are the worst o' the lot— treachery's in their blood, and because they're priest-ridden Roman Catholics, they go along with the Italians and the French. They even had their revolutionary flag flying in Bendigo when we went in to sort them out—the diggers' banner, they called it. And it was red, with a crossed pick and shovel, a miner's cradle, and a kangaroo." He laughed unpleasantly. "We burned it for 'em, and they caved in, once we'd arrested the ringleaders. It'll be the same in Ballarat, you'll see, once they cotton on to the fact that we mean business!"

Listening to him as they trotted slowly along the dusty, rutted road, Luke wondered how Jasper Morgan had come to involve himself in the diggers' cause. It was out of character; Morgan cared little for anyone but himself—although,

perhaps, they had appealed to his vanity when they had
elected him to their reform committee. He had been exces-
sively vain about his gold medal, purportedly awarded to
him by the Queen of Spain. . . .

Luke learned that two or three of the new recruits had, like
himself, been in the goldfields, though they were careful not
to dwell on their past activities; others were newly arrived
immigrants from England, whose funds, like his own, had
run out; and there were four so-called officer cadets, of good
family, who kept to themselves and offered no reason for
their presence in the police ranks. But when any of the four
deigned to talk to the troopers, it was to boast callously of
being determined to teach the damned diggers a lesson.

"They should be hanged if they take up arms," the elder
of the four opined. "Hanged as traitors—they deserve nothing else. Let's hope the Governor doesn't weaken when the
swine are put on trial, or the next thing that will happen is
that they'll march on Melbourne under their infernal red
flag!" He added, clearly shocked, "I heard that at one of the
camps they hoisted the American flag above the Union Jack.
If that's not treason, I don't know what is!"

Only the sub-inspector in command of the reinforcement
squadron appeared to Luke to have an unprejudiced view of
the situation they were about to face. A thin gray-haired
officer named Martin, he had joined the police ten years
before, having served as a sergeant in one of Sydney's garrison regiments, including a year's duty on Norfolk Island, of
which he adamantly refused to speak. But he expressed his
opinion of the conflict with the diggers plainly enough, one
evening when they bivouacked on the roadside and Luke
found him by himself, moodily drinking tea.

"Mine's not a popular view, lad," he confessed. "Not with
this lot, anyway, so I don't air it all that often. But you've
been a digger, so you'll maybe understand. First off, I don't
reckon they're aiming to start a revolution. They say they
want justice, an end to the license charges—which *are* too
high for those that never strike pay dirt—and no more police
license hunts. I think truly that's all most of them *do* want.
The police raids are calculated to stir up resentment—I've
seen that for myself—and too many of the officers abuse

their power, while at the same time some of them are corrupt and they take bribes. I won't name names, but I know some whose moral standards don't bear investigation."

Martin sighed and set down his pannikin.

"Gold has brought prosperity to this state, real prosperity that will last, even after all the gold has been dug up. It's given the country a healthy influx of immigrants, many of whom will stay and develop the outback and clear the bush to grow crops and raise livestock. That's to the ultimate good, isn't it? And the diggers work hard for their gold— backbreaking work, in shocking conditions very often—you know that better than I do, Murphy. All right, so too many of them cheat and avoid paying for their licenses, but I swear it's because they don't have the means to pay. A fairer system would be to put a tax on the gold, so that the ones who strike it rich pay for the privilege, while the others go on searching without charge. But . . ." The sub-inspector rose heavily to his feet. "The authorities don't ask my opinion, so I just do what I'm ordered to and keep my mouth shut. But I can tell you, lad, I'm not looking forward to what's ahead of us at Ballarat. Men will be killed and wounded, and the poor devils of diggers haven't a chance in hell against the force we can send against them." He eyed Luke thoughtfully. "Sergeant Fairfax mentioned you were looking for one of the reform league committee. Friend of yours, is he?"

"No," Luke denied. He hesitated, uncertain whether or not he dare divulge the real reason for his search.

Martin said gruffly, "I told you, lad, I know how to keep my mouth shut. Don't tell me if you'd rather not, but it's possible I could help."

"He's going by the name of Captain Humphrey," Luke said. "But his real name is Jasper Morgan. Back in California, where we were partners, he robbed my brother and me of every ounce of gold we'd worked for, and . . . well, it cost my brother his life."

"I see. Well, I can understand why you're anxious to find the rogue. All the same, Murphy lad, take care." He laid a hand on Luke's arm. "Don't take the law into your own hands, if you've any sense. Turn the fellow in. Remember, you're a police trooper now. Your duty is to uphold the law and see justice done. You swore an oath, didn't you?"

Without waiting for Luke's reply, Martin turned on his heel and left him. Lying under the stars, a blanket wrapped about him, it was a long time before Luke slept. Among the conflicting thoughts that came to torment him was the thought of Elizabeth Tempest, whom he had left behind him, months ago, at her parents' farm in the Blue Mountains of New South Wales. He had promised her he would come back, he recalled, his conscience tormenting him. But there would be no return for him if he found Jasper Morgan and— as Martin had expressed it—if he then took the law into his own hands and killed his brother's murderer.

At her Aunt Abigail's invitation, Elizabeth Tempest was spending a few weeks in Sydney. She had been glad enough to leave Pengallon for a spell; since Luke's departure, close to six months ago, life on her father's farm had begun to pall.

She was never idle, of course, for there was always much to do, particularly at shearing time, when—with so many men lured away to the goldfields—she and her mother, in addition to cooking for the depleted shearers' crew, had been called upon to help bale the wool or even, on occasion, to assist in rounding up the sheep.

Edmund and Dickon did the work of half a dozen men, but both were, as a result, poor company in the evening, fit only to exchange a few weary words or, in Dickon's case, mono-syllabic grunts before dropping off to sleep where they sat, often with their painstakingly prepared meals barely touched. And of late, her father had been in much the same state. . . . Elizabeth sighed.

She had enjoyed the unusual experience of the roundup, it was true, for she could ride as well as any man, and sheep were stupid creatures, easily collected into a bleating mob by the dogs and, once the pattern was established, simplicity itself to herd down from the hills where they grazed and into the fenced enclosures bordering the shearing shed. But wherever she had ridden about her father's land, she had thought of Luke or seen him in memory and, in conse-

quence, missed him the more . . . and she could not be
sure that he would come back. He had promised he would,
but that had been almost six months ago, and much could
happen in six months. Much could change, save, it seemed,
her feelings for him, and her sense of loss.

There had been no letters, only the scribbled note Dickon
had brought her the day Luke had ridden away from Pengallon and out of her life, bound on some mission of his own,
the purpose of which he had deemed of more importance
than her love.

Elizabeth sighed again. Seated in her aunt's beautifully
furnished withdrawing room, she was glad that she had
come to Sydney, even for a short while, for it eased the
heartache, and Aunt Abigail was delighted to have her com-
panionship. Abigail was old—white-haired now, and long-
widowed—but for all the toll the years had taken on her once
robust and slender body, she was still remarkably active and
possessed of an indomitable spirit and a fund of fascinating
stories of the past, to which it was always a pleasure to listen.

And socially, Sydney was an exciting place, offering every
kind of distraction to one who, like herself, was in some need
of it. There were garden parties, balls, picnics, dinners, and
. . . the horse races. Elizabeth smiled now, her smile happily reminiscent. Aunt Abigail was an enthusiastic racegoer,
and they had spent several afternoons most pleasantly at
Homebush, driving there by carriage and sharing a picnic
lunch in lovely surroundings, before taking their seats in the
fine new stands, to watch the successive tests of speed and
stamina between locally owned Thoroughbreds.

They were due to attend the Queen's Plate meeting this
afternoon, with two young officers of the garrison, Elizabeth
reminded herself, and her smile faded. If her dear aunt
Abigail had a fault, it was the fact that she was an incorrigible
matchmaker. Lieutenant Michael Lowndes and his cousin,
Ensign Peter Fowler, of Her Majesty's 50th Regiment, were
the latest of a veritable string of eligible bachelors she had
invited to make the acquaintance of "her niece from the
backwoods." It was useless to protest; Aunt Abigail simply
did not listen, and—

There was a knock on the door. It opened for the elderly

butler to announce, with a beaming smile, one of the same young men Elizabeth had just been thinking of, and she jumped up, taken by surprise at this premature arrival.

"Mr. Lowndes—I—I'm so sorry. I wasn't expecting you till noon. The races don't begin until twelve-thirty, and—"

"Miss Tempest, I know." Michael Lowndes bent apologetically over her hand. "I came, alas, to tell you that Peter and I will not be able to accompany you and Mrs. Dawson to Homebush. We've been ordered on board Her Majesty's ship *Galah,* with our company, this very day. The commander in chief"—he sounded awed—"General Nickle himself is to sail with us. It's damnably short notice, but it seems there's serious trouble in the goldfields."

"The—the goldfields?" Elizabeth stared at him, every vestige of color draining from her cheeks. If the soldiers and their general were going to sea, that could mean only the Victoria goldfields, she thought with sudden shock and alarm.

Lieutenant Lowndes confirmed her worst fears.

"Yes, the Ballarat goldfields. The diggers there—several thousand of them, by all accounts—are in revolt. Governor Hotham has sent urgently for military reinforcements. It's got to be put down, of course. I mean, it's anarchy, Miss Tempest. They're said to have hoisted the red flag and to be planning a march on Melbourne. . . ."

He talked on, but Elizabeth took in little of what he was saying. Ballarat, she told herself breathlessly, Ballarat had been Luke's destination, or so he had confided to Dickon. Could Luke be among the men—the anarchists—who had hoisted the red flag and who were threatening to march on Melbourne and the Governor in open revolt?

She was thankful when, at last, Lieutenant Lowndes took reluctant leave of her and she could ring for old Thomas to show him out. Pleading a headache, she excused herself from accompanying her aunt to the races, and an hour later, unable to remain alone in the house any longer, she made her way to the Government Domain. From there, her heart close to breaking, Elizabeth watched the troops board the *Galah,* and the ship, her upper deck lined with red-coated soldiers, sailed slowly and majestically from the anchorage and made for the open sea.

She would go home, Elizabeth decided; as soon as it could be arranged, she would go home. It was better to wait there, where she had promised to be, and pray for Luke's safe return.

The sun was sinking and the savage heat abating a little when the mounted troopers came in sight of the forest of tents and the smaller cluster of wooden buildings that constituted the township of Ballarat. Sub-inspector Martin had not pressed the men under his command, despite the urgency of their mission; he had let them take their time, with frequent halts to rest and feed their horses.

"We'll be no use to God or man if we show up all tuckered out and our horses blown," he told one of the cadets who protested at the slowness of their progress. "And you can take it from me—we shan't miss out on the action. Mr. Brownlow wouldn't have sent for us in such a hurry if he'd enough men to tackle the diggers, would he, now? And," he added shrewdly, "we're going in by a route that avoids the township. It's best if the diggers don't see us."

When they finally entered the government camp, well after dark, Luke was astonished to see that it bore a close resemblance to a fortress under siege. Red-coated sentries guarded the entrance, and others, with shouldered muskets, patrolled the perimeter as if it were in imminent danger of attack. A group of officers, spyglasses to their eyes, kept watch on the miners' camp, talking in low voices to one another, while a young man in a tight-fitting blue jacket, a revolver slung on his hip, moved from one to the other, gesturing excitedly.

The arrival of Sub-inspector Martin's contingent was greeted with very evident relief. They rode in in threes, bridles jingling; Martin formed them up in two lines and then went forward to snap a smart salute to the thickset, red-faced officer in inspector's insignia, who emerged from a stone building near the center of the camp to receive them.

"Commandant of Police Brownlow," he announced self-importantly.

"Martin, sir, sub-inspector," Martin responded, smiling. "With—"

The smile was swiftly wiped from his face when Brownlow barked at him wrathfully, "By God, man, you took your time getting here! I sent for you urgently."

"I came as expeditiously as I could, sir," the sub-inspector defended woodenly, "without knocking up the horses, sir." He paused, his tanned, weather-beaten face devoid of expression. "My men are ready for inspection, if that is your pleasure."

The young official in the blue jacket came striding across, tapping his booted leg with a cane. Despite the heavy mustache he wore, he looked only a few years older than the cadets, and Luke could scarcely believe his ears when Commandant Brownlow introduced him as Resident Gold Commissioner Rede.

They inspected the new arrivals together, the youthful Rede taking precedence, and his comments, made audibly, were, to poor Martin's obvious chagrin, the reverse of complimentary. He announced, before returning to the group of watchers he had left, "As you may observe, men, we are prepared for any act of aggression by the rebellious diggers down below. Our women and children have been accommodated in the premises of the Commercial Bank, which, like the jail, is a stone building. The utmost vigilance is called for in the situation in which we now find ourselves, but God willing, I hope to see law and order restored within the next twenty-four hours. You will be required to support Captain Wise's troops and Mr. Brownlow's police, when we go into the camp to put down the seditionists and drive them from the stockade they have erected. I hope you will be up to what is expected of you."

He walked away, still tapping his well-polished boots with his cane, and Inspector Brownlow said disparagingly, when the young commissioner was safely out of earshot, "We call that young whippersnapper the Jackass—you can see why, can't you? All right, Martin, your men may stand down—but only long enough to tend to their horses and get some grub inside them. After that I want them ready for action. Whatever the commissioner says—and he said plenty, didn't he?

—*I'm* pretty sure that we'll make our move tonight. It just depends on what word I receive from down below." He jerked his head in the direction of the diggers' camp and gave vent to a dry chuckle. "Been drilling and marching like fighting cocks all day, they have, the stupid bastards! Mad Irish rebels with pikes and their bloody papist priest haranguing them, Italian followers of Garibaldi, German bloody Lutherists, Scotchmen, and a mob of Yankee republicans trying to stage a colonial revolt out here! A real witches' brew, I can tell you, and they need sorting out. But—it's hard to believe, in the circumstances, I know—but Mr. Rede informs me that the Governor has said he'll set up a commission to inquire into their grievances! Well, I'm going to see to it that we give 'em something to grieve about first."

Martin said nothing. He saluted and gave the necessary orders, adding dryly, "Get your heads down while you've the chance, boys. I'll call you in plenty of time if there's anything doing."

The men obeyed him, stiff and saddlesore after their long ride and grateful for the opportunity to relax. But their respite was short-lived. Martin woke them, with a stentorian bellow, less than four hours later.

"Saddle up and mount! Look lively, my lads! The redcoats are sending in a storming party to take the stockade by assault. They reckon there's only about two hundred men inside it and most of them are asleep. We're to cover the soldiers' left flank and cut off any diggers that try to run."

Still dazed with sleep, Luke did as he was bidden, hating—now that it had come to the point—the prospect of engaging in armed conflict with those whom, for almost as long as he could remember, he had considered his own kind. But there was no help for it, he told himself bitterly; he had sworn an oath and must do what was now his duty. He climbed into his saddle and formed up with the others, his sheathed saber at his side, his carbine in its saddle holster, and he answered to his name when Martin briskly called the roll.

Somewhere out there in the darkness—probably within the diggers' defensive stockade—was the man for whom he was searching. The man who had cruelly and wantonly murdered Dan and the two Australians for his own gain . . .

Luke moved forward, kneeing his horse into line, his mouth suddenly dry and his heart racing. He had crossed half the world in pursuit of Jasper Morgan, and now his quarry was within perhaps less than a mile of him, he thought dully. In arms against him and in rebellion against the Queen of England's government—a legitimate target for his carbine or his saber, if, somehow, he could find and recognize him in the all-prevailing darkness.

Luke's stomach churned. It was scarcely possible to see or recognize the blue-coated troopers riding beside him . . . and the other squadron of mounted constables, under Inspector Brownlow, which had taken ground to the right after leaving the camp, was only dark shapes, heard but barely seen. It was easier to pick out the file of marching soldiers directly ahead, for their red coats and white crossbelts rendered them a trifle more conspicuous against the starlit sky.

The approach to the diggers' camp was made with caution, only the jingling of the mounted men's accoutrements and their horses' bits betraying their presence. Even these sounds ceased when they gained their objective behind a jumble of tents, and Martin's raised hand and whispered command brought them to a halt.

The horizon was lightening now, the first gray hint of dawn touching the cloud-flecked sky. The stockade lay ahead and to their right, but strain his eyes as he might, Luke could see no lights burning or distinguish any sign of movement from behind the roughly constructed barricades. They looked solid enough; he could make out piled pit props and mounds of brick and earth, with more tents behind them, scattered in haphazard fashion among the trees.

The infantry storming party was advancing steadily, their bayonets catching the dim light, their booted feet thudding on the dusty, bone-hard ground. Suddenly, as if alerted by the sound, there was a sharp cry of alarm from behind the stockade and then, startling in the stillness, a single musket shot, which woke the defenders to life.

Men rushed to the barricades, but before they were able to get off a ragged volley, the soldiers received the order to open fire. They did so in disciplined fashion, the front rank falling back to reload, the rear rank firing in their turn. A bugle sounded, shrill and clear, and led by their officer, with drawn sword, the redcoats charged resolutely up the slope and hurled themselves at the barricade to their front.

The defenders were firing back now with every weapon they possessed, and there were gaps in the charging ranks of the soldiers. Their officer fell, but he waved them on as he lay on the ground, and a sergeant took his place, yelling at them to close ranks.

Brownlow's mounted troopers now fired a volley, and they and a second line of infantry joined the advance from the flank, their gunfire having cleared the diggers' thin line and driven them back from the flimsy, crumbling barricade. The Californians used their Colts but were compelled to continue to fall back as the infantry storming party came swarming into the stockade, their bayonets locked in hand-to-hand battle with the Irish pikemen, who yielded at last, outnumbered and outfought. They retreated, leaving their dead and wounded behind them. The Americans, in their distinctive, brightly colored shirts, attempted to rally, using their revolvers to some effect, but soon they, too, were in full flight, the soldiers pounding after them.

"Draw sabers, boys," Martin ordered grimly. "It's up to us now—they're running. Do your duty!"

It was full daylight now, Luke realized, as he spurred his horse after Martin's, his saber in his hand. The rising sun threw the scene into sharp and chilling relief, lighting on bodies that lay spread-eagled on what was left of the diggers' barricades and on the approaches to it . . . soldiers' bodies, as well as those of the so-called rebels. Men were running from the rear of the stockade in wild panic, some alone, others in small groups, assisting wounded comrades.

One or two paused to fire at their pursuers, but the majority simply fled, letting their weapons fall as they sought for cover, stumbling and slipping on the pitted, uneven ground, and then staggering on, intent only on escaping the sabers of the two lines of advancing horsemen as they began to converge.

It was then, when he had all but forgotten the reason for his presence in Ballarat, that Luke observed a man on a bay horse suddenly break away from Inspector Brownlow's

troop and head at a reckless gallop for the Geelong road—a
route that would take him past the front of the stockade.

The fugitive was not in uniform, but he had undoubtedly
been with Brownlow's police in the initial attack, though
whether or not he had taken an active part in it Luke had no
means of knowing. Certainly he was running from the police
now, and . . . there was something familiar about him,
about the dark face, with its heavy mustache and the neatly
trimmed whiskers, about the way he sat his horse and the
long stirrup leathers. Jasper Morgan had always ridden long
—he had said once that his was a British hunting seat. He
. . . Luke drew a long, shuddering breath.

It was Morgan—God in heaven, after all his searching, he
had at last found the man he sought! And the swine was
running away, he would get away unless . . . Luke wheeled
his horse out of line and set off after him with no thought in
his mind save the determination to prevent his escape. To
kill him, because he had killed Dan and Frankie and Tom,
and because, however much Luke had tried to fool himself,
that had always been his intention. The devil take it, Jasper
Morgan deserved to die!

His horse was fast, it was carrying less weight than Morgan's, and Luke knew that he was gaining on his quarry. But
while he was still twenty yards behind, Morgan swerved suddenly to avoid a depression in the ground and drew level
with the front of the now almost deserted stockade. A man
was crouching there, wounded and overlooked by the
soldiers, his flaming red head just showing above the crumbling parapet. There was a rifle cradled in his arms, and his
harsh scream of "Traitor!" was cut off by the crack of the
rifle's discharge.

The bullet took Morgan in the chest. He fell with a strangled cry, and when Luke caught up with him, he was lying
motionless, his shirtfront heavily stained.

Luke flung himself from his horse. Heedless of any danger
to himself, he let the animal go and dropped to his knees
beside the man he had intended to kill. But that random shot
from the diggers' stockade had done his work for him, he
realized. Morgan was dying, coughing his life away from

blood-flecked lips—helpless and at his mercy. But at least he
should know. He should hear Dan's name before he died.

"I've caught up with you, Morgan," he said, his voice
harsh with the depths of his anger. "Do you remember me?
Do you remember my brother Dan, that you left for dead in
Windy Gully? Do you, Morgan? And the strike I made that
you robbed me of? I want you to remember us, Morgan!"

Jasper Morgan's eyes, dark with agony, focused on his
face, and Luke saw recognition slowly dawn in them.

"You!" the wounded man gasped. "God in heaven, after
all these years! You're the dim-witted boy, Luke . . . Luke
Murphy! The devil take you. I . . ."

He struggled to sit up, a trembling, bloodstained hand
groping blindly in the waistband of his breeches. It emerged
grasping a Colt revolver, the weapon Morgan had always
carried, but this time, Luke noticed with odd detachment,
there was no ornate pearl handle. Although it was leveled at
him, he was suddenly powerless to move, forgetful even of
his own weapon, the saber he still clutched in nerveless,
seemingly paralyzed fingers.

He heard the click as Morgan depressed the trigger, but
the Colt did not fire. Cursing, Morgan endeavored to rotate
the chamber, but the effort drained him of what remained of
his failing strength, and he let the revolver fall.

Still Luke did not move. Without pity, he watched his
enemy die, saw his eyes glaze over, and heard his high-
pitched scream abruptly fade into silence. His quest was
over, he thought dazedly, the long search was ended at last.
Dan's murderer had gone to meet his Maker.

From behind the diggers' stockade, the wounded marks-
man who had fired the shot that killed Morgan slid a fresh
round into his rifle. By now the red-coated soldiers and
constables of the foot police were returning to mop up what
was left of the defenders, but Rafaello Carboni still had time
to send an accursed police trooper to perdition. He raised
his rifle to his shoulder and fired, just as a redcoat's bayonet
buried itself in his back.

The bullet hit Luke just below the right knee, and almost
with surprise, he felt the leg go numb and cease to support
his weight.

He was still squatting awkwardly beside the body of Jasper Morgan when Sub-inspector Martin rode up and dismounted beside him.

"It's all over," the officer growled. "No thanks to you, Trooper bloody Murphy!" His shrewd eyes took in the scene confronting him, and he gestured with a derisive thumb to the limp body lying between them. "Is this him—is this the man you were after? Is this Humphrey?"

"Yes, sir," Luke confirmed faintly.

"Did you kill him, lad? After what I told you, did you take the law into your own hands?"

Luke shook his head. He felt dizzy and light-headed, scarcely able to sit upright, and sick with pain.

"No," he managed. "One of the diggers did. He fired from the stockade just as I was catching up with him. But . . ." He hesitated and then confessed defiantly, "I meant to kill him, Inspector. That was why I went after him. I—"

Martin silenced him. "Don't be telling me things like that, Trooper, or I'll think you ain't suitable for the police service," he warned dryly. "And maybe you're not, at that! Still —" He turned over Morgan's body with his foot, and observing the Colt, he bent to pick it up, spinning the chamber with practiced fingers. "One shot left in it, that's all. He put the other five into Inspector Brownlow and one of his troopers when he ran. They aren't sure if Brownlow's going to make it. He took two bullets in the back." Still with his foot, he turned Morgan's body again and studied the dead face with frowning curiosity. "He must have been a scoundrel, this feller, and no mistake. Couldn't be true to either side, could he? And you say he killed your brother. . . . Well, none of it got him anywhere. I reckon he's going to have some explaining to do, when he meets Saint Peter at the pearly gates, don't you?"

Luke nodded, unable to speak. Two soldiers walked past, carrying a red-haired digger between them, who, although obviously badly wounded, maintained a stoical silence until, seeing Morgan's body, he cried out something in a foreign tongue and spit his contempt. The soldiers ignored his outburst and plodded stolidly away.

Martin straightened himself and sighed wearily. "Best be getting ourselves back to camp. Can you walk, Murphy?"

"I'll try," Luke whispered. "But I—" He tried to rise and then keeled over, waves of nausea sweeping over him.

"God, lad, I didn't realize you'd been hit that badly." The sub-inspector looped his horse's rein over one arm and, with unexpected gentleness, bent and lifted Luke into his saddle. "Looks like the bone's shattered to me, boy. But I'll take you to the surgeon." He added, an odd little smile touching his lips, "You'll be out of the police if it is, and back to Sydney, maybe. Still, that's what you want, ain't it? Now you've done what you came to do."

Luke did not answer him. But it *was* what he wanted, he thought, now that his quest was over. He wanted to go back to Sydney and to Pengallon. He wanted it with all his heart.

EPILOGUE

Red stood on the lee side of the *Galah*'s quarterdeck and stared across at the piers and wharves and the clustered buildings of what was now called Port Melbourne.

His ship's boats—four of them—were lined up alongside the government wharf, on which two companies of her Majesty's 40th Regiment were drawn up, answering to their names as the sergeants called the roll. A lighter stood by, being loaded with their baggage.

Red breathed an impatient sigh. He had brought these same troops here when martial law had been imposed on the Ballarat goldfield and reinforcements from Sydney had been urgently requested by the Governor, Captain Sir Charles Hotham. Now he was to bring them back to Sydney, and, he reflected ruefully, they could scarcely be more eager to return than he.

In Captain James Willoughby's absence with the frigate *Huntsman*, in New Zealand waters, the only warship available to transport the troops to Victoria at such short notice had been his *Galah*, and he had been summoned back from his honeymoon in order to take them, together with the newly arrived military commander in chief, Major General Sir Robert Nickle.

Red started to pace the deck, his impatience growing. Those few precious days and nights, which he had spent in a state of exquisite happiness with his beautiful Magdalen, were now, sadly, a distant memory, bittersweet because they had been so brief. Indeed, he thought, he might have imagined them, were it not for the gold keepsake ring—Magdalen's gift to him at their wedding—which he now wore on his left hand.

Looking down at the small, glittering object, he swore

softly in remembered frustration. For the haste had been unnecessary, the panic short-lived, and the troops' role, like his own and that of his ship's company, almost negative.

The gold diggers' revolt had been over before they landed, effectively quelled by the police and those troops that had been at Governor Hotham's disposal when it had broken out. Fewer than five hundred men had been actively involved and up in arms. As nearly as he could gather, their resistance had lasted for only a few hours, and victory had been won at a total cost of perhaps thirty or forty lives— most of these miners'—although Captain Wise of the 40th had been killed in the attack on the stockade and an inspector of police severely, if not mortally, wounded.

The government victory had been followed by over one hundred arrests and a manhunt embarked upon—with rewards of up to five hundred pounds—to ensure the capture of those ringleaders who had managed to escape and go into hiding.

Sir Robert Nickle's arrival had, nevertheless, been a godsend, Red was compelled to concede. The distinguished old general, a courageous and many times wounded veteran of both the Peninsular and the American campaigns, had learned the value of tempering firmness with mercy. Of one hundred and fourteen prisoners taken after the capture of the Eureka stockade, Sir Robert had used his considerable influence to see to it that all save thirteen were released.

The thirteen unfortunates were to stand trial for high treason, but General Nickle had talked personally to all of them and had listened patiently to the diggers' grievances, with the result that Governor Hotham had at once appointed a commission to inquire into the wrongs they claimed had been inflicted on them, including the exorbitant cost of their prospectors' licenses.

Nickle—perhaps because so much of his life had been spent in battle with his country's foes—was a peacemaker, and his conciliatory attitude had won the gold diggers' trust and the Governor's approval. It was largely thanks to him that young Angus Broome and his brother Lachlan had both been freed and permitted to return to their father's sheep station at Bundilly—an outcome that had been greatly to the relief of Tim Broome, his own first lieutenant, Red recalled. The boys had made no profit from their exertions on the Eureka lode, but their contention that their deceased partner had deposited at the Treasury gold they had jointly mined was, Tim had told him, to be investigated.

Red smiled to himself. Neither lad, when he had seen and talked to them, had seemed unduly concerned as to the result of the investigation; they had departed, happily enough, for Bundilly a few days ago, more concerned about the reception they might expect from their father than for the fortune they might have lost.

"Sir!" It was Francis De Lancey, now his brother-in-law and restored to the *Galah*'s company, but wearing a midshipman's white patches in place of the single epaulet that had once adorned his uniform. "Sir, there's a boat putting out to us—not one of ours. Looks like the advance party at last or—" He had his glass to his eye, and he corrected himself. "No, they seem to be invalids, sir. I saw one fellow walking with a crutch on the wharf."

Red crossed to the rail and took out his own glass. With its aid, he studied the occupants of the approaching boat. There were six, apart from the men at the oars; five were in the familiar red coats and buff facings of the 40th Regiment, and the sixth appeared to be a civilian. All, as Francis De Lancey had suggested, looked like men recently discharged from the hospital, for they had their arms in slings or bandages about their heads.

"Casualties, I suppose, from poor Wise's company," he agreed. "Be so good as to see that they are suitably received if you please, Mr. De Lancey. And pass the word for the surgeon's mate—he'll have to get the sick bay ready in a hurry."

"Aye, aye, sir," Francis acknowledged. He gave the necessary orders crisply and, after another inspection of the boat's occupants, called up a party to rig a bo'sun's chair. "Look lively, my lads! And have a care when you haul those men inboard."

Marriage and fatherhood, Red reflected, had undoubtedly had a salutary effect on his once rebellious young brother-in-law. Francis was shaping well, ready to take responsibility,

conscientious in the performance of his duties, and popular
with the seamen. Magdalen had pleaded her brother's cause
when Francis and Dora had returned to Sydney, and, Red
recalled, he had listened, unable to refuse her anything . . .
although he could have no regrets on Francis's account. And
their child, his and Dora's, a winsome little creature with an
exotic name, had won all hearts with beguiling ease.

The boat came alongside, and the wounded men were
hoisted in turn to the *Galah*'s deck, the surgeon's mate in
anxious attendance. Last to appear was the young fellow in
civilian clothes, who stepped from the bo'sun's chair spryly
enough and then reached for the crutch one of the seamen
was holding out. He was about to follow the little procession
of soldiers below when, on impulse, Red strode across to
speak to him.

"You're not a soldier, lad?" he questioned.

"No, sir. I was serving with the mounted police. I was
given my discharge, on medical grounds, sir, and permission
to return to Sydney." The boy spoke well, with a slight
accent that Red could not place.

As if guessing the question he had not voiced, the onetime
police trooper added, "I come from America originally, sir
—from the Sacramento Valley. My folks are farmers there,
and I worked my passage from San Francisco to Sydney on
board a clipper schooner, the *Dolphin*. Maybe you will have
seen her in Port Jackson Harbor. She—"

"Good Lord, yes, of course I have!" Red exclaimed,
warming to his new passenger. "And I know Captain Van
Buren well. We were boys together, and I was at his wedding.
He married—" He broke off, remembering Claus Van
Buren's wedding, which, however fortuitously, had led to his
own. Memory stirred; suddenly recalling the thin young man
in the borrowed clothes who had given Claus's bride away,
he shook his head, wondering at his lack of perception. "My
dear fellow, how stupid of me—I know who you are perfectly
well! Your sister Mercy is Claus's wife, and I saw you at the
wedding! You had come, I believe, from the Tempests' at
Pengallon, and your name is Luke. Luke Bradshaw? Or is it
Bancroft?"

"Murphy, sir," Luke corrected, reddening. "I—"

"It is indeed a small world, Luke," Red put in quickly, sensing his embarrassment.

Luke's smile was warm, as if in gratitude. "Yes, sir, it is." He added, "I met members of your family, I believe, sir, at Pengallon. Your father, Captain Justin Broome, and—"

"And my brother and sister," Red finished for him. "Yes, they mentioned it." He held out his hand. "Well met, Luke, in person this time. You—what about that leg of yours? Were you wounded in the recent troubles at Ballarat?"

"Yes, sir," Luke confirmed. "Like the soldiers, at the Eureka field. But they say my leg will mend after a while, and I'll be as good as new. I reckon I was lucky not to lose it."

"Sir—" Francis De Lancey was again at Red's elbow. "First lieutenant's boat has put off, sir. And the others are loading now."

"Very well, Mr. De Lancey," Red acknowledged. He watched Luke Murphy's slow, careful descent to the lower deck, a thoughtful frown creasing his brow. The lad looked thin and pale, and the leg was obviously paining him, but it was to be hoped that it would mend, as the surgeons had predicted.

Then Tim's boat came alongside, and Red went to welcome him, as the soldiers started to ascend the accommodation ladder and Captain Thomas, their commander, claimed his attention.

It was well into the afternoon before the *Galah* put to sea and a strong southeasterly wind sent her on her way. It rose close to gale force by nightfall, and during the first two days and nights of the passage Red was continuously on deck. But his heart was singing to the music of the slashing breeze and the thunder of his ship's tautly stretched canvas, the creaking of her sturdy timbers and the pounding seas. He was going home, he thought—home to Sydney and to Magdalen —and, God willing, that was where he would stay, even if it meant resigning his commission in order that he might do so.

The sick men remained below in the care of the surgeon's mate. The troops and their officers made few appearances on deck, and the storm did not abate until a few hours before the Port Jackson Heads loomed in sight, half obscured by

pitch-black rain clouds. But, miraculously, the rain cleared
and the wind dropped, and the great harbor was bathed in
warm golden sunshine as the *Galah* shed her storm canvas
and made her stately way, under fore and topsails, toward
the familiar anchorage.

Red had his glass to his eye as the ship came to anchor. He
had started negotiations for the purchase of the small white-
painted stone cottage his mother and father had once occupied, and his spirits rose when he trained his glass on it and
saw, to his delight, that Magdalen was standing in the little
garden, a flimsy white handkerchief in her hand, waving a
welcome.

So, he remembered from his boyhood, his mother had
stood, waiting for her menfolk to come back from the sea.
Magdalen, thinking to please him, must have concluded the
purchase of Cove Cottage in his absence and moved in there
to await his return. He blessed her silently for the love and
understanding that had prompted her action and, doffing
his cap, raised it above his head in salute.

It would, he knew, be several hours before he could land
his passengers and leave the ship, but his wife was waiting
and, Red told himself, he had come home.

It was five seemingly endless weeks, however, before Luke
was told by the surgeons that he might soon expect to leave
their care. Mercy and Claus did their best to lessen the
frustration of the prolonged stay in the hospital and the
treatment he had to endure, and he was deeply grateful for
their kindness and concern and the regularity of the visits
they both paid to him.

Mercy had come alone at first, offering the explanation
that Claus was occupied with the fitting out of the *Dolphin* for
another trading voyage to the Pacific, but Luke suspected
that her real reason had been the fear of what he might tell
her concerning the culmination of his search for Jasper Morgan—information that, of necessity, must be for her ears,
not her husband's.

Thankfully, he was able to put her fears at rest. "Morgan is
dead, Mercy," he told her. "Not at my hands, although I was
ready to kill him. You see, he had joined the diggers' revolt.

He had even been elected to their reform league committee, and he betrayed them. One of them shot him from the stockade, at the Eureka, before I could catch up with him. I—I saw him die, with my name on his lips. And I reckon Dan and the other lads can rest easy now. He was given his just deserts. A life for a life, Mercy, that's what the Holy Bible teaches. Morgan has paid with his life, and I suppose I have paid as well for what I intended to do." He looked gloomily at his plastered leg.

"But you didn't take his life," Mercy said, anxious to give him comfort. She had hesitated, Luke recalled, then had asked finally, "Can I tell Claus that your quest is over? He wants to offer you employment, I know, and would do anything in his power to assist you. I'll bring him with me next time I visit you."

They had come together the following day, their happiness in their marriage and in each other evident in their smiling faces and in virtually every word they said. And Claus had offered him employment. . . . Luke sighed, remembering the generosity of that offer.

"You've the makings of a seaman, Luke," Claus had insisted. "And I'd gladly teach you navigation, so that, in time, you could take command of one of my trading vessels. We are increasing our trade with New Zealand—with the settlers there, and with quite a few of the Maori tribes—and there's every prospect of considerable expansion. The two Yates lads—Simon and Robert—have had their fill of gold-seeking. They are coming back with us on this voyage and are to act as my agents on North Island. Come with us yourself, why don't you? You could recoup your health and strength on the passage, and Mercy will give you every care, I promise you. Work for me, Luke, and your future will be assured."

But he had refused, Luke reminded himself, on the plea of a promise he had made, which, for all his present uncertainties, he meant to keep. He had let the *Dolphin* sail without him, and after Claus and Mercy had gone, he had tried a dozen times, without success, to pen a letter to Elizabeth Tempest, telling her of his return.

He could not put his love and his hopes into words. He had no skill with the pen, and each letter had seemed to him clumsy and inadequate. He must, he decided, go in person, as soon as the surgeons permitted him to depart.

They did so at last, with the warning that he must consider himself still convalescing. Luke took the coach to Bathurst, not daring to ride with his injured leg; but emboldened by the realization that his limp was barely perceptible and that the jolting of the coach had caused him no discomfort, he decided to go the rest of the way to Pengallon on foot.

It was dusk when he glimpsed the red roof of the farmhouse and its cluster of outbuildings and cottages through the screening trees, and he came to a halt, suddenly doubting the welcome he might expect.

It was then, as he stood there uncertainly, half tempted to retrace his steps, that he heard a voice calling his name. It was the one voice he wanted to hear.

"Luke! Luke, is it really you? Oh, Luke, have you come back at last?"

Instinct, Luke thought, his heart thudding, must have brought Elizabeth to meet him, for she could not have known the hour of his coming. He had sent no word. . . . Choking back the surge of unmanly tears that suddenly ached in his throat, he managed to answer her, in a voice he could hardly recognize as his own.

"Yes," he answered. "I've come back, Elizabeth. To . . . you."

She pulled up beside him and slipped from her horse, to stand looking at him, her heart in her eyes.

"I waited for you," she told him shyly. "As you asked, in that note Dickon gave me. But it was so long ago—I wasn't sure if you meant what you said. Or if you would come back, Luke. I—"

"I meant it, Elizabeth," Luke said. "I meant it with all my heart."

The memory of Jasper Morgan faded at last; even the memory of Dan's dead face faded with it as Luke took her into his arms. She was smiling now, he saw, and he held her close.

"I love you, Elizabeth," he whispered. "And I was always coming back."

The first shocking news of events in the Crimea reached Sydney via the new telegraphic link with India, and the appalling casualty list, dated October 25, 1854, was published soon afterward in the colony's newspapers, on pages edged with black.

Accounts of the tragically misdirected charge by the British Light Cavalry Brigade on the Russian guns in Balaclava's North Valley received similar treatment. Most of the editorials, however, stressed the heroism and the superb discipline of those who had taken part, while expressing horror at the terrible price their splendid regiments had been called upon to pay for what, clearly, had been an inexplicable misunderstanding of the commander in chief's order.

The *Morning Herald* stated:

> Out of a total of 673 officers and men who mustered in the Light Cavalry Brigade on the morning of October 25, over 300 were killed, wounded, or taken prisoner. Among them, we learn with deep regret, was Captain William De Lancey of Her Majesty's 11th Hussars, elder son of His Honor Judge George De Lancey, well known in the colony, who himself fought with distinction at the Battle of Waterloo.

Jenny Broome had read this report with deep and abiding sadness, and when her brother Johnny brought her a letter, delivered belatedly with the English mail, her heart sank as she made out the address at its head: *British Cavalry Division Camp, before Sebastopol, 24 October 1854.* It was from William De Lancey, and her eyes misted with tears as she read it, taking in little of the description he had given, so painstakingly, of the situation in which he had found himself the night before the fateful battle.

But the final words of the letter—written, as if at the last moment, crisscrossing the lines of lengthy description—set her weeping uncontrollably.

"I love you, Jenny," William had written. "I love you with all my heart. Wait for me, I beg you, for I have had my fill of war and soldiering. When this is over, I'll come home. Please wait until I come to you."

But William, Jenny thought, remembering the dream that had haunted her, William was dead. The report in the *Herald* had confirmed all the fears she had felt for him, all the horrors her nightmare had forecast. "Among them," meant, surely, that he was among the casualties . . . or was there a faint hope that, perhaps, he had been wounded, not killed by the fearsome horsemen in fur caps, whom she had seen in her dreams?

"I did not realize, Jenny my dear—"

Her brother came to put his arm about her. She had forgotten his presence, had been oblivious of everything save her own bitter distress, but now, grateful for his sympathy, Jenny leaned against him, hiding her tear-wet face against his shoulder.

"You never talked of him, not even when the news came through about that ghastly charge. But it's Will De Lancey you care for, isn't it, little sister? It's on his account that you've been a shadow of yourself these past weeks?"

"Yes," she admitted huskily, the brave pretense at an end. "Yes, and this letter is from him, Johnny. He wrote it the— the night before, and he sent a sketch for you." She gave him the sketch, her hand shaking, and, suddenly unable to keep it to herself any longer, she told him of her dream.

Johnny listened gravely. "Will may not be dead, you know," he offered in an attempt to console her.

"But the paper said—"

"The paper did not have a detailed list of casualties when that report was published, Jenny. It hadn't come through then. It—" Johnny broke off, smothering an exclamation. "But the mail's in—Will's letter came in the mail, for God's sake! The full casualty lists will have come in the mail, too, I'm pretty sure. I'll go to the office and find out. Don't despair yet. Just wait here—I'll be back right away if there's any news, I promise you."

Jenny waited, the letter in her hand, staring out, as she so often did, at the sun-dappled waters of Elizabeth Bay. The memory of her dream returned, so vividly that she turned away from the window, blinded by tears. And then Johnny was back. She heard his footsteps in the hall and then his voice, calling her, and the dream vanished as swiftly and suddenly as if it had never been.

"The lists *have* come in," Johnny told her, and he was smiling. "Will's reported severely wounded and in a hospital at Scutari. But he's alive, Jenny!"

"Alive?" Jenny echoed, scarcely able to believe that it could be true. "Oh, Johnny, are you sure?"

"His name's there in black and white," her brother assured her. "And I met the judge, his father, who had come to the *Herald* office on the same quest as myself. He told me that he intended to use all the influence at his command to have Will granted a passage back to the colony. He'll be home before you know it, little sister!"

"When this is over, I'll come home," William had written. *"Please wait until I come to you. . . ."* And he had said that he loved her. . . .

Jenny's eyes were shining as she looked up to meet her brother's gaze.

"I shall be waiting for him," she whispered softly. "However long it is."

Here is an exciting episode from Volume Eight in the magnificent series
THE AUSTRALIANS, *published by Dell, copyright* © *1985 by*
Book Creations, Inc.:

The S.S. *Pyramus*, bound from the port of Liverpool to
Sydney, New South Wales, wallowed sluggishly in mountainous seas, the howling, gale-force winds driving her remorse-
lessly off course to the north. Securely battened down
though she was, and with only storm canvas set, she seemed,
to the lone passenger who had ventured on deck, to be in
imminent danger of foundering.

Henry Osborne clung with numb fingers to the weather
rail, an oilskin cape about his shoulders, regretting the impulse that had led him to leave the warmth and comparative
safety of the cuddy. But its smoke-filled airlessness and the
pungent fumes of the alcohol some of his fellow passengers
had been consuming had induced such queasiness in his
stomach that, fearing it might overcome him, he had decided
to go in search of fresh air.

Now, he reflected ruefully, he would have to stay where he
was until wind and sea abated—or until the infernal vessel
capsized—for to cross the deck to the after companionway
would be to risk life and limb to no avail. The *Pyramus* was,
he had been assured when he booked passage, a sturdy,
seaworthy brigantine of close on five hundred tons burden,
well found and under the command of an experienced master, and, until the storm had struck, he had had no reason to
doubt that she was everything the shipping agent had
claimed. He— Henry braced himself, clutching at his precar-
ious handhold as the ship heeled suddenly, to plunge into
the trough of a towering wave, her bluff bows and most of
her fo'c's'le vanishing momentarily into its depths.

Tons of icy water cascaded across the deck, soaking him to
the skin and threatening to sweep him before it. As it
drained away, he heard the master bellow an order through

his speaking trumpet to the two men at the helm. The wind seemed to Henry to bear the words soundlessly away, but evidently both helmsmen heard and understood them, for, between them, they spun the wheel and brought the ship's head to the wind. Her bows rose, shuddering, and he felt the deck lift beneath his feet as, with an ominous creaking of her timbers, she gained the crest of the wave and plunged on.

God in heaven, Henry thought, his stomach heaving, why had he embarked on this voyage halfway across the world? What mad, ambitious dream had led him to sell his farm at Dromore in Ireland's County Tyrone in order to go out to Australia as a settler? True, his two elder brothers, Alick and John, had gone out there as naval surgeons and had urged him to follow them, stressing in glowing terms the prospects the colony offered to young men with some capital behind them. He had the required capital—a thousand pounds, raised by the sale of his farm, but— The *Pyramus* heeled over once again, flung almost onto her beam ends, and it seemed to Henry an interminable time before she righted herself and, pitching heavily, struggled on.

He groaned, not caring who might hear him. Worst of all, he reminded himself miserably, had been leaving behind his betrothed, the lovely Sarah Marshall, because of her parents' objections to his plans.

"Your future is too uncertain, Henry," the old rector of Dromore had told him, when he had attempted to plead his case. "Our daughter has been gently reared, in a safe, secure home background. She is not suited to the rough life of a pioneer, in the wilds of an unknown land, such as she would be compelled to face if she were to become your wife."

"But we love each other," Henry had protested. He had added, though to no avail, that he would never have considered leaving his native Ulster had he, for one moment, supposed that Sarah would be forbidden to accompany him.

"You should have thought of that possibility," the Reverend Benjamin Marshall had answered uncompromisingly, "before you sold your land, my dear young man—and before you had advanced your plan to emigrate to the point of no return."

He had been every sort of fool, Henry thought bitterly,

remembering Sarah's tears and her stricken face when he
had paid his final visit to the rectory to bid her farewell. They
had clung together, both of them too heartbroken for words,
and finally, when he had had to tear himself away in order to
catch the Liverpool packet, she had whispered brokenly that
she would wait for him. He heard her voice now.

"Send for me, dearest Henry, when you are settled and
have made your way in Australia. I will come, I swear it—
whatever my parents say!"

He wanted to believe her, but . . . Sarah Marshall was a
beautiful, attractive girl. There would be suitors aplenty,
after he had gone, young men with better prospects than his
had ever been. There was the lawyer, Patrick Hare, and a
brace of well-off farmers, once his friends: Damien Hamil-
ton, who was kin to Sarah's mother, and Guy O'Regan, his
closest rival, who—

A rending crash from somewhere above his head interrupted his thoughts, bringing his attention abruptly back to
the present. Henry watched with horror as, silhouetted
starkly against the gray, scudding storm clouds, the foretopmast lost the single sail it had borne and, split off at the
cap, came hurtling down to the forward part of the deck in a
welter of shattered spars and torn rigging.

The crew reacted with swift courage in response to the
master's shouted urging, and Henry found himself caught
up in the rush of men. Someone thrust an ax into his hand,
and he hacked and tore at the wreckage with the rest of
them, blind instinct guiding him, as the ship swung danger-
ously, broadside to the pounding waves, the whole deck
awash.

Their frantic efforts succeeded at last. The shattered mast
went by the board, and, relieved of its weight, the *Pyramus*
answered to her helm, the pumps slowly ridding her of the
water she had shipped.

Henry stood back, exhausted, aching in every limb, his
hands blistered and bleeding. The master paused for a moment beside him, his lined, weather-beaten face creased into
a grim, mirthless smile.

"Good work, mister," he said. "Thanks for your help." He
added, the smile fading, "We're going to put in to Belfast to

get that foretopmast replaced. It'll add a week to your journey, I'm afraid, but then we ain't none of us in that much of a
hurry, are we?"

He stumped on, speaking trumpet again raised to his lips.
Henry stared after him, unable at first to take in the meaning
of what he had been told.

Then, suddenly, his heart was singing.

A week in Belfast . . . time enough, God willing, for him
to ride to Dromore and renew his pleas to Sarah's parents.
Time enough, even if they again refused, to wed her without
their consent.

The hand of God had surely brought him back, and the
Reverend Benjamin Marshall could scarcely deny that it had
been the hand of God that had preserved him, with the
Pyramus and her passengers and crew, from the fury of the
storm.

The Irish coast was in sight, and the wind had abated when
Henry Osborne limped back to his cabin in search of dry
clothes.

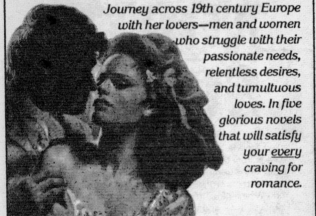